SUNDAY NIGHT

FEARS

Tom Golden

Edition 1.1
E-book edition ISBN: 978-0-9994363-1-8
Print edition ISBN: 978-0-9994363-0-1

Cover by Elderlemon Design

For my wife, Marcia
who reminded me often…

"You cannot swim for new horizons
until you have courage to lose sight of the shore."
—William Faulkner

Sunday Night Fears

CHAPTER 1

January 1983

Two o'clock in the morning.

Heart racing, hands trembling, shirt sticking to my back, I sat alone in the conference room at GEL's corporate headquarters. I stared at the phone. I told myself I'd be crazy to pick it up.

I was tired. Not a good time to be making critical decisions. Especially those that could alter the course of my tenuous career at Hamilton Pierce.

If I made the call to Pete Brooks, the engagement partner, there would be no turning back.

I studied my notes again. I was sure I was right, but would Pete believe me? This being my first audit of a public company, I was new to the accounting and auditing world. It would be my word against the CFO's.

As the Chief Financial Officer and former Hamilton Pierce audit manager, Reggie Dalton had credentials that dwarfed my own. Reggie was also Pete Brooks's best friend until he left the firm two years ago to become GEL's CFO. Pete stayed with the firm recently making partner, and this was his first assignment as an engagement partner—the guy who runs the independent audit. As a new partner, Pete would be under scrutiny by the firm and GEL's board. Pete needed Reggie as much as Reggie needed Pete. The stakes were too high for Pete. He'd take up Reggie's defense, and I'd be toast in a heartbeat.

I was supposed to be doing an audit. Not snooping around into file cabinets and desks. Now I had proof...maybe.

In a few days GEL would release earnings to the market. All signs pointed to that release occurring on time. That was what everyone expected, including all the market makers and investors making a killing on GEL's stock climb.

Here I was contemplating calling Pete Brooks to tell him his client and friend was perpetrating a massive leasing scam—an accounting fraud. What was I thinking, and why was I so convinced I was right? I couldn't be. Just a short time ago I was selling cigarettes out of the trunk of my car.

If I picked up the phone and called Pete to tell him his friend was a fraud, he would laugh me off the planet, right before he fired me. It would be reckless and careless, driven by misplaced confidence. Confidence I had no business possessing considering my track record of failure.

I dialed Pete's number. The CFO of this public audit client was a crook of the highest order; I could not let him deceive my firm into signing off on a bogus set of financials. At least, I thought that to be the case.

It was ringing.

CHAPTER 2

October 1980

Monday morning. I felt great from a well-rested weekend with Sue and the boys—well, about as well-rested as one could be after romping around with a seven and five-year-old. Still, life felt pretty good as I slipped into my routine parking spot at Benson Distributing. I was the VP and Director of Sales. Great title, mediocre pay, so-so career track. Still, I enjoyed working for them, particularly Mr. Benson.

When I entered through the employee entrance, it seemed everyone in the building was huddled around Russ's desk, which was strategically located so he could keep track of everyone and everything, including the delivery and loadout doors. Russ Morgan was Mr. Benson's brother-in-law and the warehouse manager. He was an OK guy but not very well liked. He usually came off gruff and uncompromising. Those of us who knew his history attributed that to being wounded in the Korean War, which caused him to struggle in finding a decent job until Mr. Benson set him up to work for him twenty-five years ago.

I walked up to the assembled group of about ten employees, most from the warehouse. "What's up?" I asked. A couple of them glanced my way, but it was clear they were an unhappy lot.

"Hey, why the serious faces?"

"You tell us, Sam. How we gonna operate with no tax stamps?" said Donna, one of the newer packers.

I had an inkling of what they were talking about but needed more information before I could respond. Every morning Russ would

3

come in early and run the cigarettes through the Pitney Bowes stamping machine which affixed the required state tax decals to each pack of cigarettes. The cigarette tax was a major source of state revenue, and a stamp was required on every pack.

Jake, the dock manager, joined in.

"Sam, we have over a hundred deliveries to make today."

As Jake spoke I glanced around at the other workers and was met with crossed arms, a few sighs and quizzical faces until one of them asked, "Do we still have a job?"

"Look, everyone, not sure why we don't have the stamps, but I'm going to find out. I'm sure there's nothing to worry about." I wondered if I was trying to convince myself and everyone else of something we all just didn't want to believe.

"This got something to do with the break-in last week? Like maybe the insurance company ain't payin' up?" Jake followed.

"I can't imagine there's a problem with the insurance claim. At worst, it's a lot of money, and the insurance company likely wants to make certain it's all on the up-and-up before they cut the check. But I'm sure they will."

"But you don't know for sure," one of the drivers challenged.

"No, I don't, Bob. But I've got to believe Mr. Benson's long-standing relationship with the same insurance company and the agent, who's a high school buddy of Mr. Benson's, will count for something."

"Sam, can't we fill the orders while we wait? Beats standing around here."

"Can't do it, Larry. Those cigarettes can't leave the building without tax stamps. The State of Indiana Department of Revenue would shut us down if we pulled something like that," I said. I glanced at my watch and headed toward the door to our offices. "It's not even nine o'clock. We've got plenty of time to get those orders out. I'm not worried about a thing."

"So, what should we do while we wait?" asked Norma Diego.

Norma had worked at Benson Distributing from the start. She

worked on the line filling orders. She was one of the sweetest women I'd ever met. Her whole family was that way. All six of them, minus a husband. Mr. Benson told me her story shortly after he hired me while I was making inquiries about all Benson's employees. Seemed Norma's husband made sport of pounding on his wife from time to time. "A total drunk" was how Mr. Benson described him. "Worthless SOB," he added with a disgust that implied her husband reminded Mr. Benson of someone else. Maybe someone in Mr. Benson's past, like the father he never talked about. I could relate.

"Sam's right, people. Mr. Benson takes care of all us. We should not to worry," Norma shouted out like a shop foreman in her broken English. While she had no formal rank, everyone respected Norma, and her words of assurance seemed to pacify them this morning. At least she did a lot better than I was doing to get people back to work. With no orders to fill, I wasn't sure what form that would take, but I took the moment to take my leave of the warehouse.

I went first to Charlotte's desk. She was the receptionist. I wasn't certain how she kept up with the rumor mill, but she had a lock on it. "Char, what's going on?"

She gave me a troubled look. "Don't know, Sam, but Mr. Phillips has been in there with Mr. Benson for the past hour."

I glanced toward Mr. Benson's office down the hall and then back to Charlotte. "The insurance agent?"

"Yep. It's got to have something to do with the break-in last week. They were talking to the insurance company for about twenty minutes, and they must have said something to really piss off Mr. Benson."

I was now standing at the edge of Charlotte's desk and lowered myself down closer to her. "It takes a lot to piss off Mr. Benson," I hushed.

Charlotte shrugged her shoulders and turned her head to the side, sort of the way Rocco, our family's Labrador retriever, once removed, would do when I'd walk into a room and he'd done something wrong. "Come on, Char. You're holding back."

5

"I really don't know, Sam, but I'm worried."

"Char, come on, talk to Sam," I begged. She started to cry, and I hated myself immediately.

"Whoa, Char, I'm sorry. What is going on?"

"No clue, Sam, but your name was mentioned more than once."

"This has got to be related to the break-in. I talked to Mr. Benson on Friday, and he said all seemed good and expected to get paid by the end of the day. I left early Friday assuming all went as planned and Russ would have picked up the stamps late Friday. Maybe Mr. Phillips stopped by to deliver the check personally. Not a big deal at all."

"Yeah, well, if that's the case, what's taking so long? And why did Mr. Benson have me get the insurance company on the phone?"

She had a point. I gazed out the window for a moment, thinking. "Well, I'm gonna find out right now," I said turning toward Mr. Benson's office. As Charlotte cautioned me not to go in, the door opened and both men emerged. Charlotte and I remained fixed on them as they approached us from the long narrow corridor. They weren't talking, their heads aimed at the floor—that is, until Mr. Phillips looked up at me. Most troubling was how quickly his eyes retreated to the floor when he caught my stare. I had known Mr. Phillips since I began with Benson's five years ago and had played golf with him and Mr. Benson on several occasions.

When they reached the reception area, neither was talking as Mr. Phillips began to put on his topcoat and then his hat. With his back to me, he mumbled something inaudible to Mr. Benson, who nodded and said, "I understand. Thanks, Harvey. I'll be in touch." It was all so ominous.

Charlotte tried to busy herself moving papers around on her desk. I stood watching the spectacle like I had just seen a dog run over by a car that didn't stop—speechless for lack of understanding.

As the door closed, Mr. Benson held his hand on the doorknob with his back to us and hesitated, hardly a second or two, after it had shut.

"Mr. Benson, is everything OK?"

"Sam, could I have a word with you in my office." It wasn't a question.

I had sat in that same chair during both good times and bad. Mostly good times.

"Sam, I have to let you go."

It was like I had missed the first half of a movie.

"Let me go...where?" I laughed sardonically. He couldn't be serious.

"I've done everything I could, but they won't budge."

My mouth became parched, and the blood in my veins rushed inward as if bracing for an attack. My fingers gripped the claw-like arms of the chair as I pulled upwards, wanting to pull them apart from the legs. I mumbled something even I could not interpret.

"It was *your* alarm code, Sam," Mr. Benson said.

"I don't understand. You can't possibly believe it was me. I was home in bed when it all went down last Tuesday. How could I be in two places at once?"

"Sam, calm down. I'm not accusing you."

"Well, someone sure as hell is accusing me," I said, leaving spittle on my lower lip.

Mr. Benson said nothing. I took a moment to gather my thoughts.

"So, Mr. Benson, let me get this straight. You don't believe I had anything to do with the robbery, yet you are firing me. I don't get it," I said calmly, despite roiling inside.

"You have every right to hear the whole story, so here it is." He paused long enough for me to sit up straight. My forearms rested on the chair's arms, and I clasped my hands tightly, trying hard to quell the chills that no doubt resulted from the lack of blood circulating through my arms. I wanted to give him a chance to explain and willed myself to shut up while he did so. He began slowly.

I waited until Mr. Benson had finished with the sketchy details. Simple enough. The stamps were gone; whoever broke in used my code to gain access to the building. From there, it was easy to pry open the cabinet where we kept the stamps. Untraceable. They were in and out in under ten minutes. Jake noticed the theft moments after we opened last Wednesday.

"Mr. Benson, I didn't do it."

"I know you didn't, Sam. If I thought you did it, I wouldn't even be talking with you right now," he said dejectedly. "You're the best sales manager I've ever had."

"But this is your business. How can they dictate who you can hire and fire?"

"Unfortunately, they can. Well, at least they have some leverage to do just that," he said as he shook his head, trying to lend some sarcasm to the moment.

I was still confused. There was something else he wasn't telling me, and if I hadn't insisted, he probably never would have.

"It was because of your father."

Hearing a reference to my father was nearly heart-stopping.

"What's my father got to do with this?" But even as I said it, I knew where this was going.

"It's what they learned about him that caused them to cast you with guilt." It was how matter-of-factly he said it that was so upsetting. Like he understood their position. Maybe that was because I never told him. Maybe he believed I should have. But it was none of his business. It was none of anyone's business what my father had done. I hadn't even told Sue. She could have made an argument that I should have, but there never seemed to be a good time. I mean, how do you tell your wife that your father was serving 25 years to life for murder? Nope, I never told Sue. Worse yet, I led Sue to believe my father was dead. In my own mind, it wasn't a lie. He was dead to me. I never wanted to see him again. I put him out of my mind and moved on with my life hoping he'd do the same with me. So far, so good. He'd never made any attempt to contact me. I never saw him after that night. Even when I testified against him at his trial, I did so without ever looking his way.

I didn't have a response for Mr. Benson even though he expected one. He frowned at me like a disappointed father. Memories came flooding back. Struggling to synthesize what he said, I just sat there. After a few moments, my rage subsided long enough for me to continue asking questions and probing, even though it was clear Mr. Benson felt he had given me all the information he was obliged to give me.

"So, Sam, those are the facts, and there's really nothing more I can say on the matter." He stood, picked up an envelope and moved around to my side of the desk.

I didn't stand, which is what likely compelled him to sit in the other chair in front of his desk before handing me the envelope, mumbling something about how he wished it was more. I took it and slipped it into my jacket pocket, but I had yet to rise. I had something to ask of Mr. Benson. It was not the perfect time to ask for his help, but I was running out of time and options. It shouldn't have been an unexpected request.

"Would you mind giving a call to the other wholesalers in town? Put in a good word for me. Seems to make sense to coordinate the timing with you."

He immediately lowered his head, breaking eye contact.

"I can't, Sam. I mean, I could, but it wouldn't make any difference."

I stared at him in bewilderment.

"Sam, it's like this. The insurance company told me if I didn't fire you, they would no longer insure me. No one would. After you left yesterday, I checked."

"Checked with whom?"

"All of them." He was referring to all our competitors. He had called the other candy and tobacco wholesalers in the region on my behalf. I think their answers stunned even him.

"They all have the same carrier. You're blackballed from working for any of us. You could never get bonded again, even through another carrier. I was told that all the insurance carriers share such information. Sam, it's not fair, but that's the way it is. I'm sorry.

9

I wish I could help you."

I sat there like I'd been hit in the gut with a baseball bat. I couldn't move. Worse, I had that feeling again: chest pain, heart racing, cold and clammy feeling, chills. I had had these feelings before, though it was many years ago. I became lightheaded. Aware of what to do, I did it instinctively.

Putting my head between my knees caused Mr. Benson to fly out of his chair. "Sam, Sam, are you alright? Should I call an ambulance?"

He was blabbering hysterically, but I held up my hand, signifying I was alright and this would pass. No cause for alarm. And in a few minutes, it did pass. Still, he stood next to me with that look of helplessness others had expressed before. I sat up again, saying I was fine, but I suppose the sweat broken out on my forehead and face belied my words.

Out came his handkerchief. I took it graciously and thanked him.

Mr. Benson continued standing close to me until I coaxed him to sit back down. He sat again in the chair next to me, favoring that position over his desk chair. He put his hand on my shoulder to comfort me.

"Sam, let's do this. Go home. Come back tomorrow morning. I'll make the announcement later today. You have a lot of folks here that like and admire you, son. I'll simply tell them you've decided to do something else and you'll be back tomorrow to say goodbye. Why don't you come in around nine o'clock? Your sales team will be here as well. Let's both think a little more tonight. A lot has happened today, and I think we need some time to gather our thoughts."

Mr. Benson put his hand on my forearm, which was a prompt for me to leave. We both knew thinking on it overnight wouldn't change a thing. It was a gratuitous comment. The strength in my muscles had returned. I stood up straight. Mr. Benson remained seated, head down. Without making eye contact, I said, "Sounds like a plan," with little feeling in my words. I walked toward his office door, pausing, and then said, "See you tomorrow."

Sunday Night Fears

I didn't see Charlotte as I walked past the reception desk. I walked out of Benson Distributing straight toward my company car. It would be the last time I would drive it home.

CHAPTER 3

How was I going to tell Sue?

I hadn't really paid attention to how long or in what direction I had been driving. Somehow, I ended up on Hwy 37 heading south. A sign read "Bloomington 12 miles." Maybe subconsciously I wanted to drive someplace we enjoyed together, where it all began, Sue and me. After graduating from Indiana University and moving to Indianapolis nine years ago, from time to time, we'd take the drive south, as I was doing now. We found the park-like setting of campus inviting. Since graduating, for merely the cost of gas, just $.35 a gallon back then, we could spend the day wandering about, taking in all that nature had to offer.

Somehow, sitting on a wooden footbridge while watching students as they walked by on this unseasonably warm day in late October was the perfect salve to heal an open wound. Memories of our time here came flooding back…great memories. It made me forget the bad ones—the pre-Sue ones.

I wasn't sure what was causing my melancholy mood—the fact that I had been fired or recalling a life I had willed from my memory. But maybe it was time to get it all out. After I would break the news of being fired to Sue, I'd have to tell her why. I couldn't lie any longer. At least, I shouldn't.

It was nearing 3:00 in the afternoon. I had to get back. Sue would be expecting me to walk through the door around 5:15.

When I pulled off the interstate on to Rockville Road, it was only 4:10. Sue and the boys would be home, but I wasn't ready. I pulled into a parking spot right in front of Micky's Bar & Grill.

I grabbed a seat at the end of the bar away from everyone. It had been a long time. I never sat at the bar in college. My roommates considered it strange, at first, but then seemed to accept that quirk of mine. I guess I was over that affliction and maybe working on replacing it with another.

A week ago, I had celebrated my 30th birthday, and I never envisioned this coming. I thought I was set, settled. My job, my family. I'd just coast into middle-age and beyond.

Turning thirty was a milestone, like when I turned eighteen and was still living in Jersey. Eighteen was the legal drinking age in New York back then. I didn't live in New York but close enough. A twenty-minute drive to Staten Island and I was sitting at a table at Simral's drinking a $1.25 longneck bottle of Bud…a lot to pay for a beer in 1968.

I don't remember making big plans when I turned eighteen. I was already in college. I hadn't declared a major, but I assumed I would follow in my mother's footsteps and become a teacher. It sure was better than following in my dad's footsteps.

Dad was a drunk. That wasn't fair. Alcoholic. It was a disease. He couldn't help himself. *I wonder how he's doing,* I thought, then tipped my beer back, finished it and said, "Not really."

"What's that you're saying, Sammy boy?" asked the guy behind the bar, struggling to keep up with a surprisingly busy late-afternoon crowd for a Monday.

Time to leave.

"I said music sucks," I yelled, hoping Mick wouldn't think I had morphed into a crazy drunk talking to himself. "How about a little Motown?"

"You be on da wrong side of town for dat kinda tunes," he responded, continuing the friendly banter. "We service the younger and hipper generation. Something an old fart like you knows nuttin' about," he boomed, sporting a big smile. Some tipped their drinks in agreement with Micky's comment. I feigned a half-smile and waved

13

him off.

I left a nice tip and headed for the door. As soon as I did, I paused and thought perhaps I shouldn't be so generous. I had to conserve resources. *For how long?* I wondered.

I continued toward the front door. Sue would be getting dinner ready. I hadn't even worked out what I would tell her or what I would tell the boys. I didn't know myself. I'd never been fired before.

"I'm home, sweetheart!" I said as I came through the front door.

Whenever I would walk through the door, Will and Ben would come flying into the foyer to greet me like lapdogs starving for attention. We didn't have a dog at the moment, but the boys were a close second as far as the unconditional love a dog provides. We had to put Rocco down last year when his hind legs gave out. Even the vet cried. I used to say my goal in life was to become half the man Rocco believed I was. Complete and unconditional love. I missed him so much. We'd have another dog someday, but it would be several years down the road. Even if everything worked out we still wouldn't be able to afford dog food for some time. But then, if things didn't work out, we might all soon be eating dog food.

I made my way to the kitchen, planting a big kiss on Sue. For the time being, I pushed the day's events from my mind. I'd have to face this soon enough. "Where are the boys?"

"Do you not remember anything I tell you?" Sue said with one of her manufactured attitudes—the one she used just for show.

"OK, what did I forget now?"

"School trip today," Sue reminded me. "Grades K through second went to the zoo to see the new baby lion cubs."

"My, Lord Jesus, how could I forget!" earning one of those looks which always grounded me immediately.

"Sorry, honey," I said hoping to right the ship for the possible storm ahead.

"Can we sit down and talk for a few minutes? I need to tell you something," I said while leaning on the entryway to our kitchen, watching her work.

She was folding the weekly laundry in the kitchen, which also doubled as our laundry room. She didn't stop folding but at least acknowledged my question. I hadn't really reasoned through exactly how I was going to tell her. Not only about today, but tomorrow too. And the day after…and so on.

"Of course, what's up?"

"Well, you know how I haven't been happy with my career path," I said, wanting to sound positive.

"Well, Sam Halloran, ya doo declare," Sue mocked in a poor Southern accent. "You're dissatisfied with your job, but I keep saying you are a talented man, and good things will happen if you exhibit patience and faith. You'll see."

"I know. And you have for our entire marriage retained faith and patience in me, and I love you for it. But I've reached a crossroads in my career, something I hadn't anticipated, and we may be in for a big change; one that will significantly alter our standard of living, at least over the short-term, and we need to talk."

She paused right in the middle of folding little Ben's T-shirt, giving me a cynical glare. "Change in our standard of living? We're not too far above the poverty line as it is," she said with a hint of sarcasm and a tilt of her head, both of which I'd grown to adore.

"Oh, please, it's not that bad," I snapped. It absolutely wasn't. She was exaggerating. Our home was modest but comfortable and cozy enough for Sue, me and our two boys. It possessed all the modern conveniences—dishwasher, garbage disposal, washer and dryer and air conditioning. The neighborhood was built right after WWII. It was our first home, and we loved it. Sue especially. She was pulling my strings. I dreaded what was about to come next, but I had to get into it, and soon, before the boys got home from their field trip.

Sue's constant movement made me more anxious than I already was. She would fold a few things and then whisk them off to the bedrooms to put them away, a short walk around the corner and through our living room. She'd brush by me standing at my post between the kitchen and living room acting like a swinging gate each time she passed. About to explode, I grabbed Sue refusing to yield and stared directly at her face.

"OK, honey, so here's the deal. I got fired today."

"That's not funny, honey," Sue said immediately as if I had told her the Empire State Building had fallen over. It should not have surprised me that the news of me being fired would be just as outrageous to Sue. She pushed away from me with a disgusted frown and returned to folding clothes. I remained standing in the same place with Sue a few feet from me. "Not at all funny, Sam Halloran," she said, looking at me as if she wasn't sure whether I might not be kidding.

I didn't have a response. I waited for it to sink in.

She turned toward me. "Sweetheart, fun is fun, but I have to get the clothes put away," she said, clearly dismissing my news. Total denial. "Then I have to get dinner going. I have so much to do, you have no idea, so you need to stop playing games and get out of my way, dear, and you need to—"

I walked close to her as she spun around to face me and grabbed her gently above her elbows. "Susan, I am not joking. I would not joke about such a thing." Her mouth fell wide open as she began to comprehend. I had her attention.

In that moment, I was seeing the girl I married for the first time in a long time. She was still as beautiful as the day I asked her to marry me. Just as shocked too, albeit for quite different reasons. She appeared so innocent with her little pixie nose in the middle of a field of freckles. We'd had countless discussions about those freckles until we stopped having them, and she finally believed I adored each and every one of them. Then there were her eyes, revealing whatever emotion she was feeling depending on her mood. Her shoulder-length brown hair flipped under atop a svelte figure standing at 5'5", and there you have it. The girl I fell in love with in college. The girl I wanted to spend the rest of my life with and would do anything not to disappoint. The girl trusting me to lead our family into success, prosperity and safety. By the look on her face, I was breaking her trust right now, and there wasn't a damn thing I could do about it. It was all I could do not to breakdown. I couldn't. I had to be strong for her. I needed her to continue to trust me. She needed to hear my calming and reassuring words, which I was struggling to find. I should have thought this through better.

"I have to sit," she said as if she was about to faint. I imagined what was going through her mind. I had to react quickly.

"Here you go dear. Sit. Relax," I said, gently easing her into one of the kitchen chairs. "I'll put on some hot water for tea. It's not as bad as it all seems. I have a plan," I said in-between erratic movements. I grabbed the tea kettle, adjusted the flame on the gas stove, and then noisily retrieved a cup and saucer from the cupboard. "We're going to talk about it right now." I was a good salesman, but I would be tested in the next few minutes like never before. Through it all, Sue said nothing.

As I filled the tea kettle and set it on the stove, I glanced at her from time to time, gaging her reaction like I was studying the individual frames of a movie. One I had no idea how it would end. I opened her tea bag dispensary and was confronted with a jumbled mess of different flavors. I looked at Sue's face again. She was staring at the refrigerator like there was a list of things to consider when your husband tells you he's been fired. Seconds seemed like minutes driven by the silence and her constant stare—the clock ticked, or was it my heart beating? Sue had my full attention on the next words she would speak. Everything moved in slow motion. She blinked once. Then again. Her lips parted, but no words followed. Not being a patient man, this was pure torture.

We hadn't had a real crisis during our married life, so it was difficult to figure out exactly what was going on in her mind, but I had a good suspicion she would flood me with questions after we put the boys down for the night.

"We have time," I said softly. "Mr. Benson gave me a month's severance. With your pay, we'll be fine. No worries there. So, we don't need to have it all figured out right this minute. There's time to talk about where we go from here." I was rambling. "I don't want you to worry. Let's take it slow. So, first things first."

Sue was still staring at the refrigerator. While it seemed like an hour passed, it was only a couple of minutes.

"When do you expect the boys home?" I said to change her focus. It worked.

"The boys…" she said, like she was waking up from an afternoon nap. She glanced at the clock on the kitchen wall, then at the one on her wrist as if to confirm. "We're good. I need to go pick them up at school at 6:00." It seemed she was staying calm. Maybe I was doing this the right way. Not rushing her. Letting it all float on the surface for a bit.

"Here you go, honey," I said as I gently placed her tea in front of her. I grabbed one of the random tea bags in the bin without asking her. I figured the fewer decisions Sue needed to deal with at this moment the better. I also placed a sugar cube next to her cup. "Just how you like it, dear."

"I need a spoon," she said as she surveyed my work. "Thank you," came next as I quickly handed her one.

I leaned back on the sink, continuing to survey her developing reaction. It was like viewing a simmering volcano and hoping it would not blow. Uneasy. Disturbed. But nonetheless, controlled.

"Why?" she finally asked as calmly as if she was inquiring about Earl Grey instead of cinnamon tea or as if we were thoughtfully discussing some shared event. She slowly sipped her tea and looked into my face for the first time since I told her. It appeared she was poised and ready to have a conversation, like she had processed the initial blast and was now sorting out everything that resulted from it. *Why* seemed like the perfect opening.

I proffered an answer that wasn't entirely accurate. I told her about the break-in, which was not new news. I mentioned that the thieves used my alarm code, and while Mr. Benson did not believe I was involved, the insurance company did. Her expression informed me that she was accepting what I was saying but struggling to fit it into her reality. Her reality was that I was a good person who would never lie, cheat or steal. How could others not see that? Still, Sue had a keen view the world did not always operate in a sensible and orderly fashion. I told Sue everything she needed to know at the time, which didn't include the crux of the matter—the part about my father. That would have to come later. Hopefully much later, if ever.

Sue checked the wall clock again, this time not feeling the need to confirm the time on her watch. "So, knowing you the way I do, I assume you've thought this all through and have a plan. Give me the short story. I need to leave in a couple of minutes to pick up the boys. We can have a longer discussion tonight after they're in bed."

She crossed her legs and then her arms and looked directly at me the way a judge might glower at a wayward first-time teenage offender promising he'd get his life together. "So, you don't want to sell cigarettes for the rest of your life. Get outta here," she said sarcastically with a wispy manner, taking me back to a more carefree and uncomplicated time.

"Come on, honey," I said, pleading. "That revelation should come as no surprise to you. But we need to have a serious conversation, and I do need your advice, one of those fork-in-the-road conversations. Not of my making, but, hey, I'm trying to make lemonade out of lemons here. Getting fired could turn out to be the best thing that's happened to us."

Sue pulled out another chair next to her and patted the seat. She reached out, gently holding my hands, and pulled me into her and softly, sweetly, kissed me on the lips. It felt so reassuring I relaxed immediately.

Still holding my hands in hers, she sat more erect, squinted her eyes a bit, and then said, "So, tell me what you want to be when you grow up."

I told Sue of a plan gestating within me for the past couple of months. It was so farfetched I didn't dare bring it up until compelled

19

to. Well, it seemed the time had come, so I let it fly. If it crashed and burned, so be it, but the time was now.

"I'll start at the beginning. A couple months ago, I read an article in *The Wall Street Journal* about the expected shift in focus of the major accounting firms. That for over a century, they sold only two basic services—auditing and tax. With the rise in business consulting services, they now felt they were better positioned than any other business to venture into consulting as well. They already had relationships with every public company in the world; adding consulting to their service offerings would seem a natural addition. Trouble is, the article went on, they are an industry of geeks who can't sell."

I sat back with an ear-to-ear smile and spread my arms.

"And who's the best salesman you know?"

That got me an unexpected response. "But, dear, while I agree you are a great salesman, aren't you sort of lacking the main ingredient?"

"You mean, of course, I'm not an accountant. You're right. I get it. That's where going back to school comes in."

She didn't laugh, and she didn't say "no," but she was definitely not yet sold. "I don't want to discourage you, and you know I'm up for whatever you decide, but won't that take a long time? And who's to say if you could compete with much younger, newly graduated accountants. Sounds a bit risky."

"You're bringing up some good points. Ones I've already considered, but I actually had a conversation about my chances with an HR manager at Macallan Reed. They're one of the biggest firms in the world. One of the Big Eight."

"The Big Eight? Sounds like a football conference," she said, looking at her watch and only half-listening.

Before I could respond, Sue stood straight up. "We'll need to continue this later."

"Later? I'm getting ready to give you the details."

"Look at your watch, dear," she said matter-of-factly. "In fifteen minutes, our boys will be standing in front of their school expecting their mom to pick them up. No bus service on class trip days." Sue opened the hall closet door and grabbed her Navy Pea coat. In a flash, she had the front door open and was halfway out of the house before I had a chance to object.

"Can't you ask Molly to pick up the boys today?" It was a rhetorical question. They were her boys and her responsibility. "It's a mom thing," she once confessed when challenged. Another one of those things guys didn't get.

I watched as she made her way out the front door disappointed at her initial reaction. I fell into the chair in front of our picture window wanting to catch a final glimpse of Sue backing out of the driveway. There would be time later.

Eight o'clock. Sue was busy in the kitchen grading papers. My task was getting the boys to wash their faces, brush their teeth and get their PJs on. Same routine every evening. It was a calming time preparing each of us for bed, but especially the boys. They needed time to wind down. But this was also Sue's special time when she needed to be alone. Teaching eighth-grade U.S. History didn't seem that demanding, but she always went the extra mile in her teaching.

I glanced at the wall clock over the doorway anticipating our alone time and what would be at the top of the agenda tonight. I hadn't detected a peep out of the boys since I put them down over an hour ago. Thirty minutes to bedtime for Mom and Dad. For me, more restive moments followed until bedtime. Hearing the rattle of Sue's red pencils followed by her classic sigh indicated her frustration with how tough it was to teach her students. Seconds later, the zipper closed on her briefcase.

I followed Sue to our bedroom where she made the obligatory stop in front of the boys' rooms and stood there not making a sound. I stopped, too, waiting for the all-clear from Sue. Hearing nothing out of either of them, we set about preparing for bed. It was no simple task, given we all shared one bathroom where it was impossible for two people not to bump into each other.

Tonight, though, there was breaking news on TV about a late season tornado sweeping through a small Oklahoma town. I turned up the volume to listen. An EF4 they reported. Two known dead and a small subdivision appearing to be a total loss. Sue was brushing her teeth, her last ritual before my turn. She must have overheard the TV report as she stepped into our bedroom and gurgled out some inaudible question. Even so, I was captivated by the events unfolding on TV and would not have heard her even if her toothbrush wasn't swirling around in her mouth. *What if that happened here? When I was unemployed and back in school.* A catastrophe such as a tornado would end our plan right quick. Maybe this wasn't the right move.

She clicked the TV off as I finished in the bathroom. I hustled into our bedroom eagerly anticipating our discussion. Sue was already propped up on the headboard and had chosen a magazine rather than her usual book to read. Not a good sign. That usually meant she was tired and lights-out was moments away.

Rolling into bed next to Sue, I turned on my reading light and picked up a magazine with no intention of reading it. It was more to have something in front of me. We had a lot to discuss, and I anxiously waited for Sue to begin the conversation. Earlier, I had said everything I needed to say. Tonight was her turn.

She abruptly lowered her magazine into her lap. "Sam, you have always made good decisions. There is no reason for me to think otherwise now. I know you will always have our family's best interest at heart. Why would I question it? I'm eager to hear more about this Big Eight thing."

Excited to begin, I launched into it.

"Honey, the Big Eight—"

"But not tonight. I'm exhausted."

With that curt comment, she dropped her magazine on her nightstand, flicked off her reading light, leaned over for our customary final kiss of the day, slid down under the covers and let out a sigh. I couldn't believe it. She was really going to sleep without

22

a single word about the crazy plan I laid on her earlier.

Experience taught me there was nothing I could say to dissuade her. So, I waited for Sue's familiar final phrase to follow her sigh, and it soon came.

"I love you, Sam," but tonight, there came an added assurance. "And I trust you."

"Love you too, sweetheart. And I won't let you down."

"I know."

I lay in the dark listening to her soft breathing level down as she fell asleep.

CHAPTER 4

I noticed Jake on the loading platform. He had the best clean jokes around. I'd miss his humor. I waved, but I guess he didn't see me as he walked back inside the warehouse. At least, that's what I wanted to believe.

I opened the front door to the office. Charlotte was a trapped animal behind her desk. Her eyes darted around like she wanted desperately to focus on something else—anything but to have to deal with me. Eventually, she spoke. "Morning, Sam. How are you?" The moment she said it, she rolled her eyes toward the ceiling. "Sam, I'm sorry."

"Charlotte, relax. No need to apologize." I smiled. She smiled back, the tension in the small reception area broken. "I'm here to see Mr. Benson, is he—?"

"Sam, I've been expecting you," Morris Benson said as he came around the corner behind me. He extended his hand, and I instinctively grabbed it. He shook it for what seemed a long time. It was as if the longer he shook my hand the more comfortable he'd feel about firing his sales manager yesterday. Still shaking my hand as if blowing up a bicycle tire with a hand pump, he placed his other hand on my shoulder. His body felt rigid, tense.

I wanted to leave as soon as I could.

Benson Distributing was one of my clients when I sold cigarettes for the R.J. Reynolds Tobacco Company—RJR, my first job out of college. It wasn't something anyone would have predicted me to do back in high school. I was actually voted "Most Shy" by my senior class at Metuchen High School, and they really got that one right. If someone shier than me existed, they'd be living in a basement somewhere, never to be seen. It wasn't that I didn't like people. I struggled with conversation, which was probably why I enjoyed chess in high school, especially competing on our chess team. I'd always been extremely competitive. Chess allowed me to compete without having to interact with anyone.

My time working for RJR revealed something to me. I could sell! Prior to RJR, no one would conceive of me becoming a good salesman or imagine me walking up to a perfect stranger and selling him something, anything, but especially cigarettes and plug chewing tobacco. Still, after a period of constant exposure to selling, I became good at it. My success at RJR was why Benson Distributing approached me with an offer to become their sales manager. I accepted the offer instantly.

"So, Sam, it's as I told you yesterday," Mr. Benson began, seated behind his huge ornate black walnut desk. *It must be worth a fortune*, I thought. Mr. Benson should have bought a chair worthy of a desk like that. It wasn't. It sat low, causing Mr. Benson to appear dwarf-like. Still, the desk was serving its purpose this morning. It provided some distance between him and me, which seemed to give him the confidence to tell me what I came to hear this morning. Well, most of what I wanted to hear. None of it really mattered. The situation seemed simple enough. Whoever broke in stole $25,000 worth of tax stamps. The margins in the business were so slim they'd need the insurance company to reimburse them quickly if they were to stay in business. Benson's had about 500 customers who depended on them for their cigarettes and candy. As there was little to differentiate them from their competitors, they'd have to deliver for them each and every week to keep their business. Literally, "deliver" for them. I would not be surprised to learn they would lose a few customers with the delays caused by the theft.

"So, I'm assuming with my termination you were able to settle the insurance claim yesterday." I said it in a business-like manner.

"Yes, thank God," Mr. Benson said, expressing his obvious relief.

"Did Mike make it home from Miami?" I asked for lack of anything better to say. Mike Benson, Mr. Benson's son, was on vacation but headed back early on news of the turmoil. Mike ran the inside while I ran the outside. We didn't get along for reasons I was never able to determine. Maybe he was jealous of my close relationship with his father.

"He did." His abruptness signified Mike wanted nothing to do with me. I'm guessing he's the one who told a few folks in the back I got fired and the rumor mill made short work of my reputation. So be it. I wanted to do what I had to do and leave the premises immediately after meeting with my sales team.

The events of yesterday still weighed heavily on Mr. Benson's conscience. He offered financial assistance, again. I didn't want a handout and responded immediately saying, "No, Mr. Benson. I'll be fine. You were generous with my severance check yesterday. It is more than enough. I'll be fine."

"Sam, I have no right to ask you for your help, but I must."

I suspected where he was going.

"Sam, your sales force, I told them exactly what I told you I would tell everyone. Not sure how, but the truth leaked out. Of course, they didn't believe any of it. Whatever you did with them, they are loyal to you, son. They like you very much. One in particular."

"I appreciate hearing that. Thank you."

"I think I know the answer to this, but I have to ask," he said.

I answered before he could ask. "Sara, Sara should get my job. Not even a contest. You need to make Sara your new sales manager and the sooner the better."

"I'm not surprised...but not me. You should do it, Sam. She's here and wants to talk with you before you leave. She's in the conference room."

I stood. He did too, and without much thought, I embraced him.

I was relieved he embraced me as well.

I had met Sara Proctor about four years ago while taking the weekly order at Tucker State Pharmacy. She was the Mars Candy representative; on that day she was building a promotional display near the checkout offering two-for-one Mars bars. We got to talking, which led to having a coffee. A close friendship soon developed. One thing led to the next, and two months later, Sara was my first new hire.

Never having hired anyone before, I had no formula for making such a decision, but one thing was for sure—I liked her from our first meeting. While she didn't tell me her age, I was shocked to learn it from her application. At forty years old, Sara wasn't married but had a son, Bobby, whom she adored; he was now an adult and worked at the cement plant a few miles south. Sara didn't seem old enough to have an adult child.

Sara didn't have a lot, and she appeared to be struggling financially. She didn't tell me that. She didn't need to. It was obvious in the clothes she wore. Her shoes for one thing. Shoes told the real story about one's finances. Anyone could buy a nice suit of clothes on sale and, at least for a guy, a decent tie. If someone would skimp, it would be on the shoes. The worn leather on the outside of her right heel indicated she wore a pair that had run its course. She tried to hide it with shoe polish, but the years of driving with that shoe lying on the floor mat under the gas pedal had taken its toll.

Then there was the bow on the front of each shoe. There was something about the one on her left shoe revealing it had fallen off and been clumsily reattached although not quite straight enough. Her blouse cuff, too. There was fray around the front of the cuff on each arm but especially her right one; the one she used to write up her daily sales call reports. Last, there was the second button on her blouse right below her chin. It was a decent match but didn't have quite the same sheen as the others. It had been replaced, for sure.

It was a bittersweet moment to tell her she would take over for me as sales manager of Benson Distributing, and Sara was excited for the opportunity, as well as the nice pay raise. I hadn't made many friends in my lifetime, but Sara was one I hoped I could circle back with at a later time.

CHAPTER 5

After meeting with Sara, I was spent. I didn't want to clean out my office or say goodbye to anyone. I wanted to get home. Maybe I'd come back later. Maybe not.

One of Benson's drivers gave me a lift home. On that short drive, I became flush with both anticipation and fear. Mostly fear. But there was some spark of daring ready to light the fuel of ambition in the far recesses of my brain. I was now given the opportunity of a restart.

It's not like I hadn't been anticipating moving into another career. I was fortunate the HR manager from Macallan Reed agreed to talk with me. He said I didn't need a degree in accounting. Only needed to pass the CPA exam. But he also said because I was a decade older than their typical recruit, no one would grant me an interview. The Big Eight did all their recruiting for new associates through campus. But, if I went back to school, maybe got an MBA, I could sign up through the school's campus recruiter, and all the firms would have to interview me, as long as I otherwise qualified. Meaning I had to do well. It all sounded like good advice. If I had the goal of working for one of the Big Eight firms, it was do or die—get an MBA and pass the CPA exam.

I felt I might blackout. The only thing that kept me from passing out right there in the front seat of the delivery van was my body's anatomic reaction showering me with perspiration to cool down. As luck would have it, I recovered.

The van pulled up to the curb of our home. I slowly stepped out, thanked the driver and waved him off. It was a little after 11 a.m. I turned toward the house. Felt like I was seeing it for the first time since we bought it six years ago. Nobody was home. For the moment, I was content to simply gaze at it in a manner I had not done since moving day.

The variegated tan brick gave the ranch a distinctive appearance apart from the surrounding homes with their more common red brick facades. The picture window to the right of the front door appeared inviting; maybe I should sit in our living room and stare out of it for a time.

I felt guilty standing on the front curb of my house. I needed to do something. I had to move forward in some manner, but at the moment I felt paralyzed. Lots of good reasons to move from the curb and move on to finding a new job, or go back to school...something. But still I remained there as the wind gusted, gray clouds surrounding everything: trees, power lines, our home. Not a soul in sight.

A month ago, my view of the picture window would have been blocked by the leaves on our large sugar maple tree. This being late October its dense leafage was no longer an obstruction. A gust of wind formed a small funnel swirling some leaves I had failed to rake; upward they spun off to the left toward the stockade fence. I had forgotten how the fence leaned in nearly a foot off-center. Our neighbor across the street told me it was a sure sign the fence post had rotted out. It would have to be replaced. That project would need to wait for better times.

My eyes drifted toward our roof. The dark brown shingles covering our little home were in stark contrast to the pale green ones on the detached garage to the left. Sue was not happy when I told her we could not afford to re-shingle the garage when we did the house last year. The house was leaking. The garage was leaking, too, but it was a garage. No drywall ceiling and insulation in the garage. It could wait. She implored me it would "look stupid" having two different colors. I responded we simply could not afford it, plain and simple. Sue did what she always did, knowing she was about to lose an argument. She bit her bottom lip, cocked her head in my direction and told me I'd have to make it up to her, usually meaning to take her out on a date. Which we did that night. We had a romantic and fun evening. The mismatched shingle colors never came up again. That was my Sue.

I had forgotten about date night. I wondered how Sue would react to us having to defer those.

Approaching our front door, I stopped and turned toward the curb. Observing the driveway, I noticed the cracks in the concrete and didn't remember them being so wide and uneven. I wondered what another winter of freeze-thaw would do to them. Water would seep into those cracks, then freeze, then expand imposing further damage. Even solid concrete would cede to the pressure of freezing water. Such an image seemed an apt metaphor for the journey I had ahead of me. No job. No prospects and Walter Cronkite reported last night the recession had no end in sight. When it began in January everyone said it would be over before the end of the year. Now they're saying it's the worst since the Great Depression and could hang on for some time. Again, I felt flush, weak like I had felt earlier in the van.

Thankfully, a gust of cold air whipped up, opening my light sport coat and cooling my body saving me from hitting the ground, hard.

Now gripping the porch railing, I walked up the steps to our front door pausing to ensure I was sure-footed. Suddenly, my vision clouded, heart raced. I didn't need to take my pulse. The rapid beats through my eardrums informed me I might soon pass out.

Making it inside I collapsed on one of our kitchen chairs. Sweat now cooling my body, my pulse returning to normal, vision, too. It had been years since I experienced a panic attack. I hadn't since marrying Sue.

Panic attacks had previously plagued me. My doctor said perceived threats would cause an adrenalin release. Primal. Fight or flight. Told me for most people they were rare but could be triggered by perceived life or death situations. My case was "atypical," he said.

For me, those attacks could be brought on by something as routine as a teacher calling on me in class. Most would not perceive that as a threatening situation but not me. My metabolic reaction was the same as if a wild boar were bearing down on me signaling imminent death. Why my mind interpreted minor threats in such a manner I would not come to understand for many years. Those attacks happened so often as a child most of my teachers were sensitive to my "condition" as the school nurse once told me. I couldn't believe they made a note in my file. Apparently, I was a novelty. Just as well. At least most people went easy on me, or I was certain I would have had more attacks.

But it leaked out in high school. That was good, and bad. That many were sympathetic was good. The bad part was how the girls treated me. They avoided me like the plague. Most boys, too. Except the bullies. They were relentless. In my condition, they found a new form of entertainment when they became bored. At times, they would try provoking me to see what would happen. On most of those occasions, I could scurry off somewhere to get away from them. Sometimes, I couldn't. Once, when I was a junior, they surrounded me right after the bell sounded. I was late for class that day. I was never late again. That attack was so severe I passed out and awoke in an ambulance.

School nurse called Mom. Didn't call Dad. His reputation was beastly. When Mom arrived, I overheard them telling her I should be tested for epilepsy. "Those tests have already been done," Mom told them. I didn't have epilepsy. "Merely occasional episodes," she told the nurse, "Not a big deal." But they were a big deal. To me anyway.

I didn't go to school the next day, or the next. When I finally returned to school I found I had a new nickname—The Hulk. One of Marvel Comics characters. One that fit with my condition perfectly.

Those episodes ushered in a new era for me, driving me further into isolation. Going forward, I made it my mission in life to avoid situations where panic attacks might occur. I felt cursed. In subsequent years I would have more attacks but none since meeting

Sue. I don't even remember when the last one had occurred. Apparently, I was good at willing them from my memory. I worried now, for the first time since high school, they might return. God help us all if that would happen.

CHAPTER 6

January 25, 1982

I began my last semester of the MBA program proud of my accomplishments. I was surprised how quickly I had slipped back into student mode. With only one more semester at Indiana, I would graduate with Honors.

Since I had embarked on this new direction, my confidence had improved a great deal. Still, rejection always fell hard upon me. Wasn't sure if that would ever change. I embarked on a good plan, executed it fairly well. No one predicted the bad economy would still be gripping the nation.

Then I received a phone call from campus recruiting...

"Mr. Halloran, I am calling regretfully to inform you that due to the continuing recession, the following firms have decided to cancel their spring campus interview schedules. They are as follows—"

"Wait a minute," I said. "What do you mean 'cancel?' They can't cancel," I blabbered. This couldn't be happening. I'd worked too hard and come too far.

"Mr. Halloran, it is indeed unfortunate, and it has never happened in my ten years at the University, but it is what it is. Now, if you will please allow me to continue, I need to tell you how this situation has affected your planned interview schedule."

As she continued it was as if I had trouble hearing her. Like in a gathering of people, everyone talking but I was straining to hear someone standing close and attempting to speak above the din. I could hear enough to comprehend she was saying something of grave importance but difficult to make it out.

One by one she ticked off all but one of the Big Eight firms. "Mr. Halloran, are you still on the line?"

"I am."

I had escaped serving in the Vietnam War but had seen enough war movies depicting young soldiers and how they would act after their foxhole was hit with an enemy mortar. Those still alive. Vision cloudy, hearing impaired. All symptoms I was now experiencing. Suddenly, like the opening of a *Star Trek* episode when the stars turned blurry as the USS *Enterprise* shot into space, all my senses returned with what seemed to be the caller's final comment.

"Mr. Halloran, I need confirmation that you will adjust your schedule according to the modifications I have communicated to you."

She could not have been more impersonal. Anger began to well inside of me. It wasn't her fault. She was simply doing her job. "I apologize, but this has been a bit of a shock." I paused.

"So, to confirm, you are telling me..."

I confirmed, one by one, all the firms by name that canceled and had no plans to reschedule at this time. Should they change their plans, I would be notified. I also confirmed one firm had not canceled, but there was no guarantee they would still not cancel. I thanked her for her call, out of polite habit only, and hung up.

I sat there in my recliner reading a rather difficult chapter on Keynesian economic theory and allowed the book and my notes to drop from my hands into my lap. Hands which now served to shield my face from Sue standing at the entrance to the family room. She must have overheard my side of that demoralizing call.

"Honey, who was that?" she asked in a concerned and sympathetic voice, as if she already knew that call delivered bad news.

I didn't answer immediately, and she walked into the room, still fumbling with a kitchen towel, saying more gently, "Sweetheart, what happened? Who called? Why are you upset?"

I could no longer hide my distress from Sue and took her into my arms as she folded into me. I didn't talk. She no longer asked questions. She sat in my lap as I held her tight, with her head on the side of mine, one arm around my shoulder, the other gently stroking my hair. We sat there for the longest time, neither of us saying anything.

"Hey, where is everybody?" We had almost forgotten about them, well, I had. Other things on my mind. I could tell it was Will because he continually disobeyed my instructions to open the front door slowly, so it would not crash into the closet door. I lost count of how often I scolded him for that, but today I gave him a pass. It was my fault anyway. Instead of working at a full-time job like other dads, I was fooling around at school daring to believe I could better myself. In the meantime, the house was falling into disrepair. On the list of many items needing attention was that broken doorstop which could have been replaced in minutes but had been left unattended. With all the problems sure to follow from that call, I decided to get out of the chair and greet my children bursting with excitement to tell us about their day.

After a few minutes, I decided to allow Sue to handle them. I stood motionless in the kitchen leaning on the refrigerator. Sue was standing by the sink staring at me as the kids continued to buzz around us oblivious to the pain we were both feeling. Sue broke her stare, walked up to me and kissed me gently on the lips. Clearly she was frustrated she could not mend the growing wound in my heart some nameless caller had caused.

I proceeded into the foyer, opened the closet and grabbed my coat. "Where are you going?" she said; "and won't you please tell me what that call was about."

She had a right to know. Glancing over my shoulder to ensure the kids were off playing in the family room and out of earshot, I lowered my gaze to the floor and said, "That was the woman in charge of campus recruiting. All but one of my interviews was canceled. Something about a bad economy."

"That's not fair," Sue yelled. She flipped her dish towel into the sink as she approached me but stopped, giving me the space I so desperately needed.

It was a gratuitous comment, and I turned and opened the front door.

"Sam, where are you going?" she asked with pleading concern.

I didn't answer. I didn't want to answer. I was still in shock. But Sue deserved to know where I was going. It used to scare the hell out of me when Dad, after breaking off one of the almost daily fights with Mom, would put on his coat and walk out the door. While he never said, we knew where he was headed. I just hoped I'd be asleep when he returned.

My family didn't deserve such treatment, and I said, "Honey, don't worry about me. I'll be fine. Need to clear my head. I'm going to Ace Hardware and get a new doorstop for the front door."

"I love you," Sue said from the kitchen.

I returned the affection, but the door had already closed. No matter. Sue knew my feelings for her and that I needed to be alone for a while. I'd figure out a way to deal with this latest wrinkle. I always had before, and I would again. Somehow, someway I'd make the most of a bad situation. Exactly like my chess coach had told me. Life was like a continual chess match. You against the other guy. Everyone starts out equal, but the one who figures out the other's weaknesses, then capitalizes on them with the right approach, will be the victor. He was right. This was just another chess match. I'd figure it out. I'd be the victor.

At that moment though, I had no answer for how.

I'd let a day pass to contemplate my new situation. I'd call them. Every firm who canceled on me.

When I reached a secretary trained in the fine art of screening calls I explained the reason for my call. Of course the recruiting manager was "occupied," or "not in the office today," or "with a client." The reasons didn't matter, well, all except for one.

Of the seven firms calling to cancel my campus interview, there was one firm who called to state specifically they did not want to interview me due to my age. They were still coming to campus. To my knowledge, they had not canceled with anyone except me. More than anything, that was upsetting. It wasn't because they were cutting back due to business conditions, as the others. Without even meeting me for the mandated thirty-minute interview scheduled time slot afforded each candidate, someone had determined I was not qualified because I was too old. No age discrimination laws back then.

Yes, I simply had to get through to this firm's recruiting manager. To ensure that happened I did something I never did. I lied.

"Hello, Anderson Mitchell, how may I direct your call?" said the receptionist.

His name was Bennett Cosgrove. Found him through an earlier call to their office posing as someone from campus recruiting.

"Yes, this is Sam Halloran returning Mr. Cosgrove's call. He said it was urgent." I gave her my real name. He'd never remember it anyway.

"Please hold, Mr. Halloran, I'll put you right through." It worked.

"Bennett Cosgrove, how can I help you?"

I reasoned if I could keep him on the line with my opening statement I had a chance of completing all I wanted to say. Without waiting for his response, I launched into the reason for my call.

"Mr. Cosgrove," I said, "This is Sam Halloran. I know you have made your decision, and I am in no position to second-guess a representative of one of the premiere accounting and auditing firms in the world, but for my own benefit I would like to ask why you decided to pull me from your interview schedule. I promise to just listen. I won't disagree or be defensive, but please tell me."

To my amazement he was still on the line. I expected him to seek more clarification. I expected to hear the shuffling of some papers, but nothing.

"Look, Sam," he finally began, "I empathize with you and what you are attempting to do, and if it makes you feel better, I was pulling for you, but in the end, I was overruled. Fact of the matter is you would be thirty-two years old when beginning your career with us. You'd be working with, and reporting to, staff a whole lot younger than you. You'd encounter generational differences. The selection committee, of which I am but one vote, didn't believe you could be successful overcoming those differences. A huge part of succeeding at AM relies on the individual classes getting-on with each other. I would expect all the firms have the same expectation. With your age difference, the committee simply didn't believe there was any possibility of you overcoming such a disadvantage. I'm sorry, and I wish you the best of luck."

It was a short conversation but stung with another reality. It would be difficult to "get-on" with the others, gently mocking to myself his obvious British heritage. AM had their beginnings in Great Britain, so it was not surprising to find Bennett Cosgrove was one who had made it across the pond.

Another hurdle lay just ahead. I had sat for the CPA exam the past November. A grueling exam taken over two and a half days. *Had I passed?* Any day now I would find out, but I had pushed it from my mind. The Becker CPA Review course was itself a tedious process. For sixteen weeks I attended day-long sessions every Saturday, as they religiously hammered upon us the low passing rate—only 5% would pass all four parts of the exam on the first sitting. And most CPA exam candidates were accounting majors. I was a marketing major. Sure, I had taken two beginning accounting courses as part of the business school curriculum twelve years ago, but there were a dozen courses covered on the exam I never had exposure to. Then there was auditing which was such a huge subject area, it made up its own separate part of the exam. I'd never even had an introductory auditing class!

Most of Becker wasn't a review for me; it was more or less an outline of the subject areas I would have to learn before I could begin to study for the big exam. There was more than one occasion where I had seriously questioned the wisdom in embarking on this fool's folly. Yet through it all, Sue encouraged me.

The more I contemplated my situation the more depressed I became. Then I regarded our precarious financial situation, much of which I had kept secret from Sue. She could do nothing about it so why worry her. She was teaching full-time, even took on summer school. I did what I could to earn extra money including selling Christmas trees and working on the UPS loading dock during December. Still, we needed some steady cash. I expected we could hold out until my planned start date in the fall, assuming I would have a job. My student loan payments would begin in October and add nearly $300 a month to an already strapped budget.

I sat at my desk in our bedroom, grinding my teeth, tightening my grip on my microeconomics textbook. My son Will chose to pay me a visit at the absolute worst moment.

"Ben, no! I'm gonna play chess with Dad. Leave us alone!" Will was yelling as he came sailing into our bedroom, a little too hot, with Ben close behind. Will tripped, and the plastic chess set someone had bought him for his birthday scattered all over me. White and black chess pieces flew everywhere.

"God dammit, how many times have I told you kids to leave me alone when I'm studying!" I screamed.

Will looked up at me, blaming his brother for tripping him. Bad news for both of us. I swung around and laid the back of my hand across his face with such force his head hit the corner of the box springs as he howled in pain. Ben fell to his knees, screaming in horror at what his dad had done to his brother. I froze and then fell to my knees to attend to Will, who was now crying. When Sue came in, Ben immediately reached for his mother; Will, now recovered but still crying, sailed past Sue to his bedroom and slammed his door.

Sue glared at me in horror. I stood, offering to bring calm to a scene from hell. She would have none of it.

"Samuel Halloran, I know you are under a great deal of stress, but there is no excuse for striking our children. Never!" She was trembling.

I didn't say another word. Sue's face was redder than a sunburn. She held Ben in her arms, his head buried in her chest. Her hand caressed him as if shielding him from harm...from me. Ashamed, I slowly fell into my desk chair and buried my head into my hands, imploring myself to calm down. Sue slammed our bedroom door. I could hear Will's muffled cries in his bedroom. Soon after, the front door of the house slammed shut. I ran to the living room picture window in time to watch my entire family backing out of the driveway on their way to who-knew-where. It was a little before five o'clock. Dejectedly, I walked into the kitchen, turned off the bean soup still cooking on the stove and shut off the oven where the cornbread appeared to have burned. I sat at the kitchen table and sobbed. I felt so alone, so desperate.

Sue didn't return until a little after nine o'clock. I was sitting in the family room in my recliner. The room was dark. I had been there since they left, repeating only one wish—Sue would return with our boys. She had. I now had one additional concern. We had an unbroken custom of never going to bed mad at each other. When the clock chimed ten times I feared that custom was about to be broken. I was broken. Directionless. Despondent. I had so many worries I didn't know where to begin. I was incapacitated.

Then, I caught her shadow in the doorway between the kitchen and family room. She stood there for a few moments, watching me in the dark. It seemed like a mirage. I willed myself to believe it was really Sue.

"I am so, so sorry, Sue. I don't know what else to say or do to make it up to you and the boys." At the very moment I put a period on the end of that sentence, Sue rushed into my arms. I hugged her so tightly I feared I might crush her. She was crying. Minutes passed. I felt her tears running down my neck. It felt like holy water.

"I need to tell you something. Something I have held secret from you only because I feared thinking about it myself." I knew I was about to stun my wife.

41

Sue sat up in my lap, unsettled. It was as though she realized what she was about to hear could change everything. I gazed into her eyes, deeply, somberly, as if it would be the last time I would ever see her innocence.

"When I was sixteen, I tried to take my own life."

CHAPTER 7

Sue covered her mouth with her hands, gasping for air like she might soon pass out. Then lowered one hand to touch mine, and with another deep breath, she began breathing normally. I waited until she seemed ready. I, too, needed time to think, although over the past three hours I had rehearsed what I was about to say. This day was a longtime coming. Sue moved to the floor next to my recliner, sitting on her legs, her hands wrapped around mine. She surveyed my face like a child about to hear a horror story, preparing for the worst. She didn't say a word. She waited for me to begin…and so I did.

"After seventeen years of marriage, Mom had become very adept at handling Dad's drunken behavior. Beginning in about the sixth grade, he would pick me up at school and take me to one of his favorite drinking establishments. Even in high school, sometimes he would be there at the bus circle, standing outside his car and yelling my name. If I didn't get in his car fast enough, he'd make a big scene. I had enough things to be embarrassed about. There was no point in adding to the list. I got in his car.

"At sixteen, one might think I could stand up to Dad. Especially those times when he would physically threaten Mom. On those rare occasions when I did intercede, he would push me away with the same effort one would swat a fly. But on those days with his anger enhanced by alcoholic adrenalin, he would pummel me into the ground. I was no match for him. The best approach was to go along, speak as infrequently as possible, avoid eye contact and pray I wouldn't further rile him. Such was the typical pattern. But then there was this one particular day I will never forget."

* * * *

"Now, Sammy, you know how your mother gets when I stop by to see my friends."

Friends? Sure they're your friends, Dad. You buy them round after round. I wouldn't dare say it out loud.

Invariably, there would be some sporting event, or recap of one, on the TV while we were sitting at the bar. Occasionally, he'd interrupt my wandering eye and point out something happening on the TV. I'd feign some interest in what he was discussing, but I wasn't good at deception. I couldn't care less about sports and was painfully aware that wasn't normal. I was a guy, and guys were supposed to love sports. It was weird that I didn't. I liked chess. Dad wasn't impressed. Even with what I had accomplished. In his eyes, I was still a loser. He was partially right.

When entering a bar, any bar, Dad would always stand right inside the door for a few moments, allowing his eyes to adjust from the sunlight. Once adjusted, he'd scan the bar for someone to sit next to so he'd have an audience. I always felt sorry for the poor guy who would soon be on the receiving end of Dad's commentary on how pathetic a son he'd been cursed to have.

"Take him to ball games more than any dad," he'd say in slurred and disoriented speech to the unfortunate guy sitting on the bar stool next to him. That wasn't even close to the truth, but he'd say it nonetheless.

That poor chap having to hear Dad complain about his bad luck would simply smile at him in a polite way and return his attention to the TV. Worst of all was when he'd regale his new "friend" with all my shortcomings, knowing I heard every word he was saying.

"Wish I had a son who was interested in sports," he'd say. "Millions of kids out there, and I get a momma's boy."

My chest sunk, and my breathing became shallow. I wouldn't

make eye contact with Dad. The thing to do was to ignore him.

If it was possible for me to have one favorite bar it would be the Towne Tavern. While I hated this frequent evening ritual, I could do nothing to avoid it, so I tried my best to influence which bar he'd choose. The Towne Tavern was less frequented by the bikers. They were the worst and seemed to favor the Hoffbrau Tavern down by the river. For some reason, on this day, January 26, 1967, Dad walked into the Hoffbrau Tavern and changed the course of both his life and mine.

We took a couple of seats at the bar, and Dad went into his normal routine—boring the shit out of the guy sitting next to him. Unlike the guys at the Towne Tavern, this one would not put up with Dad's bullshit, especially when he railed on his son, who the guy quickly figured out was me. When he left in mid-sentence of Dad's oratory, it pissed Dad off. He jumped up and followed the guy. But Dad was already stupid drunk and bumped into a biker dude, spilling his beer. Dad slurred some kind of an apology, but it was not good enough.

I was sitting about six barstools away and didn't hear what the biker said, but that biker laid into Dad and pelted him with two or three fists right in the face. Dad collapsed in a heap against the brass rail at the foot of the bar. He lay there unconscious for a moment while the guy and his buddies chuckled at the sight of "…a drunk who couldn't defend himself."

"Hey, pussy. Got no fight in ya?" one of the bikers yelled loud enough for half the bar to hear him, including me.

I froze not knowing what to do.

Dad groaned and began to move.

I went to him holding out my hand, being sure not to touch him. "Dad, Dad, you OK?"

He mumbled something incoherent and moved his arms. I was more scared than ever before on one of those *out on the town* bar nights with my dad.

Dad was trying to get to his feet, mumbling something that roused the bikers again. When another one of them stood up and approached

Dad, who had his hand on a stool trying to stand, the bartender warned the biker to sit or he'd call the cops. Fortunately, he obeyed and sloughed off Dad's slurred comments which seemed to substitute for any real threatening action.

The bartender turned toward me. "Take your dad home, son."

I put my arm around his waist. He pushed me away, saying he could walk "without no help from the bar ninny." I guessed he was referring to me. He yelled it loud enough everyone in the bar had to have heard the comment, yet no one returned one. Not even the biker table, in deference to me, I supposed.

I believed if I wasn't there that night at the Hoffbrau, those bikers would have killed Dad. They'd have followed him to the parking lot and beaten him to death just for fun. For years, I pleaded with God for one more opportunity. If I was so lucky, next time I would walk out the back door and allow whatever was about to happen to my dad to happen. He'd never again be a threat to Mom and me.

Dad regained his footing quickly once we hit the cold January air. He pushed me aside and led the way to his car. He was drunk, but there was no way I was about to offer to drive for the five-mile journey home. I gritted my teeth and climbed in the passenger side. I had done this often before. If I had had self-confidence I would have told him to go to hell and walked home without him. But back then, I was worthless—exactly like my father had designed and manufactured.

Fifteen minutes later, we were under our carport. I got out quickly and positioned myself next to Dad's door. "Need some help, Dad?"

"Fuck no," he growled as he slowly dragged himself out of the door. He made it difficult by pulling too close to one of the carport uprights. Still, he managed to squeeze out and weave his way to the foot of our front stairs. I held back, afraid to move past him.

"Sammy! Where are you?"

"Right here, Dad," I said as I moved by his side, offering by gesture to help him but knowing he'd never accept.

"What are you doing there? You know what to do, so do it."

I absolutely knew the routine. I was to run in the house ahead of him and distract Mom. As if that would ever work.

I entered the front door, eager to get to my bedroom—my routine on such nights. I would feel safe there. I threw a hurried glance into the kitchen where Mom was busy at the stove.

"Hi, Mom," I said cautiously, hoping she would prepare herself for what was about to walk through the door behind me. But she didn't look at me. Apparently, she was unaware this was to be one of those nights.

"Sammy, you and your dad are going to love what I cooked for you tonight," she proudly declared. "Come in here and taste it."

I didn't move. Upstairs was where I could hide. There was no telling what might happen downstairs. In a few minutes, whatever she was cooking would likely sail through the air, and I didn't want to be anywhere near the war zone.

She turned, ladle in hand, curious why I hadn't come to her. Maybe it was the blankness I wore on my face or maybe she heard her husband wrestling with the screen door. She froze, shifting her gaze from me to the front door. She couldn't see outside, but she could hear him. He wasn't even attempting to hide his drunkenness like he did most nights.

"Where's my dinner?" he slurred upon entering the house.

I took one last glance at Mom before everything went to shit. Her eyes settled on her drunken husband. I ran up the stairs and into my bedroom, slamming the door behind me. I threw myself onto the bed, covered my head with my pillows and prayed. I sensed tonight would be different.

Like the calm before the storm, there was a virtual dead silence. Then Dad's voice rose as if he could make Mom back off with an intimidating blast.

"It's none of your goddamn business what I do after work," he shouted.

Eventually, my name worked its way into the buildup of the brewing fight.

"You're drunk again," Mom said. "Worse, you've taken Sammy with you. Have you no pride? And don't think for one minute the neighbors don't know what a drunk you are. A drunk and a terrible father."

Bingo. Mom always knew what buttons to push to get Dad to spiral out of control. The yelling and screaming from both escalated.

"You've never had faith in me. You can't treat me like a man. You embarrass me in front of my friends. You embarrass me in front of my son."

Yeah, suddenly, I was his "son." About an hour ago I was that pitiful lump of skin and organs who somehow bore his last name. I was a no-good, worthless kid who was defective. Plain and simple. That's what Dad would tell me. And I'd believe him. I'd believe it was true every time he'd say it. Of course I would. He was my dad. Dads don't lie to their kids. I'd believe it even after he was no longer around. I believed it until I didn't anymore—about the time Sue came into my life.

"Get your hands off me!" Mom yelled from downstairs. Like a superhero, I leaped from my bed and ran to the top of the stairway, glaring at Dad down below. He had his arm around my mother's neck. He leered up at me and grinned like the devil he was. "What the hell are you gonna do, you ninny?" he egged on.

I didn't move. Frozen in place, I acquiesced like I usually did, knowing my dad was right. I was a worthless ninny. Spineless. I watched my mother in a stranglehold at the mercy of my father. I was scared. I wanted to come to her rescue but could not move toward them.

Someone hit the fast-forward button on the video of my life. Suddenly, all the tormenting frames were flashing before my eyes, the daily ridicule I suffered at school because everyone knew what happened at the Halloran household on most nights. "The Hulk" some would call me. There were times I wished I could have transformed into The Hulk, so I could pummel my father senseless.

But my dad was right about one thing. I was a complete ninny. I turned away from the stairs and walked down the hallway into my parents' bedroom. Where Dad kept his gun was no secret to me.

For all I knew, Dad might be strangling Mom. Still, I didn't care. Everything moved at lightning speed. A moment later, the movie slowed and returned to normal speed. I had Dad's .45 1911 ACP handgun pointed at my temple, finger on the trigger. I remembered thinking, *This is it. Screw it.*

I pulled the trigger. *Click.* I forgot to chamber a round. I was so inept I couldn't even commit suicide.

Mom screamed from downstairs.

I raced to the top of the stairs again. Even with his own gun trained on him, my father was fearless, arrogant. When he realized his son had pointed his gun at him, he said, in admiring fashion, "So my kid has a pair after all." He was grinning. This time, I had chambered a round.

I was hoping he'd let Mom go and walk away, but I guess he had other thoughts in mind. He let her go alright, casting her aside into the wall where she crumpled into a heap. Then, he slowly began to walk up the stairs, his eyes locked on mine.

"You piece of shit," he growled. "You point a gun at me, you better use it." So, I did.

He was only a dozen feet away, and I missed. He paused, then slowly continued up the stairs. I shot one more time. Missed again. He was all over me. I blacked out.

* * * *

Sue, still on the floor a few feet away, now sat with her arms curled around her knees. She was crying. Her red, teary eyes peered over her knees. I joined her on the floor and hugged her. I rocked her and consoled her.

"Honey, I'm sorry I never told you. It was such a dark time in my life. I willed it from my memory."

After a few moments, she spoke, her body and speech trembling.

"Sam, I am devastated you had to live through that."

We continued to hold each other and slowly swayed on the floor. Neither of us said anything for a long time. I had the feeling Sue wanted to say more but was afraid of what might come next. I didn't want her to be afraid. I had gone this far; I wanted to get it all out and be done with it. I prompted her to open up and say what she felt. She did.

"But why now? Why would such a horrible memory be revisiting you at this point?"

It was as if she already processed it, and when I didn't immediately respond, I watched her face contort. Her eyes opened wide, and she looked like an overripe plum when she blurted out, snot dripping from her nose, "Tell me you are not thinking the same thing. Tell me you wouldn't!"

"No, of course not, honey. I'm not thinking that at all." I wasn't, but I quickly gathered how she thought I might.

Sue seemed satisfied for the moment. The clock chimed twelve times, and she said, "You need to finish. What happened after...?"

She didn't want to say the words, but I needed to finish the story.

"I awoke on the living room floor in a sea of commotion," I continued. "I noticed red lights flashing across the living room ceiling and walls. Someone was attending to me. When he noticed I was awake, he called out. Moments later, I was talking to a police officer. I asked where my mother was. He assured me she was fine and being attended to by a paramedic. I struggled to sit up, and he helped me. There were so many people in the room, but I focused only on one. Ten feet away was my father. He had a cop on either side of him, one mashing his face into the wall, the other handcuffing him. I struggled to recall what had happened but could not. As he was led out our front door, he turned toward me. His stare was haunting, hollow, blank. One I had seen often—the stare of a total drunk. Completely vacant. I was glad to see him led away. I remember thinking, *If only one of my shots had sliced into him....*

"I gasped when I noticed the face of a man in a body bag on the floor to my right. His eyes were open, but there was no life in them.

"Mr. Miller, our neighbor, had heard the shots. He rushed through the front door carrying a baseball bat. Had he been a few seconds sooner, he might have succeeded in nailing my father before he had wrested the gun away from me in time to shoot Mr. Miller twice in the chest, killing him instantly. Moments later, Mom slammed the bat into my father's head, knocking him unconscious."

Sue sat motionless, her mouth open.

"Welcome to my world," I said sarcastically.

She closed her mouth and gave me a hollow look but said nothing.

"I'm not quite finished," I followed.

Sue tilted her head slightly and surveyed my face as if to say, *What more could there be?*

"It hit the papers the next day, Saturday," I soberly continued. "Mom and I spent most of the day at the police station. They wanted full statements from each of us. They were sympathetic, but it was easy to discern from their actions and the way they regarded us that there were things they wanted to say but didn't. At times, it seemed they pitied us. Sometimes they admonished us—Mom was a bad wife. I was a bad son. Maybe they were trying to reconcile why a husband and father could turn into a drunk who killed someone and now would pay for his crime. They weren't forgiving my father so much as they were condemning us. Me. *It was your fault,* their faces screamed. Maybe they were right. Maybe it was my fault. If I had been a better son, one interested in watching sports with my dad or starred on a school team, Dad would have been a good man. Mr. Miller would still be alive.

"I remembered leaving the police station in the late afternoon feeling more depressed, thinking *It was my fault...you ninny.*

"After Mom and I arrived home, we didn't say much to each other. We sat in the kitchen, silently. The phone kept ringing, no doubt in response to the media reports. Neither of us moved. We didn't want to talk to anyone. What could we say? *Yeah, you read it right. My father shot and killed my neighbor, the war hero. Well, he did it because I was a ninny, and my mom was a ninny as well. We pushed Dad into killing him. It was really our fault. My fault.*

"We didn't say such things between us, Mom and me. But without saying so, I wondered if those judgmental glares the cops gave us could be valid. We—I—didn't want to face that possibility.

"Mom and I needed to be alone and consider our next steps—not that we had many choices. Money was tight. It wasn't as though we could pack up the car, leave town and begin in another place. The consequences of dealing with the shame of Dad murdering a man loved by the community were too frightening to consider. Mr. Miller was a WWII veteran who received many decorations including the Silver Star, for valor, on the D-Day invasion. Dad was 4-F and didn't even serve in the war, blind in one eye courtesy of a fight he had with his father."

I stood and returned to my recliner, so I could better assess Sue still on the floor. She was no longer looking at me. I had never seen her like that: exhausted, downtrodden, lifeless. It was after 1:00 a.m.

"Honey," I said, "we're both tired. We need sleep."

"One last thing," she said plaintively, "Explain why now? What made you so upset you lashed out at Will? How do I know it won't happen again?"

I had an answer. Not that it would justify slapping my son, but it was the truth. I gazed into Sue's face, trying to predict if my answer would be good enough. Would it explain everything to her satisfaction? But then, what would explain such a heinous act? Nothing really. So, I deferred. After what she witnessed tonight, if I told her what happened on many Sunday nights as a teen, I would lose my family for sure. I gave Sue part of an answer. Not the whole answer. Maybe I would never have to go there, ever.

"Sue," I said, falling to my knees in front of her, hanging my head low, my hands clasped in a cloverleaf knowing I had one chance to explain myself. I viewed this opportunity as a gift, and I was not going to blow it.

When I had Sue's full attention, I began. "I have no excuse for what I did this evening to my son—to my family. After the call canceling all my interviews except one, I lost it inside. With all we had gone through it wasn't fair for the rug to be pulled out from under me. I found myself in the same spot when I began this quest. If I couldn't get in front of those recruiters, I had no chance of getting hired by a Big Eight firm."

Sue regarded me with no emotion, except perhaps a hint of compassion. It was encouraging she didn't simply walk away. It was certainly understandable for her to do so.

"My CPA exam grades are likely in the mail right now, to add to my concerns. I'll find out the first of next week if I passed, and if I didn't pass there will be no way my one remaining Big Eight interviewer would consider hiring me, especially at my age. All that stress was built up within me, and Will ran in at the worst possible moment—and of all things that stupid game."

"You're stressed. I get it. But what is it with you and not wanting to teach your son how to play chess? How could that set you off?"

"What do you mean?"

Sam, you know exactly what I mean. Ever since Will got that chess game for his birthday he's been wanting you to teach him. You know how to play, and from those awards, you're good at it. What gives?"

"What awards?"

Sue glared at me, casting a sarcastic expression. She knew. I said nothing and from her demeanor it was clear she couldn't move forward from this calamity until I was entirely truthful.

"I thought I tossed that box when we moved," I said.

Somehow, Sue had learned of my past interest in chess, but I'm sure I threw off signals early on in our marriage to avoid the subject.

"I used to play chess, but that was a long time ago. Bad memories I guess I blocked out."

"Well, your son doesn't understand, and I sure don't understand."

So, I began the story I had avoided for so many years.

"I was horrible at everything I touched...except chess. My Uncle Larry taught me how to play when I was around Will's age. Turned out I was pretty good at it. Great, actually. In junior high, my chess club teacher, Mr. Johnson, talked me into being evaluated by a Grand Master he knew. Mr. Johnson arranged for a meeting. I apparently impressed him enough to sponsor me into the U.S. Chess Federation. He offered to coach me once a week as well. I didn't dare mention it to my father. He'd find a reason to ridicule me about it. So, I played during the school day."

"Why did you never tell me about this?"

"That will be made clear in a moment."

Sue continued to gaze into my face until I finished what I had to say. There was no way she'd allow me to walk away from this one, so I continued. "When I was fourteen Coach Aleksey—"

"Who?"

"Sorry, he was my coach. The guy who got me involved. Russian. Really good. Like I said, a Grand Master. Anyway, he entered me in the state U.S. Chess Junior Grand Prix. I won. Surprised even him. Me too. Winning qualified me to compete in the Northeast Regional Tournament. But that required a parent signature to enter. I could have gotten away with only my mom signing, but she lived in constant fear of Dad discovering things. If he found out she signed without telling him, she would have paid for it in more pain and suffering.

"So, she told him. She waited for a Saturday morning, so he was sure to be sober. Mom sent me to my room to do my homework, but I hid around the corner at the top of the stairs to hear the discussion. His first reaction was one of confusion. He said he didn't know why anyone would take time to learn 'such a ninny game.' That was all I heard and hustled to my room. Soon after, Mom walked in with a big smile on her face and told me he was good with it. I didn't believe her until she showed me his signature on the registration form. The only condition was he would take us all to the tournament. I was elated. Finally, I could compete in something that might actually show him I was not the tragic failure he had pegged me to be.

"Sam, this is an amazing story. Why have you never told me this?"

"I'm getting there."

"So, the big day comes. It was a Saturday. Dad said he had to work in the morning, but he'd be home by noon to take us to Staten Island where the tournament was being played. I sat and watched the clock all morning.

"By 12:30, it was obvious he wouldn't be coming. Mom still had hope as she made some calls, but I knew his pattern. His boss said he'd left work right before 11:00. It was a fifteen-minute drive home, tops. Mom was furious. I told her to let it go, but she refused and told me to wait. She'd be back. I pleaded with her not to go. She ignored my requests. I had never seen her so angry. As I watched her pull out of our driveway, I knew I would not be competing that day. Nor any other day, as it turned out.

"The next time I saw mom, she was in the hospital. She couldn't talk. He broke her jaw. When I chased down the cop who came to her rescue, he told me he got a call to respond to a domestic dispute at the Towne Tavern. Apparently, Mom went into the bar and confronted him. In front of his *friends*. I didn't need to hear anymore."

Dad spent the night in the drunk tank. Sunday, too. Maybe they kept him an extra day as a favor to us. Mom arranged for me to spend a few days with a neighbor. By the time we were back together again, it was later in the week. No one mentioned the chess tournament. Coach Aleksey tried calling me at home, Mr. Johnson later told me. I never answered the phone. Never told anyone what happened. I simply crawled back into my shell at school knowing from experience this too would pass, and it did. Coach Aleksey stopped chasing me. I was certain Mr. Johnson told him what had happened or what he assumed had happened. I never played chess again. Sorry, I should have told you a long time ago. I guess I didn't want to go there."

Sue gently stroked my hair. She didn't have any follow-up questions. Sue was good about that. She knew exactly what I needed when I would retreat to "that place," as she would sometimes refer to these moments. She stood, pulling on my hand to stand with her. When I didn't react, she pulled harder until I rose to my feet, but I turned my head away from her, embarrassed. Sue wrapped her arms around me and held me for what seemed the longest time. There was nothing else I could say. I waited for Sue to speak. I prayed that in her compassionate manner, she would somehow make it all better.

Sue turned my head toward her. I was now looking directly into Sue's teacher face. "Sam Halloran, right now it's late," Sue spoke calmly but authoritatively, like she was giving directions to do something important. "We are both going to bed. When we cuddle up in our bed, here are the visions you will have. You will imagine yourself sitting in the interview next week, eyes confidently considering that recruiter. He will recognize in those eyes a confident man. Someone whom they simply must hire. It won't matter to them if you passed the exam. You will appear in every way a winner, not a whiner. They will not see you as you are at this moment. They will envision you as a future partner in their firm."

Sue paused, wiping away her tears. We stood there for a few moments while I contemplated what she had said.

"Any questions, Mr. Halloran?" Sue said as if she were reprimanding one of her students, one she liked a great deal but was momentarily disappointed in their performance.

"None, Mrs. Halloran."

"Then let's go to bed. I'm tired."

We walked to our bedroom, arm in arm, lovers and best friends.

In bed, Sue was asleep long before I drifted off. I tried hard to think those positive thoughts she had given me. If not for her confidence in me, I would have no chance of getting through next week. What that outcome might hold for me was anyone's guess but having Sue back in my corner was at least enough of a boost to get me through the night without the episode I feared most. Still, if things didn't turn around soon, nothing Sue could say would keep us together. Her choice, not mine.

Whenever things were dark for me, they often got darker. Such was my life. I had resigned myself to believe that long ago. And while my life with Sue had given me respite from my demons, I felt circumstances were building, leading to events which would destroy everything we had built together. After all, my father invested much of his time into coaching me to think that way. Like spilled red wine allowed to soak in and left to dry on a white table cloth, the stain of my father's influence would not be bleached out so easily.

Next week was do or die.

CHAPTER 8

"Samuel Halloran," the proctor yelled to the dozen or so candidates sitting in the waiting room. My competition. All of us waited anxiously for our chance to convince a campus recruiter we had exactly what they were seeking.

I immediately raised my hand and leapt to my feet. I walked up to her with all the confidence of a winner, trying hard to remember those positive thoughts Sue placed in my mind last week. Staring into her clipboard with no regard for me, she blandly said, "Please follow me," which I did most dutifully. But while walking down that long corridor, I felt like I was being led to an execution. I had rehearsed long and hard for this moment, but my mind went blank. My only desire now was that I wouldn't launch into a panic attack.

"Hello, I'm Ken Harvey. Have a seat."

I froze. I had no comment. Not "Hi," "Thanks," "Big deal"…nada. My mind was blank. Every little doubt from the day I was born was front and center. Every disappointment. Every failure. *What was I doing here? I wasn't qualified for this job. Who was I kidding? I was a fool to think I could land this position.*

I could hardly maintain eye contact with the recruiter. *What did he say his name was? Ken?*

By the way he stared at me it wasn't good. I needed to get it together. Fortunately, I dug deep and finally said something reasonable as I took my seat. "Hi, Mr. Harvey. Thanks for seeing me."

"I don't have much of a choice now, do I?" he immediately

responded.

I thought—serious comment or a joke? I was relieved to detect a wry smile. Instantly, my fears subsided. He was as human as any guy I had met. Not on a pedestal. Not as someone weighing my life's work and sitting in judgment. Not my executioner. Just a guy with a sense of humor.

"I guess that's very true," I said with a smirk, both of us realizing I was not who a college recruiter might expect to be interviewing. I was approaching thirty-two years old, married with two kids, and not even an accounting major. The odds of me pulling this off were astronomical.

"So, why are we here today?" he asked like I had wandered into the wrong office and was lost.

With little forethought, I decided to go off-script saying, "I want to begin my accounting career at Hamilton Pierce, which won't happen unless I impress you enough to believe an old guy like me won't make you look like a fool for recommending me for an office visit. How am I doing so far?" I smiled but quickly realized from his reaction I must have sounded like a complete ass. He totally ignored my comment. Even worse, the slight smile he'd been wearing turned into a frown.

The favorable image I first had of Ken Harvey had suddenly faded and the replacement was abhorrent. His thick matted-down black hair blended perfectly with his black horned-rimmed glasses as though they were an extension of it. His shirt could not be whiter especially at the cuffs where he seemed to want to emphasize his gold cuff links as he shot each cuff down from under his blue pinstriped suit jacket. Then there was the red power tie announcing to all the plebeians that Mr. Kenneth Harvey was very important. *Kneel and beg for your life* was his unspoken command. If it would have ensured an invitation to the coveted office interview, I would have done it—all day long. Everything about him resonated that he was better than me.

He picked up my resume, perusing it for a moment, then he asked,

"So, you're a cigarette salesman?" I theorized he was putting me in my place for my flippant comment. I was wasting his time. I got it. Based on my off-handed remark, which was not the image I wanted to project, I deserved his indifference.

"I *was* a cigarette salesman," I began calmly and deliberately. "A couple years ago, I came to the realization I didn't want to peddle cigarettes the rest of my life, so I began researching other career possibilities and landed on a career in auditing."

"Yeah, I see you are applying for an auditing position," he said in a cocky and dismissive fashion. "We'll get to that later. Tell me more about why you think you can be successful in my industry." I picked up on the reference and slight. Translation: *The chances of you competing against the best and the brightest and coming out on top are slim to none, but for the time being you're somewhat entertaining, and I'll humor you by making believe this was a real interview.*

"Well, Mr. Harvey—"

"Call me Ken."

"OK, Ken. I recognize I am likely not your standard candidate, but I would like to tell you why I believe I can not only be successful at Hamilton Pierce but how I can excel above most of the candidates I am competing against." My speech was stilted and somewhat rambling. I needed to get it together.

He didn't respond. Ken Harvey stared at me, displaying an air of confidence. For some unexplainable reason, though, I was encouraged; he was giving me a window of opportunity to sway him, and I might have a chance to make a favorable impression after all. He crossed his arms, relaxed into his chair and said, "Proceed."

I launched into my script.

"I took an inventory of my skills a couple years ago and recognized I was good at selling and good with people, particularly managing and motivating them, so I began to research professions where those skills might contribute greatly to not only my success but the success of the entire organization I worked for. My research spread the gamut of different professions until I began to lean toward a career in accounting and auditing.

"I read an article in *The Wall Street Journal* about a transformation occurring in your industry. Since the creation of the industry in the UK, accounting firms traditionally offered principally two services, audit and tax. The article pointed to many in the industry who viewed consulting as their future. Doing audits was risky due to lawsuits for failed audits, and success in tax was dependent upon federal and state legislation. Consultancy would appear to reveal a new world of opportunities for those firms believing they had a lock on the smartest analytical brains in the world. I believe Hamilton Pierce to be one of those firms, and I want a place in your lineup."

Giving me a measured look, he said, "OK, but why are you applying for an audit position in particular? We don't house a consultancy practice in the Indy office. Your resume here says you want to join our audit practice, and you described a scenario where a consultancy practice might do well in the future and how you might fit. But the future is not today. Today, I am here seeking auditors."

"Correct and thank you for asking. I fully recognize your practice today is confined to audit and tax. Consultancy is the future. But I have a lot to learn about your industry, and if there is one thing I love, it's learning."

He was studying my resume intensely, seeming to search for something, but then, maybe he tired of me already. I glanced at my watch and noticed half the interview was over. I had less than 15 minutes to convince this guy to extend me an office interview. Right now, I'd give myself a 50-50 chance of securing one of those coveted spots.

Abruptly looking up from his reading, he asked me the perfect question. It was such a softball, I felt it Divine and thanked God. "Give me an example where you took what you had learned and applied it to the real world."

I hesitated before answering, not wanting to sound like I had prepared for such a question. I hadn't, but I'd told the story so many times it had become a part of my DNA.

After several seconds passed, providing sufficient time to give authenticity to my response, I began. "Last summer, I took an *Introduction to Taxation* class. Even though it was completely new to me, I enjoyed the course a great deal. I found comfort in researching ways to reduce an individual's tax burden by finding tax court cases in support of a position.

"My learning experience came in handy when last fall I received notice from the IRS disallowing my Form 2106 expenses from the previous year. After my initial discussion with an IRS examiner, I sensed my defense would be too complex to be understood at that level. So, I requested my case be immediately transferred to the IRS Appeals Division as was my right by regulation."

"You represented yourself to an IRS Appeals Division lawyer. Impressive. How did it turn out?"

"I won."

"No additional tax? No penalty?" he said with a look of surprise.

"None."

Nodding his head, he seemed impressed. It seemed the perfect opportunity to close, especially given my time was about up.

"Ken, I believe I could be a staunch defender of my client's positions to their benefit as well as that of my firm, which I sincerely desire to be Hamilton Pierce. Further, I believe I will excel in this profession. As to whether I end up in consultancy, as you said, that's the future. Today, you are hiring for your present needs, which are for the auditing practice. I believe I can learn a great deal about how to best serve my clients by spending time in your audit group under the watchful eye of those who can help me become the best I can be."

I was done. One of the cardinal rules of selling was when you come to the close, as I believed I had done, shut up. Game, set, match!

Ken Harvey sat there slightly nodding his head. Then he stood, extended his hand and said, "Well, Sam, it appears our time is up. Thank you for stopping by."

I rose to shake his hand, but he abruptly pulled his back and perused my resume saying, "Oh, sorry, I almost forgot."

Scanning the document in his hands, which I had prepared and submitted before the holidays, he peered at me and asked, "You say here you sat for the November CPA Exam. If my memory is correct you should have received your scores by now. How did you do?"

Finally, he asked! With every ounce of control in my body, I tried hard to act modest when I said simply, "I passed."

Ken seemed agape and asked, "How many parts?"

"All of them. I passed all four parts. Guess I got lucky."

There was that smirk again. The smirk I would grow to love over the coming years. "Very good to hear," Ken Harvey said, suddenly shifting his demeanor to one who was selling rather than buying. His attitude changed in that instant. "I can assure you luck had no part in such an accomplishment. Given your extremely limited course work in auditing, accounting and tax, your passing all four parts in your first sitting is a very impressive performance. Congratulations, Sam. You'll be hearing from us very soon."

I nodded in acceptance of his compliment, turned and walked out of his temporary office. Inside, it was all I could do to contain my ebullience. After a slow start, I ended the interview by knocking the cover off the ball and out of the park. I was on my way!

CHAPTER 9

November 29, 1982, was my first day on the job. It was the Monday after Thanksgiving. We had a great deal to be thankful for. Everything had worked exactly as planned. Two years ago, I sat Sue down in our kitchen and told her I got fired, but I had a plan that would land me a job at one of the Big Eight accounting firms; and here I was about to walk into the Indiana National Bank Tower in Indianapolis and begin my career with Hamilton Pierce, a prominent member of the Big Eight. Stepping into the elevator and pressing the 32nd floor button, I beamed.

"Sam Halloran," I said, reaching the receptionist. "I'm one of the new associates."

The receptionist surveyed what must have been an appointment schedule in front of her. "Yes, Mr. Halloran. I have you right here. Welcome to Hamilton Pierce," she said in a friendly but professional tone.

I was still aglow and biting my lip so as not to break into a full smile. I felt my head would explode.

"Mr. Halloran, if you will turn around you will notice a door across the lobby. Enter that room and someone will be with you in a moment."

The room was filled with young men and women mingling about, talking and sipping coffee. Immediately, everyone stopped talking and focused on me as they took their seats around a large oblong conference table which seemed a little too large for the room. No one said a word. All eyes were on me, like I was a professor about to give a lecture. I stood just inside the door still open to the lobby. I needed to say or do something, but there was nothing to say, so I took my seat as well. All eyes were upon me. Fortunately, I didn't have to respond.

"Good morning and welcome class," said a tall, lanky man who walked in after me. He was dressed in a suit which made the one I was wearing look like it came from Goodwill. "Welcome to Hamilton Pierce. You are all here right on time, and I am thrilled to be the first to welcome you to your new careers. My name is Barry Phillips, and I am the Human Resources partner for the Indianapolis office."

All eyes were immediately upon Barry Phillips as he took his seat at the head of the table.

"I am also a client service partner who, together with my seven other partners, manage and direct this office, which I am proud to report now numbers 102 professionals," Phillips continued. "This year marks the thirtieth anniversary of the Hamilton Pierce office in Indianapolis, and your class has placed us into a new category of offices. It shouldn't concern you, but it is an important distinction in the firm to be an office of this size, so I thank you for representing the class that has taken us to this level. But let's move on to more important matters."

Barry Phillips seemed uncomfortable in the ambassador role. Stilted. His audience was struggling, too. I wasn't sure how to react to him, especially his apparent joy with the office's new status within the firm. By the looks of the others, it seemed we shared the same confusion, like not knowing whether to applaud or sing the National Anthem. While trying hard to listen intently to Barry Phillips, I couldn't help but consider the irony of working at HP considering what I had to accomplish to get here.

"You will find in the packet of information before you," Barry continued, "important information about the Indianapolis office that will help orient you. Please familiarize yourself with its contents. You will have time to do that in a few moments after I leave you to mingle about and get to know your fellow classmates."

As Barry Phillips talked, he glanced at every person seated around the table—everyone but me. I paid little attention to it at first, but the more I watched him, the more I became convinced he was avoiding eye contact with me. Oddly, some recruits would hazard a glance at me but would turn away when our eyes met. It was uncomfortable. I couldn't figure it out. They all had a bachelor's degree and probably hadn't even attempted the CPA exam. I had an MBA and the CPA.

Then, it hit me. I was the old guy, which was the reason everyone took their seats when I entered the room. That explained their difficulty hazarding even a casual glance in my direction. I was the odd duck in the room. Bennett Cosgrove, HR recruiter from Anderson Mitchell, may have been right when he told me I could never assimilate with a new recruiting class given I was a decade older than them. While I paid little attention to his comment, hoping my age would not be an issue, I realized he might have been dead-on. This would be harder than I imagined.

"Mr. Halloran...Mr. Halloran? Am I boring you, sir?" Phillips stared at me as if his laser focus could make me disappear so he, and the others in the room, would no longer need to deal with this anomaly.

That, and a few giggles around the table, shot me to the present. "Sorry, I don't know what I was thinking. I apologize."

Phillips, wearing a dispassionately furtive smile, said, "Yes, well, I hope your lack of interest in my comments on this first day of your career at Hamilton Pierce is no indication of the kind of performance we should expect from you." He said it wearing a patrician face.

The die had been cast. I was the outsider—the freak show. I would struggle to find where I belonged. Clearly, the divisions were drawn by age and experience—the partners on one end, the kids on the other. *How could I possibly fit in? Where would I fit in? What an auspicious start,* I thought. *Where do we go from here?*

The ugly moment was broken by Phillips when he abruptly stood and said, "Well, enough fun for this morning. You each have your assignment, and I encourage you to take it seriously, as I'm sure *most* of you will."

With Phillips out of the room, everyone stood and conversed in small groups. Everyone but me. I was standing and turning from side to side, attempting without success to join in one of those conversations. As I turned from one group to another, their ranks closed to bar my entrance. It was humiliating. There was nothing to do but stand in this small room, sipping my coffee, alone.

As the day continued, things didn't improve. Shortly after Barry Phillips left us, we were given an office tour by one of the audit managers. A woman named Elaine Porcheck took us down the hallways and between the two floors, pointing out the features of the Indianapolis office. There was such an obvious caste system at work here. I supposed being a former cigarette salesman impressed nobody.

The partner offices were interspersed throughout, probably to give the appearance of one big happy family—mom and dad were close by to watch over their little fledgling darlings. I was soon to learn how separate and unequal all the *darlings* were.

The smaller offices surrounding the elevator banks were occupied by audit and tax managers; those offices forming the outside perimeter of each floor were the partner offices separated by conference rooms and, at the far end, the library. Between them was a sea of cubicles for the senior associates, those who ran the jobs at client offices, and the administrative folks including the partners' secretaries. Porcheck explained we could occasionally use an unoccupied cubicle. She spoke like a prison warden might, pointing out the various features of the facility we were imprisoned in. I walked past a few empty cubicles and imagined sitting in one of them working on an audit one day soon. It helped me forget my initial impressions.

The tour ended on the lower of the two office floors. At the end of the hallway was a massive room filled with long tables intermittently laced with electrical receptacles. This, as explained by Ms. Porcheck, was to be our domain. Ms. Porcheck was how we were to refer to her.

Ms. Porcheck was the resident whiz-kid, having been promoted to manager after only three years on the job and only twenty-four years old. She was eight years younger than me, and she was a manager in a Big Eight firm, a CPA and from what I was to learn later, probably the smartest professional in the office, including the partners. On "Technical Training" days the partners had Elaine Porcheck brief all the professional staff about new AICPA (American Institute of Certified Public Accountants), FASB (Financial Accounting Standards Board) pronouncements, and SEC (Securities and Exchange Commission) regulations. Ms. Porcheck was the go-to person when matters of professional quality were the topic. Unfortunately, anything to do with socialization and friendliness must have been ascribed to others; Elaine Porcheck was obviously not in the room when the good Lord passed out those attributes.

If there was a stereotypic auditor, Porcheck had to be the poster child for what such a person might resemble. Her suit of armor was stylish enough, although I could not imagine a department store having a large enough mannequin to display her clothing size. She looked like a fireplug with a large square nut on top. Her chin was recessed in-between two fat cheeks atop gathered rows of fat constituting her neck, which appeared more like a scarf. Her shoulders were parallel to the floor. From there, it was a straight shot downward to her shoes, which made her feet resemble an overflowing ice cream sundae. It was an apt description, as she appeared to have had more than her share of desserts over the course of her life. From a side view, she was flat as a board, front and back. You could stand her against a wall and use her as a vertical chalk line. I'd liken Porcheck to bear-like—not the cuddly kind.

When the periodic question from one of us surfaced, she spoke with an air of aristocracy and bearing. She implied we should feel honored she would stoop to the menial duty of conducting this tour. I made a mental note to avoid her at all costs, except when I would be assigned to work on one of her jobs as her professional staff—a nightmare I hoped to defer for as long as possible.

When I returned home, one would have thought Santa Claus had made an early appearance. Will and Ben came running toward me as if I had a bundle of presents to pass out.

"Did you tell everyone what to do today, Dad?" Will was always the one with the questions. "Did you have to fire anyone? How big is your office?" He had an inflated view of my position at the firm. That was my fault. I should have given him a more realistic perspective when I first told him about my new career.

The boys dragged me into the family room as Sue and I exchanged glances in passing. She was content, for now, allowing me to spend time with the boys while she attended to dinner. She'd be all over me later with tougher questions than Will was lobbing at me right now. Hopefully my smile communicated it was a good first day and my choice of firms had been a good one—not that I had a choice. I was getting better at deception.

I sat on the floor, leaning against the loveseat with Will on his knees in front of me shooting one question after another; Ben curled up on my lap, trying to show me a drawing he made at school.

With Will being nearly two years older than Ben, he'd always taken the leadership role, proclaiming by his words and actions he was the older of the two and, therefore, deserved a higher status in all they did. This was made obvious to us when Will insisted he be allowed to get the mail from the mailbox at the curb. At first, Ben objected but soon relented and never challenged Will's presumed right to that trophy. For the peace of the household, we were happy it was fine with Ben if Will won those battles. It could be getting the mail, selecting TV programs after school or any activities occurring in the Halloran household. Will led, and Ben followed.

At least for now, Ben never seemed troubled by the pecking

order. He accepted it knowing he'd still have fun. Somehow Ben realized that by allowing Will to lead, life would be better for both. Suddenly, it seemed good advice for me. I shouldn't be so troubled by the pecking order at work. *Don't buck the system, Sam.* If I fought it I'd surely lose. I had a lot to learn, and if my new caste system at work would upset me daily, I would not have time to do the things to succeed in this new career. I needed to put it behind me.

Ben's drawing showed a man sitting at his desk, a good attempt at depicting me in my office. The one I didn't have. He blossomed when I acknowledged what he attempted to draw. While praising Ben's drawing ability, I inwardly thought how disappointed my boys would be if they only knew how low their dad was in the whole scheme of things.

Will's questions subsided. I supposed my answers satisfied him. Ben seemed pleased with the attention I gave him over his drawing. Both soon hastened to more important pursuits: chasing each other between their bedrooms and the kitchen, hollering, yelling and annoying their mother, who was now placing our food on the table.

We sat down to eat. Sue said grace as she did each evening. We began that ritual after Will was born. I believed in God, but growing up, my family only said grace for the big three meals— Thanksgiving, Christmas and Easter. When Sue first mentioned she'd like to say grace at the evening meal, I balked but quickly relented. I didn't care, and with Sue's dad being a Methodist preacher, it seemed perfectly reasonable she'd be more comfortable saying grace. A couple times she asked me to say grace, but I declined each time in a manner she determined was fruitless to pursue and eventually stopped asking.

On most evenings after the kids were in bed, it was our time to relax in front of the TV or sit in our favorite chairs with a book in our laps. Those times were usually filled with talking about our day. Tonight, all the attention would be focused on how my first day at work went. While spending time with the boys, I worried how I would approach my discussion with Sue. After only one day in my new job, I realized I had underestimated how it would bother me working with kids a decade younger.

But then, seeing how Ben yielded to his brother over what most would call "insignificant things" was an object lesson on accepting things for what they were. Ben wasn't a pushover. He'd stand his ground on the important issues. Ben's unfettered acceptance of the way things were had a calming effect on me tonight. It put everything in perspective. Thanks to Ben, for now, I was at peace; however, there still lingered concern whether I had made a terrible decision in selecting this new career at my age. Sure, time would tell, but if today was any indication of what I'd be up against, my chances of success were approaching slim-to-none. Still, Ben helped me get it together for my upcoming chat with Sue, and I silently thanked him.

"So, come on, Halloran," Sue said. "I'm busting at the seams. Tell me about your day!" Sue seemed ready to burst. I couldn't remember her ever being this happy for me. Probably because I had not given her reason to in many years. It pleased me I could brighten her day, and I hoped I could measure up.

"Oh, sweetheart. It was fine. It was a good day. About what I had expected. Not much to talk about," I said in an unusually calm and efficient manner.

"You're not getting off that easy, buddy. Talk. Now!" Sue quipped with a tone that warned me not to blow her off again.

Sue would win this one, for sure. It wasn't "a good" first day. I didn't want to burden her with all those ugly details. What purpose would it serve? This was to be my dream career, and it was too early to consider the possibility I had made a mistake. I had—we had—worked too hard to get to this point for me to reevaluate things after one day in the office. I needed to give it time. All would surely work out. I had faith. I simply needed to come up with a good story to placate Sue.

I told Sue everyone was great, from the administrative folks to the partners. My day had begun with meeting the spring recruiting class. There were thirteen of us. Our class propelled the Indy office into a new and higher-ranking category within the firm hierarchy, and Barry Phillips was pleased. I described Barry, but I left out the parts where Barry and everyone in the office shunned me. Why go there? I was sure it would turn around once everyone got to know me.

Sue seemed pleased with my report of the day's activities. She nestled in next to me on our loveseat and took my hand in hers. She laid her head on my chest, and I wrapped my arm around her shoulder, gently stroking her arm.

"Honey, I'm so happy for you," she cooed, "All your planning worked out. You're on your way to becoming a Big Eight partner. You're my man." She gave me a squeeze.

"And you're my gal."

It was true. It was the only true thing I had said since I came home.

I had learned one thing interesting today. In the thirty-year history of the Indianapolis office, I was the oldest person they had ever hired at the staff associate level. Cosgrove was turning out to be right; age would be a problem. Still, I was hopeful things would work out.

But that evening, things were not fine. When I awoke, still on the loveseat, I was shivering, cold sweat lingering underneath the clothes I had not changed from work. I would need to have my suit dry-cleaned before I could wear it again. Being as it constituted half of my entire suit wardrobe that was not good. Finances were tight after surviving two years on mostly a teacher's pay. But our debt was not my biggest concern at the moment.

It was a little after one o'clock in the morning. Sue was no longer by my side, and I remembered her saying we needed to go to bed. She did. I didn't. I reached for the afghan Sue's mother had knitted and given to us as a Christmas present last year. I was anxious and couldn't stop shivering. Fidgety. I gathered up the afghan, clinging to it like it was a suit of armor. Negative thoughts bombarded me. I struggled to consider their significance and how they might be related to my first day. Was it a prophecy foretelling of my impending failure? Was it my demons surfacing periodically to remind me of my father's repeated prediction that I would never amount to anything in life? He always said there was something wrong with me he couldn't quite figure out. I could hear his voice: "You are one screwed up, defective kid."

I was just another one of Dad's failures. "Bad sperm," he'd sometimes say. Recalling this after the day I'd endured forced a sarcastic chuckle at the ridiculousness of it all, as if dismissing it so cavalierly would shuttle its import to the bottom of a deep well, but still a part of me believed it might be true. Hearing it as a child left a different mark, one that would linger for all time, hurting again after being quelled for so long. What did it mean for it to revisit me tonight? Was it my destiny to wear this yoke all my days on earth?

My demons were returning.

CHAPTER 10

Throughout the week it seemed Porcheck was everywhere, and I would often encounter her on simple administrative tasks or pass her in the halls. Each time she treated me like a migrant worker. I suspected she had it in for me. My concern became especially clear on the last day of the three-day audit training.

Over the past two and a half days, the training had gone well, and I learned a great deal. I was gaining confidence; I might make it after all. Coming up the elevator, little did I envision that everything was about to change. This day would be different. Elaine Porcheck was instructing.

Today was the final wrap-up of the new associate training. We were to do what they called a "simulated audit." Even though this was not a real audit, it was the closest thing to performing any audit work. I was excited for the new experience but anxious, as it would serve as the basis for my first written performance evaluation. I simply had to impress.

Throughout the training, we worked on issues affecting a typical audit. We'd perform single-step audit procedures following the audit program, then as a group, we'd highlight the learning points. The audit program was the road map guiding field staff toward successfully completing our tasks, permitting the audit engagement partner to review the accounts, ultimately finding comfort in signing off on the audit and approving the company's release of their financial statements.

The different sections of the audit program—cash, accounts

receivable, fixed assets, inventory, accounts and notes payable, equity—and all the income statement accounts were assigned to the various audit team members in command and control precision. It was like a military campaign to attack, secure and defend a position. If everyone executed their job assignments as instructed and did so in a timely and efficient manner, the audit would be completed—we would capture the high ground and win the battle. It made sense, except for one thing.

I found as I went about my audit task assignments that I tended to drift away from the parts I had been assigned to complete and into areas not part of my audit responsibilities. That tendency played out in the simulated audit we were about to engage in.

To me, the audit was a treasure hunt; we had a list of things we were to find—a round stone, a bent twig, an oak leaf and so on. But I couldn't seem to stick to the assigned list. I was like a kid again enjoying the journey, marveling at nature and filling my bag with a variety of interesting objects and memories. How could I ignore the other marvels of nature—the squirrel hopping between the trees; the mushroom cluster nestled under the fallen elm; the frog resting by the clear running stream; and on and on. Many things begged for my attention. Problem was they were not on my list of things to do—my assigned audit steps. I was soon to learn this was not a game, and there was no extra credit given for "finding the hidden treasure," so to speak.

The class was divided into two groups. I was the unlucky one to be under the tutelage of Elaine Porcheck.

As the class took their seats to begin preparing for the simulated audit assignment, Porcheck stood in front of the room and explained the details of the simulation and her role in it. She paced while talking. There was an air of indignance about her.

Porcheck had a reputation for burning through staff she felt were not up to the task. More than a few new staff had met their waterloo on one of her audits. I prayed I would not become another notch on her pencil during this upcoming audit season.

75

When Porcheck and I finally made eye contact, it confirmed she remembered we didn't get off on the right foot. At least, that was my impression.

As she paused to move to a new topic, our eyes met. I wanted to avert my stare, but it was too late. We were already locked onto each other. Continuing to stare into her face. I prayed she'd intimidate some other poor soul. But she was frozen in place, three feet in front of me, staring into my face. I was so self-conscious I thought I might have dozed off and missed a question she had tossed my way. Locked in her tractor beam, I had to wait it out. Finally, she broke her gaze, surveyed her notes and moved-on to another topic.

During the audit simulation, I was assigned to audit the Cash account. My budget was two hours, which was not a realistic time frame for a real audit but appropriate for the small number of transactions in this supposedly simple exercise. I set up my work area and prepared to get to it. On Porcheck's command, I opened my packet and eagerly dug in. The only problem was I had never audited Cash or, for that matter, any account. I had never had a class in auditing. The only reason I passed the auditing portion of the CPA Exam was my ability to memorize and retain large quantities of information for a short period. That effort secured me a score of 75, the minimum passing grade.

The simulation was designed well and included other experienced staff to act as client staff. At first, I reasoned this would be a fun way to learn the ins and outs of auditing. Then, my enjoyment unraveled into a nightmare when Porcheck turned toward me, and I noticed her newly displayed temporary name tag—Elaine Porcheck, Audit Senior Associate. According to the instructions in my packet I would sit down with her to explain my audit findings. Elaine Porcheck's role would be to supervise and evaluate my work. This was not good. Even so, I tried hard to put that fear out of my mind and do the best job I could. I naively believed if I did an excellent job with this simulation, Porcheck might have a change of heart towards me.

After spending about an hour preparing workpapers from the information and documents in the packet, I felt I was doing an adequate job following the Cash audit program. I followed each step beginning with footing the columns on the year-end cash reconciliation. It seemed simple enough. I agreed the ending balance to the general ledger, then to the trial balance and on to the consolidating statements. Someone else was assigned the tie out of the consolidating statements to the financial statements which was ultimately what the partner would opine on in a real audit.

Next, I tested the outstanding debits and credits on the bank reconciliation. Those items were mostly checks written and deposits made before year-end not showing on the bank statement due to timing issues, one area my testing was supposed to confirm. Everything seemed in order. All the items I encountered were expected parts of a typical bank reconciliation prepared at year-end. The problem began when I noticed something odd on the trial balance having nothing to do with my assigned area.

The total accounts payable (A/P) balance was a summary of several sub-accounts. A/P were credit purchases like inventory or supplies to be paid, in this simulation, thirty days later. Credit card purchases would be another example of an A/P balance. I noticed one of the sub-accounts in the total A/P balance had a debit balance, which was odd. The typical balance would be a credit—a liability; money the company owed to others.

I stared at the amount for a time, working through how an entry, or a series of entries, might be booked and result in a debit balance in A/P. If inventory were purchased on 30-day terms, the entry would be a debit to the Inventory account and a credit to the A/P account, yielding an overall credit balance in A/P at period's end. The balance I was staring at was "Other payables: $96,000." All the other A/P balances were bracketed, indicating a credit balance. This one was not bracketed.

Thinking it might be an error in the spreadsheet, I footed the sub-account balances to the correct total A/P credit balance of

($356,877), which included the $96,000 debit balance. I tried to consider why there might be a debit balance on such an account and could not determine a reasonable answer.

"Thirty minutes remaining," barked Elaine Porcheck, glaring at me as if I had done something wrong.

I hadn't, at least not yet. I still had a few minor steps to complete before I could turn in my workpapers for the completed audit of the Cash account. I wasn't finished with my assignment and unintentionally ignored the time limit warning in my futile attempt to reason out the debit balance in the Other payables account. It was some odd transaction for which I had no experience, or an error in booking the original transaction. It could be a host of reasons none of which could be ascertained without examining the detail behind the $96,000 balance following the audit trail. Curious, I walked up to Porcheck and asked for such detail.

"Ms. Porcheck, I have a quick question," I said sheepishly, pointing to a spreadsheet she seemed reluctant to consider. On my second attempt, she did.

"Yes," she said in monotone fashion, eyes half-opened, surveying the room while giving me an occasional glance, informing me there could be no hope of my offering the slightest bit of relevant information. To her, I was the scum one would scrape off the bottom of their shoes before stepping into a proper house.

I instantly regretted my decision to approach her, but it was too late. She was focused on the spreadsheet I was holding and acknowledged the debit balance of $96,000. Then, she glowered at me and in a sarcastic tone asked, "So, Mr. Halloran, what seems to be the problem?"

"There is a debit balance in the Other payables account, and I don't believe it's normal," I said.

She glared at me.

I repeated myself, this time tilting my head downward, directing her attention to it with my index finger to justify my query. She continued to stare at the spreadsheet, saying nothing. I waited for what seemed a long time. Finally, she locked her eyes on my face. "I get it. And what is your question?" she said in an erudite, measured tone like she didn't grasp the point I was trying to make.

"Well, it's a debit balance in an account that should carry a credit balance," I said, alternating my gaze between the spreadsheet and Porcheck's face. "Additionally, it's an even number, which I would think odd given the types of purchases on trade credit—as opposed to a bank loan—a company might engage in." I opted to stare only at the spreadsheet, believing she was the Medusa, and my fate was near.

I fully expected her to say something, but she didn't. Finally, I raised my head from the spreadsheet and observed Porcheck's face. It mimicked a red balloon about to explode. She grabbed the spreadsheet out of my hands and tossed it to her left onto the table. Instantly, everyone focused on the unfolding melee.

"What was your assignment, Mr. Halloran?"

"I was to audit the Cash account, Ms. Porcheck."

"And, Mr. Halloran, as a new associate, would you not think there would be other staff assigned to audit the other balance sheet accounts such as accounts payable?"

"Yes," I responded, realizing I was about to be laid out by Porcheck in front of the whole class.

"And, Mr. Halloran, maybe those other accounts might be none of your business?" she said, inching closer to my face, spittle now on her bottom lip.

There was no way I could go toe-to-toe with Elaine Porcheck on any technical issue, and I had no intention of doing so. I only wanted to extricate myself from this situation. Soon. Before answering her last question, I casually drifted my eyes from side-to-side and confirmed what I feared. All the other staff had stopped whatever they were doing and focused entirely on Elaine Porcheck's grilling of me. I stood there like I got caught entering the ladies restroom. My mind was moving a hundred miles-per-hour with the only goal of surrendering and getting out with my life, or at least my job.

"I have obviously overstepped my authority, Ms. Porcheck, and I now recognize the error of my ways," I said apologetically, operating on instinct. "What would you like me to do?" My head was down, and I stood submissively like I was waiting for Her Highness's final judgment, likely to order the axe man to decapitate my head from my body.

"Well, Mr. Halloran," she said in malevolent fashion. "It would seem your misjudgment in auditing an area for which you were not assigned has been acknowledged. You should note that performing audits is a business—one in which our partners expect to make a handsome profit, part of which pays your salary. What would happen to that profit if every staff person in our firm acted irresponsibly, as you have done, and audit whatever fits their fancy, ignoring the time-honored process which ensures the only audit procedures performed on a particular audit are those listed on the audit program? I can only imagine how someone like you could explode the budget on an audit and in the process fail to perform your own audit responsibilities in an expeditious and forthright manner, as expected by the partners of this firm."

I wanted to reply, but it was senseless to engage her. I silently prayed she would bring this grilling to a quick and painless end.

"And I must point out one final observation before I dismiss you, Mr. Halloran," she said in a more casual and relaxed manner, almost smiling now. "I knew from the first time I reviewed the resumes for each new associate that hiring you was a mistake. While it is not for me to question the wisdom of our partners, it should be painfully obvious—you are a freak experiment! I cannot understand why you were hired but mark my words; I, for one, consider this experiment to be a complete and utter waste of my time. Working with you today is like trying to train a pig to fly. The day I gaze out my window and behold pigs flying is the day I might expect you to be successful in this industry. You, Mr. Halloran, are a horrible mistake in judgment, and I, for one, am through wasting my time with you."

Elaine Porcheck lifted her purse, coat and briefcase, turned from me and thundered out of the conference room, slamming the door. The eight or nine witnesses to that drubbing included several who were part of my fall class, while the others were senior associates I expected to be working for soon. Everyone just stared at me. No one said a word. I tried hard not to return their stares. I was a castrated, weaned pig.

I had to exit the room immediately to save any bit of composure and pride remaining within me. I glanced up and regarded the door through which Elaine Porcheck had departed and walked toward it as if it was my life's mission to get out of that room. Where I would go from there didn't matter. I had to get out.

The next thing I knew, I was in a hallway surrounded by people oblivious to what I had experienced at the hands of a brutal master. I glanced at my watch. It was 4:45 p.m., and I thought it a good time to go home a little early. I hopped on the next elevator with my head bowed, wanting only for the doors to close quickly. On the way down, my emotions were all over the spectrum. I tried to fast-forward in my mind to the resulting catastrophe soon to result from Porcheck's public flogging of me. Word would spread quickly. The seniors would not assign me to their jobs; the partners would determine how they could quickly extricate me from their firm. When the elevator doors opened into the lobby, I moved quickly toward the exit.

I walked to the economy lot where I could save a few bucks on parking. I had left my suit jacket, overcoat and briefcase in the training room. Fortunately, I had my car keys in my pants pocket. For the time being, it was all I needed. I didn't even consider how I would collect the rest of my belongings. Why bother? I might not be working for Hamilton Pierce much longer.

CHAPTER 11

Friday nights were special in the Halloran household. It was normally pizza night. But not tonight. I didn't want to be around my family. They deserved better.

I called Sue from a pay phone at a gas station on my way home and told her I had to work late. Also, I had an inventory observation in Greenwood at 6:00 a.m. When I got home I'd go straight to bed. No pizza for me tonight. Sue understood. She always understood. I didn't deserve her. Maybe someday I would.

By the time I arrived, the boys were already in bed. Sue was reading.

"So, how was your day?" Sue asked.

"It was a day."

"Not a good one?"

"No."

I didn't want to talk. Sue got it. While I brushed my teeth, she lay in bed. She said nothing. Talking would come when I crawled into bed next to her. I didn't want to talk tonight. I didn't want her to smell my breath.

When I finished in the bathroom, I was relieved she had turned off her reading light and had burrowed under the covers. Thank God. I needed space. I also had a half-pack of Marlboros left.

The garage was cold. Cold helped me think. The cigarettes helped me think, also. Not really. It had been years since I had quit smoking, shortly after we became engaged. Sue asked me to quit. I did. I couldn't believe I had started again. I told myself I hadn't. It was only one pack. But I really had started smoking again. Even if I quit tomorrow, the clock resets. I was angry with myself for breaking my promise to give them up. But I was currently enjoying the high a decade of abstinence from nicotine was affording me. If I could get this high every time I lit up, I might never quit smoking. Or maybe it was the Chivas rocks in my other hand giving me the high.

It was wrong being there in the dark—leaning against my workbench, smoking and drinking, teeth rattling, body shivering. I recalled my Boy Scout days when the scoutmaster arranged for a medic to instruct us in life-saving techniques. One lesson covered hypothermia.

"All the blood in your small capillaries retreats toward your internal organs to protect them. That's what causes the chills. If that happens to you in the water," he'd continued, "you'd be drowning in fifteen minutes."

But I wasn't in the water. I was inside my unheated, sorely in-need-of-repair garage. With the way things were going now, soon it would be the next family's problem. The fear of losing my house caused me to take another drag followed by another shot of Chivas. Intermittent coughing now signaling that my body was being punished. Nothing I was doing at the moment was good for me. There was a weird sort of pleasure in knowing that, but still smoking, still drinking. I didn't want to stop. Stopping would bring guilt. I didn't need guilt right now. Experience reminded me that guilt brought emotion. Emotion brought pain. Sadness and depression. Then....

I had forgotten how hot the filter tip would get when the last remnants of burning tobacco began eating into the filter on a sustained puff. As I was positioning the butt into the empty Coke can I was maneuvering another Marlboro into my lips while deftly flicking my Bic to light up. It was a technique learned from my father...somewhat chilling how easily I was able to do it now.

I didn't want to smoke anymore, but it gave me something to do. The Chivas helped, too. Both helped me forget about the day.

Exactly what he would say.

I wasn't shivering any longer. My body had adapted to the cold. Exactly like that medic had instructed us years ago. I took one last gulp of Chivas. Then one last drag. Long and hard. I felt the filter get hot in my mouth again and then shoved the butt in the Coke can on my bench, missing the hole and smashing it on top, putting too much pressure too close to the rim. The can fell over.

"Shit! Dammit!" I yelled loud enough Sue could easily have heard me. I hurriedly shut off the garage light like I was fourteen again and hiding from my dad. I didn't feel better. But then, I didn't expect to feel better.

When I entered the house, the chimes from Sue's grandfather's clock clanged ten or eleven times. I wasn't sure and didn't care. I wanted to take a shower. I wanted to clean up, especially clean out the stench in my mouth. If Sue knew I had smoked tonight it would disappoint her a great deal. Worry her, too. I didn't want her to worry. I wanted to straighten up—*Fly right, and be a man*, as Dad used to say.

Thinking about him caused my jaw to clench, sending a shiver down my spine. I worried I was becoming just like him.

I passed out in my recliner.

Sue knew. I could tell the moment she woke me at 5:00 a.m. reminding me about my inventory observation. Thank God she did. How did she know? I must have told her.

After my shower, I felt a little better. I could still taste it, though—cotton-mouth. My throat was raw.

The inventory observation on Saturday took a little longer than expected. Well, not really, but that's what I told Sue. I lied. It was over by two o'clock. I couldn't face my family. I felt so guilty. I wanted to drink and smoke more than to be with my family. Just like him.

I prayed I would quickly work through whatever was going on in my head. I prayed in between puffs from my second pack of

Marlboros in two days and swigs from the flask of Chivas I snuck out of the house.

The park was empty. Few visited the park in early December, especially when it was below freezing. At least I could sit here, smoking and drinking in peace, running the car heater with the window down. I wanted desperately to regain some semblance of the husband and father my family expected would walk through the front door of our home. I was determined to walk in the house tonight in the image my family expected. Then, noting the time, the boys would be in bed when I arrived. It was better if they didn't see their father in his current condition. Bad enough Sue might figure it out, if she hadn't already.

It was ten o'clock when I pulled in the driveway. Moments before entering my home, I whispered to myself an often-used phrase: "Tomorrow is another day." Tomorrow was Sunday. It was good I had one more day to chill out and forget Friday—forget Elaine Porcheck. I would be fine come Monday. At least, that's what I told myself.

Sue allowed me to sleep in. When I awoke, the house was empty. They were at church. I was at home. I walked barefoot to the kitchen in my underwear. The clock read 10:30. They wouldn't be home for another hour. I gazed out the kitchen window at our detached garage. I could smoke a little more before they came home. Drink a little, too.

Moments later, I was back in the garage. Fortunately, I had the good sense not to chase my cigarettes with a scotch. Drinking before noon, and on a Sunday no less, I might very well check myself into the rehab center. I smirked, then depression kicked in. It was 11:15 a.m.—they'd be pulling up the drive in the next fifteen minutes. I had time for one more cigarette.

What I was doing was wrong; I'd work through it, and things would get better. *Bet he rationalized his bad deeds in the same manner*, I thought. That pissed me off. I finished my cigarette and placed the butt in my empty scotch bottle, tossing it in the grass clippings bag. Sue would never find it there. I learned that from Dad, too.

I hurried inside and hopped in the shower. Half the day was over, and I contemplated what the next week held for me. I wondered where my jacket, coat and briefcase might be. I had left them there. I thought about Monday and what the week would bring. I didn't want to think about that.

The bathroom door opened, and Sue yelled out playfully, "Hey, sleepyhead, you OK in there?"

"Sure, I'm doing fine. Be out in a minute," I said gruffly.

I dried myself off and felt anything but normal. Sadly, I wanted another cigarette. I had at least a couple more in the pack I hid in my toolbox. Another place Sue would never check. Suddenly, I felt sick to my stomach, and I sat on the toilet. I wasn't sure how long I sat there, but it must have been awhile because softly through the door, Sue said, "Sam, are you sure you're OK?"

"I'm fine. Stop rushing me, will ya!" I yelled out. I regretted it immediately. Sue didn't respond.

When I finally exited the bathroom, I could hear the boys playing in the family room and Sue emptying the dishwasher. I felt bad about deceiving them; I felt bad about many things.

With the towel wrapped around me, I entered our bedroom and closed the door. I sat on the bed. I didn't want to face anyone at the office. I wasn't yet assigned to an audit, which meant I was supposed to report to the staff room. Word surely got out about the training session and spread like wildfire. Everyone had to know—the partners, the staff, even the secretaries. My stomach churned. Two days of smoking and drinking probably contributed to that as well. Still, I was anxious. I was anxious about seeing my family and about seeing my colleagues the next day. I was anxious about every facet of my life.

I shook, covering myself with our bedspread. Sue walked in and caught me off-guard.

"Honey, I'm worried. Are you sure you're alright?"

"Dammit, I said I was fine!" I snapped. Maybe it was seeing Ben hiding behind Sue that mollified my attitude, and I apologized to Sue. "I'm sorry, honey, I have a lot on my mind."

She moved closer and bent down to kiss me. I turned from her. "No. I think I may be coming down with something. Don't want to give it to you or the boys."

Sue didn't respond. I sensed her eyes evaluating me. "On second thought, I think I'll lie down for a while to try and shake this off," I said in as pleasant a voice as I could muster.

Sue passively agreed that might be best and backed out of our bedroom. I felt relieved knowing I might have pulled it off. I was running three days of deceiving my family. I curled up in bed, pulled the covers over my head and fell asleep instantly.

I awoke to the sound of the boys playing in the living room. My head felt heavy as an anvil, my throat like I had swallowed gravel. I walked into the bathroom for refuge, hoping to escape detection by the boys. No such luck.

"Daddy, Will won't give me my truck. Make him give me my truck," Ben appealed to me while slowly opening the bathroom door. It was impossible to hope for any privacy in our small house. I pulled it shut.

"Ben, we're supposed to share, and you're not sharing," Will responded like he was the sage teacher now. He was good at stacking the deck in his favor at every opportunity. Maybe I was witnessing a future politician. Hopefully he would aspire to a career requiring more integrity. In times like those when the boys had a dispute, seemingly without threat of physical harm to either, I'd let them go at it. They'd have to do it sooner or later when I wouldn't be there to supervise.

At about the same time, Sue cracked open the door and said, "I was about to wake you for dinner. How are you feeling?"

"Groggy, but I am hungry. Can you take the boys? I'll be out in a minute." After Sue led the boys off, I stood up from the toilet, a bit unsteady. My watch read 5:15. I mentally calculated how much time

I had before I would leave for work tomorrow morning. As if it was important to tally the time.

We sat down for an uneventful dinner. I said little. The boys didn't seem to mind. Sue noticed but thankfully let it pass.

After dinner, Sue loaded the dishwasher. I decided to watch a little TV, although it was more like staring into an empty box. Nothing was registering. It made me appear to be engaged so the boys would leave me alone. Sue knew otherwise. When we were together, or at least close by each other, we each had a sixth sense operating which allowed us to monitor the other's emotions.

Soon, the decibel level increased. Ben had violated one of the many treaties between the boys, and war appeared to be imminent. Sue yelled at them from the kitchen. A glance at my watch showed it was time to settle the boys down with the nightly mandate they hated to hear. "Time for bed, guys," I shouted from the family room. Still feeling drained, I stumbled to my feet. I walked slowly through the kitchen, noting Sue working over the sink and then into the boys' battlefield preparing to referee and assume command if necessary.

My order was met with obligatory objections from both boys reunited as allies fighting for a common goal—to stay up a little while longer. But unlike other nights, I wasn't in the mood and responded harshly. Sue picked up on my uncharacteristic attitude. Maybe she had become sensitive to my wild outbursts of late. Difficult to blame her. She was a mom first, and tonight she gathered the boys, preparing them for bed giving me a derisive stare as if to say, *"What's your problem?"*

While Sue prepared the boys for bed, I snuck into our bedroom and closed the door. I stared at the bed for a time as if it had turned into something evil, a harbinger of sorts. I ignored the warning. Languishing, I sat on the edge glaring into the mirror on the wall. I didn't like the image staring back at me. Monday was approaching. A cold chill raced up my back. For me, another day was over— another day closer to next week. Monday morning was coming.

The boys went to bed without saying goodnight to me, which was probably Sue's decision. I lay on the bed facing the wall and stared blankly at it, thinking. The door opened then closed. Sue laid next to me, touching my back in the tender way she had so often in the past. Times when she instinctively suspected something had triggered reflections back to my youth. Sue knew I was not in a good place, but as she had told me before, she felt powerless to bring me back. I had to do that myself.

"Sweetheart, is there anything I can do to help?" she whispered. I grunted. She didn't press the issue, honoring my rude request to be left alone. The bedroom door closed behind her. I was tense, too involved in working through the problem. I had been here before far too often. Only, for some strange reason, this time was different and not in a good way. I couldn't say why. It just was.

I drifted in and out of sleep. Sue was not by my side. I needed sleep, so I flung my clothes on the floor and slipped between the covers, ruminating. In about ten hours, I'd be starting my daily routine all over again. I'd be the first in the staff room, vacantly peering out the window with nothing to do. My vague reflection represented my undefined status at the firm: waiting to be assigned to an audit. Soon, the room would fill with other staff associates. At noon they would all file out, laughing and cutting up but careful not to disclose where they were headed for lunch for fear I might follow them.

I realized what I had to do—what I had done so often in the past. Think positive thoughts. Dismiss the bad ones. Push them out of my mind. Condition myself to failure and work toward recovery.

"Things will get better. You'll see. Patience," I repeated to myself over and over, hoping I would drift off to sleep. It worked, but not in the way I had hoped it would.

I didn't remember what my dream was about. When I had awakened, Sue was yelling at me to stop. No, she was begging me to stop, pleading, crying and screaming for me to stop. The overhead light was on. The boys were crying hysterically. Will was bleeding from

89

his nose, face red, eyes wide, mouth gaping as if viewing a horror film, pleading, "Mommy, please make Daddy stop. Please, Mommy." Sue was clutching the boys, one on each side of her, all three crouched in the corner. Ben's face buried behind Sue as if he could hide from what was going on in front of him. They were all trapped in the corner. Sue's eyes darted from me to various parts of the room like she was searching for a way out, a safe way around me, beads of sweat dotting her forehead and veins popping out on her temples. She breathed hard, desperate fear consuming her.

I then surveyed what my family was witnessing. There, in the wall mirror over our chest of drawers, was me kneeling on our bed, naked. My face was shades of red and purple; my nose was bleeding; my hands balled into fists; my hair was disheveled. I looked like I was going insane.

CHAPTER 12

I wanted to call.

I lay in bed casting my eyes straight up. The ceiling fan had seen better days. Maybe it was the dingy globe housing three light bulbs, two of which were dead; or the way the fan's blades slowly rotated around the motor housing, which swayed rhythmically like a countdown clock. *Tick-tock. Tick-tock. Tick-tock.* A countdown to the end. The end to this fool's journey. Then, a knock at the door.

"How did you find me?"

"It's the closest motel. You left the car."

"Would you like to come in?"

"Not really."

I fought back tears. It was all I could do to remain standing. My tightening grip on the inside doorknob kept me from collapsing in a crying heap on the filthy and tattered carpet.

"Honey, I am so very sorry for last night," I said, still not being able to maintain my gaze on the woman I loved. She was looking away, not at me. "Where are the boys?" I asked.

"They're safe," she said harshly. That hurt. Clearly, Sue was fearful for their safety from their own father.

A moment passed. "Can I come home so we can talk?"

Sue scowled at me with an unrecognizable countenance filled with resolve not much different from last night. Bits and pieces of that terrible scene raced back. I couldn't speak, fearing that if I opened my mouth she would flee.

"You hit Will. You struck your own son...again," Sue said. Her jaw trembled as she looked at me in a way that dared me to explain myself. I couldn't. I had no excuse. I wanted to deny it but knew I shouldn't dare. I sucked in the cold morning air, one hand on the door jamb and the other still clutching the inside doorknob. I looked away from Sue and tried to remember last night's events.

"You need to get some help, Sam." She dropped a small suitcase in front of me. Its thud snapped me back to reality. She walked quickly away down the battered concrete stairway of the motel. It was less than a mile from our home; I hardly remembered the walk or checking-in.

I called out to Sue, "I love you." She didn't respond or turn toward me.

I walked barefoot to the edge of the second-floor balcony and watched Sue walk to our car, then drive away. Never once did she look back. When she was out of sight, I stepped backwards into my room, closed the door, sat on the floor and wept. I sat there a long time, until the tears would no longer come.

After showering, I walked to McDonald's and brought my order to my room. It was 8:30 on a Monday morning. I knew I should have been at work. They'd be wondering where I was. I didn't care.

I sat at the vanity against the wall and ate my meal. There was nothing to stare at but the mirror directly in front of me. In the lower left corner was a crack running upward a few inches, then becoming somewhat wavy and irregular, turning downward sharply a few inches until stopping a couple inches from the frame. As it would most likely continue to crack over time, I wondered if it would continue on its downward course or turn upward again.

I took account of my own life. It hurt to think about it while focusing at that crack. I stopped mulling over the crack and instead focused on the center of the mirror. I stared back at a homeless man that I ached to run from. He blinked at me, once. Then again. I blinked...or was it him? Was I going insane?

Even though she didn't say it, Sue still loved me. I hoped that was the case, anyway. She was loving, patient and kind, but even Sue had her limits, I knew.

What happened last night had never occurred during our married life. It was a reaction to my pent-up anxiety and fears in the same way they used to own my Sunday nights from years long past. But even on those dreadful nights back in Jersey before I escaped to Indiana to find Sue, they were never so violent, so disorienting, so debilitating as last night. Maybe my high school tormentors were right after all—I was The Hulk. I was powerless to explain it, but Sue was right. I had to get help, and soon. I struck my own son in the face. I placed my head in my hands, sobbing once again.

I decided as I woke up the next day that I would rest here at the motel. Alone. I needed to be alone. I needed to think. More importantly, I needed to remember. Maybe that would help me sort things out. I called work to tell them I would not be coming in.

When I was a child, my place in the world was evident to me, and I was content to simply accept it, similar to the Untouchables in India. Well, *content* was probably not the right word. *Conditioned* would be more appropriate. I was conditioned in a lot of ways: to accept my father was an alcoholic, to accept loneliness each day at school and each weekend at home.

My childhood conditioning seemed to prepare me for what I was experiencing in my new career, except for one huge difference. I now had a loving and caring family to go home to. I thanked God for that every morning on my way to work. Sure, the life Sue and I had made for each other could have been better in some ways, but experience had taught me it could have been much worse, too. I prayed our life together had not come to an end.

Despite the childhood I had experienced, I still expected that once I broke free of it, things would get better. And they did. Now, I'd taken a bit of a detour into unchartered territory. I used to blame my father for all my problems. This time it was different. I had to blame myself.

It was a paradox, for sure. I always had trouble being satisfied in the moment. Whenever I felt most at peace, my inner voice would unceasingly push me in a different direction fraught with new challenges I never dreamed I would have the courage to attempt.

Whether to welcome that voice or run from it was never clear, but most times I wished I could quell it. That rarely happened. When I could, it lasted only a short time. It seemed my destiny to yield to that voice, as it had guided me to this new career choice. Now, I wasn't so sure it had led me to a happier place, just a different one.

* * * *

My mom was one of seven children, four girls and three boys. Her middle brother, my Uncle Albert, was my favorite. He always felt sorry for my father and treated him with respect. He was about the only kind one on Mom's side. Mom's other siblings either ignored Dad or pandered to him. Dad never realized they didn't respect him and made fun of him behind his back. Not that I had any respect for my dad, but it still hurt having to overhear them make fun of him. It did, however, give me an excuse for my own shortcomings. *It's all in the genes, right? Garbage in, garbage out. How could I expect to be somebody if I came from his stock?*

Many a night I would lie in bed stewing, dreading to fall asleep. Over and over my imaginings were consumed with worry; I would wake up the next day, without fail, to another miserable, uneventful, unrewarding day. *God, why me?* I would so often think. Why did I have the misfortune of having to slither through life the pathetic dweeb that I was? I would lie in bed and hope against hope for some miracle praying that Saturday would come fast.

Saturdays were the greatest day of the entire week. At least, that was true for most Saturdays. There was no school, no chores, no Dad in my face. Nope, Saturdays were truly a day of rest. Mom would do the cleaning and grocery shopping. Dad would flip channels from one ball game to another polishing off a case of whatever was on sale at ShopRite. He told me once, "Sammy, it's no coincidence there are

twenty-four hours in a day and twenty-four bottles of beer to a case."
I lived for Saturdays and enjoyed them about as much as I hated
Sundays—especially Sunday nights.

It would begin to play out right after *Disney's Wonderful World
of Color,* which I watched religiously even though we had a black
and white TV. Dad would be passed out drunk in his La-Z-Boy
recliner. After Disney, I'd get the first call from Mom to get ready
for bed. My stomach churned as visions of the impending week raced
through my mind. Before I had time to prepare myself, nine o'clock
would come, and I would hear Mom call, "Sammy, bedtime!" Dad
wouldn't stir; both of us were relieved for that.

I'd kiss Mom goodnight as she did the ironing, and I slowly
ascended the stairs to my prison. Sunday nights. Why I feared
Sunday nights more than any other was difficult to understand.
Maybe it was because Saturday was the only day I felt alive, when I
was a real person. I would have to wait an entire week until that
feeling would return. A week of failure at most everything. A week
of Town Taverns. A week of fights at the Halloran's. A week of
being alone. No one wanted to be around the Halloran household.
And who could blame them? They had a choice and chose to stay
away. I did not. This was my home. My prison. And Sunday night
was once again upon me.

It was like my very own Groundhog Day. Could I endure another
week? And for what? The privilege to enjoy another Saturday but
realizing Sunday was near? My Sunday Night Fears, as I called
them, haunted me for years, even long after leaving Metuchen—
even long after Dad went away. Sunday Night Fears were my worst
memories of childhood. More than the fights. More than all the
humiliating moments. More than anything.

* * * *

Since starting at Hamilton Pierce, I began a slow downward spiral.
Possibly, my expectations were too high after being on a two-year

run culminating with my securing an impossible job at such a firm. Nothing had gone right since. The constant shunning by my peers was reminiscent of my high school days when few would have anything to do with me. *Peers*, right. As far as staff classification goes, we were peers, but that was where the similarities ended. I was paying a mortgage and a student loan while trying to save for college for the boys, hoping to take a decent vacation every other year. I had nothing in common with my fellow staff associates. Few were married; none had kids. For most, the job was an extension of frat house living. They were still enjoying a hedonistic existence. Paychecks meant beer and entertainment money for them. Most still lived at home with mom and dad. A real mom and dad. A real family. A supportive one. One like I hoped and prayed I still had.

I had to stop ruminating in the negative thought, but I couldn't. Sue was right. I needed to get professional help.

CHAPTER 13

Emily Thompson's office was in a brick five-story complex of professional offices in a residential part of town on a tree-lined street. I worried I'd have to park in a strip center and walk down the row of businesses. There, between the Dunkin Donuts and Hook's Pharmacy, I'd see a sign that read: "Emily Thompson, MD, Shrink. Enter at your own risk."

I expected this day might eventually come—meeting with Dr. Thompson, or someone like her. I wanted to work it out on my own. I believed I could. Fortunately, Dr. Thompson had a cancellation and could fit me in immediately.

I grabbed the doorknob to Emily Thompson's office and held it, wondering if there would ever be a good time to meet with a shrink. Smiling cynically, I entered.

I was surprised there was no one in her waiting room, not even a receptionist. Vacant. There were no other crazies trying to bury their faces in a magazine to avoid detection. At least, that was why I brought my own magazine for such a likelihood. I stood holding the door open and attempted to rationalize why I didn't need to be there.

A sign that hung at eye level on the opposite wall read: "Welcome to the office of Emily Thompson, MD." I took a step forward and allowed the outer door to swing shut.

I stood there regarding my surroundings. Below the sign were two straight-back chairs and another along the wall to my left. To my right was another door, presumably the door to her private office. I admired that door, walking up and rubbing it with the palm of my hand. It wasn't some paper-thin oak plywood veneer, but a real solid oak door, probably eight-quarter stock with routed quarter panels. It was a piece of art, especially the beautiful patina finish which only the passage of time could provide. Most likely, it was installed when the building was constructed in 1906, according to the cornerstone I passed before entering the building.

I took a seat on the chair opposite the oak door, still admiring it. I noticed a wall button, a doorbell of sorts, to the right of it. Above it was a soiled, tattered note reading, "Please push the button once and have a seat."

I walked up, wary, and pushed the button, expecting something to happen. Nothing did. No typical doorbell sound. No sound at all. I wanted to push it again. I imagined most people would want to push it again, but reminded by the note's instruction, I did not.

I stepped backwards into the chair and reached to grab the arms to lower myself into it, moving cautiously as if it might collapse. My every movement was tentative, as if I was an intruder who might soon be caught and evicted. I stared at the doorbell and the note. Maybe it was a test. It probably said something foreboding about those who pushed the button more than once. I did not want to be one of those people, especially on my first visit. So, I sat there and waited with my magazine at-the-ready if someone else walked in. No one did.

I was surprised when the door to the doctor's office opened exactly on time. I wasn't sure what I was expecting. Dr. Thompson looked young. She was, perhaps, around my age but still seemed young for a shrink. A successful one, anyway. As soon as I said *shrink* to myself, I regretted the use of slang and wondered if she would be offended. I stood and walked toward her. She peered directly into my face and confirmed my name and birthdate. She then nodded and lowered her head in a manner one might do in a show of respect. She held the door open and stepped back so I could enter. No smiles, no handshake, no "Glad to meet you," no fanfare. It was all very businesslike and professional.

Once inside Emily Thompson's office, I scanned for a couch but didn't see one. I expected there to be a couch, but no. Just two chairs. One was an ordinary overstuffed chair, and the other was a formal 1950s' Queen Anne leather buttoned chair.

"Please have a seat," she said, still standing behind me.

I regarded the two chairs again, and it became obvious on my second look which chair was intended for her patients. It wasn't the Queen Anne chair with the small wooden table next to it. Maybe it was the open notebook on the table that gave it away, or maybe it just seemed right, but I headed for the overstuffed chair.

"Here?" I asked, pointing.

"Yes. Please, sit. Make yourself comfortable."

I sat erect with my arms stiffly aligned with the arms of the chair, watching and waiting for her to take her seat. She sat with a polite, demure smile and folded her arm under her rump. I supposed she was making sure her dress didn't gather underneath her. I was sitting directly across from her. The most obvious place to look was directly at her; it seemed a bit uncomfortable. When I was uncomfortable, I talked.

"So, how often do your clients push that button in your waiting room more than once?" I asked.

She regarded me briefly, comfortably, but in no apparent hurry to respond. "Not often."

Interesting response. It seemed a perfect icebreaker, but she didn't bite. She smiled, crossed her legs, picked up her notebook and studied it for a moment. I sat in perfect silence feeling like I was being measured. My knees were together, and I moved my arms to my lap inside the big stuffed chair, which I felt might consume me at any moment. I was sitting lower than she was. Not by a lot, but enough to make me feel a little submissive.

"Are you comfortable?" Dr. Thompson asked.

I said I was, even though I wasn't. So I lied. I wondered how often her other patients lied. Would I lie about the serious stuff? I thought I might but hoped I wouldn't. I wanted to trust Dr.

Thompson. I needed to trust her.

Each passing second felt like minutes. I wanted her to say something, but she kept reading her notebook. She flipped a page, still reading, and I wondered how much information she had about me. She was referred by my family doctor. Maybe they talked while she took notes. Maybe he had sent her my chart. I wasn't sure what to think, so I sat there waiting for her to say something. I felt it was the polite thing to do. I casually glanced at my watch noticing it was 10:06. Was it working? Surely, I'd been here longer than six minutes. She scheduled this first meeting for two hours. Could I last that long? Then, as soon as my eyes wandered about her office, she spoke.

"So, Sam, may I call you Sam?"

"Yes, of course. Sam is fine." I sounded so stupid, like a parrot. *Is Sam fine? Sam is fine.* It sounded like I was trying to convince her I was fine and didn't need to be here. She might simply write me a prescription, and it would be the last time I'd have to endure such torture.

I wanted to ask what I should call her, but before I could, she spoke.

"You can call me Dr. Thompson, Emily, Doc, whatever makes you comfortable."

I smiled and nodded my head but didn't feel the need to respond. I was anything but comfortable and quite sure it showed. I felt my eyes darting from a small window to my left, then to her, then to the stand on her left, then back to her again. I didn't commit to calling her anything. *I don't want to be here*, I thought. *If I don't move or make a sound, maybe she won't see me.* But of course she saw me, and we were about to begin.

"So, Sam. Why are we here today?"

I thought, *Lady, that was a stupid question. Why do you think we're here today?* Fortunately, I said nothing stupid, at least not yet. But then it seemed a good place to begin. She wanted me to talk. That was reasonable.

My lips felt like they were sewn shut. I had never spoken of my fears and secrets to anyone for any reason. Well, except Sue, and even with her, not completely. I simply had no idea what to say, how to say it, where to begin or if I wanted to say anything. I surmised it was like that famously rhetorical question your mom or your teacher might ask: "So, what's troubling you?" The perfectly acceptable answer and the one everyone expects you to say is, "Oh, nothing. Everything is fine."

I shifted in my seat and tried to act casual and more relaxed, like everything was perfectly fine in my world but for a few things I needed help ironing out.

"Well, Doc," I began, "it seems I can't stop thinking about my childhood." I felt stupid as soon as I said it. Sure enough, she jotted something in her notebook. I attempted to backpedal and said, "What I mean is I guess I didn't have the best parents a guy could have." It wasn't as though I was done talking. I had a lot I could say. I was deciding on what exactly to say next. Talking to a shrink was beginning to seem ridiculous.

Fortunately, something compelled me to open up. While I could reasonably cope with my hidden demons throughout my past, it now seemed my troubles were quickly becoming my family's troubles, and Sue had drawn the line. Somehow, someway, I had to get past my reluctance to talk about my issues, and I hoped Dr. Thompson had the education, experience and training to draw out those things that needed to be addressed and fixed. Finally, I captured in my mind's eye the perfect place to begin.

"It seems, Doc, that I was a defective child."

Her frown seemed to beg for more without having to say anything. She formed her lips slowly as if to respond, but I quickly interjected.

"What I mean is my father used to call me 'defective.' Oh, he had other words to describe me, but 'defective' seemed to be his favorite."

It was all I needed to say. Like moving a big boulder, tough to start, but once I did, it was easy to roll it off the cliff. Then another boulder...and another. I told her one story after another, about growing up with an alcoholic father and solicitous mother.

She took notes and said little. When I would pause after hitting a tough memory, she would encourage me to continue with "How did that make you feel?" A gentle prompt and I would continue. With each story, I returned to some very dark places. I transported back in time, and I wasn't imagining it. I was really there. It was frightening. She sensed my uneasiness and, when called for, said calming words to assure me; I was now in a safe place, and he could no longer hurt me. That was true, at least for the time being.

Dr. Thompson periodically used the power of silence, a powerful tool to make some feel nervous and anxious. At least in my case it almost always worked to get me talking. I needed to get to the core issue—what happened on most Sunday nights growing up.

So, I got into it, describing for Dr. Thompson my worst demons, how I struggled to contain them and how they had stayed hidden until recently. I even covered the whole Mr. Miller tragedy and its aftermath. When I finished, I couldn't look at her. I was embarrassed.

"Sam, did this happen to you last Sunday? Is that what prompted you to call me?" she said.

I sat momentarily stunned. A shiver cut through me like a lightning bolt might feel. I focused on a piece of lint on the carpet. I had been talking for nearly two hours. I was emotionally drained.

Perhaps it was Emily Thompson's calmness and tacit acceptance of my deeply held dark secrets. She didn't condemn. In her silence, I felt the warmth of a mother's bosom and the glow of a father's pride at his son's achievements. But then, she said something which caused years of hurt and anguish to disintegrate.

"It's not your fault."

Maybe because I didn't immediately react she felt the need to do something else. She placed her notebook on the wooden table next to her, leaned forward, and gently wrapped her hands around mine, which were clasped and trembling. Dr. Thompson stared directly into my face and unflinchingly said once again, this time more emphatically, "It—is—not—your—fault."

I exploded in tears.

CHAPTER 14

I had been at the motel three days. Sue probably wouldn't have agreed to meet me for dinner had I not told her of my meeting with Dr. Thompson. The fact that Sue agreed to meet with me rather than talk on the phone said a lot. She still loved me, for one. Equally important, it told me I might be close to getting another chance. Sue might once again trust me with her welfare and that of our boys. I was encouraged when she agreed to dinner. My hope, however, was dashed when she said I should gather up my laundry to give her, and she would bring me another change of clothes. It seemed we were taking this one day at a time. I focused on the positive. Sue and I would have dinner tonight, alone.

I arrived at the restaurant a few minutes before the reservation. I wanted to greet Sue when she entered. I was as nervous as a kid waiting for his prom date. Finally, Sue appeared. I walked toward her. I hadn't seen her this beautiful since our wedding day. My excitement was palpable when I met her at the elevators. I took her hands in mine and kissed her gently on the lips. They were soft, warm, yet cautious. I couldn't blame her. Sue was the guardian of her kids. They were my kids, too, but no one, not even I, could usurp that duty from Sue. It was her responsibility to determine if I would be allowed near them again. At least she was willing to listen to me. I had a chance to prove she and our children were safe around me. If I blew this chance, she might not give me another. I took her arm in mine and walked over to our table next to the floor-to-ceiling windows atop the Indiana National Bank Tower.

LaTour was one of the finest restaurants in Indy. I had been to LaTour for a lunch HP offered for the new recruits but had not seen it at night and was more than impressed. Entering the restaurant offered a spectacular view. The illuminated city below and the stars above offered a brilliant show on a clear but cold December evening. The oak floors with inlaid Rosewood caught Sue's attention, but she didn't remark. Still, I could tell she was impressed.

I followed her stares. The outside walls were all glass, about twenty feet high and slanted at a forty-five-degree angle meeting at the pinnacle where an immensely large chandelier set the focal point for the entire room. From the elaborate decorations, it was obvious Christmas was near. Most impressive was the massive Douglas Fir Christmas tree, which held more lights and decorations than I had ever seen. The walls, table centerpieces and other adornments confirmed they took it a step further and then some to appeal to their guests—those in an income level far above ours.

The waiter took our drink order while handing us each a menu. Sue ordered water. I did the same. Wine was a luxury Sue realized we could not afford. A few minutes later, our waiter appeared again. "Do either of you have any questions about our menu?"

"None, thank you," Sue responded confidently before giving him her order. I followed with mine. The waiter collected our menus and left us. We were alone. We began to talk about random things. I wanted to ask about the boys but left that topic to Sue's timing. Fortunately, it did not take long for her to tell me about the boys' activities over the last few days. It was as if Sunday night hadn't happened. Sue would not forget, but she was never the type to constantly dwell on anything that might disrupt the steadiness of our overall relationship.

We continued to talk through our meal. Before long, our plates were cleared, and our waiter was back to ask for our dessert order. The night was moving too quickly. I wanted to order just to extend the evening, but Sue declined, so I declined as well. After the waiter cleared our table of all dishware and crumbs, we were left alone.

Neither of us spoke. I wanted to ask but deferred. I didn't want to put any unnecessary pressure on Sue.

A moment later, I reached my hand across the snow-white table cloth toward Sue. As she looked into my eyes, I felt her hand cover mine. Everything would be fine between us. It was not yet perfect, but I was back. She had forgiven me. I had another chance, and I couldn't blow it. I wouldn't blow it; all the staff, partners and Elaine Porchecks in the world could not cause me to dismiss the love I had for my family and my will to succeed.

We tapped our water glasses together and mouthed "I love you" at the same time. When the water touched my lips, it felt like the most expensive champagne in the house.

"Oh my gosh," Sue said, glancing at her watch. "It's after ten o'clock. We need to get home. I told the babysitter I'd be home at ten sharp. It's a school night, and she needs to be home."

Sue was up before I could even place my napkin on the table. She was five feet ahead of me, scurrying toward the exit as I struggled to keep up. While standing by the elevator banks, I quietly wondered what the arrangements would be from this point. I didn't want to suggest anything.

"It's a good thing I got gas tonight, so we can run straight home," Sue said as if reminding me, again, how she was always on top of things. Then she flinched, as if she remembered I had temporary housing in another location.

"Oh, dear, we'll need to stop by the motel and check you out."

The elevator doors opened, and we piled in. "I'm already checked out. I left my suitcase with the security guard in the lobby." As the doors closed, I gritted my teeth, hoping Sue would not think me presumptuous.

She tilted her head, squinted her eyes at me, then smiled, "You little stinker. How did you know I'd let you come home tonight?"

"I'm a good salesman," I said with a Cheshire grin.

We had our arms around each other, kissing, when the doors opened to the lobby. Moments later, I tossed my suitcase into the trunk, and we were off. I pulled out of the parking garage, and Sue had already nestled herself by my side, her left arm over my shoulder. I could feel her relax into me. I had won my wife back. I hoped I could do the same with my boys.

I took our babysitter home, and when I returned, Sue was waiting for me in bed. She held out something. "A gift from Ben," she said.

It was a drawing of me sitting at my desk next to large windows with tall buildings in the background.

"When did he draw this?"

"Today, at school," Sue said as she smiled sheepishly. It was her way of telling me Ben had forgiven me. But that left the obvious next question, which I didn't need to ask. I stared at Sue.

"Will is OK. Really, he is. He's going to need a little more time," Sue said as she reached her hand out to me. "We've talked a lot. He's still hurting inside."

I nodded my head. I understood. Will was older and knew more of the world than his younger brother. Will would come around, in time. For now, I was content with where we were after what had happened the last time I was here. Hugging Sue as she patted my back, I said a silent prayer for God to give me one more chance and begged Him never to allow my Sunday Night Fears to appear again. If they did, it might be over. I quietly thanked Dr. Emily Thompson. I had a long way to go, but through her, I now had hope for the future.

CHAPTER 15

I arrived at the office at about 8 a.m. and set my things on the table in front of the window. Shortly after I got situated, others came in. Like me, they were waiting for an assignment. Unlike me, their conversations covered sports, dating, and all variety of things young twentysomethings would cover, none of which interested me in the least. They talked about things and activities I considered worthless time robbers. This morning I was happy they were ignoring me. At least no one had brought up the drubbing Porcheck had delivered to me last Friday. I was relieved. Some kind person had even delivered my jacket, coat and briefcase to the staff room, expecting me to show up at some point.

One by one, throughout the day, the other staff were assigned to an audit. Today would be the last time I would see them for a while. With their assignments secured, the staff would leave from their homes in the morning and travel directly to the audit site. Then would come Christmas break, after which the fun would really begin. When we came back from the holidays, it would be "busy season."

The veteran auditors warned the newbies how rough it would be through March 31st. All the calendar year-end public companies in the office were required to file their Form 10-K by then, and it was a mad rush to complete all those audits in three short months. My weeks would be eighty hours long, if all was going well. It would not be unusual to log in some 100+ hour-long weeks on jobs falling behind. I had warned my family about the rigors of busy season. We were prepared. Busy season would pass me by if I didn't soon get assigned to an audit, any audit. A shiver shot down my back when I feared Elaine Porcheck may have poisoned the well for me. Maybe she had already lobbied for my dismissal. I suspected that might be the case.

Having had my solitary lunch, I became concerned when I spent the rest of the afternoon in the staff room—alone. Everyone had been assigned to an audit except me. Maybe I was about to be fired. So be it. There was nothing I could do about it now.

On the window sill, I noticed a pile of magazines. Shuffling through the stack, I pulled out the latest issue of *Journal of Accountancy* and found myself quickly absorbed in an article about forensic accounting. I had heard the term "forensic" for the first time watching and enjoying *Quincy MD*, a TV show about a forensic pathologist who worked for the Los Angeles police department. The show always opened with some heinous crime—usually a murder with an unknown assailant. Quincy would survey the scene, perform some tests, talk with folks, and before the end of the show, he would solve the crime to the absolute amazement of everyone.

I had never researched the term "forensic," simply thinking it had something to do with solving crimes. I was surprised to learn its meaning—applying specific methods and techniques to crime investigation. I'd never heard the term used with accounting. I hadn't had much coursework in accounting, but it seemed odd having studied extensively and passed the CPA exam that neither forensic accounting nor criminal investigation had ever surfaced. The article gripped and fascinated me.

It was written by Joseph T. Wells, Founder and Chairman of the ACFE—Association of Certified Fraud Examiners. Joe was a former senior associate at another Big Eight firm. After a couple years, he joined the FBI, working out of Houston, Texas. I thought I understood what FBI agents did. They mostly worked to keep tabs on the mob and all their illegal activities like bootlegging, prostitution, gambling and drugs. But the article mentioned the Financial Crimes Division of the FBI formed two years ago. It was all news to me, but I wasn't surprised FBI agents worked to solve such crimes; I hadn't realized there was an entire section of the FBI devoted to working on embezzlements and other "money crimes," as the article noted, in both government and private sectors. Wells noted those criminals were "perpetrators who stole from others using calculators instead of guns." I thoroughly enjoyed the article, and when I finished, I made a mental note to learn more about forensic accounting investigation.

The end of the article also signaled the end to my time sitting in the staff room waiting for something to happen. Finally, it did.

I was assigned to my first audit!

CHAPTER 16

During the audit staff's initial meeting to prepare for beginning the audit of GEL—Global Equipment Leasing, Pete Brooks gave us the history of the company and its founder, Foster Worthington Beckworth. Close colleagues at GEL called him Beck. We were to call him Mr. Beckworth if we ever needed to address him. I could not envision me needing to. Pete, as he asked us to refer to him, was the engagement partner after recently being admitted to the HP partnership. He seemed like a pleasant, normal guy in every way, even funny. I had a good feeling about working for Pete Brooks. I wondered how he felt about working with me; had he heard what Elaine Porcheck did to me. I was sure he had.

Pete didn't seem interested in spending much time describing Mr. Beckworth, which seemed odd given the rapid rise of GEL under Beckworth's leadership. While it seemed impressive to me, maybe Pete had instincts about such things. Not me. I was thrilled to be assigned to an up and coming, relatively new, public company headquartered in Indianapolis. I couldn't wait to tell our friends I was working on GEL's audit. Everyone in the city and surrounding area knew of Beckworth from the press he continually received.

What little Pete did say about Mr. Beckworth painted the picture of a privileged kid who had all the advantages afforded by an upper-class family. His dad took a small-town grocery store and turned it into a national chain which carried the family name, *Beckworth's*. The young Beckworth, however, chose a different path, getting the idea that led to the creation of GEL seven years ago.

The name alone was a peek into Beckworth's boundless vision. Today, GEL was not only the largest equipment leasing company in the country, but they were a public company with Beckworth as its CEO and Chairman, holding over 25% of the voting stock and selling the rest to eager investors for around $600 million. The man was a genius, and I was thrilled to be assigned to the GEL audit. Not only was this my first public company audit, but it was my first assignment in my newfound career. I was beyond ecstatic.

Pete Brooks went over everyone's assignments on the upcoming GEL audit, and in jocular fashion, he told me I was responsible for auditing only one account. *Pete heard what Porcheck had done to me*, I thought. Later, he pulled me aside and told me of the significance of the Lease Contracts Receivable account—LCR, and I was fired up.

"LCR is the asset created when a lease is capitalized as required by *Statement of Financial Accounting Standards No. 13, Accounting for Leases*,"—*SFAS No. 13*, or the "Standard," Pete explained in a sidebar moment. "Like an Accounts Receivable, the asset is decreased by monthly lease payments from the lessee, the customer. The lessor, the owner of the lease, was GEL. The LCR account was only one account, but as the largest account on the balance sheet, it represented about 60% of total assets."

It felt good to talk with a partner. Pete seemed to like me instantly. As we broke, he whispered something only I would hear.

"Sam, I admire what you did to get here. I know it's been a tough start for you, but I encourage you to hang in there. I wouldn't have given you the most complex and significant account to audit if I didn't have confidence in you."

I wasn't sure how to react. "Thanks, Pete," seemed an inadequate response.

Pete seemed like such a happy guy. He laughed aloud, frequently. He'd end each of his sentences with a jovial laugh, or so it seemed, anyway. I liked him from the start and made a vow my performance would ratify the confidence he had placed in me.

Pete reached out his hand, and when I took it, he pulled me closer and said, "You actually remind me of myself. When busy season is over, we'll have a drink together and share stories."

I was stunned and sure it showed. Our eyes met, and he laughed and slapped me on the back, as two guys would after sharing a good experience in a neighborhood bar on a Friday night. "Thanks," I said to him again. "I won't let you down."

Pete Brooks laughed heartily, then addressed everyone who was gathered in the area.

"OK, you guys get to work, and I'm gonna go suck-up to the client."

Before Pete reached the door to the conference room, it opened. A rather large man entered and moved immediately toward Pete. They bear-hugged each other. Turning around to face the rest of us, they were arm-in-arm like lost brothers reuniting after a long absence.

In a blustery and commanding voice, the intruder said, "I have known this man for over ten years, and he doesn't know a damn thing about accounting or auditing."

Pete let out another bellicose laugh as the two men continued to embrace, now enjoying the obvious barbs two good friends would be expected to exchange. Pete wasted no time in countering his friend's comment.

"It should be obvious to all of you that Hamilton Pierce gets rid of bullshitters as soon as they can, and this guy is lucky I found him a job."

Finally, with arms around each other's shoulders mimicking two sixth-graders on a recess break, Pete introduced his friend Reggie Dalton, GEL's CFO. Pete then turned serious for a moment and said, "Probably the smartest man I have ever met. Reggie was way too smart to last in public accounting, so he baled four years ago and is now getting fat from stock options and other perks afforded by executive living. Reggie Dalton was and still is my best friend."

"We'll soon see if our friendship is worth any value," Reggie quipped with a devilishly sly look toward Pete. Pete laughed it off. As did the others. Not me.

As I measured the man, Pete was right about the fat part, for sure. Reggie stood only about 5'6" and was rotund, resembling the shape of a tree trunk. A full head of black hair sat atop a portly face ensconced with black horned-rimmed glasses, a decade out of style. He appeared smart, alright, and prosperous. He also had a habit of pushing his glasses up at the ridge of his nose with his left index finger. I never cared for southpaws. It was a bad sign. I lost count at the number of times he did that since entering the room. He didn't exude the image of a guy with whom I'd want to spend a lot of time. Obviously out of shape and arrogant, Reggie Dalton struck me as an opportunistic man who would run over anyone or anything to get what he wanted.

CHAPTER 17

We had an audit to perform. We were doing what they called "preliminary" audit work or "prelim." To relieve the intense workload of the busy season, auditors tried getting as much work done prior to then as possible. Accounts could be tested as of November 30th, then when we returned mid-January, they'd be updated for the month of December when the real audit would begin. I was eager to get started.

We each staked out a section of the table in the massive conference room, a totally glassed-in room inside a glass lobby standing three stories tall. Talk about being in a bubble. Everyone entering and leaving GEL could see us working away. Beckworth liked to showcase his business was beyond reproach; the independent auditors were on the job.

This was to be our home for two weeks to complete our prelim audit work, then we'd take a break for Christmas and New Year's and hit it hard in mid-January. My first busy season would be upon me. The "death-march," they called it. Basically, we did whatever was necessary to complete our work on time.

Failure to meet a deadline was unthinkable, especially those imposed by regulatory agencies such as the Securities and Exchange Commission—SEC. If we failed to meet their filing deadline, our client's stock trading would be suspended; the kind of news that destroyed companies. Missing the filing deadline for any public company was not an available option in the playbook.

Facing my first day on an audit, I was eager to get off on the right foot and fought hard to stifle my inner doubts. I felt I was smart enough, albeit ignorant in the ways of how to do an audit as confirmed by Elaine Porcheck. Her poor human relations skills aside, I screwed up. I needed to stick to *my* assigned audit plan.

I laid out my "audit tools:" a 10-key calculator, sharpened #2 pencils, two red ones for cross-referencing and tick marks, a flowchart template (although I had never prepared a flowchart), a ruler and 14-column workpaper pads. I was ready to begin. My fellow auditors did the same as we prepared for the battle to come while waiting for our senior—our commander-in-chief—to return to the conference room.

Brian Walker had attended Pete Brooks's meeting but sat off in a corner busily working on something. Pete didn't seem to mind, only briefly introducing him. We would report to Brian daily. "What Brian says goes," Pete told us. Brian didn't stand nor lift his head for his introduction; he simply waved his hand, barely acknowledging us. I wanted to have positive feelings about working for him, but this first impression made it difficult.

I thought of my family. I would be with them tonight. Fortunately, Will had resolved to check his fear of me.

A couple years ago, Oscar the Grouch from *Sesame Street* scared Will. When I found there was an Oscar cookie at the mall bakery shop, I took him there. We talked about bullies. I bought an Oscar cookie and took a big bite out of him.

"Don't hurt Oscar," he pleaded with me. He was on the verge of tears but held firm.

"But I thought you didn't like Oscar," I responded, confused, thinking I was teaching him to stand up to bullies. Then, as so often was the case with children, I realized I was learning from Will.

"I do like Oscar. He's my friend," Will said.

I struggled to understand but remained patient, allowing Will the time to tell me in his own way. "It's just that sometimes he scares me. I love him still. Maybe if he knew I loved him he would not scare me anymore." I thought of my own father, then dismissed it as a bad example. Oscar was grouchy. My father was a bad person. There was no comparison.

Yesterday, Will and I took another walk through the mall. When we sat at a table to rest, I pulled out an Oscar cookie I had purchased while he was preoccupied watching kids on Santa's lap. As I slowly edged the cookie closer to him on the table between us, Will looked at it, then at me, then at the cookie one last time before he grabbed it and took a huge bite out of it. I smiled as I watched him chew. All the while, he was smiling and observing me intermittently. He was careful not to cede even a crumb to the mall floor. When he finished, he looked at me and said, "I still love Oscar."

I quietly nodded my head and said, "I know you do. That's why I bought it for you."

A moment later, my son was hugging me. "I love you, Dad."

I picked up Will and held him tight, trying hard to keep it together. I was never good at that, but at least I was learning and growing as a father. Apparently, Will seemed satisfied with my progress, despite all my faults.

Brian Walker was your typical Big Eight recruit and, I had heard, a very competent senior. Tall, slender and good-looking, he seemed, aside from my first impression, a nice enough guy on the surface. While others considered me some freak experiment with no chance of making it, Brian, at least initially, seemed to accept me for who I was. He avoided the usual commentary about my "non-standard" status with the firm.

"So, Sam, I understand you have two kids already, is that right?"

"You are correct, Brian, but when you say 'already,' you probably forget I've been married going on twelve years."

"Yeah, that makes sense. I'm hoping when I'm your age I'll have two children. So, what's it like being a parent?"

I talked about Will and Ben until I realized I was talking entirely too much. Brian Walker was probably being nice for show. He made me feel comfortable, though, and small talk seemed to be a normal

117

part of the audit environment.

Brian then talked about his wife, Linda. She seemed to be his favorite topic, and after fifteen minutes of "Linda this" and "Linda that," I had enough, but, conscious of my low rank, I continued to feign my interest. Again, my sales training was serving me well. While I was otherwise happy to continue engaging Brian, especially since he would write my performance evaluation at the end of the audit, his constant talking made it difficult to focus on my work. I wished he'd get busy on his work areas and leave me to mine, but I didn't want to be rude. So, I kept trying to do my work and talk with him at the same time.

After about an hour, I had accomplished nothing in the way of advancing the ball on my assigned audit area. I was relieved when a woman walked in and told Brian that Reggie wanted to see him. Brian immediately jumped to attention in mid-sentence and left our conversation and the conference room like a wisp of wind, mindful that the CFO of the company was not to be kept waiting. I was glad for the break, but Brian would likely continue his chatting when he returned. I had to seek a quiet place to work.

I gathered my things and walked out of the conference room, which was affectionately dubbed the "war room" for the duration of the audit and sought the cubicle area where I expected to find the GEL staff accountants busy at work. As I searched for an empty cubicle, a voice from behind me said, "Can I help you find something?"

I turned around and was struck with the feeling I was caught doing something I wasn't supposed to be doing and fumbled a meaningless and garbled reply. I was also mindful of the mandate the auditors were expected to work in the war room. Now exposed and concerned that my discovery might bring a reprimand, I was relieved when she quickly allayed my fears.

"You're probably trying to escape chatty Brian, isn't that right?"

Caught off-guard, I hesitated to respond, but she giggled and extended her hand. "You don't have to comment. My name is Carol

Wittford, and I manage the lease accounting for GEL. It appears you and I will be working together as you audit my work."

I recognized the name from the orientation meeting and suddenly realized I was talking with the person who happened to be in-charge of managing the LCR account, my chief audit responsibility. Her comment had an intonation suggesting I would evaluate her, and I extended my hand clumsily like a schoolboy meeting his teacher for the first time.

"Carol, I'm pleased to meet you, and don't think I am searching for mistakes in your work. Trust me, even if you made some mistakes, it isn't likely an inexperienced guy like me would find any."

I cowered realizing it was a dumb thing for an auditor to say to an employee of the company being audited. In a pathetic attempt to correct my comment I was flustered and rambled something incoherent. Fortunately, Carol sidestepped the whole gaff and said, "Well, first things first. How about I help you find a place to hide from chatty Brian and put you somewhere convenient for you and me to work together efficiently."

Relieved, I replied, "That would be so kind of you, but I was told the outside auditors were to work in the lobby conference room. I wasn't expecting to get more than a few hours respite today while I reviewed the audit program."

"Nonsense. I am the accounting manager at GEL and Reggie Dalton's right-hand gal. If it becomes an issue, say I came and sought you out as I wanted you close by to improve our work efficiency. Believe me, no one will question my decision, especially your wimpy boss." Without waiting for a response, Carol turned and walked off, expecting me to follow, which I did without further comment.

With Carol leading the way at a fast clip, I hustled to keep up. It also gave me an opportunity to enjoy her physical attributes. It was impossible not to notice she was well put-together—beyond what I would call attractive. I'd even say she was seductively sexy. Friendly and beautiful. I had died and gone to heaven and considered myself fortunate to be working with an apparently kind and gracious person. I was thankful for how things seemed to be going.

To get a jump start on the audit, I spent the better part of last weekend in the HP offices. There, I reviewed the prior-year's audit program, financial statements, 10-K and supporting general ledger, trial balance and subsidiary ledgers. I told no one. The budget for doing that was only three hours. I would triple that budget, which was not good for me. Whatever time it took to complete any task on this audit, I would charge only the budgeted amount of time. I was soon to learn that practice was called "eating time" and frowned upon. Still, no one would find out. I was anxious I'd be in over my head and needed every advantage. If eating a little time here and there was the worst thing I did, I thought I could live with that.

Carol pointed out her cubicle and continued to the next one, surveying it.

"Perfect. As I suspected, this will work out just fine. One of our clerks is on maternity leave, and it seems no one has taken over her cubicle, so it's all yours. Will this work for you?"

My temporary working place would be right next to Carol's. It was perfect. "Carol, this is excellent. I appreciate your help. With you being so close and—"

I hesitated, so Carol filled the void by saying what I couldn't say.

"And you'll be away from chatty Brian."

I laughed. "So true. I'm worried hearing your pet name for Brian may stick in my head, and I pray I won't slip and call him that."

"Oh, I don't think he'd take offense. At least, he didn't during last year's audit. I'm sure he knows we call him that, and he doesn't seem to mind. Brian is your stereotypic auditor—all brains and no personality. From the short time I've been around you, you seem to break the mold. I have a sense you're different," Carol said with an admiring glint in her eyes.

"Meaning all personality and no brains?" I said.

Embarrassed, Carol quickly stumbled in disagreement. I touched her shoulder lightly saying, "Don't worry, I'm kidding, but as you likely detected, I'm a little old for a staff associate."

"Nice to see HP makes some good decisions," Carol said approvingly. "I'd like to hear the backstory someday. Unfortunately, right now I'm due in a meeting, and you've got an audit program to review, so I'll leave you to your job."

With a quick turn, Carol was off as I said, "Thanks again, Carol, for helping me get situated." Without turning, she waved her hand in acknowledgment and disappeared around the corner.

Standing in front of my cubicle, I puzzled how Carol figured out so quickly who I was. Then, I reasoned, Reggie Dalton probably told her to look for the oldest staff guy in the room saying, "That's the guy you'll be working with." Oh well. So be it. I couldn't pout about that. I had a lot to prove.

While settling into my desk, I focused on Emily Thompson's advice to think positive thoughts. I had been following her suggestions and had to admit they seemed to work. I hadn't had another episode since we met.

As I made myself comfortable in my new temporary home, I was relieved Carol was not the typical corporate accounting clerk who viewed auditors as a complete annoyance and did everything in their power to avoid them. I'd heard how some clerks resorted to giving cryptic responses in an aggressive and assertive manner hoping the auditor would accept what they had been given and not return for further inquiry. Unfortunately, that strategy often worked.

Curious and persistent, I was unlike most auditors. This was one area where age and real-world experience should help me. I was certain in any situation where I received pushback to my questioning I would persist until I had a satisfactory answer. That methodology didn't fare so well for me in the audit simulation training; however, I didn't consider that a fair test, given Elaine Porcheck was a beast without restraints. Her grilling of me and subsequent "unsatisfactory" rating of my performance now sat in my file. It was the only performance rating in my file to-date. My next performance rating would be from the GEL audit. I could not have another bad one. The door would be slammed shut on my career, permanently.

My HP advisor told me not to worry too much about the one poor performance evaluation, especially for a training exercise. It was not the most desirable result this early in my career, but that was how I was wired: challenging, questioning and attempting to do the right thing. Despite the ridicule from Porcheck, my questioning a debit balance in accounts payable was the right thing to do, even if A/P was not my direct responsibility. I should have been commended for my discovery instead of being admonished. It wasn't right.

Throughout my entire life, if I followed my conscience, it would all workout. "No shortcuts," my maternal grandfather used to say. "Meet life head-on in all you do, and you'll be a better man for it." I loved that old man and often wished he was *my* old man—the father I never had.

Carol seemed quite unexpectedly out of character. She was nice, pleasant and a looker as well.

But then I was reminded of my audit mission, which slapped me like the scene in *Animal House* where the sexually immature kid found himself in a frat house bedroom with a young, beautiful date. It was a funny movie with a memorable scene to remind me of my responsibilities at the very moment when my mind might drift off into dangerous places. I was the company's independent auditor. As required by my professional standards, I had to perform my duties objectively and with the requisite degree of professional skepticism. I realized most auditors applied such skepticism based upon their assessment of someone's character and integrity through their interactions with them. They reasoned if the employee exercising control authority was a "good" person, the risk of fraud was diminished to a relatively low and acceptable level.

I could never do that when it came to evaluating controls and the employees providing oversight. Sure, I sized-up people in the same manner, but I refused to rely on such a subjective evaluation in considering what testing was appropriate. For testing selections and my evaluation of the results, someone's character and personality were irrelevant. I expected to perform my work objectively regardless of how I felt about those involved in either the creation or review of transactions and account balances. I had trust issues, for sure. Maybe that had something to do with the lack of trust my father had created in me over the years.

Regardless, I had a lot of work to do to gain an understanding of the systems, controls and procedures surrounding the management of the LCR control account. I'd better get to it.

Two hours had passed. Carol returned to her cubicle, and I continued my review of the audit program for the LCR account. It was pushing noon, and I realized I should return to the war room. I was sure the audit team was planning where to go for lunch, and I was hoping to go with them. It wasn't that I wanted to be with those "kids," but I wanted to feel like a part of the team.

When I entered the war room, it was empty. I hesitated and took in the room. They had gone to lunch without me. I wasn't that hungry anyway. I figured I could probably get by with a candy bar from the vending machine in the employee breakroom.

I walked through the labyrinth of corridors searching for the breakroom and finally found it. I stood in front of the bank of vending machines, trying to select fast so I could get back to work. As I perused all the goodies through the glass, I could almost hear Sue scold, "Unhealthy. Back off."

The silence was broken by someone yelling, obviously displeased about something. As I casually glanced just outside the vending area, I noticed Reggie Dalton regarding me from his office. I didn't mean to eavesdrop on his meeting with someone who I could not fully see, at first. Oddly, Reggie met my stare and rose from his desk just as the other person turned around. It was Beckworth. *Mr.* Beckworth to me. Even at that distance, his stone-faced expression appeared cold and vapid. He stared at me long enough to make me uncomfortable, reached behind him and slammed the door so hard I flinched.

Without wanting to read too much into it, I returned to my task of finding lunch and made a selection.

When safely back in my cubicle, I began to get organized.

"Ditched you for lunch, did they?" Carol said from behind.

I spun around to find Carol leaning a shoulder against my cubicle entryway. It was the first time I could take her in completely. She was tall and sleek with shoulder-length blonde hair and blue eyes delicately set upon a creamy, wrinkle-free complexion that shone beautiful in any light, any time of day. If she used makeup, she applied it well. Carol was Bo Derek beautiful. And now, standing there with her arms crossed over her chest, I could plainly gaze upon her ample breasts bulging from a too tight and low-dipping silk blouse that revealed her black lace bra. Her skirt must be tailor-made, well-appointed, complementing her svelte figure. It was tight enough to reveal shapely hips and thighs and short enough to accentuate precisely molded knees atop sculptured calves no doubt formed by those high-heeled black patent-leather shoes. On a 10-point scale, she was off the charts. If she was candy sitting in a bowl on my desk, I'd be a diabetic in a week; although truth be told, I didn't think my body could survive a week alone with her on a deserted island. I finally understood how Dudley Moore felt in the movie *10*. I was quickly warming to the idea this audit could be an extremely pleasant experience.

"Sam, did you hear me? They ditched you for lunch?" She reminded me of her question. How long had I been lasciviously leering at her?

"Yes, they did, Carol. Yes, they did, indeed," I said nervously, like I got caught drooling over a *Playboy* centerfold. "Just as well though, as I really need to get an understanding of this LCR account before the end of the day. I'm supposed to make my selections to test individual leases tomorrow, and I'm a long way from being ready."

"Well, I'm just the girl next door, so you let me know when it makes sense for you and me to get together and advance your knowledge," she said with a chuckle, flipping her hair over her shoulder with a seductive tilt of her head.

"The girl next door." A curious phrase to lob at your auditor a couple of hours after meeting him. *Was that a pass?* I wondered but dismissed the thought immediately.

All things considered, it framed a pleasing picture. Carol had beauty, brains and was fun-loving. Was she married or available? I was curious. Not that it should matter. I was married and unavailable. Happily, I might add. But it did. It was part of the mystique, I supposed. I had no leanings toward her, but the fantasy was still entertaining, maybe even erotic. At her age and with her personality and exceptional body, Carol was undoubtedly married or at least in a serious relationship. Maybe she even had kids, but no wedding ring or family pictures on her desk seemed odd. I couldn't go there. Not smart. Plus, I was too busy with the task at hand.

"Thanks again, Carol. I think I'll be ready to sit down with you to better understand the LCR account later this afternoon. Would you have an hour to give me around four o'clock?"

"Not a problem, Sam. I usually work until six o'clock, so whenever you're ready, just stop by." As quickly as she appeared, she was gone.

I wasted no time returning to my work. I now faced a timetable. I had to cram as much knowledge of the LCR account into my brain and develop some thoughtful questions by four o'clock today.

A couple of hours passed, and I was fried. I needed a break, so I stood, stretched and reasoned that a quick trip outside in the cold December air might do me some good. As I walked through the main reception area, I was impressed how well-appointed GEL's offices were. I expected most of our clients would be housed in commercial complexes, all having the same tired and industrial look to them. GEL's building was situated in a park-like setting. The three open floors with expansive windows allowed the outside beauty to enter the foyer. The feeling was expansive, and while it might have seemed a waste of space considering what commercial space cost, it was a reminder what public offerings could do for a new company.

GEL's executives were not shy about spending money, and if they spent the kind of money it took to appoint their offices so well, I imagined they were spending ample amounts on their own compensation—at least for the officers and top managers of the company. I hoped Carol was considered one of those top managers. I would discover exactly what she made when I did the payroll testing as part of determining the reasonableness of cost estimation, all part of testing the company's lease capitalizations.

As I approached the revolving doors to go outside, I observed about thirty yards off to my left Pete and Reggie having a discussion. Upon exiting the building, I stood for a moment, at least partially obscured by one of the mature trees the company had no doubt spent a small fortune on outlining their building.

Gone was the open camaraderie I witnessed earlier when Pete introduced Reggie to us in the briefing meeting. They were shuffling their feet with their heads down and hands in their pockets and appeared deep in conversation. They were certainly not talking football. Suddenly, Reggie noticed me, touched Pete's elbow, and they moved away at a casual stroll. I guess I wasn't as concealed as I thought I was. That was the second time today Reggie caught me watching him and the second time he made motions to indicate it made him uncomfortable. Again, I didn't want to read too much into it, but his mannerisms piqued my curiosity.

Thirty minutes later, I returned to my cubicle and prepared for my upcoming meeting with Carol. I was getting smarter about the account I was charged to audit, but it was confusing trying to match the company's lease capitalization procedures against the governing professional standard, *SFAS No. 13*. I was hoping Carol was not just a pretty face and could clear it up for me.

A few minutes before four o'clock, I began gathering my papers and notes for our meeting. Carol walked into my cube, and in a somewhat detached and hurried manner, she said, "Sam, I'm sorry, but we're going to have to move our meeting to tomorrow morning. Forgot about an outside appointment."

Before I could answer her, she ended with, "Let's meet first thing in the morning. Sorry about the last-minute change." She turned and walked away before I could answer, but I still shouted out, "Not a problem! Have a good evening!" I poked my head out of my cube to enjoy her briskly bouncing down the hallway with her purse slung over her shoulder. Instinctively, I was compelled to follow her.

Trying hard not to be noticed, I followed Carol to the rear of the building and watched her exit through a back door to the employee parking lot. As I hurried to a window overlooking the lot, I caught a final glimpse of Carol still walking at a fast clip then sliding into the passenger side of a waiting car that already had the door opened. It was a black Porsche Carrera, which would retail for at least a hundred grand. I had checked it out as a motivator to get through the MBA program.

But who was driving? I watched the car back out of its spot, and even though I was observing through a window, I heard its wheels spin-out—all of it adding to the captivating mystique that was Carol Wittford.

Back in my cubicle, I was disappointed, thinking it unfortunate that Carol and I couldn't meet until tomorrow. At least I'd have time to make sure I had a solid understanding of the LCR account and had formulated some intelligent questions. But Carol Wittford was weighing on my mind.

Brains, beauty, and now, mystery.

CHAPTER 18

The next morning, I arrived at GEL around 7:30 and hit the coffee pot. Coffee, black, was the elixir of choice these days. It used to be coffee, cream and two sugars when I worked at Benson. I was thirty pounds heavier and never exercised. Since leaving Benson, going to school full-time and setting upon a new career, I decided it was a good idea to attend to my health and appearance.

As I walked down the hallway toward my cubicle, I passed Carol's and was surprised to find her already there. "Good morning, Carol. You're here bright and early." I wanted to pry a little about why she ran off yesterday afternoon. I was especially curious who was driving the black Porsche. I decided it was none of my business and did not want to put her on the spot. Probably her rich boyfriend, anyway.

"Good morning, Sam, and a grand morning it is," she said with an excitement that a day off or a Friday night on the town might bring. Not the greeting I expected from a corporate accounting manager first thing in the morning and in the throes of an audit. Then again, Carol's physical attributes and demeanor did not bespeak your typical accountant.

Without offering any of the missing details I craved to learn from her sudden departure yesterday, she said, "I am ready when you are to get down to the task at hand, so stop by when you're ready."

I was quick to respond. Too quick. I spilled my coffee down the front of my clean white shirt. Carol noticed and leaped from her chair, grabbing my arm and leading me to the breakroom.

"We need to attend to this immediately, or your wife will have a fit with the stain it will leave."

I never told her I was married. I wasn't wearing my wedding ring either. I'd never managed to get it resized after losing all the weight. Carol either knew I was married from some other source, or she was probing for information, none of which I was ready to volunteer. I simply followed her lead.

She grabbed a paper towel from over the sink and softly pressed it slowly against my chest and worked down, absorbing the coffee. I quietly stood by, allowing her to attend to me. She was still holding my arm up and now stood close enough I could smell her lavender scented perfume. Maybe it was her shampoo. Regardless, I was enjoying being close to her, not thinking for a second it was wrong. She continued to slowly pat the towel along the coffee trail until she touched my stomach area. In an instant, Carol became noticeably uncomfortable. She abruptly stepped back and handed me the towel. While dusting herself off at the hips, she was clearly embarrassed.

"So, work on that and stop by my cube when you're fixed up and ready to talk." Carol exited the area as fast as she entered it.

I was left soaking up the coffee spill as best I could. It was a mess for sure, but the only thing on my mind was meeting with Carol and getting answers to my questions. Only then would I be ready to make my lease selections. Otherwise, I was sure it would appear ominous to Brian if I fell behind schedule so soon into the job. I didn't want to be on his radar.

In a few minutes, I returned to Carol's cubicle. Regarding me, she immediately covered her mouth to hide an obvious giggle and said, "Your wife will be upset with you tonight when you go home."

There it was again, the probing question. So, I removed all doubt and said, "I'm sure she will be, but we've been married long enough she knows what a klutz I am."

That launched a series of questions from Carol: "How long have you been married? Any kids? What are their ages?" Before we knew it, forty-five minutes had passed, and we hadn't addressed one of the questions on my list. It seemed Carol would have been comfortable talking all day about anything other than work. Finally, I said, "Listen, I want to be judicious with your time, so we better get to my questions."

The mention of my work seemed to kick her in gear, and she invited me to have a seat in her cubicle. Swiveling her chair around, now facing me, she folded her hands on top of her crossed legs and said, "Let 'er rip."

We labored through the preliminary questions about the unfolding of the lease capitalization process. I was sure I asked more than a few irrelevant questions, but Carol was patient. She began with how the leases were obtained from the field through their captive sales force, then the internal review they went through before they made it to her desk for capitalization and input into the system.

When I questioned her about who exactly decided what leases qualified for capitalization under the four requirements of *SFAS No.13,* Carol motioned me to pause. She reached over to her desk and picked up a three-ring binder and swiveled her chair around next to me. Not certain what was happening, I remained seated, watching her organization of the records unfold. She placed the binder on top of her right leg spanning over to my left leg and opened it on the table created by our now touching legs. Suddenly, I was having trouble concentrating. Moments before, we were sitting at a comfortable distance apart, talking like two colleagues, and now we were huddled together like a couple of college kids probing each other to see if there was an attraction with little regard for the subject matter before us.

Her scent was alluring. Everything about her became sensual. The way she brushed her hair behind her right ear, lightly touching my shoulder, her forearm brushing up against mine as she turned a page. Periodically, she would shift in her chair, gently rubbing her leg against mine. She seemed to move quite a lot and acted nervous, as if I was placing her in a compromising position, but she was calling the shots here. I was merely following the bouncing ball.

Suddenly, I felt myself becoming aroused. I couldn't control it, and I was totally clueless of how to quell it. I stiffened and sat more upright in my chair out of reaction to another of her sudden movements toward me. She pulled away a little. Our thighs were no longer touching, but they were still close enough we could continue sharing the binder on the top of our legs. My arousal grew.

If she removed the binder it would be embarrassing, at least for me. I needed to get away, if only for a few moments, but there seemed to be no opportunity without making a fool of myself. I resigned to fight my urges. *Concentrate*, I thought.

It wasn't happening. What I wanted was to jump Carol. But I was married to Sue, and I was in love with Sue. How could I even think such a thing about another woman? I was an adolescent again. This would not work. I had to stop, but how?

"Carol, I need to take a restroom break," I said, although I was afraid to move out of fear of what would be revealed. So, I waited for her to get up and turn away from me.

She did and said, "Sure, not a problem."

It was an opportunity I grabbed without hesitation. I was sure it appeared odd me running out of her cube like that, but I needed to get away. What I really needed was a cold shower.

When I returned to Carol's cubicle, calmed and restored, Carol stood facing me and asked, "Are you OK now?" She was smiling like a teenager fully aware of what she was doing; she knew precisely the nature of my problem and proud she had caused it.

I tried blocking everything except leases from my mind and made no eye contact with her. I was sure it appeared weird, but I didn't care. I couldn't allow that to happen again. I thought, *Focus on the questions*. But I wanted to focus on Carol.

When I sat, she wheeled her chair next to me once more, propped open the binder and picked up where she left off in unrelenting fashion. She had to realize I felt uncomfortable. She didn't seem to care. I began not to care.

She flipped through the binder, brushing me, touching me,

flirting. No, teasing. I recalled reports where an inappropriate love affair had been disclosed about some couple, maybe I knew them, maybe not. I remembered thinking, *How could they do such a thing—married, kids, now divorced. How could they bring such hurt and shame to their respective families?* This was how.

Carol spoke again. I wanted to hear her talk. Even the sound of her voice was sensual. I was in control of my anatomical reactions, at least for the time being, and tried to concentrate on leases, sort of like a guy wanting to slow down his orgasm by thinking about something else, like baseball. I was focused and concentrated on leases, thinking that if I maintained that focus two things would happen: I would learn a lot about the task at hand, and I would probably get through this without throwing Carol across the desk and giving her what she clearly needed—what she wanted—what I wanted. Asking questions here and there thankfully helped stay my inner beast.

The more Carol talked, the more I learned. The more I learned, the better my questions became. She could answer every one of them, supported with the proper documentation. She was good. From what I could determine, her accounting for those complex transactions complied with the required accounting standards. I still had to test transactions, but she appeared to be saying all the right things.

One of my questions caused Carol to reach her left arm across my chest, turning into me, to grab a lease agreement sitting on the corner of her desk. She rubbed her breasts against my arm in the process and a wisp of her hair brushed my chin. I gritted my teeth, stiffened and began mentally naming the NY Mets starting lineup. The 1964 line up, the last time I was a fan. All to impress my father when I lived in Jersey. As crazy as it seemed, it was working.

Carol grabbed the lease from her desk, then spun her chair around in front of me, at the same time balancing the binder on my legs. She leaned forward, pointing to the lease and revealing her ample cleavage. She was working me like a pole dancer in a strip club.

Given the opportunity, I would have tucked dollar bills inside her bra. I would have done so much more to her. I was enjoying every minute of the show without regard to my learning. I'd surely pay for this later, but for now, the only thing on my mind was Carol—and not for her knowledge of leases.

Carol Wittford had me right where she wanted me, like a drunken college kid at his first striptease show. Each time she lifted her head, I had to tell myself not to gaze down upon her breasts, but still, I did. Then, there was the scent of her hair as she bent forward to point out something on the lease I was reviewing. It was wonderfully captivating. My loins were stirring again. I fantasized about what I would do to her at that moment. Not good. Something had to change soon, or we were about to be embarrassed.

"Sam, I stopped by to see how you were proceeding with the planned selections today. Are we on track to make that happen?" Brian said from behind.

Brian's timely interruption caused Carol to leap almost to attention as if a dignitary had entered. I stood, too, more slowly. With Carol in front of me and Brian behind, I felt sandwiched between two bookends, one pleasing, the other not. It was awkward standing between them. Still facing Carol, less than a foot in front of me, I noticed through her tight blouse, Carol's nipples were hard. I admired and enjoyed them. It pleased me I had caused that.

Reacting quickly, Carol grabbed the binder out of my hands and pressed it against her breasts, crossing her arms as a school girl might carry her books. She was blushing. Immediately, she turned and retreated further into her cubicle and opened her file cabinet. Not that she needed something at that moment. Well, she did need something, but she would not find it in a filing cabinet. I needed the same thing. The difference was I cursed myself for my desires. I imagined Carol praised herself for her performance and accomplishments today.

Fortunately, the entire scene was blocked from Brian's view. I turned and faced him and said, "We're good, Brian. Carol and I were going over last-minute things to confirm my understanding, and I

expect to be in a position to make the lease selections later today."
When saying the word *position*, my mind envisioned different kinds
of positions. "I was planning on stopping by to go over those
procedures with you in a couple of hours to make sure I was doing
things correctly. Does that work for you?"

Brian did not answer immediately, appearing to take it all in. He
peered around me, first regarding Carol doing whatever off in the
corner fumbling with files, and then me, as if trying to assess the
situation. I was sure Carol and I appeared somewhat cozier than most
auditor/client meetings Brian had witnessed. Brian's facial reactions
and slow, measured speech seemed to give him pause. In the end, he
seemed nonplussed by it all and said, "Sounds good. I'll expect you
later this afternoon. Carry on with what you were doing." With that,
Brian was gone.

Carol now seemed to realize how we appeared to Brian and
suggested we go to the conference room. "I think we'll have more
room to work," she said with an elfish smile.

Offering no objection, I stood and helped her gather and carry the
pile of documents and binders she would need to continue her
explanation of the management and accounting of the LCR account.

"Lead the way," I said, and Carol scooted in front of me, exiting
her cubicle. I scurried along, regarding her from behind, and wished
I had led the way. I didn't need the distraction. Her skirt was form-
fitting, more like spray-painted on her. And how she walked so
seductively with the sway of her hips, her movements communicated
she sensed I'd be admiring her in exactly the manner I was. I was
self-conscious, but what could I do? It's not my fault the view was
so stimulating. I at least felt a hint of guilt enjoying her the way I
was.

Once we got to the conference room, I waited for her to sit so I
could assume a less suggestive seating arrangement. Why couldn't
she be like most accounting clerks: old, ugly and frumpy? The eye
candy was a nice benefit, but I couldn't lose sight of my mission. I
was auditing the largest asset on the balance sheet. If they were not

capitalizing leases in accordance with the prescribed professional requirements, a lot of bad things could befall the company and adversely affect our audit opinion on their financials.

My sultry and erotic fantasies aside, I reminded myself not to be dissuaded by the experience I was enjoying. While difficult to maintain my focus, I was ever mindful of my professional duties, at least intermittently. I had come too far to blow it all on poor decision making. All things considered, I rationalized I was still doing my job. I hadn't compromised my ethics. That, I was certain. Well, maybe not professionally, but then there was the personal side. I suddenly recalled Jimmy Carter's interview where he admitted to "lusting after other women."

I had the greatest wife a man could want, and I loved her beyond words. Yet, I still could recognize lust when I felt it even though I continued to assure myself I'd never act upon it. I hoped I was right but wondered. Regardless, I was very much enjoying the pleasure of working with Carol Wittford and was in no way dissuaded by the experience. I wasn't doing anything wrong. Still, auditor ethics aside, I needed to get it together before I did something stupid.

Over the next hour, Carol and I acted like professionals. She was working diligently to ensure I had the correct understanding of the company's lease accounting and had all I needed to make my lease selections for testing. When we finished our business on this topic, I stood and thanked her for her time with a formality one would have expected upon a first meeting. Even so, we had become fast friends already. Why, I couldn't say, but the closeness we experienced when we began our discussion in her cubicle a short time ago caused me to rethink where we might be headed.

I concluded that a romp in the hay would be a bad thing to do. As I watched Carol exit the conference room, I worried she might have had a different intent. Her hesitant glance over her shoulder at me and the demure downward tilt of her chin had no other intended purpose but to contemplate her next move, one returning to the intimacy we had experienced a short time ago. I was certain she would take it to the next level; I had only to lie there and accept her loving me. Fucking me. I tried to avert my eyes, but she appreciated how I had been watching her exit; I worried what that indulgence had communicated.

With my newly acquired knowledge of leases and how GEL was accounting for them, I was ready to have Brian approve my selection process and stopped by the war room. Everyone was busy doing what they do: auditing. Brian glanced up from his snacking on a bag of chips. I took it as another painful reminder they had, again, blown me off for lunch. I didn't care, but I wanted them to know and said, "So, did you all go out for lunch earlier?"

I received a few embarrassed and guarded looks from the three other auditors in the room with none uttering a word, tacitly deferring to Brian to handle it. Unmoved, and with no show of remorse, he regarded me coldly and said, "Yes, we did. I figured you and Carol were enjoying each other so much you would dine together or find some other way to utilize the midday break."

The implication was beyond unprofessional. It was disgusting. I stared at him thinking, *This guy really has a pair, at least with an underling like me.* I felt like smacking the little twit upside the head, but fortunately, I remembered my place.

I ignored his barb without striking back.

"Brian, I'm ready to go over the LCR selection process with you whenever you are ready. Let me know when we can do that."

Not being quite done with me, he said, "You and Carol appeared quite cozy over there. Guess you're making sure the client is happy." The entire war room came to attention, first looking at Brian, then at me, waiting for my response.

Enough was enough. In an instant I engaged him. Cocking my head to the side, my index finger substituting as a metronome somehow soothing my battered ego, I said, "You are exactly right, Brian, and with my advanced age and family status I am probably the only one of us that could get away with it and not seem like a big flirt. Just taking one for the team."

Everyone in the room laughed except Brian, who I was certain meant his comment as a dig and was not pleased I could return service so well. All he could manage was a sarcastic grunt. He put his head down over his work and gruffly said, "I'll stop by in a bit to go over your selections. Be sure you are ready."

"Got it, chief. I'll be ready whenever you are." I turned and left the conference room, favoring the retreat I had established in the cubicle next to Carol's. I took the route passing Carol's cubicle. She wasn't there.

I needed to calm down before Brian stopped by. A moment ago I had forgotten my place. I suspected I would pay for my lapse in judgment. It was stupid to challenge him, especially in front of the other staff.

I focused on a different issue. This one had nothing to do with my professional success. I believed Carol would welcome me into her bed at my asking, and at this very moment, I wanted to ask.

CHAPTER 19

"Don't ever do that again," Brian said.

I whirled around in my chair to see Brian standing there. He was rigid, his eyes squinted, fists clenched at his side seemingly filled with resolve. There was no doubt what he was referring to, but I felt compelled to inquire out of contempt for his riding me, especially in front of the other staff and said, "What are you talking about?"

"You know exactly what—"

"Gentlemen, am I interrupting?"

Saved by the real boss, Reggie Dalton popped in, and his timing could not have been better. "I'd like to go over your selection process for the lease testing of the LCR account. I understand from Carol you're ready to make those selections." He was staring directly at me while talking, almost deliberately ignoring Brian. Before I could speak, Brian said, "Reggie, you are correct. Sam is ready, but I need to go over his process and approve it so—"

Reggie's interruption was more forceful this time. Glancing deferentially toward Brian, he said, "That's fine, but can the three of us do that now so I can get my IT guy pulling the selections? He's got a lot of projects on his plate, and I want to get that important procedure out of the way as soon as possible."

He was staring at Brian so intently, almost daring Brian to refuse his suggestion. Being the wimp that he was, Brian simply said, "That would be fine, Reggie." Reggie looked at me, expecting my approval as well. I quickly calculated it would be best for me if Reggie joined in this process. Brian couldn't play games taking advantage of his position as the senior auditor.

At Reggie's suggestion, we moved to the conference room where Carol and I had met earlier. I discussed the selection-making process being sure to first indicate I was following the same process used in the prior year, which was music to an auditor's ears. Neither Reggie nor Brian offered comments.

Believing I had walked through the process and explained it well, I glanced at Brian first for some confirmation. Avoiding eye contact with me, he said, "I think this is all in order, Sam. You did a very good job putting this together." It was a gratuitous compliment, but I was quick to accept it. He then looked deferentially at Reggie.

Reggie stood and said, "Very well, Sam, let's head over to the computer room, and Brian," he addressed him dismissively, "I'll stop by the war room after Sam and me are through here. I have some things I need to go over with you." The message was clear to Brian: *Sam and I had this, and he was not invited to join us,* which was fine and dandy with me. Brian mumbled reluctant agreement with Reggie's plan, but I could tell he was more than a little ruffled. He wanted to have the last say. He was *my* boss. At least he was savvy enough to know when to keep his mouth shut.

Reggie and I walked out together, leaving Brian in our dust. I was certain Brian would hobble me later in some way as retribution. I didn't care. Reggie was running the show, and for the time being, he and I were on the same side.

We walked down the hallway to the computer room. It was the first time I was alone with Reggie. He asked me the question I expect all CFOs and client staff would be interested in knowing. "So, what's the story behind you deciding to get into the auditing business at your age?" Considering the trip to our destination was a short one, I gave him the short story. But as we approached the computer room, he held up his hand, instructing me to defer the discussion, which I was happy to do.

The computer room was noisy, and with a brief introduction, Reggie signaled me to instruct Wyatt Duncan, the IT Director, on the protocol he needed to follow in the selection process. Reggie appreciated from his audit days that instructing, monitoring and certifying the selection process for confirmations was in the realm of the independent auditor's responsibilities. He dutifully stood and listened, without interruption, as I instructed Wyatt.

I told Wyatt which files to query, random start and interval to use in writing the proper selection code. When completed, I would review the code prior to him inserting the tape into the IBM mainframe. The lease selections would result. I'd confirm those balances and lease agreement details as part of my testing of the LCR balance. Above the din of the whirring sound made by the spinning tapes and mechanics of the systems in the room, Wyatt's agreement indicated he understood the task at hand; he acted like he knew the drill. In a few minutes, I had finished with my instructions to Wyatt. We were done for now, so Reggie and I exited the room. Wyatt would write the code, and I would return to monitor the actual running and selection of the leases. Later, the entire selection process and its output would all be tested by an intern I would supervise.

When we left the computer room, I thanked Reggie for his help, but he was not done with me. "You're the new kid on the block, and I wanted to lend a hand on this important task. I am also painfully aware how Brian can be such a twit." His smile was begging agreement, but I demurred to comment.

"It's time for my afternoon coffee," Reggie declared. "Would you care to join me?"

It was a kind offer and one I was eager to accept. A guy at my level never expected to have a one-on-one chat with a public company CFO, especially a former Big Eight firm audit manager. I, too, was keenly aware of my responsibilities as an independent auditor and responded saying, "It's a kind offer, Reggie, but I'm supposed to witness the selection process, so I better stay here until it's done."

Reggie offered a wry smile and said, "I'm aware of what your responsibilities are. How about I tell Wyatt to write the code but not begin the selection process until you return. You and I can get to know each other better, and you can still fulfill your independent auditor responsibilities." He said it with a sarcastic tone as if those responsibilities were all show, and *real* auditors didn't follow them to the letter. *Everything in moderation* was his subliminal message. Maybe his casual attitude on the issue was telling.

Before we left the computer room, Reggie told me we'd meet at my cubicle after he instructed Wyatt to wait for my return. I paused briefly to consider the process. *Had I missed any steps?* I wondered. Reggie stared at me as if willing me to leave. He had a commanding presence compelling others to carry out his instructions without question. It worked on me, as I returned to my cube.

Reggie collected me in a few minutes, and I followed him through the lobby and past the war room. I sensed all the auditor's eyes following us through the reception area and out the revolving door. I assumed we'd be getting into Reggie's car, but to my surprise, Reggie walked over to a black stretch limo expecting me to follow. Of course, my fellow auditors would be wondering why I was hanging with the CFO of the company. All of them except Brian, who would be green with envy. I was enjoying my important status while it lasted. Brian would be roiling inside.

I waited for the driver to get the door for Reggie and felt like a true executive when he did the same for me. Inside the limo, it felt like a different world. The rich feel and smell of leather conveyed wealth. For the first time since beginning my new career, I had a taste of where I was headed.

Reggie and I went for his afternoon coffee but not to the shop around the corner. No, he took me to his country club.

When the limo pulled under the covered portico at the restaurant entrance, a white-gloved valet opened the door. Reggie did not immediately react. He glanced at me as if to say something but didn't. He exited the car and climbed the red carpeted stairs leading to the entrance. I dutifully followed him, acting like I knew what to do. I had never been to a country club, let alone as a guest of someone with the stature of Reggie Dalton. At the top of the stairs, another white-gloved valet tipped his head to Reggie as he opened the door for us to enter. He tipped his head to me as well. Like a fool, I tipped my head in return. I was sure it made his day.

Reggie appeared to know exactly where he was being led by the maître d'. As he was being assisted into his chair, I grabbed at the chair in front of me whereupon another waiter politely assisted me. I honestly could not understand what all the fuss was about. Attending to Reggie first, a waiter asked, "The usual, Mr. Dalton?" Reggie responded with a nod, unfolded his napkin, relaxed into his chair and said, "So, Sam, please continue from where you left off."

At first, I was puzzled but then realized he was referring to his earlier question about my drastic career change at my age. But to be sure, I confirmed saying, "You mean what's a guy my age doing here?"

"Exactly," he said with a carefree chuckle as someone approached with a box of cigars. "Sam, do you care if I smoke?"

"Of course not."

"You might peruse a selection for yourself."

"Thanks, but I used to sell those things out of the trunk of my car, so I'm going to pass, but thanks for the offer."

"Not these, Sam. These may not be Cubans, but they were grown of Cuban seeds in similar soils in Guatemala. I can assure you, these are not the cigars you sold out of the trunk of your car."

"How do you know what brand of cigars I sold?" I quipped losing the deferential tone.

I caught a wily grin as he dusted off his jacket. He ignored my question and instead said, "So, I'm waiting with great anticipation for your story."

The waiter lit Reggie's cigar, giving me a moment to consider my response. I was attempting to measure this man who suddenly seemed very interested in a staff associate at his company's auditing firm. I wanted to ask him why but passed.

"I was a marketing major in college," I began. "Not like I had a clue what I'd be doing with such a degree. When my senior year rolled around, I realized all I was qualified to do was sell something. Turns out, the Division Manager for R.J. Reynolds Tobacco Company saw something that impressed him." I purposely paused hoping to engage Reggie who was puffing on his Guatemalan Cuban. I wasn't sure he was listening to me. I was wrong.

"And did you come to learn what that was?" Reggie asked, at least appearing to show sincere interest.

"The ability to persuade," I proudly said.

Reggie Dalton smiled with a quizzical tilt of his head saying, "Persuade?"

"Well, to sell is to persuade, is it not?"

"It is, indeed. Please continue."

I told Reggie Dalton how I steadily improved in my ability to win people over to my way of thinking each year while at RJR. Reggie continued enjoying his cigar, but his eyes were locked on mine. When I paused, in another attempt to engage him, he nodded his head, indicating I should continue.

I told Reggie about my decision to leave RJR for a better opportunity at Benson Distributing—what I did for Benson and what Benson did for me—and my decision to return to school leading me to this new career in accounting. I left out the part about getting fired.

"And here I sit before you," I said as I ended the story.

I was surprised Reggie seemed impressed. His eyes did not divert their penetrating stare the entire time I was talking. Even when he sensed a waiter bending to ask him something, a wave of his hand sent him scurrying off without finishing his question. If Reggie Dalton wasn't engrossed in my story, he was sure faking it well. As far as he was concerned, I was the only other person in the room. I had never met anyone like him, and if forced to describe him, I wasn't sure what adjectives would come to mind: confident, assured, capable...dark. When that descriptor entered my thoughts, an

143

ominous sign revealed itself, suggesting other attributes one would not want listed on their resume: pedantic, petulant, arrogant. It may not be fair, but I might also add deceptive.

"Yes, indeed. Here you sit before me." He signaled the waiter for the tab, which was immediately presented, and he signed it. It was clear he was preparing to leave, but it all seemed so abrupt and confusing. Why no follow-up questions? Did I bore him? Did I overstep his invitation to relay my story?

Then something bizarre happened. He offered me a job. Well, not exactly, but he suggested I consider a job with GEL. It was both exhilarating and unsettling. Reggie suggested I consider becoming a candidate for GEL's recently posted accounting position—Financial Reporting Manager. I was aware, also, that it paid three times what I was making. But before he made me an offer, I cautioned him, saying, "I would have to report it to my firm, as it could be considered a breach of my independence."

Reggie smirked. "So, it seems you are not just a pretty face after all. You're up on the rules and regs, which is impressive given you are so new to the industry."

He leaned forward and took another puff. "Look, I'm not making you an offer...yet." He paused for effect. Then, turning toward the window away from me, he exhaled a long stream of smoke and continued. "All I'm saying is GEL is now on top of our industry, and we have our eyes set on even greater opportunities in other industries, maybe other countries." He paused again, turned toward me, and continued. "And we need lots of good people to keep us there and take us to the next level. Good people like you. Like I said, I'm not offering you a position at this time. I'm simply making conversation with a bright and ambitious professional. So, I don't think you have anything to report to *Papa*, but that's your decision." He said it with confidence, knowing I would not report it. If I did, I would be removed from the engagement immediately for independence reasons.

With that, he set down his cigar butt, stood, wiped his face with his white linen napkin and tossed it onto the table before walking toward the exit without saying another word, like a king at court. There was no need for him to announce his movements. Everyone in the room would be focused on King Reggie.

I followed him through the doors to the main building and out to his waiting limo with its heated black leather seats. Neither of us spoke. In the car, Reggie pulled out a portfolio and wrote in it during the entire trip back to the company without saying a word, not even about the open manager position. We sat across from each other in relative silence the entire return trip. I thought we had a good discussion at his club. He offered me a job, well, sort of, and now the silent treatment. So be it. Telling my story was a sales pitch. I was always in the habit of selling myself. I played this like any other sales job. The next person who speaks loses. I was determined to sit there in complete silence, unless he spoke first.

Maybe Reggie had subscribed to the same logic. Twenty minutes later, when we returned to GEL's offices, I thanked Reggie for his hospitality and his courteous treatment of me, especially considering I was so new to the profession. He said, "The pleasure was all mine," as he dropped me off at the main entrance. I closed the limo door and watched as it sped out of the parking lot with Reggie still inside, no doubt off to some important meeting. As I watched the car work its way to the main entrance and eventually out of sight, a fact occurred to me.

Reggie Dalton was thirty-five years old. Only three years older than me. Even with my late start in this new career, I could picture myself there...even beyond. It was motivating. I needed to be patient. There'd be no more teasing Brian, and I'd stay away from Carol, even though I felt I could enjoy the show without ever touching the merchandise. I told myself I could but wondered.

I needed to take it one step at a time. My primary goal was to do a good job on the GEL audit, enough so that Brian Walker would give me a good evaluation, not necessarily glowing, but good enough to neutralize the bad one already in my file.

Entering GEL, I thought, *Wouldn't it be interesting if next year I was Brian Walker's client? That'd be a hoot!* I laughed silently at the thought and savored that image as long as I dared, but as tempting as Reggie's offer was, I would never seriously consider it. It was too soon, and it wasn't enough. There was much more to learn.

As I walked through GEL's offices, I refocused on the task at hand: making those lease selections with Wyatt. Such a mundane task, indeed, but first things first. The good stuff would come for sure. I felt it now.

After entering the computer room, I sat down with Wyatt to review the code he had written while I was with Reggie, noting it appeared in order. Not that I had any programming knowledge, but his code appeared to match that of the prior year and include my current year parameters. Good enough for me.

Even though I dismissed the accounting manager position, I couldn't stop thinking about what it might be like to work at a company like GEL. Working directly for such a brilliant and successful guy like Reggie Dalton would be an amazing learning experience. I didn't much care for his personality, but still, I could learn from him. Beckworth, too.

Having to sit while the computer executed the lease selections was a good reminder of how boring a job could be without challenges.

An hour later, Wyatt informed me the selections were made and the individual customer confirmation letters printed. He helped me gather the nearly 600 confirmation letters and the control listing (to be used later as a completeness check) into several envelop boxes which I would take to my cubicle. I was about to experience one of the boring and mundane tasks auditors accept as part of their job: preparing the confirmation letters for mailing. At least I was looking forward to having the services of an intern to help with my testing tomorrow. It would give me a chance to supervise another staff professional, or at least one in the making. A nice change in the routine. Plus, I missed supervising others as I had done at Benson.

As I walked to my cubicle, I passed Carol's. I was warmed inside when I saw her sitting at her desk, and she noticed me. She came bounding toward me saying, "Whoa, it looks like you could use some help with those. Give me some." I gladly did and thanked her. Things just seemed better when she was near.

"Seems you've got your work cut out for you. Let me know when it's time for us to sit down and go through the questions I'm sure you'll have as you begin your testing."

Her comment surprised me, as I expected my testing would be routine, so I said, "You seem pretty sure I'll have questions. Are you saying I'll find a lot of exceptions?"

Carol seemed taken aback by my comment and said, "Not really, but I do expect you to find exceptions as you'll more than likely struggle with reconciling our capitalization decisions with the *Standard*. I trust you have your very own copy of it with you?"

"Thanks. I do have my own copy. I've been sleeping with it so much my wife is threatening to kick me out if I continue with such bad habits."

"Well, if she does, keep in mind I have a spare room in my apartment. I would be more understanding of what you'll be going through over the next week." As she set down the box in my cube, she said, "Have at it and ring my bell when you have some questions. I'm totally at your service."

As Carol walked out of my cubicle, I couldn't help admiring another of her skin-tight, short, form-fitting dresses.

And what was with the comment that she had a "spare room" for me at her apartment should my wife throw me out—"ring my bell…I'm at your service." Sure, one could consider it playful banter between two friendly professionals, but, in combination with her overtly friendly attitude and the way she cloaked her sexy body in tight-skinned garments, I had to wonder if her spare room comment was an invitation.

I was sure I was reading too much into Carol's comments probably trying to feed my own ego. I willed myself to concentrate.

Focus, Sam, focus. Believing that good advice, I settled into reviewing the lease selections against the *Standard*. Also, I had to prepare for tomorrow when I would instruct an intern how to assist me with the confirmation process. Before leaving the house, I warned Sue this would be a long day, and I'd be working late tonight.

Later in the evening, I relaxed in my chair and rubbed my eyes. It was only then I noticed it was going on eleven o'clock. I had been sitting in the same chair for the past six hours studying the *Standard*, suddenly realizing I skipped dinner. Now I was feeling hunger pangs. It made sense to call it a night. I had to report again at 8 a.m., as Brian would surely not cut me any slack even though I was the only auditor working late. He was a punctual guy and expected his staff to follow his lead. I was almost certain he would be planning his retribution for that stunt I pulled with Reggie earlier today, and it would be unwise to give him additional reasons to take me down. Not that he needed a reason.

Driving home, I considered my plan and how I was tracking to it. I was comfortable with how things were going. At this point in my trek, with the past slowly fading in the rearview mirror, things seemed to be going well.

Some years ago, I had several meetings with my father's shrink during one of the rare times he tried to win his battle against alcoholism and depression. That became his life's work, as he would do it only to stave off Mom kicking him out of the house and threatening divorce. Divorce was a big stain in those days, especially for Catholics like us. It showed the world you were weak. His shrink had suggested I, too, might one day fight depression.

"It's in the genes," he would say.

It had been over a week since I visited with my shrink, and like my father, I did so…or else. It was good to talk with someone who understood my struggle. The readings she had suggested were helping. They showed I was not alone in my struggles. Yet, another part of me, the one filled with self-doubt, feared I could never shed my demons. After all, I was my father's son and would never amount to anything approaching successful. It was my destiny, like Dad had frequently told me.

I lay in bed trying desperately to go to sleep, tossing and turning. It was impossible to get those feelings of self-doubt out of my mind. Why it was visiting me now, I could not answer. Things seemed to be going well...maybe too well. My pessimism was working me again. It seemed times like this, when things appeared good, it never lasted for long. The memory of what happened a short time ago, the nightmare that turned my household into a den of horrors for Sue and the boys, could not happen again. I tried to recall the advice from the last book I read, the one by Eckhart Tolle: *Something about living in the present...I am a good person and should focus on all the good things I am blessed to have...think at all times positive thoughts.*

"Please, God," I said softly aloud. "Not ever again."

CHAPTER 20

Driving to work at the GEL offices felt surreal. Yesterday, Reggie Dalton, a CFO of a public company, offered me an accounting manager position. He must have seen something in me I didn't. It felt good.

My temporary confidence boost dissipated rapidly as I turned into GEL's parking lot. Brian Walker was pulling in. If I didn't stop to allow him to grab the first parking spot we both approached, we would have collided. I yielded to him. Hell, he didn't even slow down knowing I would stop.

I walked up behind him and said cheerfully, "Good morning, boss. How is Brian today?"

Brian casually glanced over his shoulder, then turned back and walked, briefcase in hand. Glibly he responded, "Fair, I suppose. And you?" He could not have been more disingenuous. I didn't respond.

We parted, him headed for the war room and me toward my comfortable hideaway. I was relieved I didn't have to sit across from him all day in that massive conference room. *Thank you, Carol.* Every time I thought of Carol Wittford, I smiled.

Back in my own cubicle I felt safe and secure. Everything I needed was right where I had left it last night, except for the coffee stain on the carpet next to my desk. I didn't remember that being there.

"Good morning, Mr. Auditor." Already, I could recognize Carol's voice, maybe her scent as well. Even though we were separated by a cubicle wall, being close to her enveloped me in a shameful happiness. Seeing her and working with her had become the highlight of my day.

"Good morning, and how is Carol this morning?" I immediately responded.

"Excellent and ready to tackle the day's challenges like the whiz kid I am, at least in my own mind, anyway."

"Well, *I* think you're a whiz kid," I said, continuing the game of talking over the cubicle wall. "And by the way, you have been an enormous help to me in understanding the accounting for the LCR account."

"So, how is it going?" she asked as she walked into my cube space.

Today, she chose a low-cut, cream-colored dress that stopped about mid-thigh, sleeveless, matching high-heels, no hose. Her perfectly tanned legs glowed with a sheen that appeared bathed with fine oils. I held that image for a time and later visualized us lying on a beach, me rubbing her entire naked body with scented oils.

"So, what's on your agenda today?" she asked.

"Well, after my studying the *Standard* for lease capitalizations last night, I am comfortable I understand the four major requirements under which a lease can be capitalized. So, I suppose I'm ready to begin testing the selected leases against the *Standard*."

"How many did you select?"

"I didn't select them. Relying on the gods of statistical sampling, should they exist, my predetermined confidence level and expected error rate produced a random start and interval which pulled around 600 leases to be positively confirmed and tested."

"Wow, sounds like a lot."

"Considering you have nearly 20,000 leases on file, it really isn't. Think about it, from a relatively small sample we will need to form an opinion on the entire LCR balance, which makes me think whoever invented the science of statistics must have been a pretty sharp guy."

"Or gal," she playfully added.

"Come on now. You don't actually believe a *woman* could have come up with the science of statistics?" It was all innocent and playful jousting. I wasn't trying to make some kind of statement.

"Unfortunately, you are correct, but imagine how much better the world would be today if women had been allowed to express themselves a hundred years ago. Actually, it was an Iraqi who first discovered the world of statistics over a thousand years ago. I can't remember his name, but he developed the first code breaking algorithm based on frequency analysis. He wrote a book called *Deciphering Cryptographic Messages* which contained detailed discussions on statistics."

"OK, you have impressed me, again. So, how do you know so much about such a boring topic?"

"Now you've insulted me," Carol responded impishly, continuing our carefree early morning ribbing. "I started off as a statistics major at Purdue, then switched to accounting late in my studies which is why it took me five years to finish my undergrad degree."

"So, why did you switch?"

"The usual reason. I was chasing a guy who was an accounting major."

"And did you catch him?"

"Unfortunately, I did. But that's a story for another day."

Carol's demeanor quickly changed as we had stumbled upon a topic she clearly wanted to avoid, and I was happy to oblige. Recalling unpleasant past relationships usually changed attitudes in a hurry. It happened to me every time I recalled my father. I would not go there with Carol.

Our playtime had expired. Carol turned from me. Taking her leave, she said, "So, I'm in all day if you need help, except I have a four o'clock meeting with the officers."

"Is that a planned meeting?" I asked. It was none of my business, but Carol responded nonetheless.

"Interestingly, it wasn't on the schedule. Got a call last night around eight o'clock from Reggie's secretary putting it together. Apparently, Mr. Beckworth called it. Flew up last night. Must be something important for him to leave his Miami condo for the frigid north."

I was surprised to hear Foster Beckworth would be flying up again, but I didn't feel comfortable mentioning his name. I had understood he wouldn't be around for the audit. "They typically have meetings involving the officers put together at the last minute?" I asked quizzically.

"Not since the IPO," Carol responded. "That was one crazy ordeal, but since then everything has been pretty organized and routine. Besides, what are you, Sherlock Holmes all of a sudden? Why the interest in my meetings?"

Her abruptness startled me. It was like I had overstepped my bounds. "Sorry, I've always been a curious sort of chap and love a good mystery. Forget I asked."

"Forgotten. So, I'm around most of the day if you need anything."

Carol was gone from my cube, but her scent lingered.

The morning flew by, but then I was interrupted by a supple voice at my cubicle's entrance.

"Mr. Halloran."

I popped my head up, noticing a child standing erect in the middle of my doorway. Well, she seemed a child upon first glance, but I quickly learned otherwise.

"Mr. Halloran, my name is Patricia Walters-Pickering. I'm the new intern, and I was told to introduce myself to you."

"Well, good morning, Patricia Walters-Pickering. I am happy to meet you. Come on in and pull up a chair," I said as I sat relaxed. I watched her nervously moving about as if she had a mental checklist she was going through, careful not to miss any steps. I put her at about nineteen years old. Short, skinny with no figure, or if she had one, well hidden. She was modestly dressed in a fluffy blouse buttoned to the neck, around which she wore a small cross that

153

dangled from a delicate silver chain. She wore a wool skirt cut to mid-knee, and she was African-American with an afro reminding me of one of my fellow protesters at college during the Vietnam War era. Tanya was her name. We had made a pact to attend every rally we could in front of the Administration building, but never would either of us throw the rock through the window. After an hour of protesting, someone else would throw the rock. It usually signaled the end to the evening, as they would be handcuffed and hauled off to jail. I liked spending those times with Tanya. I'd lost track of her after Sue and I became engaged. I hoped she was doing well.

As Patricia shuffled about, I was feeling guilty for not greeting her properly. I should have stood and extended my hand. It must have been a combination of the shock of her youth and my inexperience at supervising professional accounting staff. The older I got, the younger they seemed.

"Patricia, first off, if my father shows up, you can call him Mr. Halloran, but please call me Sam. Are you good with that?"

"Yes, sir."

"And please dispense with the 'sir.' I feel old enough around here without you adding to it," I said in a stern, yet jocular fashion.

"I'm sorry, sir, I mean, Sam. But calling you sir is not a reference to your age. I'm from Louisiana. Referring to adults as sir and ma'am, well, it's a Southern thing. It's how we all are raised. I don't mean to offend."

"None taken, but you're in the North now, and my first piece of advice is to ditch the 'sir' and 'ma'am.'"

"I'll try, but please be patient. Everything is so new to me."

We went on about ten minutes getting to know each other. Patricia was a junior at Indiana, so we had something in common. I think I moved up the power curve in her mind when she learned I received my MBA from there.

Dispensing with the background stories, I began describing what Patricia would be doing. First off, I would have her reperform the computerized lease selection process. I walked her over to a nearby cubicle and instructed her to sit at the desk where I had stacked the binders she would need for her testing. I handed her a thick computer run. The double-spaced green-bar paper—the Control List—contained the computer-generated listing of leases to test from the code Wyatt wrote—all 600 leases. Those tests should confirm Wyatt followed my instructions for the selection of leases from the total population of 20,000 leases. I placed my hand on a stack of letters next to the binders and explained that for each of the leases on the Control List, a letter had been generated which we would mail to the customer. I then placed in front of her a binder listing all 20,000 leases—the LCR Ledger. I showed her how to test the computerized selection process against the Control List.

"OK, Patricia, our random start is 66. You begin at the first lease and count down 66 leases in the LCR Ledger. After the initial selection, our count sequence interval will be 34. Every 34th lease is one that should have been selected."

I held up the Control List indicating the 600 lease selections. I told her for each count sequence we would match up the lease listed in the LCR Ledger to the same lease in the Control List to ascertain the selection program operated as we expected.

Patricia listened intently. "So, how about you begin as I observe?" I suggested.

Without further instruction, she counted down the LCR Ledger to the 66th lease, highlighted it and matched the lease number, name, and the like over to our Control List, noting it was one of the 600 leases we had selected for testing. Noting next our interval of 34, Patricia counted down 34 additional leases, highlighted it, then noted that lease also appeared on our Control List—the second lease selected for testing. She would repeat that for every 34th selection—about 600 times. Tedious, for sure. I was glad I didn't have to do it.

"So, that's the process, Patricia. If this matching doesn't work out in this manner, that would be considered an exception. Inform me immediately should you find any exceptions. Got it?"

"Yes, sir...I mean, yes, Sam."

"Any questions?"

"Just one, Sam."

"Earlier, you pointed to a stack of letters you said were generated as representing one for each of the selected leases on the Control List. Should I not also ensure there is a letter for each of those selections and all the information matches the Control List?"

Holy shit, I thought. Given the cross she was wearing, I praised myself for not saying that aloud. But she was right. The whole purpose of these selections was to generate 600 letters to be mailed to lessees confirming the details of the lease.

"Good catch, Patricia. You are exactly correct."

I didn't admit I had forgotten that step. The faux pas reminded me of my lack of auditing experience. I needed to be more careful. If I made a critical error in my testing of the LCR account, it could spell trouble for me. Hopefully our review process was such that Brian or someone up the line would catch it, but it sure wouldn't bode well for me.

I smiled at Patricia and returned to my cubicle across from hers, figuring she had enough to keep her busy for some time. I sat for a while watching her work. Patricia Walters-Pickering would do fine. She seemed smart and conscientious. But then, what did I know at this early stage of my own career?

After we ensured the computerized selection process was executed as I had instructed, I would have Patricia stuff into envelopes the confirmation letters and include a SASE returnable to our Indy office. When I would stop by the office, usually on Fridays, I would retrieve and log them into the Control List. When the letter stuffing was completed, I'd find some other mundane task for Patricia to do. That wasn't fair. Everything I would have her do would be necessary and an important part of our audit, and I reminded myself to be sure to tell her.

I helped my intern carry the binders to a nearby conference room where she wouldn't be distracted. Feeling comfortable I had Patricia busy, I returned to my cubicle and reviewed the audit program for

LCR testing to ensure I was performing all necessary audit steps under the program. The biggest part of the test was to confirm all the operating leases were properly capitalized in accordance with the accounting rules. I couldn't entrust this most important task to an intern. It had to be done by me.

I quickly scanned the audit steps for my LCR testing. At least by the number of steps, it appeared I was about halfway completed.

"Hey, Mr. Auditor," Carol's familiar voice wafted over the cubicle wall. I perked up like a puppy dog. "It's seven o'clock, and I haven't heard a thing out of you since I got back. You still awake over there?"

It was good to hear her voice, and I was about ready for a break. "Oh, damn. I must have fallen asleep!" I responded.

Carol came whizzing around to the entrance of my cubicle on her roller chair acting like she believed me with her mouth open; my tension finally eased, and I leaned back in my chair. The relaxed mood was exactly what the doctor, or shrink, in my case, had ordered.

"But come on, kid. Could you imagine Brian or, worse yet, Reggie catching me sleeping the day away with all the pressure to get this preliminary work done?"

We laughed as Carol said, "I love when you call me *kid* from time to time. It's so cute but not very accurate. How old do you think I am?"

I knew exactly how old she was from reviewing her personnel file as part of my earlier payroll testing, but I lied and said, "I don't know, but I'd guess late 20s?"

She patted my forearm, let out with a big laugh and dipped her head toward me so her hair brushed alongside my arm, not so innocently.

"I'm thirty-one, silly. Same as you, right?"

"Well, true when I started with HP, but I turned thirty-two in October, and you *just* turned thirty-one."

Suddenly, the laughter stopped as she said, "How did you know

I just had a birthday?"

Whoops, that was a slip, but I quickly recovered saying, "Because I noticed you have a Virgo pendant hanging on your charm bracelet. Not too hard to figure out."

She leaned back in her chair grabbing her wrist, dropped her jaw and said, "Wow! OK, I'm impressed. You are a good auditor. I'd better be careful now. And while we're on the topic of astrological signs, what can you tell me about Virgos?"

We were starting to go down a path instinct informed me was best to avoid. "You got me there, kid," I said sloughing it off. "I don't have a clue what your sign says, but we'll have to defer this discussion for another day. I need to check-in on the home-front."

"OK, I see you're not going to be any fun tonight," Carol said as she jumped up and turned to push her chair back to her cubicle, but she didn't move away immediately. "So, we'll defer to a less busy time. Maybe when this is over, I'll make you buy me dinner to thank me for all the help I'm giving you."

She couldn't have been serious, but maybe she was. Her eyes lingered on my face a moment longer than they should have. The measure of her last glance was one of her sultry, bad-girl looks. She used them sparingly, but meaningfully. It was painfully obvious Carol was better at this cat-and-mouse thing than I was. Not knowing how to respond, I simply smiled and lowered my head to break eye contact, thinking it was an innocent comment. But then, perhaps not.

I looked up again as she turned the corner of my cube. The smile on her face said a lot more about what she might be thinking and planning. Still feeling uncomfortable, I smiled and waved but had to wonder again what was going on between us.

Having told Carol I had to call home and "check-in," I needed to find a phone. I didn't have one with an outside line in my cubicle. Besides, I wouldn't want to call Sue where Carol could overhear. But still, I hesitated. Everything about Carol was front and center on my mind, and I wanted to linger a bit longer if only to savor the possibilities.

Inside the war room were two phone booths where one could make private calls. I felt such a relief when Sue answered. I loved to hear her voice. Everyone had finished dinner, and the boys were doing their homework.

Sue was writing a letter to her mom and dad. I apologized for working late, and she relieved my guilt by saying, "Not a problem, Sam. You told me about busy season, so I'm prepared for this."

"Yeah, but this is the middle of December, and we're only doing prelim work. The real overtime begins in January when we return for the year-end testing. I'm told it's intensive with long hours, seven days a week until they release earnings and then file."

"Sweetheart, none of that makes sense to me but I'm fine. We're all fine, so you do what you need to do and don't worry about us. I'm so happy this is working out as you had planned."

There were times like these when I fell in love with Sue all over again. "Sweetheart, I love you very much," I said, acknowledging her deep sense of devotion to me.

"Love you too, dear. Now, get back to work, and I'll see you when I see you."

I hung up the phone and considered how lucky I was to have her. I felt guilty for my recent thoughts about Carol.

Then, I told myself what I was doing was all a part of my job, to make nice with the client. That was all I was doing with Carol. Still, I needed to keep it in check. I shouldn't beat myself up too much. There was not a normal man alive who didn't have those same lustful imaginings from time to time. Look, but don't touch. So far, so good.

It was eight o'clock in the evening, and I had at least another two hours of work ahead of me. As I opened the door to our conference room on my way to my cubicle, I suddenly stopped as I glimpsed Carol approaching the revolving doors and exiting the GEL lobby. I was surprised to catch her again entering the passenger door of that black Porsche Carrera waiting for her in the drive-up lane. So, she had a boyfriend who was apparently rich. None of my business…

Was I jealous?

159

CHAPTER 21

"So, what are your Holiday plans?" Carol asked as I was clearing out my cubicle.

It was Christmas Eve and the last day of our prelim work. Brian said we could leave by noon since the company was shutting down for the Christmas holiday. I didn't think I'd be wrapped up with all my work by noon. Carol said she had no plans for the evening, and she'd be happy to stay and help me. That seemed odd. Not that she offered to stay and help me, but I wondered why she wouldn't be with her family the night before Christmas. Even if she didn't have a husband or kids, surely she had parents. Or maybe the dude with the Porsche...somebody.

As usual, I had underestimated the time it would take to get all my prelim work wrapped up, and it was going on five o'clock. True to her promise, Carol stayed.

All things considered, I felt I did a good job my first time on a real audit. Wrapping the cord around my 10-key, I was thinking about the holiday and how I looked forward to spending Christmas with my family.

Carol and I continued to talk over the cubicle wall with no concern of being overheard. Everyone else had cleared out. They would be with their families now. I would be with mine soon.

The PA system was still playing holiday music, hinting Christmas was around the corner. I was humming along and feeling good about my accomplishments since beginning the GEL audit, thinking of how proud my family was of me.

I went to the war room to drop off some binders. It was eerie with the place so empty, except for Rufus, the maintenance guy. Rufus was busy taking down the fifteen-foot Christmas tree in the GEL lobby. Christmas had yet to pass, but it would be depressing to see it after returning from the holidays. He told me he'd rather take it down now.

I walked past Rufus and returned to my cubicle. Seeing him busily taking down the tree caused me to think about the new year ahead. 1983 would be an exciting year, and I was eagerly anticipating it. I had a good feeling about what the new year would bring. Satisfying feelings warmed me when Carol's voice seemed closer. I turned. She was standing in the doorway. She looked different. Sexy, alluring, sultry...different.

She had balanced her sleek frame in-between the sides of the entrance to my cube, her arms extended outward. She was showing more cleavage than she had earlier in the day. My eyes settled first on the lacy fringe of her bra. I stared at her longer than a married man should. She didn't speak, nor did I. My eyes followed her frame downward, slowly, taking her all in. She wasn't wearing hose. Barefoot, too. As she rubbed her shin with her foot, slowly up and down, I caught the shimmer of her knees. Her calves were taut, muscular. Watching her caused my groin to stir.

Carol unbuttoned her blouse. I watched and enjoyed, making no attempt to stop her.

She pulled her blouse out of her skirt. Slowly. Her eyes locked on my face while my eyes wandered inch by inch over her entire body. She was beyond beautiful. Goddess-like. Neither of us spoke. I stood motionless as if I was in her bedroom closet hiding from view and watching her disrobe, watching her in secret, afraid to move lest she find me out and stop. I didn't want her to stop.

Maybe it was the way she was admiring me now. Her lips were slightly parted. A shimmer of light rested on them. When her tongue began slowly moving between the corners of her mouth, back and forth, I wanted, more than anything, to take her mouth into mine. I wanted more than that. It was obvious Carol did as well.

She was standing only a few feet away, desirous yet vulnerable. She began moving closer. Not all at once. Gliding. Deliberately. She was performing for me. Luring me in, not only physically, but emotionally. The stirring below which began a few moments ago was complete.

The instant I wanted to hold her, she was in my arms. Her lips were on mine. I accepted them so willingly, too willingly. It was wrong to take another woman into my arms and kiss her as I was now kissing Carol. I could stop. But I wouldn't. A moment longer and I would stop.

She lightly bit my lower lip, then pulled back for a moment, smiling and teasing. Then, she brought her lips to mine again, delicately, at first. Her tongue engaged haltingly, as if she were licking whipped cream from a ripened strawberry. Savoring it.

She pressed her mouth on mine harder. Her tongue swirling inside my mouth, engaging mine. I shivered, about to lose control. She was a maestro knowing this part of the show was like turning a key, allowing me to enter a room, her private playroom which was once out of bounds but now opened for my total enjoyment. I was playing without a care in the world. Whatever consequences awaited me, I would willingly suffer them in exchange for the pleasure I was currently experiencing.

I was married, but my actions belied that fact. Carol knew I was married, but clearly, she didn't care. My one arm was gently but firmly positioning her head to absorb optimum pleasure from pushing her lips onto mine. I wanted to hold her there forever, tight against my body, although there was no need. Carol had no intention of doing anything else but kissing me back, hard; her tongue and mine dancing uncontrollably. My other hand was caressing her where, before, only my eyes had touched. She positioned her hips allowing my thigh to nestle between hers and began moving her hips. I followed. Our hips now moving rhythmically, attempting to simulate making love.

But we weren't making love, not yet, anyway. I failed to notice where her hands were; they were busy unzipping her skirt. This had to stop. I had done nothing wrong. At least, that was what I told myself. Every muscle in my body was taut and quivering uncontrollably, like an addict might feel. I would stop soon.

I did not want to betray Sue and have sex with Carol. But at the moment, I was enjoying sheer ecstasy, and at least for the time being, I did not want to stop, nor did I have the willpower to stop.

Carol maneuvered us farther back into the corner of my cubicle. Kissing me more softly, as if she realized she had won, she unbuttoned my shirt, then slid it off, letting it drop to the floor. Carol was advancing the agenda. I could have stopped or at least slowed the progression. I was sexually naive, but it was obvious where this was headed, what she clearly wanted. Still, I had no guilt. This was wrong.

But I didn't care.

In an instant, we were all over each other. Carol's skirt fell to the floor. I pulled her blouse up and over her head, revealing the black bra that earlier lent me enough of a peak to stimulate. I flipped her around, pinning her into the corner. She allowed me to take control. It was clear she wanted it that way. There in the shadows, I paused in an effort to prevent my climax. It was too soon. I wanted to enjoy Carol for a little longer, longer still, as long as I dared.

I turned her around toward me and leaned my head back, so I could take her in. As I did, she removed her bra. It seemed sinful to stare. Her body was sculpted as if done by a master. My heart was pounding. Carol was the most beautiful woman I had ever seen. I could not believe she was standing in front of me this very moment, nearly naked. She grasped my hand and gently pushed it down toward her waist. She let go, expecting me to know what she wanted. My inexperience showed as I fumbled around without purpose. I was disappointing her.

Grasping my hand again, she led me farther. I acquiesced and allowed her to drive. I accepted where she wanted my hand to rest.

As I playfully flicked at the top of her panties, she pushed downward still on my wrist.

"It's OK, Sam. I am ready for you. Take them off. Take me down to the floor. I want you inside me. Make love to me, Sam. Do it now."

I ignored her and continued to play with her panties, my fingers slowly walking, inching closer and closer until I reached my destination. She grabbed my hand shoving it into her crotch. Hard. We were kissing again. Even more passionately than before. I pressed firmly on her vagina and it set her off. I feared what might come next. This was my limit. Carol had other plans.

Reflexively, I pushed away. She would have none of that and pulled me back into her. I pushed away again this time releasing her.

"Carol, no. Stop. We can't. I'm married."

"Take me, Sam. Take me now," she yelled. Demanded.

She came forward still, attacking me like a wolf on her prey. Her arms gripped me intensely. Her tongue danced wildly across my bare chest, biting gently at my nipples, trying feverishly to pull me down, my arms now under her armpits holding her, resisting, caressing her. She was drawing me in again.

Still I held back, silently pleading to let me go, yet hoping not. Just a little longer.

I wanted to yield to her, to take her in the manner she was pleading me to do. Then, I thought of Sue and the boys. If I had sex with this woman, I couldn't face them ever again. Fortunately, my love for them was enough for me to push Carol off, but still I wanted her. I sensed she knew.

Carol pulled at my pants. They dropped to the floor, then my shorts. I pulled her up to my chest. She resisted and pushed me against the wall. She fought me like an animal. She was winning. Her tongue traversed my chest, stiff like a pointer. It traveled lower, to my navel. I felt it dance, then linger. It felt so good. It felt so wrong.

A shiver ran up my spine, and my muscles tensed. Primal urges began an automatic process eventually ending with me inside her.

That could not happen. Yet, I could not, would not, stop her. I wanted to take this as far as I could without ultimate penetration. But Carol wanted me inside her. From her moans, the way she continued kissing me, her movements, she was trying desperately to control my movements all toward satisfying her desires. I struggled knowing this should not advance but prayed it would. I never wanted this feeling to end. I was certain my moaning showed the ecstasy I was enjoying. It motivated Carol all the more.

Seemingly in complete frustration over my unwillingness to take her down to the floor, Carol slid her hand into my crotch and grabbed me. At that instant I came. Nothing could have been more embarrassing. She moaned in frustration, yet it only made her more aggressive. Before I could react, I slid to the floor onto my back. Carol maneuvered on top of me. She was still on a mission to make love to me, but it was too late; like an electrical circuit had been cut in my brain my senses were returning.

Without regard for anyone who might hear she said, "I want you inside of me. Now. Make love to me, Sam."

Lying on my back with Carol on top of me, I pushed her off saying, "Carol, it's too late. I'm sorry."

Still, she hung on to me, even as I attempted to push myself up to a sitting position against the wall. Now, she was acting upon her urges. She was not yet satisfied and determined to continue.

"Carol, I'm sorry. It's just—"

Angry at first, she yelled, "Damn you. Damn you, Sam!" Then she was consoling, softer, more loving. "Let's keep trying. I need you inside of me."

My body quivered like I had run a marathon. I was cold. My muscles were spent. I lay there on the floor and found my arms now limp along with the piece of my anatomy Carol had finally given up on.

Even as Carol slowly stood up I only caught a glimpse of her gathering her clothing. In a moment she was gone from my cubicle. I was left there, pants and boxers wrapped around my ankles, still wondering how this all happened so quickly. My heavy breathing now subsiding, I took note of what had transpired over the last fifteen minutes. Guilt was already working its effect on my awakening mind. *What were you doing, you dumb ass? What were you thinking? You're married! You have a loving family. Why?*

I worked hard at rationalizing. *It wasn't my fault. It was all so primal. But I didn't do it. I didn't go all the way. I stopped short of adultery. I was good. Right?* It was a question rather than a statement. I did things tonight I could never relay to anyone, especially to Sue.

I stood, pulled my pants up, buckled my belt and then sat in my office chair, hands on my head, reliving it all before it faded from my memory. How I had felt with Carol, my God, that had never happened to me. It scared me. Not even with Sue had I felt like that. Never.

Then reality hit, guilt too. How did we get to this point? We both flirted, but people do that all the time. *Why did I let it go this far? This was all my fault. Where would we go from here?*

Moments ago, I was lost in the wonderment of what we had done, now reflecting upon how quickly it had all happened. Carol intended to make love to me. Like a teenager, I could not perform to her satisfaction. *How could I ever face her again?* I sat there paralyzed. Part of it was physical, the other part mental. She had disappeared from my cubicle, which was good. I did not wish to face her now. Maybe never. But that couldn't be. We were still working together. I'd return next month to finalize the audit. I still needed her help to accomplish that. My job performance, getting a good evaluation; everything hinged on Carol continuing to help me.

We had to talk about what happened between us tonight. We had to set the ground rules for going forward. Better now rather than later.

I threw on my shirt and buttoned it up. I assumed Carol went back to her cube to get dressed and resume some semblance of normalcy. I stuck my head in searching for any sign of her. Her desk lamp was on, purse on her chair, coat hung on the side wall and her high heel shoes neatly placed in the corner. But no Carol. Where could she have gone? Maybe she went to the restroom to freshen up.

I sat and waited in her cubicle for her to return. I was anxious to talk through this and grew impatient. I walked to the women's restroom. I waited for a few moments, then went inside and called her name. No Carol.

I walked throughout the offices. Periodically, I would call out for her. Coming upon the door to the GEL lobby, I cracked it open and was relieved to see Rufus still working on wrapping and boxing the Christmas ornaments. He was humming *Jingle Bells*, obviously believing himself alone. It was a good indication he didn't witness the exhibition we had staged. But no sign of Carol.

I returned to her cube. Still no sign of her. All her belongings remained. It was 6:45 p.m., and I worried what Sue might think. I told her I'd be home by five o'clock. It was Christmas Eve. I had to call her.

Immediately, I grabbed my audit bag and coat. I scanned for any more of my possessions, knowing I would not be returning until January 10th when the year-end field work would begin. I made my way to the war room where I could call and tell Sue I was sorry for my tardiness. She had to be worried.

I picked up the phone but hesitated before dialing. *Was I sorry for what I had done? Was I compounding the big lie by telling Sue I didn't call earlier because of work?* I squeezed the phone with both hands, trying to will away the shame I felt.

What had I done? Did I have sex with another woman? Surely not. She touched me. But I didn't have sex with her. As I dialed our home number, guilt was having its way with me. I felt sick to my stomach, especially when Sue picked up.

Hey, Sue, sorry I fucked one of the client's employees.
That's all right, Honey. Did you enjoy it?
Sure did, but to be honest, I didn't go all the way.
That's good. Going all the way would be bad.

I love you, dear. I'll be home very soon.

Love you, too. Promise you won't fuck anyone but me ever again.
I promise.

That was weird! The entire time I spoke to Sue, I imagined something different. I needed to get hold of myself and gave up my search.

On my way home, I recalled the actual conversation I had with Sue. If I didn't already feel guilty enough for acting upon my lust for another woman, my guilt doubled when Sue told me being late was no big deal. The boys were eager for me to come home so we could enjoy the night before Christmas. It would have soothed my conscience a little if she were angry. But Sue rarely, if ever, was angry with me. When I did something to upset her, she'd simply grit her teeth and say something sarcastic. But if she realized what I was apologizing for...she would explode in raw anger, knowing I had destroyed all we had built together...our family. It hurt even more to picture her reacting that way. *What was I going to do?* At this point, I had no idea.

Sure, I felt guilt for what happened tonight with Carol. But that wasn't the worst of it. I was lusting for another woman for the first time since I married Sue, the woman I was still madly in love with.

So, why my interest in Carol? I could not explain it, especially after what happened tonight. I wanted Carol so badly, yet after today, when I could have had her, I pushed her away. I did not have sex with her, but I would now dream of it. I would lie with the woman I loved and think of Carol.

I was confused and clueless where it all might lead. One thing was for sure: While I had considered myself as sexually naive, such was no longer the case. I now possessed a very dark secret.

I finally pulled into my driveway, and I could not get Carol out of my mind. Two emotions played upon me. First there was Carol, the person. I had grown to like her in such a short time. Then, there was the Carol I now felt emotionally bonded with and wondered—feared—where it might lead. I prayed that second emotion for Carol, the one I dared not pursue, would dissipate. I prayed hard for that to be the case, but deep down, I realized a new and sensual relationship had developed tonight. One I hoped wouldn't end anytime soon.

Through our living room picture window, I regarded Sue playing with Will and Ben in front of our Christmas tree surrounded by all our presents. I felt a drop of water hit my hand. I had betrayed my family.

CHAPTER 22

I continued watching my family through the window, their visions no doubt filled with the promise Santa would soon arrive. I recalled how much fun we'd had as a family enjoying past Christmases with the wonderful wife and two great sons I was blessed to have. I always believed Christmas was made for children. Our two would chomp at the bit on Christmas morning when they would race into our rooms, jump on our bed and plead and beg, "Santa came!" Ben would say. "I saw all the presents he left for us! Hurry, Mommy! Hurry, Daddy!"

"Calm down, Ben," Will would say, trying to act like the older and more mature brother. "Our presents aren't going anywhere. We need to be patient and wait for Mom and Dad to tell us it's OK to open them; otherwise, Santa will not be happy with us."

Will may have acted calm and controlled, but he was as eager as Ben to rip open every one of his presents. At nine and seven, the boys still believed in Santa Claus. And why wouldn't they? We kept that secret as all parents were supposed to do. We did our part to protect the great myth of Christmas.

The story played out a little differently when I was seven. It was then I learned there was no Santa Claus but in a manner most kids did not.

* * * *

"Sammy, what on God's earth are you doing?" Mom asked in an

angry tone. It was Christmas morning. I was otherwise occupied.

"Morning, Mommy. Merry Christmas! Look what Santa brought me," I shouted with glee as I played with my new Hasbro Fighting Lady. It was at the top of my list that year. The Hasbro Fighting Lady was an aircraft carrier complete with a complement of jets and navy sailors and a realism unlike my other toys. It was at least three feet in length and intricate in its design. I was so wrapped up in playing with my Fighting Lady nothing else in the world seemed to matter. Nothing until Dad joined Mom on the stairs that Christmas morning of 1957.

"What the hell are you doing, you little shit?" Dad screamed in a visceral display of his displeasure. It didn't seem to make sense, but his anger caught my attention. Dad's yelling always brought me to attention because of what would follow. In one sense, I clearly heard what my dad had said, but in the other, surely he was not serious. He couldn't be mad at me. Not today. This was Christmas. It was the happiest day of the year, and I was the happiest kid on the block. Until Dad came bounding down the rest of the stairs, shoving Mom against the wall as he made his way down to the landing.

"Tom, don't yell at Sammy," Mom pleaded. "He didn't know. Please, Tom, it's Christmas."

Dad didn't care it was Christmas. He didn't care I was playing with my new toys, happy and content, living in my own fantasy world, dreaming of me captaining a great ship, battling the bad guys and saving us from certain doom. I was so absorbed in what I was doing, I didn't realize how angry Dad was.

Then, Dad's foot came crashing down on the deck of that grand ship. It wasn't so grand anymore. Plastic pieces flew everywhere. I jumped back and hit my head on the corner of the coffee table and saw stars. *This couldn't be happening. Today was Christmas. Didn't my dad realize today was Christmas?*

Mom was on him in an instant. Still dazed from hitting the coffee table, I hardly felt the back of his hand across my face driving me to the floor. I immediately cowered, not knowing what was coming next but expecting the worst. I screamed and cried even though experience had taught me it would make him madder; however, I wasn't focused on why my dad was mad at me. He wasn't just *mad* at me. He was enraged.

He was trying to throw off Mom, now clawing at him. It gave me a chance to hide under the coffee table, protecting me from the beating I feared was coming. He grabbed my ankles, first the right one, then the left. I was holding onto the table legs, holding on for dear life and thinking if I could stay under the table, I had a decent chance of getting through this attack with minimal injury. I honestly couldn't remember Dad ever attacking me this way. Sure, he'd taken the belt to me like every other dad disciplined their kids. That hurt, but it was controlled discipline. This was different. This was an attack, the worst I had ever experienced.

He yanked me from under the coffee table, and I looked into his face for the first time that Christmas morning. The veins popping out of his neck turned purple, and his eyes were the size and color of the ashtrays he had scattered around the house. Continuing to scream at me, it was as though he was taking out every frustration cast upon his own pathetic life; if he could teach me this one lesson it would make his miserable existence all the more justified. "You're just a kid and need to learn life is tough," he would say in the heat of disciplining me. Even when he was drunk, I didn't feel then as I did now. I truly believed my father would kill me.

"For God's sakes, Tom, you're going to kill him! He's your son! Let him go, you low-life piece of shit!" Mom screamed at the top of her lungs.

I wasn't sure if Mom intended to hurt him, but I never heard her speak to Dad like that. Maybe she felt drastic means were necessary to save my life. I was certain Mom felt Dad would put me in the hospital if not kill me and later say that I fell down the stairs.

In one final show of dominance, he grabbed me by the hair, pulling first my head and then my whole body off the floor until I was dangling in mid-air. As quickly as he attacked me, he let me go, and I crumbled into a pile on top of a hundred pieces of grey plastic, the remnants of the biggest, baddest, grandest ship in all the world…Hasbro's Fighting Lady.

I was dazed at the stark realization of those pieces scattered on our beige carpet. Among them were chards of glass from the vase Mom leveled against the side of Dad's head. Some had smears of blood on them.

"Run, Sammy. Go to your secret place. Run, Sammy, before he wakes up."

I jumped to my feet and bolted for the basement door without a word to Mom. Within seconds, I was on the shelf the previous owner of our home had constructed in the basement. I winnowed myself through boxes, things Mom was not ready to pitch. Mom was a hoarder, which seemed a useless thing to do, but that Christmas morning, not yet fully aware of the extent of my cuts, bruises and abrasions, I was glad Mom was a hoarder. It gave me a place to hide.

* * * *

I never told Mom why I didn't wait for them that Christmas morning, so we could go downstairs together to open our presents. I didn't tell Mom what I was thinking that Christmas morning as I sat at the top of the stairs.

Seeing the presents below through the banisters confirmed Santa had come to my house. I was overjoyed, especially since the day after my birthday, Dad exploded when I broke the trigger on the plastic gun he had bought me. He said Santa would know how I disrespected my toys and wouldn't bring me any more for Christmas.

"Santa's gonna pass you by this year, stupid," Dad said.

Since my birthday, I lived in fear there would be no presents for me under the tree. Gleefully gazing downstairs that morning, Dad was wrong. Santa didn't forget me.

But sitting there I remembered. Every Christmas morning, my parents and I would gather around the tree to open presents, and something would cause them to argue. A simple misspoken word and they were off and running. I would try and divert them, so I could enjoy opening my presents but always to no avail. Every Christmas morning, I would cry as I opened my presents while my parents screamed at each other. That was a given. I would cry and pray for them to stop.

That Christmas morning when I was seven, I desperately wanted to open the presents Santa had brought me in peace, which was why I slid down the stairs on my rump, one stair tread at a time, contemplating how to avoid the fight that always came Christmas mornings. Little did I imagine I was setting up a torrent of fury I would never forget.

No, there was no Santa Claus. Christmases never seemed the same since 1957. That was until I experienced Christmases with my own two little boys. They helped me forget the past, and I loved them for it. Finally, I could enjoy the feeling of giving, the exact same feeling I was experiencing sitting in my driveway with my family inside waiting for me to come home from work. I had two weeks off and that was gift enough for me.

Later that evening, Sue and I were sitting in the living room with a glass of wine and holding hands. The kids were fast asleep in their beds as we cuddled closer. We were looking forward to spending some real family time together. At that moment, life seemed so perfect.

So, what the hell was I doing with Carol? What did that say about me? I was afraid of the answer. I supposed it would all simply have to play out.

CHAPTER 23

"Honey, I don't remember the boys being happier with their gifts than this year," Sue said, flopping down on the living room sofa next to me, throwing her arm around my neck and planting a big kiss on my cheek.

"Whoa, kid! What's this all about?" I said, rebalancing my notebook on my lap but happy for the interruption.

"Ha! You called me 'kid' again! When was the last time you called me that? If you're trying to seduce me, it's working."

"I call you that all the time," I said, knowing Sue was right. I hadn't called her *kid* in some time.

"Liar, liar," Sue said smiling, maneuvering into my lap and nuzzling my notebook off to the side.

"Hey, don't. I'm trying to work here."

"Don't you get mad at me, Sam Halloran," Sue said in that firm but loving way she occasionally schooled the boys. She knew I wasn't angry. She wanted to play. The boys were playing with their Christmas loot in the family room. Maybe it was time for Sue to play, too.

"You give me your attention, buddy, or I'll hurt you bad," she said, persistent and unrelenting.

I yielded and tossed my notebook to the floor, holding Sue in my lap with her straddling me, arms around my neck, big beautiful smile splayed across her face. She nestled her face to the side of mine whispering, "Tonight after we put the boys down, you're gonna get lucky."

175

"Oh, I am, huh," I said, absent the usual passion. My thoughts were elsewhere.

"Yes, you are, my handsome CPA."

"So, now that I'm a CPA you want to bed me?"

"Of course. I want to be your mistress. We'll have sex every day and be naughty to each other. We'll quit our jobs and travel around the world keeping track of all the places we make love. We'll make a big map and put it up on the ceiling over our bed."

I flipped Sue forward, catching her before she fell to the floor. "What has gotten into you woman?" Whatever she was doing it was working on me now. Sue dragged me to that sensual place with her. Her magical spell had finally captured me. We stared into each other's face.

"I love you, Samuel Halloran."

"And I love you, Susan Halloran."

I slid her to the side and cradled her in my lap, her legs and feet on the sofa. We held each other as I stroked her hair. Sue looked totally serene. I was getting there, but not entirely. Sue was completely immersed in me, happy. She didn't need to say anything. I could see it in her face and feel it in her relaxed body. When Sue was happiest, she would not say a word as she lay with me in bed, on a blanket at the park or in my arms as we were now. I only wished I could feel so carefree.

It had been nearly a week since my romp with Carol. Still, I thought of her constantly. Prior to Sue interrupting my work, I picked up my notes to break the spell Carol held over me. However, when Sue mentioned the word 'mistress' Carol consumed me once again. I cursed myself but then was warmed imagining Carol in my arms. Last week's events still held a firm grip on my emotions. It was not that I loved Carol. I just wanted her.

Sue and I made love last night, which likely put her in a playful, sexy mood. That was good. I enjoyed having sex with Sue. Last night was amazing. We hadn't made love passionately in a long time. I enjoyed every minute but cursed myself afterwards. The entire time

I crawled over Sue's body, in the dark, in our marital bed, I thought of Carol.

"Do you remember when you first called me 'kid'?"

"Of course I do."

Shortly after Sue and I became engaged, we discussed our age difference. I was nineteen and Sue was twenty-two. It bothered her she was three years older. A lot, actually. So, I began calling her 'kid.' She loved the nickname from the start, and I used it all the time. But that affectionate term took up residence in a lost part of my soul that stayed hidden behind the curtains. Carol hadn't entered the picture yet, but stress had. It was right about the time when the rigors of school and studying for the CPA exam consumed my life. Then, too, the financial pressures began taking their toll on me. It was the first time in our marriage I allowed the stress of life to weigh me down. Even sitting here on Christmas break, when I should have been relaxed, I was stressed out. Totally. The stress of wanting to succeed in my new career; the stress of wanting to provide for my family; the stress of making sure I performed well on the GEL audit. And yes, the stress of dealing with emotions I had never had—loving two women at the same time.

But that wasn't true. I loved only one woman, and she was lying in my lap. The other one…she was just a plaything, something I felt deprived of during my teen years. If I'd previously had sexual experiences in the normal course of growing up, I would have worked it out of my system, and someone like Carol would not affect me in the way she did now. I wanted to believe it was true.

"OK, kid, I need to do some work, so up," I said as I helped a reluctant Sue to her feet.

"Hey, you're on vacation. What's the deal?" Sue said jokingly. She wasn't objecting.

"Sorry, kid, but I have something I need to resolve. Something I want to delve into when I return to the field on this audit. I'm going to the law library for a couple of hours."

"You're no fun at all," Sue said, refusing to release me. She puffed out her lower lip as if pouting. She was totally fine with me leaving for work. I appreciated that. I kissed her a couple times until her lips became normal again. She enjoyed it and wanted more, nipping at my lower lip signifying as much; however, my thoughts kept straying to the new *kid* in my life.

It took me down memory lane driving to the law library on Indiana University's Indianapolis campus. While completing my MBA, I went there often to study between classes and many evenings and weekends. Having so much classwork coupled with studying for the CPA exam, there was no way I could concentrate with the boys bouncing around. The Indiana University Law Library became my sanctuary.

Once again, I needed some alone time to better understand GEL's revenue recognition practices. The library had always provided a quiet place to think through complex issues. It wasn't an audit program step. I chuckled to myself as I recalled Elaine Porcheck beating the crap out of me for doing the same in the audit simulation training. I was finally over that ass-kicking. My confidence was shored up and what she thought of me didn't matter so much anymore.

I had a favorite hiding place in the library stacks and went there immediately. Sure enough, it was deserted, and I'd be alone. It was two days before New Year's Eve, and the campus was still on break. Not a soul in sight. Perfect. I laid out my notes and began thinking through the problem.

In the orientation meeting, Pete had given us the concept of how lease capitalizations would work and passed out summary notes. It covered the general concept, applicable accounting standards, and provided several examples. For now, I would focus on how the company recognized revenue. At the present, I was less concerned with measuring the company's compliance with the *Standard*. I began that elusive business case.

Concept: The revenue recognized from the leased equipment would be the present valued stream of income represented by the monthly lease payments over some multi-year contractual term, net of costs.

Example: An eight-year lease requiring monthly payments of $60 for 96 months would gross $5,760. Subtracting product costs and present valuing, the remaining amount of about $2,200 would be recognized as net revenue when the lease was signed.

The *Standard* characterized the transaction as a sale—as if sold for cash or financed in much the same way people bought stuff every day. *But was it a sale?* I asked myself. It sure seemed like a lease to me. Absent the lease accounting rules, the logical revenue recognition practice would be to recognize revenue when the cash was received or became due. That would be $60 a month…not $2,200 when the contract was signed. It seemed convoluted, not natural, contrived. I closed my notebook and stared off into the stacks like I would do when studying, trying hard to understand a particular concept. It was then I noticed a familiar face.

"Yoshi! Yoshi Fukuda, what are you doing here?" I shouted and leaped from my chair.

"Hey, Sam," Yoshi yelled from across the reading area, as if we had forgotten where we were. Neither of us cared. Not a soul in sight. We embraced each other and expressed our good wishes for the coming New Year.

"Didn't expect to see you here," I said.

"You're going to think me crazy, Sam, but I accepted a part-time adjunct position here in the undergrad business school."

"Teaching what?"

"What else? Accounting. That's what I do, right?"

Yoshi Fukuda was an assistant controller at the Allison

Transmission plant on the west side of town, not far from where we lived. We met in statistics class during my first semester in the MBA program. He was a math whiz and the only reason I was able to ace that class. Through his tutoring, we had become fast friends. I regretted losing touch with him, and we began immediately catching up.

"Get outta here! You're working at Hamilton Pierce as a staff associate? So, you did it! You actually became a CPA! I'm very proud of you, Sam."

And from the expression on Yoshi's face, he truly meant it. It probably surprised him more than made him proud after seeing how I struggled to grasp the concepts of statistics.

"So, are you still at Allison?"

"I am, indeed," Yoshi said with a downtrodden, dejected look.

"I thought your plan was to take your newly minted MBA degree and jump ship to a bigger and better opportunity."

"You remember those chats we had." He paused as if to reflect upon dreams not realized. "Shortly after graduating, I tried to leave Allison, but when word spread I was unhappy and might leave, the bastards threw a bunch of money my way and promised me continued success and promotion, some day. Whore that I am, I took the money and stayed." We laughed, heartily. It was so good to be with my old study partner and friend.

"So, you're a big shot professor now. But school's out for break. Why are you here in our old stomping ground?"

"Because teaching is harder than I imagined it would be. These kids are a lot smarter than when I was an undergrad. Or maybe they aren't afraid to challenge the professors like we were back in the day." We laughed again.

"So, that's my story. Why are you here?" Yoshi said.

"Well, I'm trying to think through a set of facts on this audit I'm doing. With the boys screaming and carrying on with their Christmas booty, I needed to find a quiet place where I could think. Naturally, I remembered this place, and here I am." Before I finished my sentence, I was already thinking about involving Yoshi and wasted no time in asking.

"Say, Yoshi, I don't want to impose on you—"

"You could never impose on me. Please, tell me you need my help again. My ego needs a boost!"

"Yoshi, you're the smartest numbers guy I know, and I'm thinking you, more than anyone, would be the perfect person to run this by. Are you sure you wouldn't mind?"

"Are you shitting me? Let me have it!"

"OK, man. So, here it is...."

Due to the confidential nature of my work, I couldn't disclose the client's name. He'd have heard of the company for sure. Not a week went by without some story appearing in the local papers about GEL's success and continual rise as a Wall Street darling. Even though I didn't tell Yoshi, I was certain he might figure it out. It was easy to determine HP's local clients, especially the public ones, and GEL's revenue recognition methods were the topic of many of those articles. But knowing Yoshi the way I did, he'd be discrete. All he cared about was having another complex problem to work through. He lived for such challenges and thrills. We'd be a good pair in business. Yoshi would be the inside guy with operations and numbers; I'd be the outside guy managing our clients. It was maybe something to ponder, but not now. Now, Yoshi would help me solve my problem.

"So, Yoshi, the company I'm auditing leases various types of equipment. Everything from a desktop computer to earthmoving equipment. They went public two years ago. The business model was this: The customer indicates exactly what they want to purchase, or rather, lease. Virtually anything the customer wanted. It could be a car, computer, airplane or a tractor...anything. Then, the company would negotiate the best price from the dealer, purchase it and lease it to the customer. It was the perfect mechanism for cash or credit-strapped customers to get the equipment they wanted quickly and affordably. No down payment. Simply sign the lease agreement in which they promised to pay the agreed upon monthly lease payment for the contract term. That was it. Once the contract was signed, the customer received the goods and walked away very happy. They had exactly what they bargained for at minimal cost and risk to them. At the end of the lease, the product was returned, or they could opt for a lease to own arrangement. Lease terms varied based on the product and its economic life."

Yoshi listened intently. He was a great listener and a more than competent analyst.

"Marketing approach appears interesting and unique," Yoshi said. "I gather they are successful enough to afford an HP audit. Nothing you said seems unique from an accounting perspective."

"For the most part, that's true, but the accounting can be unique," I added, more or less repeating Pete's description at the orientation meeting.

"What's unique about leasing? You bill the customer monthly and book it as revenue," Yoshi quipped in his usual cocky manner. He was really smart and liked to show off sometimes...which was most of the time. But I loved that about his nature.

"Maybe, but this company prefers to record them as sales-type leases—capital leases," I said with little purpose.

Yoshi's head tilted up and his eyes widened saying, "Ah, capital leases. You mean where they capitalize the future income stream of monthly payments and book all the revenue at the time the contract was signed. But that's got nothing to do with the business of leasing, so what's there to brag about?"

"You got it, Yoshi. I agree, the accounting for operating leases was simple versus the complexity of capital leases. What I don't fully understand is why the company is doing so amazingly well in such a simple business. So well, in fact, they are acquiring leasing companies across the country at a blistering pace. They brag to the investor community that their uniqueness with regard to revenue recognition is to account for their leases as *capital* instead of *operating*."

Yoshi furrowed his brow, then said, "Well, it's not a choice. If the terms of the lease meet the requirements for capitalization, then they'd have to do it. But I agree it seems odd one could entice investors into an IPO for a mundane business such as leasing equipment. But I must be missing something and need more to go on. I need numbers, I need their growth chart, their business strategy, their cash flow. Talk to me, Sam."

"Agreed. Let me give you more facts." We sat and I pulled out GEL's 1981 Form 10-K filing and went through the numbers. Attempting to cover the company name, Yoshi laughed saying, "No need for that, Sam. I figured you were talking about GEL. I'll be discrete." And he would.

I began lobbing information to Yoshi like I was a tennis ball serving machine: when the company was formed, their growth in revenue, margin and net income since inception, proceeds from their IPO, use of funds, the current year secondary stock offering and their plans for continued expansion through acquisition of other leasing companies. He listened intently not even taking notes. He never took notes. He told me once it slowed him down and interfered with his continual analysis of the problem. When I talked about GEL's acquisition strategy, he held up his hand and stopped me.

"Why are they in such a rush to acquire other leasing companies? Where do they get the cash to make all those acquisitions? Doesn't this unnecessarily increase risk by spanning management across unlike entities around the country? I mean, why do that? How do they benefit?"

"Whoa, slow down, Yoshi. Why would it seem strange to have an aggressive acquisition strategy? They're aggressive."

"But how are they financing these acquisitions? These are high interest times," Yoshi said. "What are they paying in interest?"

I flipped through their latest quarterly filing. "On average, 15%."

"Holy shit! 15% is a fortune. What margins could justify such a high financing cost?"

"I think their margins are around 35-40%. That seems more than adequate to justify the investment, don't you think? And besides, they used the proceeds from their secondary stock offering this year to pay off the bank debt initially used to close on the acquisitions."

"Well, that would explain a lot," he said. "Equity is a lot cheaper financing source than debt, especially these days." Yoshi paused, again reflecting. I dared not break his concentration. "So, it would seem we have to begin to think like an investor. Why would an investor want to buy this stock?"

"Good question. We were told at the orientation meeting investors were impressed by the company's steadily rising Earnings Per Share—EPS. Not only that, the audit partner said the company seemed to have an uncanny ability to accurately predict their quarterly EPS and hit them almost to the penny."

"Every quarter?"

"Yep, they hadn't missed a quarter in the last two years, and if they did, they earned more than projected."

Yoshi was rubbing his chin and said, "No wonder they're a darling of Wall Street. While I agree it's truly exceptional, it's also a red flag."

"Red flag? I just read about red flags in an article about forensic accounting." I caught the reference Yoshi was trying to establish. "Yoshi, you're not saying you think the company is fraudulent?"

"No, but it is a red flag to be able to hit quarterly projections every quarter, especially for a new company and growing so rapidly. I'm just saying for now, it's something you should keep in mind."

"Noted. Let's move on. I don't even want to think about something like that." I did but not now. I had to first understand the business model.

"Well, Sam, I hate to shatter your innocence, but financial fraud is a growing concern. You auditors are on the front line."

"Meaning what?"

"I'm saying that if a public company is engaging in fraudulent accounting and the auditor doesn't catch it, it probably won't get caught. At least, not on a timely basis. Maybe it would take a market collapse to expose it, but it would be nice if the investment community could depend on the auditors to sniff it out."

"I guess that's a discussion for another day. I can tell you this from my exam study, the auditor is not responsible for finding fraud, and there was not one question on the CPA exam addressing fraud."

"Well, OK, but all I'm saying is you need to be aware there are some red flags here, and I'd hate to read about you on the front page of the *Indianapolis Star*: "Company Executives Caught in Massive Fraud—Auditor Sam Halloran Missed It!""

We had a good chuckle, like that might ever happen, but it got me thinking. Maybe Yoshi had a point.

"OK, pal, I get your drift," I said. "But let's get back to the central issue here. I want to get comfortable and understand their business model. That will help me audit the account properly. What else do you need?"

"Fair enough. Let's go through an example of sales-type accounting. Can you run me through one?"

"We need to find a chalkboard," I said.

"Follow me," Yoshi said and was ten steps ahead of me in seconds.

"Where are we going?" I asked as I hurried to keep up with him tearing through the library. We entered the crossway above Fee Lane on our way to the School of Business wing.

"As I told you, I'm an adjunct here," he said, glancing over his shoulder at me with a sheepish grin. "I have the classroom keys!"

Moments later, I was in one of the large horseshoe shaped lecture halls with a piece of chalk in my hand. "Got my HP12C calculator fired up. I'll put an example on the board," I said, continuing to read from my handout.

> EXAMPLE: Customer leases a garden
> tractor for $60 a month for a term of 8 years.
> No money down. Due upon contract signing
> is first month's rent.
>
> Input monthly PMT = $60

Input i = 5%
Input n = 96 months
Solve for PV= $4,740
FV = $5,760 ($60 x 96 months)
UI = $5,760 - $4,740 = $1,020 amortized to income ratable over 96 months (Unearned Interest)
PV= $4,740 (net revenue) - cost to purchase of $2,500 = $2,240 gross profit recognized at signing of contract.

Yoshi studied it for a few moments, then said, "So, this is an example of when they *convert* an operating lease to a capital lease or sign a new one? Right?"

"Yep, the way I understand it is when they acquire another leasing company, they essentially dump all overhead—fire folks, get rid of the building and equipment and simply bring all the leases in-house to Indianapolis to manage."

"How many leases do they have in inventory?"

"Thus far, they are managing about 20,000 leases."

"Seems like a lot of leases for a relatively young company," Yoshi said as he picked up the 10-K, noting the small sales numbers in the early years leading up to the IPO. Pointing to the document, Yoshi said, "So, this huge spike in revenue and net income looks like they made a slew of acquisitions just prior to the IPO. I'd bet that was when then changed their accounting policy for leases."

"Correct. That same year they made eight acquisitions. Then capitalized a bunch of leases—hence the big spike you're seeing in revenue and net income."

Yoshi continued to study the document in his hands, regarding my comments. After a few moments, Yoshi bounced his index finger in the air and said, "Sam, I think I know why they are going through the trouble to account for leases as sales-type capital leases instead of operating leases." Yoshi became animated. Experience had taught me good things always happened when Yoshi became excited about something.

"If, in your example," Yoshi pressed on, "they continued to account for the acquired leases as operating leases, they would record only $60 in revenue each month per lease. If, however, they somehow converted those acquired operating leases to a new contract, one meeting the guidelines for capitalization, they could book $4,740 in revenue at the contract signing of only one lease. They are essentially recognizing all the revenue from the deal which they would not otherwise get to recognize for years. That's a huge advantage!"

Considering the example I'd put on the board, I hesitantly said, "I get that, Yoshi, but they are simply following the accounting rules."

"How convenient for them," Yoshi remarked sarcastically. "Sam, I think their growth strategy mandates they buy operating leases and somehow get the customer to sign a new lease—one which included provisions requiring them to convert the lease to a capital lease, a sales-type lease, thereby *requiring* them to book several thousand dollars in revenue, on average, for each lease they convert. Awe, shucks," Yoshi said smiling and shaking his head as if admiring the company's strategy.

I tried focusing hard on what Yoshi was saying. The clear advantage of using sales-type lease accounting allowed—no, required—the company to recognize revenue not otherwise recognized for years if accounted for as an operating lease. "I see your point, Yoshi. But so what?"

"Here's so what. Let's say GEL acquires a leasing company holding 3,000 leases. Now, keeping this simple and sticking with your example, assume their average monthly lease revenue, in terms of cash in the door, is $60 per month for each lease. That would mean in the first month they would recognize $180,000 in total gross revenue on all 3,000 leases. But, if they converted all of those to capital leases in the first month, they would gross $4,740 in revenue for each lease—about $14.2 million in total! Now, consider the effect of capitalizing 20,000 leases, or take it out a few years. 50,000 leases...You see the possibilities?"

I stared at the example on the board, then at Yoshi, then back to the board.

"Sam, close your mouth!"

A cold chill raced down my spine as I considered the possibilities of how GEL's revenue recognition method could attract investors.

"But I doubt they are converting all those leases as soon as they acquire the company," Yoshi said. "If they did, the revenue for month one would be enormous, but month two would be next to nothing. So, what I think they might be doing is pacing themselves."

"Pacing themselves. What do you mean?"

"Think about it, Sam. Using one of the new spreadsheets like Lotus 1-2-3, they could input the details of their inventory of operating leases, then determine how many they needed to *convert* in order to recognize the needed revenue to hit their target EPS."

"So, not all their leases—"

"Exactly, just enough. Pacing themselves," Yoshi said. "What you just did on your calculator for one lease, they could replicate for thousands of leases using a spreadsheet on a desktop computer. Next, they simply divide up the list to their sales force who calls the customers somehow incentivizing them to sign the new lease contract, one that *requires* GEL to record it as a capital lease. Revenue floods in the door. Once they hit the revenue yielding their projected EPS, they stop converting leases. Goal achieved. Next quarter, the ritual begins again. It would also explain why they need to continually acquire more and more leases. They need a steady flow of leases in inventory, so they can continue this practice of revenue manipulation."

"Yoshi, I'm not an experienced auditor, but even I know the words *revenue* and *manipulation* do not belong in the same sentence. What are you really saying here?"

"I'm suggesting what you may have here is a pyramid scheme."

"You mean a Ponzi scheme?"

"No, I said it right. Pyramid scheme. A lot of people think they are synonymous. In practical application they are. Those early entrants, in this case, the company's early investors, reap rewards from the later investors. If they hang on too long and the company fails to continue to acquire and convert more leases, the stock tanks. If you were an early investor, increased your investment, say, five-fold and then bailed, you'd make out good. The later investors are stuck holding the bag as the company's stock price tanks. Same thing with a Ponzi. The difference is a Ponzi scheme deals entirely with interest rates. Charles Ponzi paid outlandish rates of return to his earlier investors using new funds bilked from later investors who were left holding the bag."

"So, a distinction without a difference."

"Yep," Yoshi said sardonically. "Whatever you call it, it's illegal."

I sat down in one of the classroom seats and buried my head into my hands. I was fast realizing my audit client could be a massive leasing scam, and from what I could tell, my firm had not detected it. Worse off, I was the foot soldier now in charge of determining the appropriateness of the accounting for the largest asset on GEL's balance sheet—LCR. The weight of the responsibility I now felt was enough to make me sick with concern. My mind was racing.

"How can I be sure?" I said.

"I expected you might ask that. Here's what you need to find out. First off, take a look at activities surrounding the lease customers and conversions. Are GEL salesmen calling large numbers of acquired customers enticing them into signing new leases? Leases which just happen to be constructed so as to require being accounted for as capital leases. How are they motivating the customer into signing a new lease? For example, let's say an acquired customer had a year left on the lease; what is GEL doing to motivate them to sign a new extended term lease?

"Next, consider the timing. Do those customer calls seem to

occur in the normal course of running a business? Or do you detect patterns whereby a bunch of them occur near the end of a quarter and then stop abruptly? Remember, when they get the customer to sign the new lease, the revenue generated from the conversion must be recognized when the new contract is signed. So, consider all those thousands of operating lease contracts sitting around…just waiting. Waiting for the go from top management to make conversions.

"Literally, Sam, such a call would be like starting the printing presses for making money—generating revenue. Every converted contract is more revenue to the company. In *form*, the company is only following proscribed accounting practices. In *substance*, they are printing money."

I was frantically taking notes as Yoshi continued to analyze and instruct me. "One more thing," Yoshi said, pacing back-and-forth in professorial fashion. "Examine how the company accounts for write-offs."

"Write offs of what?"

"Capital leases. Presumably, some customers will go out of business, go bankrupt, or for whatever reason, stop paying on their lease agreement. How does the company account for write-offs knowing the contractual stream of revenue would no longer be assured? The company would be required to write off the remaining asset, the receivable, knowing it's not going to be paid."

"The LCR," I said, quietly considering the consequences to myself.

"The what?"

"LCR. The asset created when they capitalize the lease—Lease Contracts Receivable—that's what I am auditing."

"Well, OK, buddy. Then, it's all on you," he said smiling wildly. "Like I said, I'd hate to read about you in the papers."

CHAPTER 24

Walking into GEL's lobby on January 10th was in stark contrast to when I was last there in December. There was part of me that hoped Carol would not be returning, but that was ridiculous. Not only would she return, but I would work with her this very day.

Thinking about working together so closely during the day and occasionally into the evening caused my loins to stir. I cursed the feeling, yet I wanted to satisfy it again. It was wrong, yet I was powerless to stop wanting her.

Again wanting no part of working in the war room with Brian and the other auditors, I walked immediately through the massive lobby being thankful I had arrived early enough to avoid their stares. I walked to my cubicle with the will and determination I needed to get into my work, perform it correctly and get out of this place and on to my next successful audit.

While rounding the corner to my destination, I caught Carol Wittford bent over talking with someone in the cubicle across from mine. I was intimately familiar with her shape, especially from behind. As if she could sense me, she popped up and greeted me with the biggest smile, forcefully extending her hand.

"Welcome back, Mr. Auditor. I'll bet you're ecstatic to begin your year-end fieldwork," she said, rolling her eyes to emote the sarcasm in her voice.

It was not exactly the greeting I had expected, but it was clear she was putting on an act because others were listening. I played along. Not much of a choice. "And a good morning to you, Carol, and a

Happy New Year, too," I said with a smile.

"Oops, yes, I always forget the Happy New Year part this time of year," she said.

Carol's reaction surprised and relieved me. There, it was done. I worried over our first encounter needlessly. It was over fast and uneventfully.

Before I could say anything more, Carol said, "Sam, I'm late for a meeting. I'm sure you'll want to get right to it, so I'll leave you for now."

Walking into my cubicle, I tried hard to block out the visual forming in my mind created by my familiar surroundings. It was 7:30 in the morning, and I could hardly afford time to ponder the events of the last time I was here.

A few moments later, none other than Foster Worthington Beckworth walked past my cubicle and stopped at Carol's, but she had gone to her meeting. He didn't linger, and another moment later he returned along the same path. He shot me a derisive glance in passing.

I sat in my cubicle staring blankly at the fabric covered wall in front of me, drifting off. I had never been through a busy season. It would be a challenge, especially having to rationalize doing the clandestine investigation I felt necessary after meeting with Yoshi Fukuda. I wished he were here to make this journey with me. He called me shortly after we met and said it was good to run into me, so good he had made a big decision. Apparently, I made him feel guilty he hadn't acted upon his plan in the same manner I had. "You did what you said you'd do, and you're realizing your dream," Yoshi said. "I hadn't, but that's about to change."

It turned out, Yoshi quit his job at Allison. He wasn't certain where he would work next but felt confident it was the right decision. To clear his mind, he would embark on a six-week church mission to Sierra Leone, Africa. "Always wanted to do it," he said. He told me he would not be reachable but would catch up with me when he returned and then thanked me again for forcing him to rethink. The news was unexpected, but I wished my MBA friend well. After I hung up, I had selfishly regretted that Yoshi would not be close by to continue coaching me through this investigation I was about to begin. Now I was flying alone without my wingman.

I heard muffled voices from the hallway. Carol's voice registered first, then Reggie Dalton's. They were speaking in serious but low tones. I quieted myself to listen but could not make out what they were saying. When the voices stopped, I rose to have a look. There was no one in the hallway or in her cubicle. Oddly, there was no sign of her. Desk lamp off, no coat and no purse. It was as if she hadn't come in yet, but, of course, she had.

I was anxious to meet with Carol but willed myself to stop thinking about it. Lots to do. The first item on my list was to organize the confirmations binder. Since my prelim work, the positive confirmation letters we had sent to lessees were mailed back to our downtown office. Not all would be. That was to be expected. I would perform alternative procedures on those selections to validate the information those letters were seeking to confirm. Fortunately, most were coming in with the customer confirming the details of the lease. This was good.

Even sitting in my cubicle, I imagined the scent of Carol. It had been two weeks since.... I tried not to think about what happened between the two of us the last time we were together. *Together.* Interesting way for me to characterize what had occurred upon our last meeting.

Again, guilt invaded my thoughts every time I relived it. Remembrances of the nuns at St. Eugene's Catholic School who reminded us we'd burn in Hell for having such thoughts, let alone acting upon them. The trouble was, I didn't care about Hell right now. I'd ask for forgiveness later. Now, I was catching up on a life which had escaped me...until meeting Carol.

Carol's passion for me brought with it great satisfaction if for no other reason but to prove my father wrong. It seemed my subliminal goal for the rest of my life, to prove him wrong. *Why was I thinking about that bastard?* He was out of my life. But memories still lingered. Hurtful memories. Memories I had hoped I would never recall for the rest of my life, including the one most likely responsible for my allowing Carol to seduce me. I hadn't thought about Sandy in many years.

* * * *

"This seat taken?"

"No, of course not," I said before looking up at the person who said it. When I did, it was only briefly. I turned away from Sandy Mitchell and stared out the school bus window. I wanted to stare at her. Sandy was beautiful. Everyone wanted to set their gaze upon Sandy. Who wouldn't? She was captain of the cheerleading squad and the most beautiful girl I had ever laid eyes upon. Now, she was sitting next to me. I was petrified.

"Where are your books?" Sandy asked with a tone establishing I should carry books home to do my homework. We were in the same English and U.S. History classes with two of the most demanding teachers at Jefferson Junior High. Both always assigned a ton of homework and today was no exception, so it must have seemed odd to Sandy with all the homework assigned that I would not be carting home books.

"I got my homework done in study hall," I lied. I wasn't sure what else to say. I couldn't tell her the truth: I didn't care about homework. I didn't care about a lot of things back then. I was preoccupied with being an outcast.

"Oh, OK," Sandy said with some astonishment at my response, but she was unwilling to debate the point.

As the bus clicked through its gears and climbed up to speed after the stop sign, my mind was racing to think of something to say. The more I grappled with what to say, the less I could think of anything. I couldn't even make casual conversation. I felt like I was about to stand on a stage addressing an audience of 500 people. Adrenalin was coursing through my body being this close to a beautiful and popular girl. She smelled like a floral shop with no individual flower's scent distinguishable. I didn't think a freshman could smell so good. It only complicated my situation.

It was a twenty-minute ride to my stop. The time usually dragged. My usual routine was to stare out the window and think random thoughts berating myself. I was unpopular. Few would carry on a conversation with me. I was nobody. Maybe Sandy didn't know. I should say something to her. But what?

"Well, aren't you going to ask me why I'm on this bus?" Sandy asked coyly.

"Yeah, good point. You don't take this bus, so why are you here today?" I responded.

"That's the spirit. Good question," she replied, smiling playfully. She could have responded in mocking terms. Others would have. But Sandy was nice. I had never paid much attention to her, but now it seemed I should have. She wasn't like the others. Odd combination—beautiful and nice.

"No one is at my house tonight. My parents are visiting my sick grandpa at Middletown Hospital, and they won't let me spend the night alone. So, I'm spending it with my Aunt Sally. She lives on Werner Court. Maybe you could help me watch for that stop."

Inexplicably, my knees became the focus of my attention, but I could sense Sandy watching me. I couldn't believe such a beautiful girl was sitting so close. Our legs weren't touching, but her dress was laying up against my leg. My stomach was gurgling.

She's making normal conversation. I couldn't do that. Soon, Sandy would realize she was talking with a socially inept person, and she would stop talking. Then all would be as it should be. But Sandy didn't stop talking.

"So, what stop do you get off?"

"My stop is the one right after Werner Court, so I'll be sure and tell you where to get off."

It was a decent sentence. My stomach calmed, and I looked her way while saying it. Maybe it was her non-judgmental demeanor, but I was gaining confidence.

"OK, well, since you live so close and you've already done your homework, maybe you can help me with the assignments tonight? Maybe after dinner?"

Before I could respond, Sandy took control of the moment as if her question was rhetorical, and I would help her tonight.

"So, I'll see you later tonight, but maybe you can help me with something right now?" Sandy continued to talk about things, but I couldn't focus. I was in awe of her presence, enjoying the best bus ride I had ever experienced. My confidence grew by the minute.

Sandy's speech was racing as she opened her English book and slid it across to me such that half of it was on my leg and the other half on hers. She also scooted a little closer and like the true dweeb I was, I scooted away, closer to the window. It was an automatic reaction I regretted as soon as I did it. But Sandy didn't seem to take notice.

"I'm really having trouble diagramming this sentence." Sandy was pointing to one of the questions in our homework assignment on the freshly printed mimeograph paper.

I paid more attention to what she was asking. I wanted to help her. After staring at the question for a few seconds longer, I began drawing out the sentence diagram on her paper when she playfully yelled, "Don't write it out there, silly. Klein will see it's not my handwriting, and I'll get in trouble."

She laughed, and I could tell from the way her long blonde hair brushed against my forearm she was looking at me. I laughed, too. She pulled out a blank sheet of paper and said, "Here, silly. Write it here."

I felt myself smiling. I had forgotten how good it felt to smile.

I wrote out the entire sentence diagram on the separate sheet of paper Sandy laid on her book. "There you go," I said. "It's pretty logical if you take it slow." I proceeded explaining to her each part of the sentence. Sandy watched intently and leaned into me. This time, I did not slide away from her.

"You're so smart, Sam. You could be teaching this class." It was an exaggeration, but to some extent, she was right. I wasn't good at a lot of things, but sentence diagramming came easy. English was my best subject even though I never pulled higher than a "C" in the class. It wasn't because I didn't know the material. I had always done well on the tests. I blew off the homework assignments which cost me points toward my final grade.

The bus wheels screeching caused me to glance up. I became sad instantly.

"Hey, this is your stop," I said matter-of-factly, but I felt pangs of sorrow knowing Sandy and I would now part.

Sandy leaped up and grabbed my arm, pulling me up as well saying, "Come with me. You can help me finish the rest of it right now."

What an idiot I was. I couldn't believe I resisted saying, "But this isn't my stop."

Fortunately, I came to my senses. Maybe it was her determined tugging on my arm, but I stood and followed her.

The bus pulled away in a roar, black smoke belching out of its exhaust pipe. We coughed as Sandy, still holding my wrist, pulled me along to escape the fumes. Her laughing caused me to laugh with her. When we stopped running, Sandy's hand slipped from my wrist down to my hand. She laced her fingers with mine. I didn't resist. Maybe I was catching on.

We stopped and stood there eyeing one another, still holding hands, not speaking. Now I could enjoy her beauty. We were about the same height. It was easy to stare at her, like a painting in an art gallery. Calm, absolute, inviting. Her skin was pure, not unlike a bar of creamy Dove soap right out of the package. Untouched. Her glistening bluish-green eyes and silky blonde hair curls rippling over her shoulders suggested an innocence I myself had lost many years ago. Sandy was undeniably perfect in every way. Clueless what to do next, I could have remained there the rest of the day.

Sandy smiled, turned and walked along the street holding my hand. We didn't talk. I felt so comfortable with Sandy, I didn't care to talk. Holding hands and walking with her, I was in ecstasy.

"That's my aunt's house," Sandy said pointing to a small brick ranch. "She won't be home for another couple of hours, so we'll have some privacy."

Sandy must have noticed my unsettled look and followed with, "I mean so we can get through this homework, and you can be on your way." The whole conversation was awkward. It wasn't Sandy's fault. It was all mine. She was trying to make conversation like any fifteen-year-old would, except I was too immature to play along matching her comments. My thoughts were racing by so quickly as I struggled to think of something witty to say.

"Hey, Sammy! Sammy boy! Whatcha doin?"

I didn't have to look over to the car that had slowed down matching our gait. It was the irascible voice of my father, his slurred speech informing me he was already drunk. I purposely didn't regard him.

"Do you know that guy?" Sandy whispered.

I didn't respond. I closed my eyes, clinched my free hand into a fist and prayed he'd drive on by, hoping Sandy wouldn't learn the truth. But he didn't, and she was about to.

On my lead, we picked up the pace. We were close to Sandy's aunt's house. I felt we could make it and get away from him.

"Who's the babe? Aren't you gonna introduce me?"

"Sam, who is that guy?" Sandy asked as she shifted her glances between him and me.

"Ignore him," I said.

"Hey, pretty girl," he said.

Sandy stopped and confronted him saying, "Whoever you are, leave us alone, or I'll call the cops."

"Ignore him," I said to Sandy, still holding her hand but more tightly now. I jerked her along toward her aunt's house, insisting she not engage him. But Sandy was determined not to be intimidated.

"Hey, pretty girl. I'm trying to help you out. That little boy you're with is a waste of your time. I know that for a fact 'cause he's my son."

That did it. Sandy stopped instantly like she had stepped in wet concrete. She glowered at me as if I was somehow responsible for this humiliating scene and asked accusingly, "He's your father?"

"Sorry to say he is," I said cringing, gazing downward and surrendering any hope of getting Sandy away from this brewing confrontation.

The next thing my father said was something I believed was beyond the pale, even for a drunk like him. "Don't bother with him. His pecker is too small to satisfy a babe like you."

My head was ready to explode as I turned my attention from Sandy toward my father with a rage I had never felt. I let go of Sandy's hand. My shoulders stiffened, arms taut and fingers curled into fists, I moved toward his car. He must have seen my rage, too. He let out one final hideous chortle, then floored it as his wheels left rubber on the street pavement, and in a flash he was gone.

Adrenalin coursed through every muscle in my body, but I now had no antagonist to attack. All I could do was helplessly watch him disappear down the street.

The sound of a door slamming shut snapped me back to the present. When I turned in its direction, Sandy was gone. I called out her name as I turned from side to side. She did not respond. I assumed she had run into her aunt's house, which I was standing in front of, alone. I waited for a sign from her house. A light flipping on. Something. But there was no sign of life. Sandy was probably petrified. I doubt she had ever experienced anything like that. Of course not. She was like the rest of her upper-middle-class friends. She had normal parents who loved and cared for each other and their little girl. Their princess. She was sheltered from the horrors I faced daily. This whole experience had to scare the life out of her.

The next day at school, I searched for Sandy. I wanted to apologize but couldn't find her. She was absent. Same on Friday. It wasn't until Tuesday of the following week I glimpsed her walking toward me down the hall, but she quickly darted into one of the classrooms. She had to have seen me. She was trying to avoid me. I would make it easier for her. I never again attempted to talk with Sandy Mitchell. Encountering my father must have been so traumatic she would do anything to avoid it ever happening again. That would be easy. Simply steer clear of me and she would achieve that goal. I wished I could have done the same.

* * * *

CHAPTER 25

Approaching midnight. My eyes were on fire. Contacts killing me. Had to get out of there.

I had been working at my cubicle all day and was surprised Carol hadn't popped in. I needed to take a walk, so I stood and made my way to the vending area to get a Coke. I also needed to get my contacts out.

I returned to my cubicle and pulled out my audit program and the questions I had accumulated along the way, including those Yoshi helped me formulate. I remembered Carol had shown me what she called "her cheat sheet" which explained the entire lease accounting process. A decision tree, of sorts. She pulled it from one of her desk drawers. It would certainly be helpful working my way through my questions if I had it front of me. But Carol wasn't here. *Why had she not returned all day?*

Maybe due to the lateness of the hour in combination with my exhaustion and desperation to understand the company's complex lease accounting process, I was motivated to do something I never imagined I would consider. I walked into Carol's cubicle and rifled through her desk files searching for the decision tree diagram. I found it! Then, I noticed another file.

The typed label read "COMPLAINTS—1982." Without much deliberation, I pulled it out. In the center of the file folder was another typed label: "CONFIDENTIAL." I'm not sure what compelled me to ignore the obvious warning and open the file, but I did.

The first document I came across was apparently from one of the company's lease holders. It was a typed letter dated August 24, 1982, and it was addressed to Carol Wittford. The writer acknowledged an earlier phone call with Carol about a host of issues having to do with duplicate billings, poor follow-up and more. The letter was not long and ended with: "I hate your company, your people and your equipment! Cancel my lease and pick up your shit!" My knees buckled as I slid into Carol's chair.

An hour had passed. The other letters were similar to the first. Complaint letters from GEL's customers, some with attached documents to support the writer's claims. I stopped reading and perused the remaining contents of the file. It contained other letters addressed to various GEL employees: the CEO—Beckworth, VP of Operations—Duncan Fowler, whom I had not met, CFO—Reggie Dalton and Carol Wittford. All of them had more of the same complaints and ended with something like "pick up your equipment and cancel my lease."

I leaned back in Carol's chair and tried to make sense of the contents inside the file. I had momentarily forgotten where I was. Suddenly realizing I was sitting in Carol's cubicle instead of mine, I jumped up and retreated to my cubicle with the file.

Reclining in my chair, the file resting on my chest, I clutched it with crossed arms as if protecting a valuable treasure. Discovering the *Complaints file,* as I now dubbed it, suddenly filled me with fear.

My mind was racing trying to determine the impact of what I had just found. I was too exhausted to figure it out now. Needed sleep. I made my way to the war room and turned on the copier.

While it was warming up, I tried to get comfortable in one of the high-back leather chairs surrounding the war room's large, oval-shaped table. I fed the letters I had already read into the copier, then sat again and opened the Complaints file. The next several documents were more of the same. Letter after letter.

At 3:20 a.m. I stopped reading, pushed the newly discovered file away from me, crossed my arms, leaned back in my chair and considered my meeting with Yoshi Fukuda. Suddenly, I didn't feel so tired. While I didn't have his questions in front of me, I remembered him telling me to discover how the company accounted for write-offs. Sure, it made sense that with 20,000 leases some customers would cancel. I considered the accounting ramifications of a canceled lease.

If a customer canceled a lease, there was no longer a guarantee the expected monthly lease payments were assured. That wasn't difficult to reason. The lessee simply canceled the lease, meaning, "I ain't sending you no more money!" I talked aloud. Getting slaphappy due to the lateness of the hour. I forced myself to think it through, step-by-step. I fed more letters into the copier.

Sure, there could be a dispute, maybe even a lawsuit to enforce the lease, but at any rate, the company must book some type of loss provision recognizing the future expected stream of lease revenue might not materialize, at least partially.

In provisioning for the possibility of nonpayment, GEL would have to book a credit to the LCR account with a corresponding debit to the income statement, either a direct credit to LCR or to a contra-account to be netted against the LCR balance. I didn't recall seeing any such contra-account in the financials. So, maybe GEL wrote the lease off? Which would account for why I found no contra-account. That made sense. I would check into it tomorrow with Carol. I made a mental note to run Yoshi's other questions by Carol at the same time, assuming she'd be in.

Still, my suspicions were growing. I considered if there were any implications to the rest of the lease population, those not sampled in my testing. I didn't count the letters in the Complaints file, but there were many, maybe a hundred or more. The irate customers who wrote those letters might be indicative of a larger problem with the company's operations. It would take time to write such letters. It would be easier to simply make a phone call to GEL rather than write a letter cancelling a lease. It could be that other customers did just that, possibly several hundred more. They never took the time to write a letter. It was not only possible, but probable.

Assuming these letters might be just the tip of the iceberg and there were many other disgruntled leaseholders demanding their lease be canceled, why had I not heard about this before?

Then, it hit me like a boulder—the confirmation process. Searching for invalid leases or incorrect information was the reason we circulated letters to GEL's lease customers. That process should have exposed the fact that some customers were dissatisfied with the company and wanted, no demanded, their lease contract be canceled.

But recalling my cursory review of each returned letter, I noted no exceptions. Not a single one. I focused on that new fact. Not one returned confirmation indicated any errors in the amounts or terms of the selected lessees or dissatisfaction with GEL's service, equipment or billing practices. Why hadn't I questioned that before? Because this was my first attempt with the positive confirmation process! Sure, I knew enough about it to pass the CPA exam, but this was real life, and I had no practical experience. I must be missing something. There had to be a reasonable explanation.

It made sense for some customers to cancel. Even Yoshi suggested that would be normal. Carol would clear it up in a hurry. She would likely show me documentation supporting the write-off for each of the leases from the Complaints file, in the same way they would write off an accounts receivable no longer collectible, a direct hit to earnings in the period in which they became aware of the loss. That's the accounting rule.

Of course, that was the only logical answer. For every customer complaint letter in the Complaints file, the company would show me that the lease for the customer was written off. Carol would show me. I hoped that was correct. The alternative was unimaginable. But then Carol supposedly had already walked me through the entire lease accounting process. Never once had she mentioned write-offs or all the letters from disgruntled customers filed away.

I did not have an answer. At least I was pleased with my reasoning and surfacing the right questions. Good questions. But I was tired. No, exhausted. Yet, with the company's earnings release quickly approaching, I could not simply walk away from this issue, or at least I shouldn't. After the earnings announcement, it would be too late to do anything about it from the standpoint of HP issuing their opinion. We'd still have time to withhold our opinion before the actual filing with regulatory authorities, but what an embarrassment it would be for the firm...for Pete Brooks, the guy who expressed sincere confidence in me.

The LCR testing was my responsibility. If there was a problem of any magnitude with customers, hundreds of customers, so dissatisfied with the company, Brian would ask me: "Why didn't you surface this issue during your preliminary work?" I was certain all the blame would fall on me.

I felt lightheaded. My lack of sleep had to be a contributing factor. But I was certain the possibility of me having incorrectly performed some audit procedures was enough to bring on symptoms like I was experiencing. I felt sick to my stomach.

In the breakroom, I slammed down a 7-Up. After a few minutes, it was working. When I returned to the war room, my shirt was sticking to my back and chest—another anatomic reaction to my building anxiety.

By 4:15 a.m. I was anticipating this would be an all-nighter. I called Sue knowing full well I'd be rousting her from a sound sleep. She'd be panicked hearing the phone ring at this hour but more so if she woke at 6 a.m. discovering I hadn't been home. After relaying my situation, absent the details, she yawned into the phone and said it was no big deal and for me to be careful and thanked me for the call. All such administrative duties attended to, it was time to pour into that file and go to work. On what I was not certain, but finding the Complaints file was an anomaly needing further investigation before I could decide on its import to the audit, if any. I snickered to myself when thinking my only guide was *Columbo*, a TV detective series I watched religiously during the '70s. It starred Peter Falk as the bumbling, yet savvy, detective in pursuit of the evidence proving a big crime about ten minutes before the end of each episode. It sounded silly, but I wished I had taken notes to help guide me now. I'd have to rely on my memory and instincts.

I opened the Complaints file again and read the next letter in the stack. Still struggling for a plan, I hoped *Columbo* was a true depiction of how such cases were solved. I hesitated. I could be opening a big, dark, deep hole I would one day regret as I stood in the unemployment line kicking myself for ever having opened it. Then, I realized I could be fired just for rifling through Carol's desk.

Whatever my thinking and rationalization, none of it mattered as I continued working my way through the file, seeing where it led me. I hoped something would click, that somehow, I would see the way forward. I was unsure if that was a good strategy, but what else could I do? I could call no one. They'd laugh me off the planet. No, I had to figure this out myself, and I had to do it quickly.

Suddenly, my high school chess coach's teachings came to mind. He would often have me replay famous chess matches. He had constructed a board that swiveled so I could turn it around to play both sides, following along in recorded matches. Different gambits came to mind. I was surprised I could remember them by name so long after I had given up the game. *All because of him.* I couldn't think about that now. I'd think about that later. Now, I just needed to keep replaying in my mind all the facts, all the moves that had been made. Therein lay the clues to solving this problem.

At five a.m., I felt like I could fall asleep any moment. But I couldn't. I had to keep going until I had a plan. I didn't expect to solve this issue tonight, but I had to have a plan, at least a list of questions I could ask Carol. Carol would help me solve it. Carol would know exactly what to do. She could probably solve this in less than an hour by showing me the proper documents. I was stupid to waste all this time trying to figure it out myself. I was ruminating so much now it seemed absurd to continue. I needed sleep.

Sunday Night Fears

Before falling asleep at the conference table, my final thoughts included: *I don't yet have a plan. Only questions and probably not the right ones. I am so in over my head.*

CHAPTER 26

Through the war room's glass wall, I noticed Brian approaching the revolving doors. I shot up straight. Standing, I gathered my thoughts, shocked I was still in possession of the Complaints file. I grabbed it and the copies I had made and headed for the war room door wondering if Carol was in her cubicle. She'd notice for certain the Complaints file was missing.

I considered my appearance. I couldn't let on I'd spent the night here. Brian would be all over me inquiring what I was working on. I wasn't even close to being ready to disclose my findings. The last thing I needed was Brian reviewing and evaluating my work, punching holes in my logic. He'd surely show me what I was missing, how the company had written off those bad leases throughout the year. Why hadn't I considered that earlier, and why had I wasted all that time? No, bad timing. I had to disappear.

"Good morning," I said as I hustled out the war room door the moment he opened it.

"So, what brings you in so early, Sammy boy?"

Now about twenty feet past Brian and moving at a good clip, I glanced over my shoulder saying, "Wanted to get an early start, boss." He hated it when I called him that. At the moment, I didn't care what Brian thought of me. I needed to disappear to some quiet place and think hard about how the Complaints file discovery might affect my testing of the LCR account. I wanted to be right about what I thought I had discovered, but then knowing the possible implications to the company, to my firm, to Carol, I wanted to be wrong. Still, I couldn't ignore what I had found; I couldn't stop investigating.

I casually glanced into Carol's cubicle. Empty chair, no purse, no coat. She hadn't yet arrived. I returned the Complaints file to its original location in her desk drawer. At least I hoped that was the case.

I was eager to study the letters I had copied. Surely, I was missing something. Why couldn't I let it go? Smart auditors had poured over GEL's accounting in the past. Hell, HP audited all five years of financials for inclusion in the IPO. If there was a problem with the largest account on the balance sheet, who was I to be the one to uncover it when others before me had not?

It was 8:30 in the morning on a Tuesday. Carol should show up at any moment. It would be better if I wasn't here when she arrived. I needed to disappear, but where? I was always either here, the war room, or on the *John*. Eureka! The perfect place to get some serious alone time.

I sat on the toilet seat contemplating my next move and quickly realized my foolishness. It was less than two weeks before GEL's earnings release. Everyone was walking around expecting HP, rather, Pete Brooks would be signing off on the financials as a foregone conclusion. We were all working diligently towards a perfunctory conclusion. Likewise, everyone expected LCR would be signed off by Pete as well. And why not? I had found nothing in my testing to support a different conclusion. But now, upon finding the Complaints file, that could all change. I was missing something. I needed time to think. *But look around, Sam. You're working through a complex issue while sitting on the toilet*! I thought.

I walked out of the men's room and headed for my cubicle. Finally, there was Carol walking out of hers in the opposite direction toward the executive offices. She didn't see me approaching. I recounted the steps I took to replace the Complaints file. What if she suspected something?

Suddenly, another chess gambit came to mind—The Fool's

Mate—checkmate in two moves…just two moves! It wasn't difficult to see how it got its name.

It hit me like a rogue wave. Carol has been playing me for a fool all along. *Stay close to him so he becomes captivated with your body and seduce him into signing off on the LCR account. Fuck him until he bleeds. Anything to make sure he signs off on LCR.* That was the mission Reggie gave Carol. And I'm guessing she agreed. It would not be the first time in my life someone I trusted would deceive me.

Carol had not yet returned. I was standing in the hallway outside her cubicle. I was being ridiculous. I couldn't keep avoiding her. Before the holidays, we were inseparable. It might tip them off if I seemed to avoid her now. It wasn't smart on my part. This was shaping up to be a game of survival. I needed to sit and think through the implications and what my next move would be. I can't keep retreating to the safety of a toilet seat every time I needed to think.

As I turned to enter my cubicle, I caught Carol rounding the corner. She noticed me and walked directly toward me, eyes locked on my face. I admired her in slow motion. I didn't want to show her that much attention, but she was the only one in the narrow corridor. Fortunately, she was sporting a pleasant demeanor. A relief, for sure.

I admired her gait. I'd seen it often. The walk. Like a runway model, strutting and displaying her assets. As she approached, she slowed her pace most likely for my enjoyment. She was as stunning as ever. Maybe even more so. She stopped a foot in front of me, close enough I caught her scent.

"Good morning, Mr. Halloran."

She had the same executive presence, same captivating smile, same alluring perfume. Trying to act normal while still maintaining the faux formality, I said, "And good morning to you, Ms. Wittford." She smiled, displaying a temerity I hadn't seen before.

Being this close to her was not good. In high heels, Carol was at eye level. As she passed, she rubbed her elbow against my forearm, which I was certain was intentional. A few feet past, she turned to face me. I turned toward her and tried not to stare, but it was impossible not to notice and appreciate her chiseled looks. She stopped and stood there, smiling, not saying a word at the moment, allowing me to enjoy her like a free sample in the sweet shop at the mall. "So, we should catch up. Is now a good time?" she said with a school girl glint in her eyes.

"Now is a good time, indeed." She had me again. Influencing my compliant and immediate response was likely the guilt I felt for grabbing the Complaints file and believing her friendliness towards me was all a ploy to keep me duped. Guilt remained for a lot of things: our holiday romp, taking the Complaints file, continuing to lust after her. I still believed I did the right thing by taking that file. At least, I hoped others might see it that way.

Carol dropped her purse on her desk and shot me one of her classic alluring poses. Her every action belied my rejection of her on that fateful evening. She appeared ready to pick up where we left off. *What game were we playing now?* I wondered.

She peered into the mirror hanging on the side of her cubicle wall, tussled her hair playfully with her fingers, then shot me a quick glance through the mirror, probably to see if I was watching. I was. She was controlling me and loved every minute of it. Like a puppy dog, I stood and waited for her to lead the way. Finally, she walked past me close enough to brush against me one more time like she was sprinkling me with fairy dust. In passing, she flipped her head back saying, "Follow me."

We walked through a door leading to the employee exit but turned to the right and headed down a metal stairway. I hadn't been this way before. With no comment, I followed her. At the foot of the stairs, Carol led me down a narrow hallway. We soon came to a nondescript door which opened to a conference room with a round table and an office speaker phone in the center of it. I didn't take time to survey the rest of the room. I was still watching Carol's every move, even as she turned to close the door quietly behind me. I waited for her to take a seat, but she didn't sit and appeared nervous and unsure of herself, which was so uncharacteristic of her. She stood several feet away, fidgeting with her hands, looking down and away but facing me. It was like she had something to say.

Suddenly, her demeanor changed from a few moments ago when she was flirting. "Sam, I think I need to do some explaining."

At last, she was about to address what had occurred between us on Christmas Eve.

"Carol, no, there's nothing to explain," I said.

"Of course there is. I was wrong—"

"No, Carol, *we* were wrong." I explained to Carol we were colleagues, well, in a professional sense. I was her auditor. I was independent and objective, but nothing in the rule book excluded friendship. At least, I didn't think there was. She nodded in agreement, demurely. On that night, when she entered my cubicle she reacted upon her emotions. It was not uncommon for two colleagues to have a brief moment when they pushed the boundaries. There's no intended evil in that. I told her what she did, what we did, had happened a thousand times before when two people worked so closely together.

Carol listened intently. She said nothing but moved closer, putting her finger ever so gently against my lips to hush me. She had something to say. I relented and quieted myself.

"Thank you," she said in a most sincere and respectful manner. She lowered her hand from my lips and then her head. Stepping back, she rested her arm on one of the chair backs, purposefully creating some distance between us, a barrier too. It didn't seem her style. Something was up. Her jaw clinched as if providing her the strength to say what she had to say.

"So, that accountant I told you I had chased at Purdue—do you remember we touched on that topic a few weeks ago?"

She was staring directly at me. I nodded with no verbal response.

"Well, I did catch him, and we immediately fell for each other. So much so, we married in our junior year in college. My parents were furious. They did not approve. It wasn't like they had anything against Jim, whom they had met at a dinner when they visited for homecoming. That dinner went well, and we had a good time without incident. My parents, well, certainly my dad, cautioned we should take it a lot slower. He meant *I* should take it a lot slower. Of course, I didn't listen. How could I? I was in love. Or thought I was.

"My dad called me about a week later. To 'check-in,' he'd said. You can imagine how disappointed he was when I told him we had gone to Vegas and gotten married. A muffled cry informed me Mom must have picked up an extension but soon realized it was Daddy crying, although he'd never admit to it. He told me he had always dreamed of giving me away one day. That would not happen now. Trying to sound positive, they said they understood. Mom forced herself to say something like, 'We remember what being in love was all about.' Some other awkward pleasantries were exchanged. Both wished us well, then hung up the phone. They were hurt, more hurt than I had ever remembered them being. I sensed Daddy wanted to chastise me and tell me what a big mistake I had made, but he didn't. I was his little girl, and he still loved me dearly. I wanted to think that."

We were still standing. It all seemed so awkward. Why was Carol relaying this story to me? Still, I remained quiet. Something was up with her.

"Daddy's intuition was right. Time would prove how right he was. About a month into our marriage, I suppose my dad felt it was time to give me one of 'life's lessons,' as he would call it. He cut me off. He told me I was a spoiled little princess taking full advantage of all the luxuries afforded corporate executives like him; I had no sense of making it in the world under one's own steam.

"Jim had a different upbringing. His family had struggled financially for as long as he could remember. He told me the only way he could afford attending Purdue was through the grace of the United States Government—the GI Bill. He did a tour in Vietnam as a medic. He never talked about it. Later, it would explain a lot.

"Jim had been accustomed to doing without and scraping by. I had not. Our first year of marriage was pretty much bliss as one

213

might expect any first year would be. We didn't have much, but then, we didn't need much. We had each other, which was all we needed, if you know what I mean."

I did know exactly what she meant, considering they likely made love constantly. I smiled behind pursed lips. It wasn't a happy smile, rather obligatory and offered without commitment. It communicated I was listening, offering no judgment, approval or otherwise. Carol continued to regard me occasionally with a quick glimpse as if seeking my approval for her actions. I stared at her blankly and unemotionally, trying hard to stay neutral. I dared not physically comfort her, ruling out another repeat of the intimacy we briefly shared. I tried keeping Sue front and center on my mind.

Carol continued to walk me through their first year of marriage. Why, I had no clue, but I allowed her that time. "After graduation we bought a house in the suburbs of Milwaukee, Jim's hometown. Jim had worked at Burger Boats a few miles outside of Milwaukee. Through that experience he had figured he could do what had made Burger Boats so successful—build boats for rich people. So, he started his own luxury boatbuilding business with a SBA loan. At the same time, he would build a comfortable life for our family. At least, that was the plan," Carol said cavalierly.

Carol delivered "A beautiful baby girl we named Laura." Carol felt certain that a new grandchild would be the perfect opportunity to reunite with her parents. It didn't work out that way. They refused to visit her in the hospital. Her dad was stubborn, she told me, and adamant they would not provide Carol, or her growing family, any financial or emotional support. She stubbornly accepted believing her family would persevere. She was certain her mom and dad would come around in time.

Maybe my impatience showed, but Carol begged for my continued attention and would "get to the point soon." I acquiesced even though, now having found the Complaints file, I was becoming more and more suspicious of her. She continued, but at a faster pace. She told me how it seemed Jim's new boatbuilding business showed early promise but then slowly disintegrated into a struggling enterprise.

Then the drinking started. Not right away. It was when Carol became pregnant with Josh, her second child. After she brought Josh home from the hospital, it seemed Josh had several medical issues. It wasn't what her husband wanted to deal with while he was struggling to keep his business afloat.

"No pun intended," Carol mused with a timorous smile.

I tried again to move things along, saying with some empathy, "Carol, it distresses me such a nice person like you would have to endure such hard times. I don't want to seem callous in saying this, but I don't see what this has to do with the job you and I are doing at GEL." Carol suddenly broke down and cried. She covered her face. The tears soon turned to sobs. I immediately realized my mistake in abandoning my empathetic posture. I helped her into a nearby sofa against the wall. I took a seat next to her and tried, professionally, to comfort her; first by gently rubbing her shoulder, more of a patting, then lightly taking her hand while her other was wiping tears with a tissue she had pulled from somewhere. When Carol turned quickly toward me and embraced me, I allowed her to melt into my chest, my head now buried in her flowing blonde hair. Her touch, her scent, her extreme vulnerabilities worked toward softening my coarse posture. But I forced myself not to be taken in by her story as it now seemed she still wanted some emotional bonding with me. She had me exactly where I expect she wanted me, and I tried fruitlessly not to empathize with her.

Soon I became angry with myself for falling for her yet again, allowing her to manipulate me. Still embracing Carol, I tried to assess my current circumstances, realizing I was in a very compromising position. Before I could extricate myself from her arms, she went into press mode.

"That's when he started abusing me." Carol then released me, deviously well-timed to check my reaction. Whatever my expression, it seemed to encourage her to continue. "First, it was a slap in the kitchen one evening after I told him how desperate our financial situation actually was. No matter how long I labored over our personal books as well as his business books, it was no use. Bankruptcy would seem the only way out for the business and for us personally. Apparently, it was the wrong thing to say as I soon learned.

"He slapped me across my face so hard he knocked my head into the kitchen cabinet, which dropped me to my knees. Then, he reached down and slapped my other cheek. He stopped only when Laura showed up in the kitchen. She had awakened earlier and was now crying and visibly upset as she raced into my arms. Jim said something incoherent, then stormed out of the house."

Carol paused, continuing to deal with a tissue taking on the shape of a golf ball. I stood and walked over to a counter, grabbing a handful of tissues. I handed them to her and returned to my seat next to her. I felt sorry for Carol, but in the back of my mind I was thinking about the Complaints file. She might have noticed it out of place and wondered if I had seen it. I no longer trusted Carol but felt powerless to leave her while in the grips of telling me such an emotional story, so I stayed and continued to listen. Still suspicious of this meeting and unsure where it was leading, I didn't dare say a word. All my senses were guarded and alert.

After a few sniffles she continued, "With Jim gone from our house and Laura in my arms crying, I hugged her tightly and tried to explain why Daddy was being mean to Mommy. After calming her down, she fell asleep in my arms. I carried her to her room and glanced at Josh still sound asleep in his crib opposite Laura's bed. I was thankful he had not awakened, too. I lingered a few minutes in the kids' bedroom, ensuring they were asleep. With that accomplished, I went downstairs to the kitchen to attend to a growing knot on my forehead.

"As I closed the freezer door after getting a cold icepack, I was alarmed to see Jim standing in the kitchen. Startled, I jumped back, dropping the ice pack on the kitchen floor. Jim approached me, and

I covered myself, expecting another barrage. He grabbed my arms and pushed me into the corner of our cabinets, pinning me there. I was petrified and braced for the worst, knowing it was useless to fight his strength and power over me. I closed my eyes expecting to be hit. Instead, Jim was crying.

"His vise grip on my arms relaxed. As he slowly and gently began to envelop me with his arms pulling me towards him, I reluctantly began relaxing my defenses.

"He blamed the booze and promised it would never happen again. I forgave him. And, of course, it wasn't the last of those episodes. Jim took to smacking me as his weekly stress reliever. Then, Jim went too far."

Carol averted her stare toward a door on an opposite wall. She seemed to stare at it for a time and then winced. Her body movements telegraphed the pain she was about to relive, pulling another chapter from a troubled past. I knew the feeling all too well.

In a guarded yet deliberate manner, she said, "Josh was still an infant. One Sunday, I was working with our personal finances, searching to find a way to tell Jim it was truly over. There was no escaping it. I was aware Josh had been crying more than usual but deferred attending to him while wrestling with the books...until Laura screamed, 'Daddy, stop! You're hurting little Josh!'

"I flew into the nursery and leaped on Jim. I was no match for him as he easily deflected my advance. As if to prove he was still a man, he picked me up from the floor by my hair. Josh continued to scream while Laura pounded on Jim's legs, screaming for him to let me go. With seemingly all of his frustrations channeled into his right fist, he pounded my face as he continued to hold me up by my hair delivering his blows one after the other. It was the worst pain I had ever experienced. I passed out.

"When I awoke in the hospital, Mom was by my bedside. Confused as to where I was or how I landed there, I soon realized I was without my kids. I sat up in my hospital bed trying frantically to call for Laura and Josh. My mother comforted me and told me my children were alright and with a neighbor; I should lie back and rest. She would remain with me. I took her advice, settling into the soft pillow, allowing the Percodan to do its magic. I didn't expect Daddy to be there. He would be too proud to be by my side. After all, he did warn me. As I drifted off to sleep, I wasn't angry with Daddy. I was so sad for my current circumstances and quietly cursed myself for not taking his advice about the person I would marry.

"In addition to a broken nose, my cheek bone was fractured, which would later require several surgeries to restore. I had hoped upon seeing my mother things would soon return to days when I was Mommy and Daddy's little princess. That was not to be."

As I continued to listen to Carol's horrendous account of her violent marriage, I felt myself melting. Faint scars appeared above her cheekbone. I hadn't noticed them before. My earlier skepticism had been mitigated by not only her story but how Carol had told it. Here was this tough, confident professional I had, in a relatively short time, grown to like and admire, crumbling in front of me. I felt helpless to alleviate her pain and suffering and had, a while ago, abandoned my cynicism. Continuing to hold her hand, I patiently waited for Carol to continue. With her other hand now on top of mine, her grip tightened, appearing to give her strength to continue.

"The hospital released me five days later. Mother was there to take me home. She stayed with me, helping around the house with the kids and the cooking. Well, she hired a cook, nanny and a cleaning person, but it was still great to have her close by. Most days she would flip through fashion magazines and watch soap operas. I mostly lay in bed intermittently crying about my plight. Jim had disappeared. I never saw him again, and I couldn't tell you whether he's alive or dead. I often hoped for the latter, but today, I don't care other than I never want to see him again.

"A few days of that routine brought my mother to my bedroom, asking if I felt strong enough to visit with her in the living room. She didn't waste any time in giving me a dose of reality. She would soon leave to go with Daddy on a planned trip to Europe. They would cruise the canals in southern France. My mother's face lit up like a beacon when she told me their plans. Finally, she paused as her mood turned somber. She reached into her purse, pulled out an envelope and slid it toward me across the table. She said she wished she could do more. It was the best she could do, given Daddy held most of the purse strings and was adamant, saying I had brought all of this upon myself and my family.

"My mother's limited support, financially and emotionally, was enough for me to grab hold of the lifeline she had thrown me, and I was lucky for it. I also considered myself fortunate to have a shot at a second chance. My accounting degree would soon come in quite handy."

Carol stopped crying and relaxed comfortably on the sofa. She pulled her hand back from resting on mine, and I pulled back, too. She was slowly reverting to the person I knew. She seemed to relax a little, like a huge weight had been lifted. I was still puzzled about why she felt compelled to bring me down here and tell me that story.

Carol ended her story by explaining how she had come to GEL. "After a relatively short stint working for McAllister, a regional accounting firm, I set out to find a corporate accounting position. That's when I landed my position here three years ago. I was assured that by working diligently, I would be amply rewarded. That promise turned out to be the first truth told to me in a very long time. I owe a lot to this company, Reggie in particular. He literally saved my life."

When Carol finished, she was sitting erect and askew of me. She wasn't so pretty anymore. No longer the diva I had been worshiping. Her hair had lost its sheen and body. She was disheveled, mascara running down both cheeks. Her nose was bright red, almost matching in color the former whites of her eyes. With her hair now pulled behind her ears, I noticed them sticking out.

As Carol rose and walked to a small sink in the kitchenette, I watched her the entire time until she was around the corner. She still had a killer figure, which made me wonder why she hadn't rebounded from a failed first marriage. Before I could stop myself, I said, "But, Carol, so you had a bad first marriage. You are still a very desirable woman. You're bright, and you're beautiful. You'll get into a rewarding relationship for sure."

I continued to sit on the sofa watching Carol adeptly using a washcloth and peering into the wall mirror. I refocused on Carol, the accounting manager for my audit client, the Complaints file and where this was leading. I had to shift gears. I had to learn more.

Carol's tale of woe was done and over. I felt compassion for Carol, but I was now on a mission to determine what Carol knew about those hate letters I had read last night from the Complaints file. Why had she not told me of them?

I was considering how I would begin the discussion and was not confident I had formulated the best approach. Fortunately, Carol excused herself and stepped into the restroom next to the kitchenette. It gave me a few moments to take stock of where I was.

With little hesitation, I focused again on the Complaints file. Was she aware I'd found it? Maybe she told Reggie I was on to them.

I stood from the sofa, nervously pacing, waiting for Carol to emerge. I wondered what was coming next. Should I allow Carol to continue leading, or should I take over the agenda? I was ill-prepared for this cloak-and-dagger intrigue and desperately wanted to focus on my audit responsibilities. I suddenly realized I had been doing that. I had successfully completed and signed off on most of my audit program steps. Technically, I was almost done. Then why was I down here in a basement conference room with Carol Wittford listening to her pour out her soul as if I should care? I mean, I did care...even though it was not part of *my* audit responsibilities to care. *Screw you, Elaine Porcheck*, I thought.

Suddenly, the Complaints file and Yoshi's questions were front and center. Now would be the perfect time to hit Carol with them since we were down here secluded from both her boss and mine.

But then I remembered Peter Falk in *Columbo* and the techniques he used to extract confessions from the bad guys. When Columbo had reached that point, he had all the answers. He no longer needed information; he needed the perpetrator's confession, and he had a plan. Due to his extensive research and investigation, Columbo deftly delivered each question with specific purpose, like stair steps, and with each answer moved the perp closer and closer to the inevitable confession. The perp did not understand where he was being led. Then came the moment of the big confession. He was trapped, confessed and appealed to Columbo's compassion. Only then did Columbo smile and place that awful cigar in his mouth…THE END.

My path forward became clear. I wasn't there yet. I had questions, but there was more I needed to do, more information to gather on my own, exactly like Columbo. Once I had exhausted my own list, only then would I be ready to confront Carol, and maybe Reggie, too. I had to be ready for Reggie. If I let Carol in on my investigation too early, she'd surely tell him. Reggie might even inform Pete of his job offer to me and insist I be removed from the audit for independence reasons. Pete would do it; he'd have to follow the rules, and I'd be history. The time for my questions was premature. I had to be patient.

Then, as if sensing she was taking too much time and I might lose sympathy or whatever emotion she was trying to engineer, Carol exited the restroom. She had used her time well. Gone was the tussled hair, running mascara and makeup. It seemed the moment she stepped out of the restroom she became reinvigorated with a new purpose, a new direction she would take. Carol's attitude had shifted. "So, we have an audit to wrap up. Rest assured, I am totally committed to finalizing that to your satisfaction. I suppose we should head upstairs and work hard toward that end."

I nodded my head and offered a circumspect smile, still unsure why she brought me to this place. In the short time I had known Carol I now realized there was a motive in everything she said or did.

Carol moved close and touched my shoulder. She gave me a peck on the cheek and said, "Thanks for listening." It wasn't one of those sultry and seductive kisses which, by her past actions, signaled the red light was on and the door was open. It was more like a brother-sister greeting of affection. She appeared to be working hard to take us back to an earlier time not so long ago when Carol's effusive personality drove everyone around her, including me, to join in the excitement of the moment, even if that moment were long hours of hard work. The Carol I had grown to appreciate, but in a professional rather than lustful way, was hopefully returning. She appeared to want to move on, and I was happy to do the same, at least for now.

CHAPTER 27

With only a week to go before GEL's earnings release, I was stuck. Paralyzed would be more like it. Not because I didn't have a plan. I had a plan, but I lacked confidence in it and feared making a fool of myself. But as luck would have it, this morning I had another session with Emily Thompson.

It had been less than a week since our last session. I was a little surprised that Dr. Thompson hadn't questioned why I wanted to meet with her so soon again. But then, she didn't seem the type to question someone in need. I was certain she saw me as one of those people.

I wondered what kind of relationship one was supposed to have with their shrink. I felt I had a good one with Dr. Thompson. While we were not friends, I talked with her like she was. I had little experience with close friendships. My best friend in the whole world was Sue. She was always a friend and a lover. Maybe Dr. Thompson was sometimes a friend, always a confidant. Whatever she was to me, she was very helpful this morning.

Since meeting with Dr. Thompson, I had not had another episode. Sue never brought it up. Occasionally, she'd ask how it was going with Dr. Thompson. She wasn't prying. She respected my privacy. She was comforted enough knowing I was continuing my sessions with her.

Emily Thompson never told me what to do; in the way she responded, I'd usually walk away with a clear purpose in mind about what the way should be. This morning was one of those sessions.

"Good morning, Doc."

"OK, so today I'm 'Doc,' is it? How do you decide what you call me each time we meet?" she asked with a wry smile.

"Not sure. I don't think about it. I just let it happen," I said.

"So, are you usually this carefree about most things?"

"Come on, Doc, you know the answer to that."

Emily Thompson smiled as she picked up her tea, green tea. She was a health nut. At times, she'd extol the virtues of "good food for the body and soul."

I wanted to hear more about Doc Thompson's views of the soul, so I asked her to explain. She took another sip of her tea, smiled, then said, "So, tell me about your week," ignoring my question.

"I'm pretty stressed out this week, Doc."

"Oh, so how can I help?"

We opened each session about the same way. This morning I told her, without specifics, how I faced a real dilemma: whether to simply follow the plan laid out for me (the audit program) or follow my instincts, even though doing so could get me fired."

I would imagine most people would offer advice favoring the safer route. Emily wasn't like most people, though. She asked me several questions. She flipped through her notebook—what I wouldn't give to have a glimpse of what she wrote about me.

It was like watching a surgeon at work. Meticulous. Studied. If she stuck to her pattern she'd ask a couple more questions before she was ready to advise me, not by telling me what to do but leading me to determine which door to open.

"You told me previously that embarking on this new career was a long shot. Now that you've been there a couple months, what do your chances of success look like?"

I was honest with her and said, "They are not looking good."

"Would you like to expand?"

"Not really. Too much to talk about, and I don't want to confuse the issue with superfluous material." Such as my convoluted feelings for Carol. I wasn't ready to go there yet with Dr. Thompson.

Hopefully it was over with Carol anyway, so why muddy the waters? I did tell her that I was conducting an investigation…clandestinely. She didn't respond.

She paused and thoughtfully looked into my face. She was unshakable, carefully pondering her next question. "Do you still have the same goals and aspirations for where you expect this new career will take you?"

"I do."

She reviewed her notes for a few moments, flipping through a couple of pages. It was painful watching her evaluate me.

"Sam, I'm aware from our past sessions you have an embedded fear of failure. It has shaped all you have done in the past and much of what you do today, interfering with all you want to become. Can we explore this a little bit today?"

"If you wish."

"It's not up to me. You know the routine. If you don't want to go there, we can take a pass."

"Fine. What do you want to know?"

"Only what you want to tell me."

"Seriously, are we gonna play this game again?" I said with a bit of an edge. If I was her, I'd walk out if someone got this way with me. But not Dr. Thompson. She had the patience of Job. She just sat there staring at me. I hated when she did that—contemplative, silent. It usually worked, as it did today.

"Here's the deal, Doc. Maybe there are experiences in my past where I've taken risks and succeeded, but none come to mind."

"I don't think you are being fair to yourself. What about your marriage?"

"What about it?"

"You took a big risk there, and it seems to be working out for you, right?" It was the perfect time to get into the problems I was having on that topic. Still, I simply could not bear Dr. Thompson knowing what I had done. "Sam, how about we try this tack. Instead of focusing on the chances of success, focus instead on the fact that if you don't try there is no possibility for success."

"Sounds like a suicide mission."

"Only if you do so recklessly. Are you being reckless in your work?"

"No, I'm being thorough. I must be. There's too much at stake. I have to be right," I said with determination.

"OK, then. Is this the type of situation where you can eliminate risks by conducting more testing?"

"Yes, you are exactly right. But I'm having trouble formulating what procedures I should perform to get to the right answer. The safer bet is to stop what I'm doing and simply sign off on the account I've been auditing. Everything else I'm looking into is a side story. Just instinctively, I feel like I could be dealing with a massive leasing scam, and people at the company are trying to blackmail me into ignoring it."

Dr. Thompson didn't say anything. She just looked at me.

I had overstepped. "Sorry. I've told you too much. Forget what I said."

"Forgotten, but, Sam, I'm merely trying to get you to take an honest account of where you are in this investigation of yours. From what I gather, you have taken steps to minimize the risk that you are wrong. You're questioning what you are doing, which is a good thing. You're being honest with yourself. Are there further things you can do to minimize your risk?"

It was slowly becoming clear to me where Dr. Thompson was leading me. Talking through it was helping...calming, if nothing else.

I was finally getting the point she was trying to make: the wall of fear I had faced so many times throughout my life was getting in the way of my decision-making.

I sat there, hand on my chin, bouncing my index finger off the end of my nose and staring straight into the carpet. Dr. Thompson said nothing. She was letting the stew simmer. I had a feeling she would speak soon and take this home.

"Sam, you might consider this," Dr. Thompson spoke softly but reassuringly. She reached behind her and removed one of her books from the shelf.

She opened the dog-eared book, flipped a few pages and paused. "I found it," she proudly proclaimed and began to read: "*You cannot swim for new horizons until you have courage to lose sight of the shore.* It's a quote from William Faulkner."

I simply looked at her and smiled. I thought momentarily, then stood up and said, "Thank you, Doc. You did it again." She returned my smile with the confidence of a home run hitter who had just won the World Series.

I walked out of Emily Thompson's office with a grin on my face and my gut churning.

CHAPTER 28

I arrived at GEL's offices around 9:30. I had warned Brian I'd be late due to a doctor's appointment.

"Are you coming down with something? 'Cause if you are, stay away from me. Everyone else too," he said.

At least he didn't tell me I couldn't take time off to see the doctor.

I got right down to work by reviewing the audit program. The financials remained. I needed to completely tie out all the workpaper binders to the consolidated financial statements. Three hours later that tedious and boring task was done.

While I flipped through my assigned portions of the audit program, I stared for a time at the steps listed beneath the caption "LCR—Lease Contracts Receivable."

Of the twelve specific steps listed, all of them were checked as completed. Only one remained. It was an overall sign-off. I stared at it. If I checked it and passed on my workpapers a lot of stress would be lifted. Even if they later found a big blow in the LCR account, they couldn't fault me. I had completed every assigned step without exception. So, if fraud existed in the LCR account and I didn't catch it, I would be blameless.

Then, considering my other option, if I pushed the envelope and continued my investigation refusing to sign off until I was satisfied, bad things could happen to me. Pete Brooks wouldn't force the company to delay their earnings announcement based only on my suspicions. I let out a sarcastic chuckle.

I sat with my chin resting on the palm of my hand and blankly stared at a half-finished glass of water sitting on my desk as I recalled that Faulkner quote.

Glancing toward the entrance to my cubicle, I opened my briefcase and pulled out my newly compiled file containing all the documents pertaining to my investigation. I felt confident Brian would not disturb me. He'd be busily preparing for Pete's final review.

Noon approached. There was no sense in going back to the war room to go out to lunch with my colleagues. As for Carol, I hadn't seen her all day. I spread the file out on my lap and faced my cubicle's doorway, so if someone came in, I could quickly close the file. I jumped every time someone walked by. I couldn't concentrate. This wasn't working.

I needed to clear out.

I closed my file and stuffed it into my briefcase. I fought off fears of detection. Screw it. I was on a mission. I also grabbed the LCR Ledger. I would find a quiet nearby fast-food restaurant to review those letters and consider my next steps. I could also grab a bite to eat.

While driving to Burger King, I wondered if Carol suspected what I was doing. It still seemed odd why she took me to the lower level conference room, and it was especially odd for her to tell me about her first marriage and two kids. Strangely, she had never mentioned them. What grade were they in? Who watched them during the day while Carol was at work? No pictures in her cube. So odd.

I devoured my hamburger and fries. For a few moments, I stared at the stack of documents in front of me. Fortunately, I was in a booth for four and had ample room to spread out. On one side, I fanned out the letters I had copied from the Complaints file. On the other was the LCR Ledger full of all 20,000 leases supporting the LCR account. In the center was a blank pad of paper and in my hand, a pencil. On top lay a single sheet of paper with some of my earlier notes, including Yoshi's questions I had yet to find answers to. I had no excuse now. Everything I needed was in front of me. It was time to begin.

I first focused on the letters. While reading one of the letters, my concentration faded. I did not understand what I was looking for.

I thoughtfully reasoned through it. Those letters alone did not necessarily mean the lease was canceled. I had to determine if they were still listed in the LCR Ledger. Since the sum of that ledger tied to the financial statements, GEL was representing all their leases were valid. If the leases referenced by the Complaints file letters were no longer listed in the LCR Ledger, it meant they were written off, and I had no issue. The letters would be meaningless to an auditor if the company had removed the leases as an asset. I recomposed myself and then reasoned through how I might make a connection between the letters and the LCR Ledger in front of me. I was pleased with my approach to solving this mystery. Alone here, I could reason through each of the letters in the same way.

I selected the first letter and reread it. The date was August 24, 1982, well within the company's calendar year, which ended on December 31. In the letter, the customer indicated what he wanted done in not so pleasant terms and attached one of their monthly billings which contained the lease number: 04201981ATLBOND.

I was guessing that lease should have been canceled. If it was canceled, it should no longer be listed in the LCR Ledger.

The function of the number was not immediately evident, but the last four letters BOND likely represented the name of the lessee, Bondurant Construction Company. The numbers could represent a date. Maybe it was the date when the lease was initiated. I soon confirmed that to be the case. It was beginning to come together, slowly.

As it was possible for more than one lease to be initiated on the same day, they used the first four letters from the customer name as a further differentiator. The initials ATL must represent the office which initiated the lease, in this case being Atlanta, Georgia, which I also noted as the address on the letter. Simple enough.

I quickly scanned the LCR Ledger, noting it was summarized by lease number, then the office. So, the number had to be a date. In that way they would automatically be ordered by date. It made perfect sense.

On this date, April 20, 1981, there appeared to have been nine leases initiated in their Atlanta, San Diego, Chicago, Austin and New York City offices. I scanned the ledger and found the lease I was searching for—Lease #04201981ATLBOND. Upon discovering how easy it was to find a lease by its number, I was excited and reached for the next letter in front of me, then stopped.

Now, I had an issue! If GEL had canceled that lease, as demanded by the customer back in August, it should no longer be listed in the LCR Ledger. Canceled leases don't generate payments. No payments, no lease, at least no valid lease, anyway. No lease, no asset.

But I wasn't certain it was canceled. I only had a letter in my hand from a very irate customer. At least they were unhappy when they wrote the letter. Maybe GEL worked it out with them, and the lease was not actually canceled. Maybe Carol called them and smoothed it over, whatever their gripe was. That was a possibility.

As I considered it, I turned my head to the side, and there on the wall of the Burger King was a pay phone. Only one way to find out.

The LCR Ledger had all the customer information including their phone number, so I dialed it.

When I was transferred to their accounting department, I used a pretext—a lie.

"Hello, I work on behalf of GEL. I am inquiring as to why last month's lease payment of $1,140 was not yet received."

After a brief period on hold, the clerk informed me that lease was canceled in September. I thanked her and apologized for the confusion, then hung up the phone. I shivered at the reality of what I had done.

No matter. I was finally advancing my investigation. This was my first evidence proving GEL was accounting for their leases

231

incorrectly. The customer had canceled the lease within the current calendar year. It should have been written off necessitating a hit to net income, the main calculus in determining EPS, and the principal driver in GEL's rising stock value. With that lease still listed in the LCR Ledger, it remained on the company's financial statements as an asset. Big problem. This could be an innocent oversight. One bad lease would not amount to overwhelming evidence of a leasing scam. Not by a long shot. But it was a start, and I grabbed the next letter in the stack.

This letter had no copy of their lease attached, but under the company address it read:

Re: Lease #09241981SDCUTL

Again, I flipped through the LCR Ledger following the numerical order I had previously established and quickly found the lease. The numbers matched exactly appearing to be a private residence for James Cutler. True to form, the last four characters of the lease contract number were derived from his name. It matched perfectly to a listing in the LCR Ledger...all making sense.

I made a call to the Cutler residence. Another pretext. Mr. Cutler was at work, but his wife was certain he had canceled the lease as she handled the bills and didn't recall making any payments for some time. She also enlightened me to another issue. She asked when GEL was planning to pick up the equipment, a small Kubota garden tractor. Not expecting this circumstance, I paused for a moment and told her I'd get back to her.

Besides the fact GEL had stopped collecting on the lease, there was also a strong possibility they had assets they should have repossessed but had not. If they did not pursue repossessing the equipment serving as the basis for the lease contract, how messed up was this company? I made a cursory note to follow up on repossessions. I noted no accounting or physical signs of repossessed equipment during my audit work. Not even an audit program step—

Screw you, Elaine Porcheck!

It took another hour to make additional calls in the same manner. I couldn't reach everyone, but I now had eight customers confirming lease cancellations. They were no longer customers of GEL and no longer paying on their lease contracts—eight canceled leases that should have been removed from the LCR Ledger as soon as they were no longer valid assets of the company. All should have been written off, the leased equipment repossessed. Yet, all were in that ledger and therefore included in the financial statements of the company as of December 31, 1982. All were bogus.

By the time I returned to GEL and retreated inside my cubicle, the day was about gone. It was approaching 6:00 p.m. The audit was pretty much ahead of schedule, which was why Brian told everyone earlier they could leave at five o'clock. Perfect. I had a lot to do knowing there were canceled leases not being accounted for properly, or so it seemed. As for the other issue Mrs. Cutler had surfaced regarding GEL not picking up their equipment, I could not confirm that had been done with my other calls. One referred me to someone in their asset maintenance department. I didn't want to push my luck running the risk someone would become suspicious of my bogus credentials, make a call to GEL and expose me. The fallout from such a call was inconceivable. Here I was, calling my audit client's customers and posing as a GEL representative. I was an auditor who was lying and misrepresenting himself. I'd say that would be grounds for termination, for sure. I could even lose my CPA license. Better to quit while I was ahead.

The entire audit staff was gone. I hadn't seen Carol all day. It was just me and the night cleaning crew. I moved the ball forward today and had some things to contemplate. I needed to evaluate the issue at hand and decide tonight if I had a problem worth pursuing or ascertain where the resolution was and put it to bed. Sounded like a logical approach.

Taking advantage of the empty war room, I gathered the ledgers and other documents I needed and spread them out on the large table.

I began thinking through the problem and the evidence. It was not lost on me that I had selected eight letters from the Complaints file, and all eight turned out to be canceled leases even though they were still listed in the LCR Ledger. It was not a scientific study but still seemed a good basis for concluding every letter included in that file likely represented a canceled lease. I did a quick calculation in my head assuming every letter was tied to a bad lease—it amounted to about a $1.2 million write-off to the LCR account. All of that would hit the income statement—hard. With Earnings Before Interest and Taxes (EBIT) for the period ending December 31, 1982, of just under $50 million, that $1.2 million would represent 2.5% of EBIT. I remembered from my training that 5% was the threshold after which an investor might consider the financial statements to be materially misstated. I had extrapolated that amount from all the Complaints file letters assuming they were all bad leases. What if the actual number of canceled leases were double or even ten times that? Now, we'd be talking major impact.

Midnight. I was tired and stood to stretch. Thinking I needed some fresh air, I walked toward the war room door and noted the binder containing the lease selections we had confirmed by mail sitting on the chair next to Brian's chair. I picked it up. I had assembled it and given it to Brian for his review. He had yet to sign off on it. It was probably queued up for him to review tomorrow. I held the binder. My mouth dropped. Yes…not only was it unlikely, it was inconceivable!

I was frozen in place. How could there be eight bad leases, maybe even a hundred if I considered the entire contents of the Complaints file, yet none had been selected in our circularization (confirmation) process?

We had circularized the company's file of 20,000 leases and selected, through a statistically valid process, 600 leases for positive confirmation. All letters were sent out to customers. All those returned letters, along with my alternate procedures, were contained in the confirmations binder I now happened to be holding. I flipped it open and sat down at the table again.

My memo outlining the results of the entire process was in front. In it, I concluded the results of our testing confirmed the validity of the LCR balance on the company's financial statements. Based on the results, it was entirely appropriate to conclude our sample was representative of the population. No issues. I performed that testing myself. I called customers not responding and verbally confirmed the details of their leases. I called customers where the information they reported differed from the company's books and records. In all, I was successful in resolving all possible exceptions. There were no unresolved exceptions. My testing was conclusive, perfect.

Maybe too perfect.

My earlier phone calls today confirmed the eight leases—*The Bogus Eight* as I now coined them—were all included in the population of 20,000 leases. They were all supposedly eligible for selection in the confirmation processing Wyatt ran—yet none were selected.

What if that selection process had chosen one of The Bogus Eight for positive confirmation? They would have been included among the leases where I would have mailed a confirmation. They would have responded, or I would have called them to confirm the details of the letter.

What would have happened if I had done that? Most likely, exactly what had resulted from today's phone calls.

Thinking through how the results of the circularization process would have changed if I had selected a canceled lease, I would have walked away from my testing with an entirely different conclusion about the validity of the LCR balance. If the company knew about The Bogus Eight yet left them plainly listed in the LCR Ledger they presented to me to test, they were stupid...or they were comforted in the notion there was no way one of them would have been selected. But how would they be so certain those canceled leases could not have been selected?

I reanalyzed every step I had performed in the confirmation

235

selection and mailing process.

At 1:15 a.m. it hit me. Patricia Walters-Pickering. My intern. She reperformed the selection count sequence. What if she did it wrong?

I leaped from my chair to the audit black boxes in the war room. I rifled through its contents hunting for the Control List where she documented her testing until I found it. It had her initials, mine and Brian's on the cover. This was a dead binder, as we called the binders successfully passing field review, which signified it was done correctly. I never expected to unearth it again. I carried it over to where I had the LCR Ledger already at my temporary work station on the conference table.

I was no longer tired. I was invigorated—maybe I was on to something! Maybe my intern screwed up the counting process, which might explain why none of the confirmation selections included any of the canceled leases. It was ridiculous, but how could a college junior fail an audit step merely requiring one to count? The only way to be certain would be to reperform my intern's work. It had already been a long day, and I wasn't nearly finished.

I flipped open the LCR Ledger and counted down manually, reperforming the intern's process. The random start number was 66, then following intervals at each 34th lease.

One, two, three, four…66. Got it. Holding my finger as a place marker on the 66th lease, I traced it over to the Control List, noting it was selected for positive confirmation. It was highlighted on the ledger and a check mark appeared on the Control List. All was in order. Good start.

By 5:30 in the morning, I had completed about forty selections. I had hardly made a dent. It was painful, but there was no other way to test the selection process. I could wait and ask Brian to assign another staff person to help. I chuckled aloud. Laughing gave me another shot of adrenalin as well. Exactly what I needed to keep going.

Before I began the count to the next interval, I had to pause, blink hard and focus. I worked my way down the list, finally arriving at the 34th lease in sequence. Fingering that lease item, I stared longer than usual at the black print formed by the thousands of ink dots on that green bar paper. Something was wrong. This lease was not selected for confirmation. I must have miscounted. I began again, working my way down the list and arriving at the 34th lease. I stared at it and focused my eyes, tracing back and forth. The lease I was fingering was not selected for positive confirmation. Oddly, the lease underneath it had been highlighted and selected—the 35th lease. The wrong one!

I considered the implications. I understood computers and programs were complex, but no matter how sophisticated the program, computers could count! Further confirming the wrong lease had been selected, I reviewed the actual confirmation letter. It was true. The wrong lease was selected for confirmation.

Two questions came to mind. First, how could the computer miscount, and second, why did the intern not note that as an exception?

Because my intern did a sloppy job! Because she was an intern! That was why.

Refocusing on the task at hand, I made note of the information from the lease that should have been selected and continued in my counting. I went on to the next interval count. Good. And the next. Good. And on and on…and then it happened again about an hour after the first mishap. The wrong lease, the 35th lease, was selected for confirmation. What was going on here? Again, I wrote down the information for the lease that should have been selected and continued with my reperformance procedures.

It was approaching eight a.m. I was exhausted but not too tired to contemplate my current situation. I had been up all night. The GEL employees and my audit colleagues would soon arrive. How could I explain what I was doing here in the war room? I couldn't.

I still had time. Brian had told everyone they didn't need to come in until nine o'clock because it was Saturday. I hoped that timing also applied to the GEL staff assisting us with the audit. I didn't want anyone to know what I was doing. I wasn't ready.

I gathered the workpaper binders and ledgers I had been utilizing all evening to reperform the lease selection process for positive confirmation and took them to my cubicle. I spread them out on my desk, a side table, the floor, any flat surface. I had to keep going even though there was a risk I might be caught.

By 10 a.m. I had found more mistakes from our selection process. I now had twelve leases that should have been selected for positive confirmation but were not. They were skipped over.

I stopped my testing. I could have continued reperforming the counting process, but I felt I had enough evidence to prove something was amiss with the programming. I was too tired to think through the possibilities. I wished I could close my eyes, just for a little while.

I made a photo copy of each of the pages in the LCR Ledger containing the count sequence exceptions. Each exception needed further investigation. There could be more. I hadn't decided how I would, or even if I needed to, complete that task. Sleep deprivation was winning. I was too exhausted to think about it any longer. I needed sleep.

Sue! I hadn't called her last night. She'd be worried sick by now.

The "hello" that was delivered into the receiver on the other end was spoken by a nervous and frightened sweetheart of a woman. I hoped for Sue's forgiveness.

"Honey, I can explain," I said humbly.

"Oh God, you're alright. Oh, thank you, God. These were the worst 154 minutes of my life!" The preciseness of her accounting for each minute emphasized how much she had worried. "I have been sitting by the phone since waking up, agonizing over if I should call the police or what I should do. Where are you?"

"Sweetheart, I'm sorry. I'm fine. I'm really sorry."

Then she began crying. I felt horrible.

"Honey, I'm still at GEL and I've had a helluva night. I'm eager to tell you about it, but I can't now. Please trust I will be home no later than six o'clock tonight. I'm so sorry I forgot to call. Please forgive me."

"You know I forgive you, but please don't forget again. It was bad enough you were out the entire night. I couldn't imagine what I'd do if something bad had happened to you."

Another minute later, I finally got off the line. Even though I hadn't seen another soul, I scurried to the safety of my cubicle like a little boy who had broken his mom's favorite Hummel and ran to avoid detection.

I pulled out the twelve copies of the green bar paper. Each page bore a lease that should have been selected for confirmation but was not. I had to decide my next step. I wasn't certain what that might be. I was flying alone and blind. Of one thing I was certain—this anomaly could not be ignored. Computers could count! That this computer couldn't was too unbelievable.

All signs led to paying another visit to Wyatt Duncan.

CHAPTER 29

Fortunately, computer geeks usually worked weekends, and Wyatt was not to disappoint this Saturday morning.

"Wyatt, remember me?" I asked as I walked into the computer room.

"Of course, Sam. Good morning."

I presented the twelve copies of green bar paper to Wyatt and said, "Just a quick additional test I need to perform. Could you please print out the customer record for each of the highlighted customers?"

Wyatt examined the pages of the twelve errant leases and said, "But that's what you've already got in the LCR Ledger. I could run it again, but you're going to get the same thing."

"I'm sure you're right, but it's a step included in my audit program. I'm not experienced enough to evaluate the usefulness of it. Is it possible to write the code differently so you are certain to print out every record for each of those customers in the master file? It might be a different program than you had previously done for the LCR Ledger printout."

"Sure, Sam, not a problem," Wyatt said as he turned from me to attend to my request. "But I didn't write that code. It was written last year by my predecessor. I tweaked it a bit to incorporate the parameters you gave me, but those were minor edits. I didn't think I'd need to rewrite the entire code. Right?"

I thought about it for a moment and said, "I think that's OK, Wyatt. I'll have to think about it," I said after a brief pause. I honestly didn't know and cursed my inexperience.

Wyatt had already sat in front of his keyboard talking to himself, very geek-like.

At 11:14 a.m. I glanced at the computer room door and considered that, by this time, Brian and at least some of the auditors had surely shown up. If my luck continued nobody would walk into the computer room over the next few minutes.

I took a seat and observed Wyatt type the program code. I couldn't recall Carol mentioning if she'd be coming in on Saturday. I kept nervously watching the door and praying Wyatt could complete the task for me without incident. Soon, my wish was granted.

"Sam, step over to the printer, and you'll see the printout in a few seconds."

True to his prediction, I moved in that direction, hearing the soothing sound of the dot matrix printer doing its thing. Before long, I was tearing off the one sheet of green bar paper and glancing at it, noting that it included the records of twelve leases. After thanking Wyatt and recovering the copies I had given him, I dashed though the door and made my way to my cubicle.

Sitting erect in my chair, I began reviewing what Wyatt had printed out. I set it next to the original LCR Ledger where I noted the twelve exceptions. For that grueling labor, this had been my bounty. Twelve leases, that were exceptions to the count sequence, should have been selected for confirmation but were not. Now, I was hoping to learn why.

The two listings I was comparing side-by-side displayed the exact same information for each column and in the same order for each of the lease customers exactly, except for one thing. On the listing Wyatt just printed out, there was one additional column on the extreme right with no heading. In that column, for each lease listed, I noted the letter "X." I did not understand the meaning of that character. There was no legend on the page, and I had never seen it displayed on any printout or document pertaining to lease contracts or lease customers including the LCR Ledger I was comparing it to.

Its appearance as part of the customer record for those twelve leases was a complete mystery.

Staring only at the new printout, I studied it and tried to discern its meaning when I was interrupted.

"Good afternoon, Sam."

Carol was standing in the doorway of my cubicle. When I spun around, she appeared startled by my appearance and said, "Wow, you look awful. Are you alright?"

"Thank you for your kind assessment. I happen to feel awful," I said returning to my work.

"Sam, I'm so sorry. You should go home."

"I can't," I said in a monotone voice, dismissively. "We are in the final stages of clearing the books for the upcoming earnings release, and I need to stay here and keep working."

I tried to appear engrossed in my work spread out in front of me, and I was hoping she'd take the hint.

"OK, but I'm right next door, Sam. If you need anything, please don't hesitate to ask."

"Thanks, Carol," I said without lifting my eyes from my work.

I waited a few moments longer to ensure she was gone, and I continued with my examination of the twelve lease selection errors with the "X" next to each—the X codes. I stared at it for a few moments, then glanced again at the LCR Ledger. There was obviously something in Wyatt's recent programming code causing it to printout lease records which included those X markings—or maybe there was something *extra* included in the previous code used to printout the LCR Ledger. Perhaps something causing it to skip over those twelve leases.

My immediate mission seemed clear. It was true, computers could count but only when programmed to do so. Computers could also miscount...but only when programmed to do so. Learning accounting and auditing was a challenge enough for me, and now I needed to add computer programming?

I feared I was nearing the point where I could no longer conduct my investigation clandestinely. At the same time, I shuttered at the reaction I would receive from Brian if I brought this to his attention. He'd probably fire me on the spot. I was not ready to reveal my work to him. I needed more in the way of solid evidence. Right now, all I had were anomalies and hunches. If I laid this in front of him, he might confront Reggie directly. That would not be good, as it would give him a heads-up and he could cover the trail. Brian would believe Reggie, his client, over me. No, I still needed to pursue this on my own.

Maybe it was time to talk to Carol. She was the LCR queen, and we were friends. Or at least I could continue that ruse.

I decided it was too risky. What if she was in on it? In on what? I was getting ahead of myself. I needed to remember HP did this audit last year and found no problems. At least none worth ditching the audit, as I was working towards suggesting. The result here was the worst imaginable. The path I was on was not one whereby we'd be writing up some suggestions to improve the company's internal control system or some other inane auditor ding. No, the path I was on, if I was right, would cause my firm to withhold blessing the company's earnings release until this lease issue could be resolved. Even before that could happen, I'd have to prove the whole thing was material to the financial statements. Only if it was material would Hamilton Pierce withhold its audit opinion, or worse yet, issue an adverse opinion. If that happened it would collapse GEL's stock price, possibly resulting in its bankruptcy and eventual demise.

And what about that prior-year's audit? The Complaints file was labeled with a date—1982. That could only mean there was at least a 1981 file likely filled with similar letters, so what if bogus leases were contained in last year's LCR balance? GEL's 1981 financials could also be materially misstated. If that were the case it would prove even more devastating for my firm. The lawsuits would fly. All hell would break loose. *Damn,* I thought, *where was I going with this?*

I was so unnerved I found myself standing, staring blankly at the documents on my desk. I hadn't even realized I'd stood up. I needed to take a break. My lack of sleep and exhaustion could be clouding my judgment. A brisk walk in the cold air of a winter's day might be good.

As I exited the building, the stark sunlight caused me to close my eyes and turn from the light until my eyes acclimated. I sauntered along the side of the building behind a row of trees which offered some protection. I expected the cold but not the bright sunlight. As I stood between the trees and the building, I was startled to see that black Porsche Carrera pulling into a parking spot not far from my position. I gasped at the sight of Reggie Dalton exiting that beautiful car.

He gently closed the door and stood admiring it, holding his stainless-steel coffee mug, careful not to drop the newspaper he had tucked under his arm. Even though I was comfortably hidden from view behind the trees, I crouched a little, leaning against the building. Frozen in place, I watched Reggie casually stroll toward the entrance. I didn't move a muscle until he was comfortably inside the building.

So, she was sleeping with her boss. I found it hard to believe. He was a slouch and slovenly. She was comely and desirous in ways that would attract a real man, a husband who would love and care for her. What did she see in Reggie Dalton?

By the time I was inside the confines of my cubicle, it was approaching midafternoon. I was getting my second wind, which was surprising, especially considering I had been up and working for over twenty-four hours. I wasn't sure if it was the brisk walk outside or the revelation of Reggie jumping Carol at all times of the day, but I was now very awake and aware.

GEL's earnings release was scheduled for Friday. Less than a week away. I had to complete my work and disclose my findings to someone with the authority and the balls to do something about it. Under my current pace, I was a long way from such a meeting.

I needed to shortcut my investigation and get right to the total potential effect on the financial statements, quickly. It would be the first question asked of me right after, or maybe even before, I offered my findings.

When I walked into the computer room, Wyatt was hunched over his keyboard like he was on a mission.

"Wyatt," I said. He jumped, startled like a fourteen-year-old caught with a *Playboy.*

"Holy shit!" he belted out.

"Hey, man, I'm sorry I startled you."

"You can't sneak up on someone like that, dude."

As I focused on Wyatt's computer screen he wasn't gazing upon a magazine, but he also wasn't working on company business. He was playing some computer game. I devilishly grasped at an opportunity that was suddenly not beneath me to exploit.

"So, Wyatt. How do you think Reggie would react if I told him I caught you playing computer games during working hours?"

"Oh, man. You wouldn't off me like that, would you? I thought we were friends."

"I'm just playing with you. We *are* friends."

He playfully mimicked a punch to my shoulder and said, "Thanks, dude. I knew you were just playing me."

Shamelessly taking advantage of the situation, I said, "But while we're on the subject of *friends*, I need a favor."

"What? Dude, you told me this morning you were done pulling my chain with that audit crap."

"I did, and you're right, but Brian asked me to use my excellent relationship with you and have you print out a report for us. I don't think it would take too much of your time, and I will be indebted to you."

"But, man, I've got a pile of report requests from Reggie and Carol to get done today, and I'm not gonna have time to throw your report on the pile."

I took the opportunity to remind Wyatt of the meaning of

friendship by saying, "I understand, but if you had so much work to do, I'm surprised you found time to play computer games while on the clock."

"Man, you told me you'd forget that."

"And I will as soon as I walk out of here. Come on, Wyatt. Let me tell you what I need, then you decide."

His mannerism communicated a tacit acquiescence, and I explained what I needed. "So, what I want you to do is to take the December 31, 1982, listing of leases, the LCR Ledger, and run a query on that entire file."

The next person to speak loses.

"What's the query?"

CHAPTER 30

As I walked by Carol's cubicle, I noticed her desk light was on, but she wasn't there. Maybe she was somewhere screwing Reggie Dalton blind.

It was well past Wyatt's deadline. I moved quickly to the computer room. Wyatt was standing over the printer, mesmerized, as if watching a gripping, frightening horror film.

"Wyatt, what's the deal? Where's my report?"

Pointing to the printer in front of him he said, "Right here, dude. It's still printing."

I walked up and stood next to him. I surveyed the printout and almost collapsed in disbelief.

There it was. A printout onto green bar paper of each lease file appearing exactly as it did on the LCR Ledger I had been testing. It was so familiar, at first, anyway. They were similar but not the same.

On these green bar pages I was staring at line after line of lease customer information, and at the far right of each line lay an X in the last column, exactly like the twelve leases Wyatt had run for me earlier in the day. I was staring at hundreds, which could turn into thousands, of similar leases. Still printing.

Something had to be gravely wrong with my logic. All of these records before me could not be bad leases. My God, if that were the case, the financial impact to GEL would be devastating. But there it was. The pages were printing out about one page every sixty seconds. Ten more minutes passed. Another ten pages printed off, each page contained about twenty leases. Still printing.

Wyatt and I stood next to each other staring at the printer, both in awe of what we were seeing. Me, because I understood the implications and Wyatt, because he was seeing a computer run revealing something I was certain he had not known existed, even though he did not yet comprehend its full impact.

Finally, the printer stopped. The whir of the large computer tape rolls stopped spinning. It was eerily quiet. We looked at each other like a pair of hunters in the deep woods when a sound caught our mutual attention. Here, though, it wasn't a sound, rather, the absence of sound. Wyatt moved a hand toward the top of the printout. He tore off the report, then handed it over without a word. It was like he knew life was about to change.

I gathered the printed list into both hands. I laser focused on him as though the next thing I would say would carry the greatest authoritative warning. "Wyatt, I can't tell you at this moment what this represents, but I can tell you that if you mention this to anyone—anyone—you might just go down the rabbit hole with the lot of them." Wyatt nodded his head, reluctant to make eye contact with me. We didn't speak another word. I returned to my cubicle with the report and sat at my desk, numb with fear of what lay ahead.

Flipping the pages one by one, it was obvious for the first time in a long time what had to be done. The next logical step was to call these "former" customers and verbally confirm the details of their lease contract with GEL. Based on my earlier testing, I feared the result of those calls. There was no valid lease. Maybe there was at one time but not anymore.

One thing I could do immediately was check out the Bogus Eight. Sure enough, each of them was included on what I now called the "X Code Report."

I had some phone calls to make.

But I couldn't call all of them. A quick calculation of the number of pages before me yielded an estimated 6,000 leases. The implications were unconscionable.

Somehow, someway, the programming code Wyatt had run in

December had been altered. How that could have occurred without my knowledge would be a matter to resolve on another day.

With earnings release less than a week away, I had to act quickly and responsibly to resolve this issue once and for all. Everything I had done on this investigation of mine had brought me to this point. I knew what I had to do: select some customers from this new listing to call.

But then, it hit me. It was a weekend. Businesses would be closed.

At 6:30 p.m. I guessed Wyatt and I were the only ones in the building. I couldn't be certain. While I hadn't seen Carol for a couple of hours, I had heard Reggie talking with someone earlier. I guessed he was probably sitting in his office smoking one of his Cuban cigars. Or maybe they were together, again. I pounded the desk in disgust, then admonished myself for even caring. I did care though...I was jealous.

I forced myself to face reality. I would have to wait until Monday before I'd know for sure. I would call many of the phone numbers listed next to each name on the listing I was now stuffing into my briefcase. I would go home and review it. I might find some residential listings and make calls to them tomorrow, Sunday. They'd surely be home. Sunday would be a great time to contact a homeowner.

Without killing anymore time thinking about Carol, Reggie, Brian or anyone associated with the audit, I grabbed my briefcase and left the building. Moments later, I was standing at my car and fumbling with my keys to open the door. It was cold, dark, no moon. I was shivering and perspiring. The temperature had to be in the single digits; however, I was sweating like I was on a beach.

I continued fumbling until realizing I was trying to insert my house key into my car door.

CHAPTER 31

When I arrived home, it was approaching eight o'clock. Sue met me as I opened the door, kindly not mentioning I was two hours later than promised. As she approached me, I warded her off saying, "Honey, I'm exhausted. I think I'm coming down with something."

"You look tired. Why don't you get ready for bed? I'll make you some soup."

I had been awake over the last thirty-some hours and derived all my nutrition from GEL's vending machine. I should have been famished, but I felt awful. It wasn't from hunger; I was certain it had to do with sleep deprivation. All I wanted to do was crash. "No soup. I just need sleep."

I sat on the edge of my bed thinking through next steps. Somehow, I had to finish my procedures on this investigation and then meet with Brian to lay it all out. I still couldn't get comfortable with that part of the strategy.

Finally in bed, I curled into the fetal position and pulled the sheets, blankets and bedspread tightly up to my neck. I was shivering uncontrollably. My body ached, and I was beginning to feel nauseous. Then it hit me.

I alone controlled where events might lead. I had only to keep quiet about it. What was it to me? An audit. Like the one performed on GEL last year and the thousands of other public company audits around the globe. This was audit season, and the markets were poised for earnings releases like the one GEL would announce this coming Friday. I could simply let it happen exactly as planned. That was the safer play, for sure. There just wasn't time to call enough customers to be certain. Why take the risk that I might be wrong?

In an instant, I had resigned myself to accept my investigation was over. I would let it die and move on to the next audit. I was relieved; I finally relaxed, stopped shivering and quickly fell into a deep sleep.

I awoke to the rustling wind. It was still dark outside. This was the most depressing part of winter, dark when I left for work, dark when I returned home. Maybe it was an ominous sign. But then came a positive note. I sniffed the air and was immersed in a joyful feeling. Bacon!

I loved the smell of bacon. It was probably the best smell in the world. The distinct sound of a metal kitchen utensil being tapped against the rim of a pan, confirmed my lovely and considerate wife was busy in the kitchen. Sue was fixing me breakfast, my favorite breakfast. I cast off the covers and sat up. For a moment, I remained on the edge of my bed taking account of where I was and how I felt. I was in my home, the smell of bacon in the air, and the clock read 6:10 on a Sunday morning. The kids would not be awake yet. Also, I felt great! No shivering. My stomach was fine. I was well-rested and ready to enjoy the day in comfort and at home with my family.

The wafting aroma informed me at least a pound of bacon was cooking in the kitchen. Hearing it sizzling in the skillet, its aroma permeating the entire house, I could almost taste the bacon. I leapt from bed, starving.

I grabbed Sue from behind, giving her a hug.

"Hey, you! Stay away from me if you're getting sick. I cannot afford to share it with you. Not enough sick days," she said in a playful yet stern tone as she was now cooking my scrambled eggs. Still with one arm around Sue and the other shoving an entire slice of bacon into my mouth, I garbled out, "Not a problem, sweetheart. I'm fine."

I sat at the kitchen table allowing Sue to plate up the eggs. They were perfect, especially with the melting cheddar cheese completely enveloping them. I shoved another strip of bacon in my mouth, then sampled the eggs, followed with a large bite of toast. I washed it all down with coffee.

"My goodness, Sam," she said looking at me with her mouth open but leaving the outline of a smile.

"What?" I loaded up my fork for another barrage on my mouth. "I'm famished."

When I had finally finished eating I walked to the bathroom, in desperate need of a shower. I hadn't showered since Friday morning and was soon comforted under sheets of flowing warm water. I could have enjoyed standing there all day. Ten minutes later, the water became tepid; I was reminded how small our hot water heater was and climbed out and got dressed.

As I was dressing, I contemplated the decision I thought I had made last night: halt the investigation and simply follow the bouncing ball. Brian would complete his review. Pete Brooks would pay us a visit in the field. Sometime in the next few days he'd sign off, and GEL would move forward with their earnings release on Friday. The formal signing of the firm's audit opinion would follow, and I would be on to my next audit. Scheduling had already informed me a week from Monday I would be assigned to the audit of some startup private company with big dreams of going public one day.

The kitchen phone rang. Sue picked it up after two rings.

All my hygiene attended to, I gave myself a last glance in the bathroom mirror and concluded I looked pretty good, especially considering the last couple of days.

I laid down my comb and turned from the mirror to exit the bathroom to find Sue standing in the doorway. She looked devastated—eyes red, tears running down her cheeks. Her question came out of nowhere.

"Are you having an affair?"

Whatever my reaction it seemed to confirm Sue's worst thoughts. "I knew it. You bastard. That's why you haven't been coming home.

You've been with her! How could you do this to me? To our family!" Sue ran into the bedroom and slammed the door shut. The push button lock set. I tried to get her to open it and tell me what happened. She wouldn't. Sue was locked away from me, crying, sobbing, not talking. I had a bad feeling who the caller was.

Just then, Ben ran by me quickly entering Will's room and slamming the door. I was sure he sensed what was coming and cuddling up with his brother seemed a wise move. I ignored him.

I went into the kitchen and grabbed a paper and pen, then returned to our bedroom door. Still locked. I stood by the door and asked to be allowed in. She wouldn't answer. Frustrated, I said, "I'm going for a walk." I slid a note under the door. It was time to be honest with Sue.

I slipped on my shoes and a jacket too light for the weather, then headed out the front door. Walking was the right remedy for sure. With each step, it became clearer what I needed to do. By the time I arrived back home, there were no doubts remaining. I had a plan: a newfound conviction and resolve.

Briefcase in hand, I stuck my head inside Will's room. Both boys were huddled together on the floor in the corner. I was glad they had each other. I knelt and told them that Mommy and Daddy had a disagreement. We'd work it out, and they shouldn't be worried. I got them started playing one of their favorite games and explained that I had some things to do at work. I told them Mommy was taking a nap, and they should let her rest for a while.

One last time, I knocked gently at our bedroom door. There was no answer.

I told Sue I loved her, and I would see her tonight. As soon as I turned away, the door opened. Sue stood before me with swollen, teary, red eyes, but she was no longer crying.

"What do you mean '…lustful affair of the heart?'" Sue asked accusingly. "Are you in love with her?" Sue had read my note.

Looking directly at her, I said, "Honestly, honey, I don't know what emotions I feel. Confusion would be one. I do know this, though: I love you very much." I turned from her and continued, "Someone I have been working with has had feelings for me. She flirted. I flirted back. She tried seducing me into having sex with her. I considered it, but then my love for you turned me from it."

Maybe it was my unguarded pause that hit her the hardest. "Well," Sue said tearing up again, "true love doesn't give way to another woman." Sue turned from me, but this time I grabbed her arm, turning her into me. She slapped me. Hard. She had never slapped me before. I let her go, and she retreated into the bedroom slamming the door. "I don't believe you," she cried out. "She told me to let you know the 'kid' called. You even used your pet name for me with her. You've called me 'Carol' during the night. I don't believe you!"

"Dammit, Sue, I'm trying to tell you. I did think about her in a way that betrayed us. But then, I thought of you. There is nothing there. I am in love with you. Always have been, always will be. I'm not going anywhere...unless you tell me to leave."

"Leave. Get out. Now!"

I was stunned and stood by our door wanting to say more but then felt I had said enough. I assessed that I did not do such a good job convincing Sue I was through with Carol, but perhaps I hadn't yet convinced myself, and it showed.

CHAPTER 32

Moments later, I was in my car and driving to a familiar place, albeit taking the long way. I needed to clear my head.

The Burger King was packed with a busy brunch crowd, but the booth next to the pay phone was open, as if I had called earlier to reserve it. I wasted no time in spreading out.

After spending about thirty minutes reviewing the X Code report Wyatt had printed for me, I took the phone in one hand, dimes in the other and dialed the first household selected at random from those listed under "Residential."

I randomly selected only a couple dozen or so customers to call, realizing it was not a statistically valid sample. Still, I was keen to sample from all of GEL's offices, all prior acquisitions, enough of a sample to convince me of the premise under which I was operating. If I hit upon more canceled leases, I'd be satisfied. Fearing the worst, I picked up the phone to make the first call.

I used the same pretext as before—the same lie. One by one, every customer confirmed what I already knew to be true. There was a lease, but it had been canceled. I forgot to ask if the leased equipment had been picked up. Nerves. A couple of them volunteered it had not. Still, the fixed asset issue seemed secondary and pointless. I hung up the phone. I was convinced enough.

Tomorrow would be judgment day—the day when I would sit down with Brian. I would show Brian all my evidence, and he would view me in a different light, for sure. He would tell the staff how they had misjudged me. How brilliant I was. It would be a new day for Sam Halloran. I would be the hero who found the fraud and saved the partner from signing a bad audit opinion—every partner's nightmare. The "experiment" Hamilton Pierce tried had actually worked out to save the firm from a costly embarrassment.

Then reality hit. It suddenly seemed insane to walk into GEL's corporate headquarters tomorrow morning and sit down with Brian to tell him of my discovery, what I had been doing over the past month. It wasn't that my confidence was shaken. It was more about strategy—just like a chess game. Nope, running this by Brian would be the Fool's Mate.

If I brought this to Brian's attention he'd have me lay it all out in the war room with the other audit staff watching and listening. Knowing him, he'd likely take extreme umbrage at the fact that a first-year associate dared to conduct such a clandestine investigation of a client right under his nose and without his knowledge. "Are you crazy," he would ask, "or just stupid?" Then he would fire me right there on the spot.

No. This was too big for Brian's small mind. I needed to take this to the partner. I would lay out my case for what I believed to be a massive leasing scam that would erase nearly half of the company's net income for the past year. Worse, this fraud was perpetrated by the officers of the company compelling HP to withhold its audit opinion and notify the SEC. I had no idea how such a process would unravel but had to trust that doing the right thing was all I needed to concern myself with.

I would call Pete Brooks tonight telling him of the fraud I had discovered and arrange a meeting where I would lay out all the evidence. That was it. If I was going down, it would be with the engagement partner as my judge.

I would either be a hero or find myself unemployed.

CHAPTER 33

I got home late, and everyone was in bed. I slept on the sofa. I awoke early, showered, dressed and left the house before Sue and the boys awoke.

The drive to GEL's office was short. I walked through GEL's lobby on a direct path to my cubicle. I was on a mission and didn't glance toward the war room. At 7:15 in the morning, it would be empty. Very soon Pete Brooks would be arriving to perform his final review in preparation for his sign-off. Or, at least, that was what everyone here would expect. Once completed, GEL could release earnings on Friday, as planned. But I knew differently.

Carol was at her desk, which was surprising at this time of the morning. I ignored her for reasons I didn't care to consider. Maybe it was because she was screwing her boss. Maybe because I was sure she had to know about the X codes; she and her boss were perpetrating a massive leasing scam. Maybe it was her phone call to my wife. I wanted to spit in her face.

I slid behind my desk wanting to avoid her. I did not get my wish.

"Sam, can we talk?" There she was, standing at the entrance to my cube. I wanted to confront her about the phone call. I deferred. My overall mission was too important to strike at her now. She had become nothing more than a cog in the wheel to me. I would be dispensing of her very shortly. She'd regret ever meeting me. Soon.

Without turning to make eye contact, I said, "Been very busy, Carol and still am. I can't talk now."

My actions and tone said, *Get away from me, bitch,* but she was not dissuaded.

"Sam, we need to talk," she said as she inched a little closer to me.

"I'm *really* busy," I said with more attitude. "Let's talk tomorrow." By tomorrow, it would be too late. Pete would have already shut the audit down. No earnings release. No GEL. It would be over.

"Sam, we need to talk now…about the X codes."

I was livid. I flew out of my chair and confronted her dead-on saying, "You did know! You knew, and you kept it from me. You lied. Get the hell out of my face! I have nothing to say to you." I turned away from her hoping she'd leave. She didn't.

"Sam, you don't know everything, but I am prepared to give you the missing pieces. You need to hear me out."

Well, at least she didn't deny it. Maybe there was more I needed to know. It now sounded like there was.

"I'm listening," I said, regarding her in a skeptical manner.

"Not here. Follow me," she said, already on the move.

It was clear she wasn't asking. She was telling me to follow her. She was around the corner and halfway down the corridor before I could react. Hustling to keep up with her, she glanced back, making sure I was following.

She led me to a familiar flight of metal stairs. We'd been through this route before, to the basement conference room where she told me of her estranged marriage. I never figured out why she felt compelled to tell me.

I followed her into the room and laid my notepad on the tabletop.

"Not here," Carol said. She went to the left, to a door with a keycard security pad. I noticed her regarding it last time thinking it might be a closet where they kept, well, things they needed to secure.

She slid her keycard and opened the door, glancing back to ensure I was following. "In here," she said.

I followed her into a darkened room. "Where are we?"

When she closed the door and flipped on the lights, I was blown away. It appeared to be a living room complete with a massive wood coffee table in front of a plush L-shaped sofa. It was the perfect place to watch the 60" plasma screen TV mounted to the wall. I had seen one of them a few weeks ago in the Gregg Electronics Store. Way out of my price range. More like the price of a nice car. Carol said nothing as I slowly turned in a circle taking it all in. The room included an exquisite bar with a smaller TV at eye level on the back bar flanked by crystal glassware on one side and bottles of liquor on the other, behind what appeared to be leaded glass set in a black walnut frame. I admired it.

To the left of the bar was a set of closed double doors. I imagined where they might lead. Carol was now standing in front of those doors facing me. I had seen enough. I didn't understand why she had brought me to this basement apartment; I didn't care. I had Carol alone. I approached her and demanded answers. I was filled with rage and emotion when I grabbed her biceps. My face inches from hers, I said, "You knew, Carol, you knew all along! About the X codes, about hiding cancellations, not writing them off. You bitch." I jerked her back-and-forth but still held on to her, tightly.

"Stop, Sam, you're hurting me."

I was incensed and couldn't remember ever being this angry. That wasn't true. I was this angry often growing up as a child. But this time I feared I might do something with it.

Compelling myself to hold it together, I stopped yelling. Not because I understood. Not because I cared about Carol. I might want to fuck her like the whore she was, but I was still livid with her deception. She put at risk my job, my life and my marriage.

As I loosened my grip on her forearms, she melted and collapsed into me. I shoved her away, recalling how she had played me all along. At this point, I could not stand to touch her. Gone were any feelings of emotion I had previously held for her. She collapsed onto the sofa, her head in her hands, sobbing like a child. "Sam, I'm so sorry. I had no choice." She took a gasp of air as if to continue, but I cut her off.

259

"Bullshit," I said as I remained standing. "We always have choices." My tone could not have been more hateful and judgmental."

"No, Sam, you're wrong. Please hear me out, then you can decide what to do, and I won't get in your way. Please, sit for a moment and let me tell you why."

Maybe it was the smell of her perfume or that she was still a very desirous woman. Even with her hair a mess, she was alluring. She was playing me again. I hated her for it, but then I could not ignore that I still desired her. Her low-cut blouse revealed that same black lace bra, her voluptuous breasts, her outstretched arms...all lured me back in. I was about to allow her to explain. I sat on the sofa but kept my distance.

"Begin," I said, "but I'm not guaranteeing I'll stay to listen. You were part of it. I'm certain of it. Steps have been set in motion that will stop the audit partner from signing off on the audit. Nothing you say will prevent me from following through."

"I understand," she said, wiping away her tears.

Likely realizing she had accomplished the most critical task of calming me down and committing me to listen, Carol took a few moments to compose herself. She flipped her blond hair behind her ears, blew her nose and wiped her running mascara. I watched, a little too closely, as she attempted to smooth her skin-tight skirt that was now seductively halfway up her thighs. I hated myself for it, but again, I fantasized. Maybe this was her plan. I wondered if there was a bedroom behind those double doors she stood in front of a moment ago. I cursed myself for still wanting her.

Waiting for her to begin what was likely to be another tale of woe, I imagined this must be the place. Of course. This was the place where she and Reggie retreated, often, to do the dirty deed. Right here in their offices. Even as I stared at her like the whore I had labeled her, I was aroused by her presence, especially in this place. Alone with her.

But then, I considered the anger I held for her was possibly not because of her deceptiveness; maybe I was jealous of her relationship with Reggie. Whatever the reason for my feelings, I forced myself to keep the presence of mind to get as much new information out of her as I could, trying hard not to be seduced by her captivating beauty and vulnerability. My senses were on full alert for what she might pull next.

"I'm waiting," I said, displaying my increasing impatience. "You need to start talking, or I'm walking out of here."

A few more sniffles and a last smoothing of her skirt, she sat up straight thrusting forward her ample breasts. Headlights to show me the way through the darkness, I supposed.

"I know what you must think of me," she finally began, "and I don't blame you. But I ask you not to judge me until you hear why I did what I did."

I wanted desperately to lash out at her, but that would have been counterproductive. It was best to let her find her own way. If she didn't get into the scam soon, I'd say something, but for now, I'd let her talk.

"When I began working here three years ago," Carol began, "it was exactly what I needed. I was going through a horrible divorce. I'd married the wrong guy who got his rocks off by abusing me, both physically and mentally. Somehow—"

"Carol, you've already told me all of this."

She pushed back sternly and said, "Please, Sam. Let me tell you what I need to tell you in my own way. I will give you what you want. Just please listen."

I was beginning to lose it again and flung my hands up in the air. "What do you mean you'll give me what I want? How do you know what I want?"

She looked at me like a teacher would at an unruly student. Calmly, she said, "You are about to be a hero. I will agree to cooperate with your firm, and I will work with federal law enforcement and regulatory authorities to lay out the entire fraud. Names, amounts, schemes, dates, everything," she said. She waited for permission to continue, motionless, steely-eyed, steady, determined.

Her instincts were perfect. Again, it seemed she always said the right thing to gain my favor and attention. I lifted my head, crossing my arms into my chest but remaining skeptical and attentive and asked, "You'll do that for me? Why?"

"For several reasons—for my children, for my own battered self-esteem, and yes, for you, Sam."

This was going in the right direction. I shouldn't be too anxious and needed to back off and lower the temperature in the room. I took a deep breath through my nostrils as my mouth was clinched tight, still angry she had deceived me all this time, almost ruining my career. Maybe my marriage, too. Still, the added pressure I foisted upon her was not doing either of us any good. I forced myself to stay silent. To chill out a bit.

She took my pause as permission to continue.

"Through our horrible marriage, we managed to produce two beautiful children." Carol opened a locket on a chain around her neck, and then leaned closer, showing me their pictures. I couldn't tell if this was another way to seduce me or if she genuinely wanted to share those pictures.

"Laura is eight, and Josh is six," she said in a whimsical manner as if injecting her children into the conversation erased away all her problems. "They are my life. Everything I did was for them. My job here was my respite. Reggie took me under his wing and taught me everything about the business. He promised me great things, and he's delivered at every turn. He and this job chaperoned me through the most painful time in my life. He saved my life and Laura and Josh's lives. I owed Reggie a great deal."

Same story, different chapter. I had run out of patience and cut in. "Maybe I'm an unsympathetic bastard, but I've already seen this movie. Lots of families suffer similar circumstances yet it doesn't justify whoring yourself out and committing securities fraud."

"Three years ago," she continued, ignoring my outburst, "Laura was diagnosed with stage IV leukemia. She was given six months to live. Today, my precious daughter is alive, and her prognosis is guarded but hopeful. All of this is thanks to the brilliant and dedicated doctors and nurses at MD Anderson in Houston, Texas. Laura's been in and out of treatment since being diagnosed but has been cancer-free for nearly a year now. Josh is there, too, with my mother. They live in a comfortable but modest house close to the hospital. They've made a new life for themselves in Houston. I fly there most weekends."

Carol was getting emotional again. I did some quick math. From my payroll testing, I recalled Carol made $54,000 a year. Her salary was good, but it wouldn't begin to cover medical bills, let alone the house for her mother and kids. Then, there's the expense of Carol flying down there to visit them. Maybe I was a heartless jerk, but in my mind, nothing justified what she'd done.

She likely sensed she was not getting through to me and cried again. At least this time she could contain it to a shorter period.

"Sam, there's no way I could afford all the expenses associated with Laura's care. Even if I wanted to leave GEL, I could never get health insurance anywhere else with Laura's condition. Past and ongoing medical treatments have totaled over a million dollars. Reggie has made sure all those costs were covered. I know you must think—"

"I'm sorry, Carol. You've been lying to me probably since the day we met. Why should I believe you now? In fact, you told me your parents were well-off, so why couldn't they afford to help you?"

"Fair question. You have a good memory, but you should also remember my dad cut me off. Mom later told me he had run into a few financial difficulties of his own. When he would not help Laura, his only granddaughter, stricken with this life-threatening illness, my mother filed for divorce and was shocked with her lawyer's discovery.

"Turned out, dear ol' Daddy had a gambling addiction and got in with the wrong people so deeply he ended up blowing his brains out one Sunday morning while sitting in his Benz in their garage. Shortly after, the lawyer informed my mom that Daddy had cashed in his life insurance policy years earlier without her knowledge. As for the estate, there was nothing left except piles of debt. My mother found herself broke about the same time I reached out to her for help with Laura."

"Still, you prostituted yourself for personal gain even if you did it for your kids," I said in as judgmental a tone as I could muster. "I'm not buying any of the rationalization you're trying to sell me. You're a liar and a cheat."

"Well, you got that right," Carol said in a remorseful tone. "And don't forget, Sam, I am a whore, too."

While I didn't disagree with anything she said, her self-deprecating comments were instructive. She was a beaten woman.

"Let me ask you something, Sam. You have two boys, and by the way you talk about them, it's clear you love them dearly. Put yourself in my situation. Say your oldest son needed very expensive medical care. You could appeal to charitable organizations or trust in the county hospital. You know your child's situation is dire. Then comes an opportunity with someone reaching out to help, virtually guaranteeing your son would have the best medical care available. Your son will live.

"You're certain it would make you feel obligated to him, but would you honestly care when your child's life is at stake?

"Later, the crisis passed, your child is alive and well. Is that when you turn against your benefactor? Or are you so thankful to him you would do anything to repay the favor that saved your child's life?"

It was the first time since we began this conversation that I sat with less judgmental eyes and simply listened.

"You are faced with a situation," Carol continued, "where you find yourself compromising your integrity to save your child's life. It's not difficult to rationalize. You help perpetate and then cover up a fraud which ultimately may cause some fat cats on Wall Street to lose a few bucks. Maybe a big auditing firm like Hamilton Pierce must pay millions in settling shareholder claims to make their bad audit go away and their partners make ten percent less next year. Think about how much you love your son and look me in the eye and tell me you wouldn't do whatever it took to save his life."

I lowered my head without saying a word. Carol's emotional outburst seemed to sap her remaining strength. She continued to whimper and dab her nose and eyes with a tissue. She was a mess.

I stood, walked to the kitchen, grabbed the tissue box and handed it to Carol. She took it with one hand and touched my hand with the other. No sexual overtones. Just in need of human contact. I finally relaxed back into the sofa but didn't say a word. After a few minutes, Carol broke the silence.

"You are probably thinking I brought you down here last week to…" She glanced over to the closed double doors, holding her gaze there.

I followed her stare suspecting behind them lay a king-sized bed in a bordello of sorts for her and Reggie.

Carol turned toward me and continued, "I respect you too much, Sam. True, right from the start I had been trying to seduce you. When I first brought you down to this place that was indeed the plan." Carol dropped her head as if ashamed and said, "Behind those double doors is a bedroom…and a hidden video camera…and microphone. The plan was to compromise you into turning a blind eye while the company's financials received the HP seal of approval, and we returned to our own lives. That was the direction I was given, and I agreed to it but obviously could not go through with it when I had the chance."

I recalled when Carol had lured me down here. It seemed odd at the time but now learning what the plan was brought a sense of relief. I might have gone through with it.

"After hearing you talk about your family and especially your wife, Sue, I didn't have a chance with you, although I wanted so desperately to think I did."

Go to Hell, I thought, but I didn't say anything.

"All that was confirmed when I threw myself at you, and you rejected me. That hurt more than you will ever know, not so much because I failed in my mission to seduce you, but because in the short time we have known each other, I grew to like you very much. At times, I fantasized about how it might be different if you and I were a couple. I admit I called your home yesterday hoping to drive a wedge in your marriage. We suspected you discovered the X codes. Reggie wanted you to be distracted from the audit, and I was desperate. He stood next to me and demanded I make that call. When I saw you this morning, I realized I couldn't go through with it any longer. We had it out yesterday when I balked at making the call. His intimidation won over, but still, I think Reggie suspects I'm no longer working his plan. I feel so ashamed." She buried her face in her hands and sobbed quietly.

With her head in a submissive position, her hands clasped on her lap, she sat there, vulnerable, waiting for me to react, hoping I might give her some indication I understood and maybe even forgave her. My trust in Carol was growing. She was a willing participant in some despicable actions, but a rare sense of compassion was paying me a visit. I reached out to her and gently, compassionately took her into my arms. She hugged me so tight I was surprised with her strength. She shivered uncontrollably. We sat and held each other. I allowed her to decide how long she needed comforting. It was a while.

Her predicament was weighing upon me. I had mixed feelings for sure—admonishment for her crimes but sorrow and, yes, pity. Still, I had a job to do.

When she finally released me, we stood facing each other. I held her hands and said to her, "I'm going to need your help. Can I count on you?"

"I will do anything I can. And thank you, Sam. I am lucky to have you for a friend." She hugged me and broke down again.

I held her, not so sure about how true the *friend* part was, but I let her have that one. She sure needed a friend right now, and I needed her. Her verifying the scam would make my job a whole lot easier.

I relaxed my embrace. She did the same, and then I moved to her side, placing my right arm across her shoulder. My palm gripped her bicep, pulling her into my side as if to steady her for a difficult walk into the light of day. Together, we would begin to unravel this massive leasing scam, first to my engagement partner and then to the authorities. I would willingly help Carol face whatever legal problems would befall her, not that I knew how it would play out. I imagined the U.S. Department of Justice would gladly give Carol immunity for her testimony against Reggie Dalton. I suspected he was the king fish behind this fraud, most likely partnering with Beckworth, too. Both their heads on spikes would probably satisfy the vultures soon descending upon GEL demanding blood once this scam became public.

As Carol and I walked into the conference room and to the front door of this sordid place, before I could grasp the doorknob, the door burst open.

There stood Reggie Dalton, surly and angry, drawing distinct creases down his fat, bulging cheeks and across his forehead, gun in hand. I don't remember if I let Carol out of my grasp or if she pulled away, but somehow, I had the presence of mind to kick the door back, stopping his forward progress. Even as I did, it was too late.

The gunshot was deafening. I cringed as if already shot. But I wasn't shot. An instant later, Carol collapsed into my arms.

At first, her body was rigid and heavy. Everything was in slow motion as I watched the shooter's face ripple in horror; his shot hit the wrong target. The gun fell to the floor.

Trying to steady Carol from falling, I stared directly into Dalton's face wondering if he would pick up his gun, point it at me and pull the trigger once again. I was powerless to change the course of events.

But he didn't shoot again. He looked at Carol, then to me. Raw fear contorted his face. Dalton's hands flew up. He appeared disoriented, stumbling backwards and crashing into the wall opposite the doorway. His eyes opened wide at the realization of what he had done. He turned and disappeared. The relief of that moment enveloped me like a cooling shower, drawing all my strength away. I fell to my knees still holding Carol in front of me.

Laying Carol down to the floor as gently as I could, I tried to cradle her on my lap. Carol was holding her stomach and grimacing. She was in serious trouble. As hopeless as it seemed, I tried maneuvering both of us toward the conference table where there was a phone, but I was going nowhere. I was slipping on an ever-increasing pool of Carol's blood.

The bullet had likely sliced through an artery. Instinctively, I inserted my finger once finding the entry wound in her abdomen, blood oozing between my fingers. Her entire front was bathed in a deep red. I was paralyzed with fear and trembling. I glanced over my shoulder for some pathway to the phone. To call for help I'd have to leave Carol lying on the floor. She'd bleed out in seconds.

She had not said a word, nor had I. With my free hand, I held her left hand, which was now covered in her blood, and said franticly, "Carol, hang on. I'm going to call for help," but I couldn't leave her.

Her grip on my hand was like a vise, and she whispered, "Don't leave me, Sam."

I again tried to pull away, but she resisted even though I now detected weakness in her grip. Anything I could do or say seemed inadequate. "Carol, I'm so sorry. Let me get you help."

"No. Don't let me die alone. Please, Sam."

I didn't leave; I couldn't leave her. I tried to provide comfort as best I could.

Carol appeared very weak now. Trying to talk. Having great difficulty, pulling ever so gently on my shirtsleeve. Then, in hushed but distinct words, she said, "Tell Laura and Josh how much I love them…promise me…tell them…."

Before I could reason through what Carol had asked, I said, "Yes, of course I will."

A moment later, her body fell limp, a last breath of air slowly escaping.

"No, Carol, hang on!" I yelled, but before I could say another word, her head fell to her chest.

CHAPTER 34

January 3, 1998

I had finished relaying the saga of my first public company audit (excluding my personal life issues)—the GEL audit.

There was not an audible sound in the University of Chicago auditorium filled with over 1,200 of Hamilton Pierce's newest staff associates from offices around the U.S. Some were crying, most were paralyzed where they sat. For over two hours they listened, silently, to my presentation as each class of newly minted auditors had done over the past several years. Eerily though, it seemed this class was more subdued, more moved than previous classes. Maybe I did a better job presenting, knowing I would soon mark the fifteenth anniversary of Carol Wittford's death.

A long pause ensued. I drank from a bottled water. My audience slowly began coming back to life.

Carol had done some reprehensible things, but I didn't fault her now. As the years passed, my experiences had both broadened and softened my attitudes toward wrongdoers, perps, felons, crooks, fraudsters, whatever. I had seen many.

The GEL audit was my first and last audit. SEC enforcement became immediately involved in investigating not only GEL's transactions since its inception but, also, the prior audits performed by my firm. The Government's investigation had taken a year to complete. With my firm's cooperation, I had become SEC Enforcement's principal witness. Through it all, I found my interests had turned away from the field of auditing to a new area—Forensic

Accounting Investigation.

My views of those who strayed over to the dark side had been influenced after conducting numerous fraud investigations and seeing perpetrators up close and personal. I had come to sympathize with Carol Wittford in a way difficult to explain, perhaps resulting from my own maturity…maybe because the memory of Carol would never leave me due to the tragic way she died.

I began, once again, to speak to my audience.

"I understand you weren't given much background on why the firm has me recount my GEL audit experience to every beginning class of new auditors," I said. "That was by my design. I wanted you to hear the GEL story before we talked about the learning points this tragic tale offers. I'll cover the major learning points, then I'll take your questions."

At this point in my presentation, I unleashed my prepared speech. "Somewhere along the way, probably in your auditing classes, you learned the meaning of professional skepticism. You know from those classes that professional skepticism requires a questioning mind and a keen evaluation of audit evidence. I'm sure every one of you could recite the official definition forward and backward. But I know, and the firm knows, it is difficult to truly understand what it means to possess skepticism in all you do, unless you become embroiled in a case of fraud.

"Maybe you didn't follow through on that one red flag; the company controller seemed like a good fellow, and he conned you into accepting his explanations unsupported by objective audit evidence; you were too busy to give it a second look. It could be that scenario or one of many others. Whatever the case, trust me when I say you do not want to experience what I did on the GEL audit firsthand.

"But, the firm is realistic. While instances of financial statement fraud are rare, encountering fraud on one of your audits could result in grave harm to our brand and possibly your own career.

Accordingly, the partners want to do whatever we can to avoid such a scenario. Hence, my presentation to you today."

From center stage, I surveyed my audience. I wanted to ensure what I had said would have a chance to sink in. I also wanted them to completely focus on what I had to say next.

"As a new associate, you might think your opinion does not matter. You're wrong, just as I was wrong to think that on the GEL audit. However, if I held to that opinion and allowed the partner to sign off, imagine the consequences. Your opinion matters. And here's the most important takeaway from today: "*You*, not the partner or the manager, are the ones who touch documents, create spreadsheets, perform the analytics, interview the clerks and review the details. If fraudulent transactions exist in the books and records of the company you are auditing, and *you* don't find the fraud, it most likely will not get caught."

I paused again for effect, then after a moment, I continued with several more learning points before eventually wrapping up. "So, there you have it. Please remember my experience on the GEL audit and realize it could happen to you as well. Thoughtful attention to this important topic will avoid tragic consequences for all involved."

I concluded my formal presentation and strolled about the stage for a minute or two hoping what I said would find a home in the recesses of their minds.

The quiet that had existed in the auditorium for the past two-plus hours was gone and replaced by everyone talking to each other. Maybe that was a good sign. Hopefully they were sharing their thoughts about my presentation and not simply discussing their upcoming weekend party plans.

After a few moments, I asked, "Now what questions do you have for me?"

Fifty hands immediately shot into the air. Fortunately, sufficient proctors managed the excitement, bringing calm and order to the Q&A while passing the microphones to eager questioners in a responsive manner.

I was not surprised to hear the first question touch on the personal, rather than the technical. Sometimes they began with, "What became of Reggie Dalton?" but today, the first question hit home...hard.

"How did you feel about Carol Wittford being murdered? Do you think she got what she deserved?"

My initial emotion was one of anger but then realized it was an innocent question asked by a likely bright, ambitious and eager-to-learn young woman.

"I apologize for my hesitation in responding to your question. You touched on a very sensitive issue I have spent years trying to rationalize. Even fifteen years later, I find myself attempting to come to grips with the realities of those events."

The questioner had retaken her seat. The audience was again silent, waiting for my response.

"As I relayed in my story, Carol was faced with some difficult personal decisions, and as a father, I could certainly identify with her struggle. Nothing in my mind justifies committing such a deliberate and heinous act, a crime involving moral turpitude. I could never justify such an act...but then, I was not walking in Carol Wittford's shoes. Who was I to judge her? If circumstances turned out differently, maybe in the prior years' audits, I might have witnessed a better ending.

"For example, if our staff were doing the right things in the previous audits, exercising the appropriate degree of professional skepticism, the leasing scam could have been detected in its early stages and foiled long before this ended so tragically."

I was hoping the throwback to previous audits would have redirected them to the technical side, but that was not so.

"Next question," I said.

One of the proctors handed the microphone to another young female, and I wanted to yank the microphone away and give it to a guy—my generational slip believing a *guy* would get off the personal questions.

"What happened to Carol's children? Did you honor her dying wish?"

After another long pause, I displayed a jocular smile and sarcastic chuckle. "I sure wish you folks would ask me something about the technical side of this audit. Your questions are bringing back some difficult memories." I hoped my personal reflection would have dissuaded her from pursuing her question, but as I regarded the questioner, then the rest of the audience, it was obvious they wanted desperately to hear my answer.

I channeled my anger, frustration, and guilt away and outside of my body, just like Doc Thompson had instructed me to do. I was still seeing her, although not as regularly.

Momentarily calm, I struggled to answer.

Pausing gave respite to near-paralyzing memories. As I considered what to say, how much to say, I recalled the day I met with Carol's mother and children for the first time.

* * * *

Immediately after Carol's murder, I began a very painful journey, first contacting Carol's mother, Helen. I assumed that soon after the police and paramedics came onto the scene of Carol's murder, one of them would call her mother in Houston. They would be cold and procedural in informing her that her daughter was murdered. It wouldn't be fair to Carol's memory or her mother. I assumed it would fall on her to inform Carol's children; before that, I had to be the one to call Carol's mother.

The pain of having to make that call was trumped only when I made the trip to Houston a week later to attend Carol's funeral and then met with her children to honor my promise.

It was difficult to meet with Laura and her brother, Josh. Helen introduced me to her grandchildren as someone who worked with their mother. "They were friends" was how Helen characterized our relationship.

Josh was crying and being consoled by his grandmother. Laura acted quite differently. She stared at me, listening intently as I described how her mom and I worked together on the GEL audit. Laura was hanging on my every word as if it was her mother, not me, talking with her.

When it came time to honor my promise, I bent down and held Laura's hands. I had held the hands of my own children often but never under such circumstances. Laura offered no resistance. I took that as a sign of trust. I had been fighting back tears believing it might scare the children, but as I held Laura's hands, I remembered when I held Carol for the last time. A tear slid down my cheek, and I gently coached Laura closer. Our foreheads touched. Instantly, the flood gates opened.

"Why are you crying?" Laura asked.

I didn't answer her question directly, opting instead to tell her what her mother so desperately wanted me to say to her children. They were truly Carol Wittford's last words.

I pulled back so I could lock on Laura's eyes. I struggled hard for strength. God heard my call.

"Laura," my voice began weakly but strengthened, soothing as I continued, "The last thing your mother told me was 'Tell my children their mother loved them very, very much.'"

I had hoped I had relayed it exactly as Carol intended. I wanted to wipe away the tears cascading down my cheeks, but I did not want to let go of Laura's hands. At least, not yet. I would allow Laura to choose that timing.

Josh was still being consoled by Helen, who was rocking him in a chair next to the fireplace. His whimpering stopped. Maybe he had fallen asleep. I would try to spend time with him later in the day.

Still crouched in front of Laura holding her hands, our foreheads no longer touching but eyes still locked on each other, I patiently waited. Aside from asking me why I was crying, Laura had not uttered a word. I had no experience in dealing with this. What could I do? What else could I say?

275

As long as Laura stared into my eyes, I could not move. I supposed she was measuring me in some way. It was times like these, when personal sensitivity was needed, I wished Sue were by my side. She'd say the right thing in the right way.

For a brief moment, Laura's eyes broke with mine. I was relieved and started to stand. Suddenly, Laura tightened her grip on my hands in the same way Carol did during her last moments. When I returned to my crouched position, Laura asked, "Did you love my mother?"

My chest sunk as I lost my breath. I looked into Laura's eyes as she held my hands, not so tightly now. Laura's grandmother had left Josh napping in the chair and was standing next to Laura, gently stroking her granddaughter's hair out of her eyes. Helen perhaps had heard Laura's question and realized this child needed comforting.

Finally, through the grace of God, I managed to respond, saying, "I loved your mother for how much she loved her children. As a father, I know there could be no greater expression of devotion than a parent's love for their children."

Laura embraced me.

* * * *

"Yes, I did honor Carol's dying wish," answering her question.

Standing on stage, after recalling that most difficult trip to Houston, I could say no more about that visit. I was fraught with emotion, neither feeling compelled nor willing to add to my answer.

A young man held up his hand.

"I'm confused," he confidently declared. "You mentioned your decision to call the engagement partner, informing him of a problem with the audit…to tell him of the fraud you discovered, and lay out your evidence. But then you ended your story with Carol being murdered and the company CFO running off. I'm guessing when you made that call to the partner, it would have set in motion GEL's collapse. It would have been too late for Dalton to do anything about it. As CFO, he would have been the first to know it was over. So, why did he come after you and instead murder Carol?"

I stood staring at him for what seemed forever.

"Young man, what is your name?" I asked.

The young associate froze in front of me, paralyzed. His face reddened, and his expression seemed to foretell of his impending doom. I quickly tried to allay his angst and calm him by saying, "Son, you're not in trouble. It's actually the most perceptive question anyone has ever asked me after relaying that story, and I want to remember who asked it."

"Robert Freeland, sir."

I smiled. In answering Robert Freeland's question, I would be released from the guilt I had been carrying since the day of Carol's murder. It was time.

"Robert, you are correct. I told you I had the phone in my hand; I dialed the partner's number; and, yes, he did answer…but I hung up the instant he spoke. He had no idea it was me who had placed that call. It all happened in the early morning hours of the day Carol Wittford was murdered."

The audience let out a collective gasp.

"So, you see, I never completed that call to the engagement partner. I only wished I had. I wished I had so badly that sometimes at night, in my dreams, I replay that call to the engagement partner as if I had followed through with it. Sometimes I dream a completely imagined meeting with him in those early morning hours, laying out all the evidence, receiving his praise and accolades. The next day walking into the Indianapolis office of Hamilton Pierce to the cheers and applause of everyone. All the partners lined up thanking me for saving the day in the nick of time. Reporters with their microphones and cameras rolling extolling me as the brilliant auditor who stopped the bad guys just in time. I would have been the hero Carol Wittford prophesied.

"But none of that happened. Why? Because I was afraid. I didn't follow through with that call because I feared I might be wrong. I was afraid of being embarrassed, or worse yet, of being fired. Bottom line, I feared committing yet another failure.

"Failure…rather, fear of failure, is something I've struggled with my entire life, even to this day, even though I'm a partner. A pretty successful one, I might add."

I paused for a moment, scanning the audience to see how this was being received. I thought of my father and of his prophecy that I would never amount to anything. I painfully recalled my childhood struggles. I thought about my family and my success as a partner at Hamilton Pierce.

Emily Thompson told me I should talk about those things, but this was not the place. By the expressions on my audience's faces, they seemed unsure of what to think of me. I didn't care what they were thinking. It seemed reasonable to bring my answer to a quick conclusion before someone sent the guys with the straightjacket to rein me in. With that in mind I went into wrap-up mode.

"Folks, the bottom line is this: If I had done the right thing at the right time, Carol Wittford would still be alive today, and Laura and Josh Wittford would never have suffered a loss no child should have to endure. I caused them to lose their mother essentially before they grew to know her."

I said it as forthrightly and confidently as I could, but there must have been weakness in my delivery. Off to my left, Veronica appeared from behind the curtain, making her way to center stage to bail me out as she had done so often before. We were off script. So, this last comment would be my swan song for today, and Veronica, who was as familiar as anyone with the GEL audit and its aftermath, could finish fielding their questions. I was somewhat embarrassed but relieved my time here was about over. I was also in need of a stiff drink.

Returning my attention to my audience and taking my cue from Veronica's entrance, I said, "As it seems my time has ended for today, let me leave you with this: Yes, today is about impressing upon you the importance of exercising professional skepticism and what it requires of auditors, but there is an added benefit to your witnessing my presentation—to believe that failure is not a crime. It is permissible to fail. It's expected you will sometimes fail. Seriously, it is. Don't allow the possibility of being wrong prevent you from doing what you believe to be right. Don't make the same mistake I did."

Fighting off the emotion about to manifest itself in me, I turned toward Veronica, introducing her to the audience saying, "This is Veronica Martinez. Veronica is a director in the Chicago forensics practice, which means she oftentimes runs my most difficult engagements. Please give her your undivided attention as she will be taking over for me now. I wish you all the best and good fortune with your careers at Hamilton Pierce."

I turned and winked at Veronica, now smiling at me as she took my microphone, and I exited the stage.

Considering I sort of lost it there, I was surprised to hear such a loud and sustained applause as I walked off. Even after I was well off the stage and halfway to the exit, they were still applauding. It was nice to feel appreciated, but I wanted out of that building quickly.

My stomach had asserted itself. Suddenly, I was having severe cramps. I raced off to the restroom.

When I exited, I could hear Veronica speaking. I glanced at my watch and ditched getting back to my busy schedule, opting instead to listen to Veronica finish up for me.

I found a discreet place behind the curtains where I could manage a peek at her through the center slit. Watching, I took pride in the way she addressed the audience. I hearkened back to when I first hired Veronica out of college eight or nine years earlier. She was a real catch, for sure.

I watched her glide across the stage deftly moving her hands, the inflections in her voice all timed perfectly to emphasize her words.

She was impressive. I had taught her years earlier how to command an audience as she was doing today. It was rewarding to watch her on that stage. She had become an excellent speaker, but it was her judgment honed by conducting many complex investigations that would allow her to handle what was about to play out.

CHAPTER 35

Veronica described her role in the practice and appeared prepared to field more questions from the audience. It didn't take long for hands to pop-up.

A young man who waited patiently for the proctor to hand him a microphone, spoke boldly into it. "How did that guy ever make partner?"

Maybe because I was focused on Veronica, or maybe my stomach was still behaving in an odd manner, I didn't hear the young man. Fortunately or unfortunately, Veronica clarified. "I'm sorry. Are you talking about Mr. Halloran?"

"I am," blurted out the young staffer unabashedly. "I am, indeed."

I still wasn't sure what he said, but from the audience's reaction and rising sound level in the auditorium whatever he said was causing a stir. From Veronica's movements and hesitancy to speak, it appeared Veronica, too, was caught off guard.

Whatever was afoot, Veronica, having been in some dicey investigations around the world, was never one to stumble. She would handle it. I was certain of that. His question had flustered her, but she quickly recovered to take command of the moment.

Calmly yet assertively, she said, "You may be referring to Sam's admission that he made some mistakes. What you will no doubt learn throughout your career is the firm encourages exactly what Sam was proffering today. We want you to take chances, calculated risks. We want you to do bold things, obviously after considering all options and consulting with the appropriate partners and risk management

281

consultants in the firm."

It was a considerate and professional answer delivered with the proper tone and demeanor. I still wasn't certain what all the fuss was about, but I surmised from the actions of the young new associate he had not been satisfied by her response. Apparently, he had a point to make.

"But he really blew it," he said. "His actions got someone killed. Someone who had kids. Kids who had to grow up without a mom. Kids who are probably completely screwed up today because of Sam Halloran's poor decisions."

That was clear enough. My first reaction was to leap onto the stage and respond. Almost immediately though, I had a different reaction. One of remorse. When his words soaked in, it was hard to dispute them. His manner was terse and uncompromising, but the substance of what he referred to was the source of fifteen years of my angst related to Carol Wittford's untimely death. I allowed the slit in the curtains to close and sat back into my chair. I had to get out of there. The memories, the guilt, it was becoming too much to bear.

Before Veronica replied, there spoke another voice from the audience. A familiar one.

"And who are you to judge the actions of a partner in this firm? You, a new associate at Hamilton Pierce, still wet behind the ears and now sitting in judgment of a senior and extremely successful partner of this firm."

Even shouting, that voice was familiar. As every head in the auditorium turned to see who was speaking, a young lady appeared from the top corner. She was making her way toward the aisle and motioning for a proctor to hand her a microphone. A building murmur accumulated from everyone wondering what was happening.

The young lady descended the steep steps to the left of the young man she was now calling out. Admonishing would be more like it.

As she came into view and climbed the stairs to the stage, Veronica stepped back, yielding to the yet unidentified female. Unidentified to the audience but not to me. Well, Veronica recognized her, too. I hadn't seen her in a while.

I almost pitied that young man for the ass-kicking he was about to endure. I smiled.

She had boldly walked to center stage, every eye on her, but she was in no hurry. She now had the high ground, commanding her audience in exactly the manner I had taught her to do. The next events would play out on *her* timetable.

I wanted to go on stage so badly but allowed nature to take its course. She would defend me better than I could defend myself. Anticipating what was about to happen, I fidgeted with excitement, feeling almost giddy with anticipation of what was to come.

Veronica yielded the stage to the mystery guest and walked toward me. I continued to watch the events unfold as I caught Veronica staring at me through the curtain slit and smiling.

When Veronica reached me, she turned to face the audience and stood to my left. I whispered to her, "What's she doing here?"

"Shut up, old man. Watch." Few could talk to me like that, but we were like family.

We watched the boy who dared to criticize me now paralyzed in place. He'd remember this day for a long time.

Combining an assertive voice with a commanding presence, she glided across the stage, each step deliberate, holding the microphone in one hand with the other acting as a metronome to her assertive words, like daggers being flung at him. With it, she gave the audience chapter and verse expanding on the principles of failure I had briefly touched upon.

After taking enough of a tongue-lashing and embarrassment in front of his peers, the young man stood, supposedly to protect his honor and regain the high ground, and interrupted her, saying, "You act like you were there. You can't be much older than any of us. Why do you think you know so much about what happened?"

Veronica, watching her, softly said, "Do it." I braced for what was coming but silently cheered. I was not disappointed with what followed.

The young woman stopped talking and lowered her head, allowing her long blond hair to fall gracefully forward, encasing her narrow face. She gripped the microphone with such firmness that in her sleeveless dress her arm muscles tightened like sturdy staffs outlining a chiseled body. Then slowly, but deliberately, she walked almost to the edge of the stage directly in line with the young man, staring him down with such intensity it was amazing he still had the backbone to remain erect.

Finally, she spoke, calmly but assertively. "You are correct. I was not there when those awful events transpired to take the life of that mother. But I was in Houston, Texas, when a magnanimous and caring new associate with Hamilton Pierce held my hand to tell me how much that mother loved her children.

"If you're wondering how, I think you said, 'screwed up' those kids turned out, I can help you with that. The youngest, Josh, after graduating valedictorian of his high school class, enrolled as a premed student at the University of Illinois. He's doing well.

"And the little girl, Laura. Well, I think even you are smart enough to figure out that she is standing in front of you holding this microphone, which she will gladly use to teach you how to respect others if you—do—not—stop—talking!"

The audience erupted in cheers and applause.

Over the applause, Laura continued to address him. "Especially about those who are clearly superior to you in every way imaginable and are not here to defend themselves. So, if you would be so kind as to allow me to finish the story."

Quieting herself, she continued in a calming voice. "You see, that partner you so willingly denigrated made one additional promise to Carol Wittford as she lay dying in his arms. When I was mature enough to grasp the meaning of why Sam Halloran would make trips to Houston, first annually, then more frequently, he told me what he failed to tell you today."

Laura paused. Absorbing her emotion along with my own, I didn't try to resist my tears this time. They flowed like a river. I listened and remembered.

"My mother also asked Sam Halloran to look after her two children. As he told the story to me on my thirteenth birthday, he agreed to do that before considering the enormity of what he was committing to do. At the time he had made that promise to my dying mother, he was struggling to provide for his own young family. Yet, not only did he make that promise, he followed through. I love that man as if he were my own caring father."

Laura paused, probably to gather her composure and settle down now that the attacker had wisely taken his seat. Like a protective lioness, Laura likely sensed the threat was over.

Returning to center stage, Laura turned and faced her audience and said, "All I can tell you is that Sam Halloran, or 'Pop' as Josh and I affectionately refer to him today, is the most honest, sincere and compassionate man I have ever known. He cares about people, and he especially cares about all of you. He wants the same for you as he does for his own children and for me and my brother...to be happy, secure and successful. I hope you took good notes because the advice you received here today could make all the difference in how successful you become in your own careers."

There was a momentary silence throughout the auditorium, probably to ensure Laura Wittford had finished saying what she likely felt compelled to say. Laura turned and walked toward Veronica, handing her the microphone. She no longer needed it. Mission accomplished. With the young lad now slinking to the nearest exit, the audience erupted in raucous applause, leaping to their feet. She and Veronica hugged affectionately. Laura then exited stage left with a causal yet humble glance and waved to the audience as she disappeared behind the curtains.

Backstage, Laura was moving quickly toward the exit door. She didn't see me. "Hey, kid," I yelled, getting her attention.

285

Laura looked up and without a word ran to me. We embraced. She was crying.

"Pop, it's so good to see you."

"Sweetheart, it is so, so good to see you as well."

"I hope you're not mad at me, Pop. He disrespected you, and you were not even there to defend yourself, so I couldn't control myself. Please don't be mad at me."

"Are you kidding? I'm just disappointed we didn't film that performance. You were amazing!"

We finally released our embrace. I held on to her hands. She leaned back, and I took her in, saying, "You look beautiful. Stunning, just like your mom. She'd be so proud of you."

The memory of Carol caused us to embrace again, this time only briefly.

"Let's get out of here," I said to her while still holding her hand and pulling her along. "Why didn't you let me know you were coming to Chicago?"

"Pop, we've got to talk."

"Not here," I said. "I want to get as far away from this place as possible. Then we'll talk. And I get to go first."

Laura didn't respond. She'd expect I'd be happy to see her but also that I had to know what she wanted to talk about. It was what I feared would happen one day.

CHAPTER 36

We hopped in a cab.

"Laura, it's going on five o'clock. How about we go straight to dinner?"

"I'm good with that."

"So, how long are you in town?"

"That depends."

"On what?"

"On how receptive you are to what I want to discuss."

I didn't answer her. The cab arrived at one of my favorite Chicago restaurants—Le Colonial on Rush Street, just around the corner from my condo. I didn't have reservations, but it was early, and I was known to them. A *neighbor*, as some would say. The best Chicago restaurants always made room for their neighbors.

We exited the cab. Laura walked inside while I settled with the cabbie. She, too, was familiar with this place. She'd always felt comfortable here, and I was hoping our conversation would not lead to creating a bad memory.

When I entered the restaurant, Laura had already taken her seat in the right corner booth with her back to the wall. She seated herself so I'd be forced to sit directly across and face her, ensuring I could not divert my attention from her planned agenda. I had taught her well. Laura was now poised and ready to hit me with her big sales job. After what I had been through today, I wanted to avoid the battle I expected would soon begin—we had been down this road before. When I arrived at our table, Laura's face foretold of her conviction.

Quite honestly, I didn't stand a chance.

"So, this is the way it's going to be," I said to her as the waiter pulled out my chair to assist me.

Smiling coyly, she said, "Hey, Pop, you're a good teacher. But *I* was smart enough to listen, which makes *me* responsible for how I turned out."

Right again. I was so proud how she had "turned out." But she was still a young professional in the making with a lot to learn. I wanted her to stay in auditing for a least a few more years.

I reached across the table and held her hands.

"It's always great to see you. But you really should have let me know you were coming."

"And give you a heads up? Not a chance. That wouldn't be very strategic."

I simply sighed, smiled and shook my head. She'll make an awesome partner someday. Laying my eyes upon her again, I said, "My God, look at the woman you have become. I'm so proud of you."

"Pop, stop it, I'm a professional now and a far cry from the innocent little girl you first met in Houston fifteen years ago. And that's why I'm here. We have something serious to discuss."

I wasn't ready to go there yet and said, "Not so fast, sweetheart. How's your grandmother?"

"She's excellent, and she told me to scold you for not keeping in touch with her on a regular basis." But she followed, "Gram said, 'Tell Sam I miss him very much.' She knows how busy you are, and she could not be more appreciative of all you've done for us."

"Heck, Helen is the toughest grey-haired lady I know. She doesn't need my help or anyone's for that matter. But she's right, I have not been the best at keeping in touch. I'll call her soon."

I wouldn't. Not because I didn't care. I was entirely too busy building the Chicago forensics practice, which I felt was where this conversation was about to move.

"Pop, I want to transfer to Chicago."

"There you go again, mixing business with pleasure too soon. How's your brother?"

"Pop, you know Josh is fine, you talk to him more than any of us, and yes, I'm planning to stop by campus before heading back to San Francisco. And, yes, I keep in touch with Will and Ben as you well know. So, can we dispense with the family updates for now and please talk about why I'm here?"

I wanted so much to avoid this conversation. The work we did was often too dangerous to worry about having a loved one involved. But, long ago, I had seen in Laura one of the attributes I admired in myself. She was persistent—so much so it was just a matter of time before she would win this one. In the end, Laura would transfer to Chicago and become a valued member of my forensics practice. If I continued to say "no," she'd threaten to transfer to another practice, maybe New York. It would drive me crazy, her being in another city and performing financial crime investigations for some other practice leader. It was something I would never permit to happen.

I expected this day would come. I would approve Laura's transfer to Chicago but not tonight.

Often in the past, when we talked by phone, she would broach the idea of transferring to be closer to all of us, but I think mostly me. More accurately, Laura wanted to be a part of my forensics practice. From an early age she took a keen interest in what I did for a living. She took her first accounting class as a high school junior, aced it and all those that followed.

All too soon, she headed off to UT-Austin majoring in accounting. When it was time to search for a job, I made sure she received the attention she deserved in the recruiting process. But, there was never any doubt she'd get an offer from Hamilton Pierce on her own excellent credentials.

Laura would do well in Chicago. The city had been good to me, especially after I started the forensics practice, and it became so successful. It had been only four years since my boss put a gun to my head, saying, "Sam, you're needed in Chicago." He was right to press me, but it was difficult leaving Indianapolis. I had many good memories of raising a family there and didn't want to leave. I had some bad ones, too, but I tried not to think about those.

Finally, the package they offered me was too rich to ignore, but beyond that, there was another reason I accepted the transfer—I could grow a practice so much larger than I could ever do in Indy.

As our notoriety grew, so did our practice. Right from the start, I had no trouble recruiting the best and the brightest staff from within the firm, poaching from the auditing practice and from our competitors. Soon, everyone was describing our Chicago forensics practice as "auditing with an attitude," implying we recruited sharp auditors but only those with a keen sense of adventure, those enjoying the investigative side of auditing but abhorring the routine, tick mark, check-the-box compliance mentality. Our staff quickly became bored when things were calm. We hated routine. It was only when everything was in complete chaos were we the happiest. There was no static routine to what we did.

I had found my niche—catching bad guys. But, there were bad guys, and there were *really* bad guys, Beckworth and Dalton being only two of them. They were evil, and for some reason the more evil and sinister my targets, the better the hunt. I reserved a special place in my heart when guys like them were brought to justice. I had an idea why I felt that way.

Today would have been perfect in every way except for some bad memories foisted upon me once again. It would seem I could not escape my past. Even before reliving that tragic day on stage, news of my father once again surfaced. The current prosecutor from my home county in New Jersey called this morning, right before I went on stage. He said it was a "courtesy call."

Turns out my father was released from prison. Time served. Debt to society paid. *Bullshit!*

He served a thirty-year sentence and was released from Rahway State Prison last month. I didn't bother to ask why it took a month for my so-called "courtesy call." Twenty-five years for the murder of my neighbor, Mr. Miller, plus five more years for his participation in the 1971 Thanksgiving Day prison riot. Five hundred inmates held six hostages, including the warden, for twenty-four hours. Six officers were injured, three with stab wounds, in the early hours of the riot. Prosecutors went for life without parole claiming my father was one of the leaders. Best they could negotiate was an additional five years. In a ridiculous sort of way, it was nice to hear my father had finally found something he was good at...leading a prison riot.

I never contacted him the entire time he was in prison. Now, once again, I'd be looking over my shoulder. Only this time, if he ever tried contacting me or any member of my family, I would kill him.

CHAPTER 37

A couple days later, Laura and I had dinner together expecting Josh would join us. He couldn't. Something about a hot date. Go figure. Laura left for home this morning, although her *home* would be changing shortly. She was thrilled when I told her at dinner that I would approve her transfer.

I enjoyed having dinner with Laura as much as my own two boys. Will worked for Goldman Sachs in NYC. He often told me he shocked even himself by entering an industry "…with even less free time than accounting!" But he seemed to be doing well and enjoying the Big Apple. Ben had followed in his mother's footsteps and was student teaching at Sue's school in Indy.

Ever since the GEL investigation had concluded, my life began an uptick. While I still had my ups and downs, I continued to better myself in all things, mostly centering on family and career. Well, absent Sue.

We never slept in the same bed or lived under the same roof after that Sunday. While we made several attempts at reconciling, Sue had told me it was my conflict with the memory of Carol she could not get past. Difficult to fault her. It was the most complex relationship I had ever had. Even Doc Thompson couldn't help me sort through it. After about a year, Sue and I divorced but remained friends. Neither of us remarried. Sue still lived in Indianapolis. We talked occasionally, mostly about the boys. While Sue was aware of my continuing relationship with Laura and Josh, that topic never came up. I understood. Deep down, I still loved Sue. We had written many chapters together, some with dog-eared pages, some torn. I still hoped there remained at least a few chapters unfinished. But, as she told me once, "There are some things I can't ever let go of." I respected her logic. I had put Sue through a lot. Maybe someday....

It was a rare idle moment gazing out my 52nd floor corner office in the Chicago Loop. I was the partner-in-charge of the largest forensic accounting practice in the U.S. firm, growing larger every year. Money was no longer a problem for me. It was just one way to keep score, but I had another scorecard: fraudsters. I had enough experience to know it wasn't only about my pursuit of them.

Recounting the GEL investigation on stage saddened me. Fifteen years ago, I had made a tragic mistake. And for what? My own insecurities. And did the bad guys pay? No, of course not. Because it was just a "money crime," as the press termed it. Another "victimless crime," they'd said. I suppose Carol's murder was just a sideshow to them.

Foster Worthington Beckworth pleaded nolo contendere to SEC charges of financial statement fraud. No jail time. His punishment was being barred from serving as an officer of a public company. I lost track of him. Had Carol survived to testify against him, he would have gone to prison. His buddy, Reggie Dalton, was still on the run and wanted for the capital murder of Carol Ann Wittford. There was no trace of him since that tragic day. The Feds immediately froze all his accounts but were certain he had squirreled away enough to live out his life comfortably on some deserted island. I tried not to think about him. No one else was implicated in the fraud. The day after it became public, GEL's stock dropped 85% in the first hour of trading, quickly suspended by the NASDAQ. GEL eventually filed for bankruptcy, their assets sold off for cents on the dollar. Most of the money was gone, spent or disappeared. Yoshi Fukuda was right. It was all a big pyramid scheme.

Staring out of my office window, I had every reason in the world to be content, satisfied. I wasn't. I put on a good show, for sure. The fact was, I was bitter. I needed another investigation like GEL. I enjoyed catching the bad guys who stole millions and hurt others. Most of them hid behind their Wall Street lawyers, making it difficult and tedious for us to nail them. But we would, eventually. It would be somewhat rewarding but not like I felt with GEL.

GEL was different. Someone I cared about was murdered. Someone I loved was lost. That made it personal. Of all my investigations, those where tyrants attempted to rule, to take advantage of others, only because they could—for that group of criminals, it would be personal for me. Clearly, I needed that feeling again, to make it personal.

I could not answer the obvious question of *why*. I just did. Maybe it was because I triumphed over insurmountable odds in the GEL investigation. Or, maybe it was the first time where other people, better people, smarter people, believed, quite wrongly, they could beat me. In the end, it was I who proved to be the smartest. I exposed them for the crooks they were. Were it not for me discovering and exposing that fraud, there was no telling how long they could have continued. I stopped them. I wanted to keep stopping them.

There was another reason I needed that fix. I craved another opportunity to face-off with the demons I was still carrying around, those that hovered over my every action, waiting for me to fail. Those that used to visit me the first day of every week—my Sunday Night Fears. While I never had another incident since meeting with Dr. Emily Thompson, my demons had not vanished. I was warming to the realization I wouldn't shake them no matter what I did, no matter how successful I became, no matter how many bad guys I caught. Likely, my demons would win out in the end. I knew why.

My father…my asshole father. Why couldn't he simply die?

"Sam, sorry to barge in."

"No problem, Maggie, what's up?" I asked my secretary, happy to return to the present.

"I've got Walter Hopkins holding. He's the—"

"I know Walter well, put him through."

"Walter, you old fart. How are things in Philadelphia?"

"Philadelphia is doing fine," he said, bypassing his usual penchant for banter. "Can't say the same about Guatemala. Sam, I just hung up with Steve Lemly, the CFO of my largest client, Hampton Enterprises. They received an anonymous letter suggesting a huge problem with the general manager of their liquor distillery."

"Can you fax me the letter?"

"My secretary is doing that now, but let me give you the nuts of it. Steve said they've had concerns about him in the past ever since he managed the plant construction ten years ago. He's always given their internal auditors a tough time, ours too. We found ways to get comfortable with his financials in the past, but now he won't allow internal audit or our team access to the plant."

"That's not good."

"It gets worse. The plant he runs is Hampton's largest facility with nearly a thousand employees, mostly women. As you will read in the fax, he takes liberties with many women employees often resulting in tragic results. You can see for yourself when you read the letter, but he has his own small army and has allegedly bribed every cop, judge and politician in the country. The writer claims he's the cousin of El Jefe, Mexico's top drug kingpin. Sam, this guy sounds bad. You'll make your own assessment, but this may be one you'll want to pass on. I've already warned Steve of that possibility. Anyway, Steve's ready to hire you and wants me to set up a conference call."

"Set up the call, Walter."

We left it that Walter would set up a conference call for later in the day. I reclined into my soft leather chair, gazing out over the Chicago skyline thinking...*another chance to prove him wrong.*

Appendix

Dear Reader

Thank you for reading my first book in the Sam Halloran series. If you enjoyed it, I would greatly appreciate you writing a review on Amazon.

Before sitting down to write *Sunday Night Fears* I did some research and was surprised to learn there are few, if any, successful novels on accounting fraud. I find that hard to believe. Look at all the successful legal thrillers. Ok, so maybe accounting has a reputation for being boring. Not so for those investigating accounting fraud. Forensic accountants are the Navy SEALs of the accounting industry. Their work is exciting and can make for some gripping thrillers. I know because that's what I do, and I would like to continue writing in this genre and subject matter.

Every so often I run across inauthentic novels. The author takes liberties with how things are really done. I hate that. Sure, it's fiction, but it's not fantasy! True, the story is the most important element in any good fiction novel, but wouldn't it be refreshing to pick up a book with a great story *and* know it really happens in just the way the author described! I would think so...at least for many. Those are the readers I want to reach.

Like *Sunday Night Fears*, I want my novels to ring true depicting how forensic accounting investigations are actually performed. I have a completed first draft in the second of the Sam Halloran series inspired by one of my most challenging investigations. On an otherwise calm Friday one of my partners called. The fax of the anonymous letter sent from his largest audit client told of a despicable and ruthless general manager of their Guatemalan plant...and how he terrorized his captive workforce of mostly women. The investigation was one of the few times I feared for my life. I think you will thoroughly enjoy the read.

So, if you would like to see more of how it's really done, set in a gripping tale, please encourage me to continue by writing a review.

Again, thank you for taking the time to read *Sunday Night Fears.*

About the Author

Tom Golden is a retired PricewaterhouseCoopers (PwC) Partner and former leader of PwC's Chicago Forensic Accounting Investigation practice. Tom has a national reputation in forensic accounting and fraud investigation. He has been quoted/profiled in a number of worldwide publications including *Journal of Accountancy, USA Today, The Financial Times, Business Week, Chicago Tribune, The Age* (Melbourne, Australia) and *Fraud Magazine*.

He has extensive testifying experience and is a frequent speaker, having conducted fraud investigation training seminars for both U.S. and foreign organizations, the FBI and IRS. Tom was the lead author of the award-winning Wiley book *A Guide to Forensic Accounting Investigation*, now in its second edition. He earned his MBA from Indiana University, is a CPA, Certified Fraud Examiner (CFE), former chairman of the Board of Regents for the Association of Certified Fraud Examiners (ACFE) and has been awarded the title of Regent Emeritus. He was one of the fraud experts appearing in the 2017 film *All the Queen's Horses* documenting the largest municipal fraud in our nation's history.

Tom was an adjunct professor at DePaul University, developing and teaching the school's first Forensic Accounting Investigation course in 2002. Tom also served on the board of the Better Government Association (BGA), five years as its Chairman.

While Tom has retired from PwC he simply cannot turn down continued requests to conduct high-profile investigations—and likely, for the right ones, never will. Together with his wife, a retired school teacher, they sold their Chicago condo and headed west about a hundred miles. They purchased some land building a home in the middle of the woods. Before leaving, they made a stop at PAWS and rescued a mixed-Labrador puppy. Their sons' families live a short distance away—allowing precious time to spend with their four grandchildren. Life is good!

About the ACFE

Founded in 1988 by Dr. Joseph T. Wells, CFE, CPA, the Association of Certified Fraud Examiners is the world's largest anti-fraud organization and premier provider of anti-fraud training and education. Together with more than 80,000 members in more than 150 countries, the ACFE is reducing business fraud worldwide and providing the training and resources needed to fight fraud more effectively.

The positive effects of anti-fraud training are far-reaching. Clearly, the best way to combat fraud is to educate anyone engaged in fighting fraud on how to effectively prevent, detect and investigate it. By educating, uniting and supporting the global anti-fraud community with the tools to fight fraud more effectively, the ACFE is reducing business fraud worldwide and inspiring public confidence in the integrity and objectivity of the profession.

The ACFE offers its members the opportunity for professional certification. The Certified Fraud Examiner (CFE) credential is preferred by businesses and government entities around the world and indicates expertise in fraud prevention and detection.

Learn more about the ACFE at www.acfe.com

Tell them Tom Golden sent you!

iii

Acknowledgments

Tom Golden is a frequent speaker. Please visit his website at www.tomgoldenspeaks.com.

Or, feel free to email him at tom@tomgoldenspeaks.com.

When Tom completed writing *Sunday Night Fears,* he chose to independently publish on the advice of several consultants in the publishing industry bypassing the literary agent query process. Through their coaching he selected, and now recommends, the following professionals to you:

Publishing industry consulting: www.janefriedman.com
Editing: www.authormarkspencer.com
Proofreading: www.bronteelise.wixsite.com/brontepearson
Website design: www.webdesigncity.com
Publicity: www.bbnmarketing.com
Social Media: www.createifwriting.com/coaching-webinars/

The author is not responsible for websites (or their content) that are not owned by the author.

And a final acknowledgment from Tom...

In mentoring my colleagues over many years I've often said no matter how smart you are, no one can be successful without someone else giving them a hand up the ladder of success. There are many over the course of my career to whom I owe a debt of gratitude but none more than two of my former PwC partners: Bob Decraene and Dave Whitman. I am sincerely grateful for all they have done for me.

Speeches and Seminars

Tom's presentation style is unique and can be tailored to each specific audience. Whether he speaks from a podium or freely moves around an open stage, he delivers common sense techniques which internal auditors and financial executives can use to spot and avoid fraud. Tom's presentations highlight his real-life experiences conducting large-scale investigations bringing to life his investigative techniques to create an experience sure to enhance learning in a memorable, oftentimes humorous, fashion. He literally "wrote the book on fraud," and you are guaranteed to walk away a savvier business person having attended one of his sessions.

Tom enjoys speaking about fraud almost as much as performing investigations. Some of Tom's favorite topics are listed below.

He especially enjoys teaching others how to prevent fraud or chase down perpetrators bringing them to justice. That is why he discounts, by half, his fee to schools.

He can be contacted at tom@tomgoldenspeaks.com
Join Tom's Readers Group by visiting his website
www.tomgoldenspeaks.com

Fraud "Auditing" 101

Your internal auditors likely graduated from a good college or university after studying for four to five years to earn that B.S. in accounting or Master of Accountancy degree. They may have spent several years at a Big Four accounting firm. You think they are "Fraud Fighters." You are mistaken. Unless they have specific experience dealing with fraud or some specialized training, it is likely that your auditors are clueless about how to recognize fraud and what to do to prevent it. This course is intended for internal auditors and will give them proven techniques for detecting fraud they can incorporate into their annual risk assessment and current internal audit schedule.

The Art of the Interview

Imagine how valuable it would be to get the perpetrator to admit they committed the crime, with intent. Arguably, there is no better evidence of a crime than a voluntary confession.

An experienced investigator knows that simply presenting evidence of a theft or financial impropriety is not enough to convict. It is incumbent upon the prosecutor to also prove intent, or scienter...that, at the time the crime was perpetrated, the suspect *intended* to deceive, to do harm.

The ability to sit down with targets, or those who possess knowledge of crimes, present them with the evidence and obtain their admissions is just about the most valuable skill a successful investigator can possess. They don't teach you this stuff in college.

Trust but Verify

Message to all those exercising control authority...you were not hired to be human lie-detectors relying entirely on what you are told by others, particularly company employees and outside vendors. Your job is to acquire and review valid evidence in an objective and independent manner and sufficiently verify that the information supports the transaction(s). Anyone who trusts without sufficient verification is, quite simply, someone not doing his or her job. It's really that simple.

All those involved in performing and monitoring control activities: executives and managers, internal auditors, all the way down to the accounting clerks who touch documents, need to change their view of TRUST and the basis upon which it is granted. They need to do it now, and they need to do it on a permanent basis. This seminar is designed to bring a dose of reality to your employees.

Have another presentation in mind...reach out to Tom
tom@tomgoldenspeaks.com

8 ⁻/0

40720466R00187

Made in the USA
Middletown, DE
01 April 2019